THE BRAVE

THE BRAVE

Nicholas Evans

WINDSOR
PARAGON

First published 2010
by Little, Brown
This Large Print edition published 2011
by AudioGO Ltd
by arrangement with
Little, Brown Book Group

Hardcover ISBN: 978 1 445 85431 1
Softcover   ISBN: 978 1 445 85432 8

British Library Cataloguing in Publication Data available

AudioGO   13.12.10

Printed and bound in Great Britain by
CPI Antony Rowe, Chippenham and Eastbourne

For my sister, Susan Britton

The free have lost what mattered,
The brave stay home in bed.
The white hat now bespattered
With the blood of needless dead.

Our heroes all are banished.
We rode them out of town,
The valiant who vanished
When the sun was going down.

Shane Van Clois,
'Men in White Hats'

THE

BRAVE

SEMPER FORTIS

The boy followed the guard along the corridor, watching the sway of his wide backside and the belt with its handcuffs and baton and the big bunch of keys that jangled as he walked. The back of the man's blue shirt was stained with sweat and he kept wiping his neck with the palm of one hand. It was a part of the prison the boy hadn't been allowed into before. The walls were bare and whitewashed and there were no windows, just fluorescent boxes on the ceiling speckled inside with dead bugs. The air was still and hot and smelled of stale cabbage. He could hear distant voices, someone shouting, someone laughing, the clank and echo of metal doors. Somewhere a radio was playing the Beatles' new number one, 'A Hard Day's Night.'

The boy's weekly visits usually took place in the long hall next to the waiting room. He was almost always the only child there and the guards knew him by now and were friendly, chatting with him as they led him to one of the booths. Then he'd have to sit there staring through the glass divider, waiting for them to bring his mother in through the steel door in the back wall. There were always two guards with rifles. He would never forget the shock of that first time they had led her in, the sight of her in her ugly brown prison dress and handcuffs and ankle chains, her hair cut short like a boy's. He'd felt a pain in his chest, as if his heart were being prized open like a mussel shell.

When she came in she always scanned the

3

booths for him and smiled when she saw him and the guard would bring her over and sit her down in front of him and remove the cuffs and she would kiss the palm of her hand and press it to the glass and he would do the same.

But today it was different. They were going to be allowed to meet in a private room, just the two of them, with no divider. They would be able to touch. For the first time in almost a year. And for the last time ever.

Wherever the guard was leading him seemed a long way inside the prison. It was a maze of cement corridors with a dozen or more barred and double-locked doors. But at last they reached one made of solid steel with a little wired-glass window in it. The guard pressed a button on the wall and another guard's face, a woman this time, appeared in the window. The door buzzed and clicked open. The woman had plump cheeks that glistened with sweat. She smiled down at him.

'You must be Tommy.'

He nodded.

'Follow me, Tommy. It's just along here.'

She walked ahead of him.

'Your mom's told us all about you. Boy, is she proud of you. You're just thirteen, right?'

'Yes.'

'A teenager. Wow. I've got a thirteen-year-old too. Boy, is he a handful.'

'Is this death row?'

She smiled.

'No, Tommy.'

'Where is it then?'

'You don't want to be thinking about that.'

There were steel doors all along one side of the

4

corridor with red and green lights above them and the woman stopped outside the last one. She looked through the little spy hole then unlocked the door and stepped aside for him to go in.

'There you go, Tommy.'

The room had white walls and a metal table with two metal chairs and there was a single barred window through which the sun was shafting down and making a crisscross square on the cement floor. His mother was standing in the middle of it, quite still, shielding her eyes from the sun and smiling at him. Instead of the prison uniform she was wearing a plain white shirt and slacks. No handcuffs or ankle chains. She looked like an angel. As if she were already in heaven.

She opened her arms and held him to her and it was a long time before either of them was able to speak. He'd promised himself he wouldn't cry. At last she held him away from her to inspect him then smiled and ruffled his hair.

'You need a haircut, young man.'

'Everyone has it long now.'

She laughed.

'Come on, sit down. We haven't much time.'

They sat at the table and she asked him all the usual questions: what was going on at school, how had the math test gone the previous week, had the food in the cafeteria gotten any better? He tried to give more than one-word answers, tried to make it sound as if everything was fine. He never told her what it was really like. About the locker room fights, about how the bigger kids taunted him for having a convicted murderer for a mother.

When she ran out of questions she just sat there and stared at him. She reached out and took his hands in hers and stared at them for a long time. He looked around the room. It wasn't as frightening as he'd imagined. He wondered where the gas pipes and valves were.

'Is this it?'

'What, sweetheart?'

'You know, is this the actual chamber?'

She smiled and shook her head.

'No.'

'Where do they do it then?'

'I don't know. Somewhere back there.'

'Oh.'

'Tommy, there's so much I wanted to say . . . I had a whole speech prepared.'

She gave a false little laugh and put her head back and for a while didn't seem able to go on. He didn't know why, but it made him feel angry.

'But . . . I've forgotten it all,' she went on.

She rubbed the tears from her cheeks and sniffed then took hold of his hand again.

'Isn't that funny?'

'You were probably going to tell me how to behave for the rest of my life. To be good, do the right thing, always tell the truth.'

He pulled his hand away.

'Tommy, please—'

'I mean, what would *you* know about that?'

She bit her lip and stared down at her hands.

'You should have told them the truth from the start.'

She nodded, trying to compose herself.

'Maybe.'

'Of course you should!'

'I know. You're right. I'm sorry.'

For a long time neither of them spoke. The shaft

of sunlight had angled to the edge of the room. There were golden flecks of dust floating in it.

'You're going to have a fine life.'

He gave a sour laugh.

'You will, Tommy. I know you will. You'll be with people who love you and who'll look after you—'

'Stop it.'

'What?'

'Stop trying to make me feel good!'

'I'm sorry.'

He would always regret that he hadn't been kinder to her that day. He hoped she'd understood. That he wasn't so much angry with her as with himself. Angry at his own powerlessness. Angry that he was going to lose her and couldn't die with her. It wasn't fair.

How long they sat like that he had no idea. Long enough for the sun to move away from the window and for the room to fill with shadow. At last the door opened and the plump-faced guard stood there, with a sad, slightly nervous smile.

His mother pressed the palms of her hands together.

'Well,' she said brightly. 'Time's up.'

They both stood and she hugged him so hard he could hardly breathe. He could feel her body quaking. Then she held his face between her hands and kissed him on the forehead. But he still couldn't look her in the eye. Then she let go of him and he walked away to the door.

'Tommy?'

He turned.

'I love you.'

He nodded and turned and went.

7

ONE

They found the tracks at dawn in the damp sand beside the river about a mile downstream from where the wagons had circled for the night. Flint got off his horse, the odd-looking one that was black at the front and white at the back, as if someone had started spraying him with paint then had second thoughts. Flint knelt down to have a closer look at the tracks. Bill Hawks stayed on his horse watching him and every so often glancing nervously up at the scrubby slope that rose steeply behind them. He clearly thought the Indians who had kidnapped the little girl might be watching. He pulled out his gun, checked it was loaded, then holstered it again.

'What do you reckon?'

Flint didn't answer. To anyone else, including Bill Hawks, the tracks just looked like holes in the mud. But to Flint McCullough they told a whole story.

'Must have ridden downstream in the water so as not to leave tracks around camp,' Bill said. 'You can see this is where they came out.'

Flint still didn't look at him.

'Uh-huh. At least, that's what they want us to think.'

He swung himself back into the saddle and steered his horse into the water.

'What do you mean?'

Again Flint didn't reply. He rode across the shallows to the opposite bank, then followed it downstream another thirty yards or so, his eyes

9

scanning every rock and clump of grass. Then he found what he was looking for.

'Flint? Mind telling me what's going on?'

'Come see for yourself.'

Bill rode across to join him. Flint had dismounted again and was squatting on the bank, peering at the ground.

'Darn it, Flint, will you tell me what you're up to? What are we waiting for? Let's get after them.'

'See here, among the rocks? More hoof marks. Deeper ones. The tracks on the other side are kinda shallow. No riders. It's an old Shoshone trick. They turn some horses loose then double up to send you off on the wrong trail. This here's the way they went.'

Bill Hawks shook his head, impressed and a little irritated, as people often were, by Flint's brilliance.

'How much of a start have they got on us?'

Flint squinted at the sun.

'Three hours, maybe three and a half.'

'How many of them?'

'Three horses, five or six men. Plus the girl.'

'Let's go.'

Flint mounted up and the two of them rode away along the riverbank.

'Tommy! Bedtime!'

It was his mother, calling from the kitchen. She always got the timing wrong. Tommy pretended he hadn't heard.

'Tommy?'

She appeared in the doorway, wiping her hands on her apron.

'Come on, now. It's half past eight. Up you go.'

'Mum, it's *Wagon Train*. It goes on for an hour.'

10

She looked confused. The familiar evening smell of gin and cigarette smoke had wafted with her into the sitting room. Tommy gave his most angelic smile.

'It's the one I love most. Please.'

'Oh, go on then, you little rascal. I'll bring your milk.'

'Thanks, Mum.'

Flint had found the little white girl a few days earlier, wandering alone in the wilderness. Her dress was torn and stained with blood and her eyes were wide with terror. The major questioned her gently about what had happened but she seemed to have lost her voice. Flint said she must have been with another wagon train that had run into a Shoshone raiding party and that somehow she had managed to escape. Then, last night, the Indians had crept into camp and snatched her from her bed.

But Flint McCullough, who was without any doubt the bravest and cleverest scout in the entire world, would find her, kill the Indians and bring her safely back.

In this evening's episode Flint was wearing his tight-fitting buckskin jacket with the fringed shoulders. Tommy, naturally, was wearing the same. Well, almost. His mother had made his jacket out of some beige fabric left over from her new bedroom curtains but the result was too big and baggy and, to be honest, nylon velour didn't look anything like buckskin. Still, it was better than nothing and he had a hat and a gun belt with a real leather leg-tie on the holster that were both a bit like Flint's. And the black Peacemaker six-shooter with the white handle, the one his sister Diane had given him for his birthday, looked so convincing that Tommy thought he could probably use it to rob a real bank. For this evening's adventure he had loaded it with a new roll of caps, the pale blue ones which came in a white tube and made a much better bang than the cheaper red ones you got at Woolworth's.

It was early September and the evenings were closing in. The air that drifted through the big bay window was cool and smelled of rain-soaked dust and apples rotting on the lawn. A blackbird was singing loudly in the old cherry tree and down across the meadow that stretched away from the foot of the garden, a cow was calling for its calf. Tommy was sitting at one end of the enormous new sofa. It had red and green flowers all over it that made you dizzy if you stared at them too long. It had come with two matching armchairs and they took up so much space you now had to squeeze sideways to get to the television set, which stood in one corner of the room in its important mahogany-veneered cabinet.

The house had once been a farmworker's cottage on to which his parents had built an ugly extension. Despite a unifying coat of whitewash, the place seemed at odds with itself. It stood in an acre of garden on a gentle, wooded hill from whose crest you could see the steady encroachment of the town as, one by one, farmers sold their fields to developers. Work was already under way on a massive four-lane motorway which would go all the way from Birmingham to Bristol. Tommy's father could often be heard complaining that the area wasn't really countryside any more.

But Tommy loved it. He'd lived here all his life.

He didn't care much for the front garden. It was too small and prim and civilized. But if you walked out through the back yard, up the crumbling red brick path, past the old greenhouse and the derelict raspberry cages, you found yourself in a world altogether less tame. And it was here, where the willow herb and nettles and brambles ran rampant and nobody but he ever ventured, that Tommy spent most of his waking hours. It was his own, secret Wild West. Indian country.

He'd made a few friends at the little local school that he'd been going to for the past three years and sometimes went to their houses to play. But his mother rarely allowed him to invite them back. Tommy didn't really mind. He knew the other boys thought he was a little odd and too obsessed with westerns. They often preferred to play soldiers or cops and robbers and even if he could persuade them to play *Wagon Train*, there was always a fight about who got to be Flint McCullough. The fact was, Tommy preferred to play on his own. Anyway, all the best cowboys were loners.

He had Flint's walk off to perfection. And the way he tilted his chin and lifted an eyebrow when he was thinking or squatting to study some tracks or poke the embers of a fire to see how old it was. In the wild end of the garden, in the little clearing where he'd whacked down the brambles, Tommy even had his own horse, the fallen limb of an old sycamore with branch stumps exactly where the stirrups should be and some brown string tied to another stump for reins. He would swing himself into the saddle just like Flint, easily or in earnest, depending on what the story playing in his head required.

13

There were deeper things to emulate too, things that were more difficult for an eight-year-old fully to grasp. These were all about what was going on *inside*. Flint could read a man's character as shrewdly as he could read hoofprints in the dust. He kept his thoughts to himself, rarely smiled and only ever spoke when he had something crucial to say. In his solitary adventures, Tommy would assume these manly traits, humming the theme tune or the more dangerous music they played whenever Indians appeared. And when the plot required, he would speak (aloud, but not so loud as to be overheard by anyone walking up the lane beyond the hedge) in Flint's western drawl.

He didn't always play *Wagon Train*. He liked being Red McGraw from *Sliprock* too, the fastest draw of them all. He would stand like Red, looking dangerous, in front of his bedroom mirror, his hand hovering over his gun, and recite the words with which the show always began:

In the town of Sliprock, lawless heart of the Old West, where the many live in fear of the few, one man stands alone against injustice. His name is Red McGraw.

Sometimes, for a change, he'd be Rowdy Yates from *Rawhide* or Cheyenne Bodie or Matt Dillon. Maverick was okay too, except he spent too much time sitting around in saloons and wore funny town clothes. Tommy preferred those who wore buckskin and rode the range, fought Indians and caught rustlers and outlaws. What he definitely never played, wouldn't be seen dead playing, were any of those silly, cissy cowboys, the ones who carried two shiny silver guns, like Hopalong Cassidy or The Lone Ranger, and had holsters

14

with no leg-ties. How could you be a serious gunfighter without a leg-tie? Worst of all were the ones who *sang*, like Gene Autry and the ridiculous Roy Rogers.

His mother had reappeared now, a glass of milk in one hand, a plate with a slice of apple pie on it in the other, a fresh cigarette jutting from her lips. Without shifting his eyes from the screen, Tommy took the milk and pie.

Flint and Bill Hawks were hiding behind some rocks now, spying on the Indian camp. Night had fallen and the Indians were all asleep around a campfire, except for the one keeping watch over the little girl, and even he looked as if he was nodding off. The girl was tied to a log and looked pretty miserable.

'Be careful now. No spills, please.'

She took a puff of her cigarette, blew the smoke at the ceiling and stood with her arms folded, watching for a while.

'Oh, he's the one I like, isn't he? What's his name?'

'Flint McCullough.'

'No, the actor I mean.'

'Mum, I don't know.'

'Robert something or other. He's so handsome.'

'Mum, *please*!'

Just as Flint and Bill were about to launch their rescue, on came the commercials. Tommy's mother groaned and left the room. To his parents commercials were 'common'. Respectable families only ever watched the BBC which had the good taste not to show any. Tommy couldn't see what the problem was. In fact, the commercials were often better than what went either side of them.

15

Tommy knew most of them by heart. Like Diane, he'd always been a good mimic and sometimes when his parents had visitors, his mother would ask him to do the Strand cigarette man. Under protest, pretending to be more reluctant than he really was, Tommy would leave the room and a few minutes later slouch in again wearing his father's old trilby and raincoat with the collar turned up, puffing moodily at an unlit cigarette he'd taken from the silver box on the lounge coffee table, and say: *You're never alone with a Strand.* It always got a big laugh and sometimes people even clapped. For an encore, while he still had on the outfit, his mother would ask him to do Sergeant Joe Friday from *Dragnet*.

Oh, Mum, he would groan with fake embarrassment, which would naturally prompt a pleading chorus of *Oh, go on, Tommy, please!* So he would duly adjust his face to its most serious, manly expression and, in Sergeant Friday's deadpan delivery, announce that the story they were about to see was true and that only the names had been changed to protect the innocent. *The facts, ma'am, just the facts.*

By the time he'd finished his apple pie, Flint and Bill had everything pretty well sorted out. The Indians all got shot or ran away, the little girl was rescued and when they got back to the wagons, her daddy had turned up. He had a bandage around his head but was otherwise okay. They gave each other a tearful hug then sat down with everybody else around the fire for supper. It was bacon and beans, which was the only thing Charlie the cook seemed to know how to make.

Just as Flint had so cleverly guessed, it turned

16

out that the other wagon train had been attacked by a Shoshone war party who apparently wanted the little girl to be somebody's squaw, though Tommy wasn't quite clear what that might involve. Anyway, she got her voice back and it all ended more or less happily, as it nearly always did.

Tommy took off his cowboy hat and sat fiddling with the brim, eyes glued to the screen until the theme tune and the credits had finished.

'Come on, Tommy,' his mother called from the kitchen. 'Up you go. Your father will be home any minute.'

'Coming.'

He carried his empty glass and plate through to the kitchen, which had recently been *modernized*. Everything was now covered with pale blue Formica. His mother was standing by the stove, stirring a pan and looking bored. On the radio, the BBC newsreader was saying that the Russians were planning to send an unmanned rocket to the moon.

His mother's real name was Daphne, but she hated it, so everyone always called her Joan. She was a short, rounded woman with plump arms and fair skin that flared red whenever she got cross, which happened quite often. In fact, her reddish brown hair always looked cross, especially on Fridays when she had it re-dyed and set into a helmet of tight, wiry curls.

Tommy washed his glass and plate in the sink and left them on the draining board where his mother's cigarette lay propped in an ashtray, oozing smoke. Beside it stood a cut-glass tumbler of gin and tonic. She always poured her first the moment Big Ben struck six o'clock on the radio.

17

This was probably her third.

'What time will Diane be home?'

'Late. She's getting the last train.'

'Can I stay up?'

'No, you cannot! You'll see her in the morning. Go on now, up you go.'

Diane was twenty-four and lived in London, near Paddington Station, where she shared the top floor of a big old house with three other girls. Tommy had been there only once when his mother took him to London to see a doctor in Harley Street. Diane came home almost every weekend and the moment she arrived the house was at once filled with light and laughter. She always brought him a gift of some sort, something funny or unusual and often, in his mother's opinion anyway, entirely unsuitable for a boy his age. She would bring the latest records that everyone in London was dancing to or the soundtrack of some new musical she had been to see. On her last visit she'd brought *West Side Story* and they played it again and again on the gramophone, singing along with it until they knew every number by heart. Tommy had been singing *I like to be in America* ever since.

Diane was more fun than anyone else in the whole world. She was always playing tricks on people, even total strangers. She would phone up, pretending to be someone else and do naughty things that grown-ups weren't supposed to do, like swapping the salt and the sugar or propping a mug of water on the top of the bathroom door so that whoever walked in got soaked. Their mother would erupt (which was precisely what Diane wanted), while their father would put down his newspaper and sigh and say, *Diane, please. What sort of example is that for the boy? Could we perhaps try to be a little more responsible?* And Diane would say, *Yes, Father, sorry, Father*, then behind his back, pull a face, imitating him, or put her thumbs in her ears and stick her tongue out and go cross-eyed and Tommy would try not to laugh and usually fail.

Diane was an actress. She wasn't really famous yet but everybody agreed she soon would be. There was already another, older actress called Diana Bedford, so she used their mother's maiden name and acted under the name Diane Reed. Tommy was enormously proud of her. He had photographs of her and newspaper articles and large posters of the plays she had been in pinned to his bedroom wall, alongside all his western posters and pictures.

The photo he liked best was the one from a glossy magazine in which she was wearing a black satin evening gown and big sparkly earrings and a white fur stole draped around her shoulders. She was outside the Café Royal, a famous London restaurant where all the stars went, and it was night-time and she had her head tilted back and was laughing as if someone had just cracked a great joke. Tommy had never seen anyone more beautiful. The headline said *CATCH A RISING STAR* and underneath it said: *Diane Reed—Face of the Sixties*. His mother, who managed to pour cold water over almost everything, had observed that since it was still only 1959, perhaps this was jumping the gun a bit.

As he lay in the bath tub, Tommy was aware again of the feeling at the top of his stomach. It was a ball of dread that was getting steadily bigger, like the stacks of strange new clothes on the spare-

19

room bed. Two pairs of grey flannel shorts, two grey sweaters, four grey shirts, six pairs of grey knee-length socks, four pairs of underpants and vests, sports shorts and shirts (one white, one green), a dozen white cotton handkerchiefs, a green-and-yellow-striped tie, and finally, the dark green blazer and cap, each emblazoned with a yellow badge of two crossed swords and a shield with the school motto, *Semper Fortis*, written on it. Tommy's father said this meant you always had to be brave, in a language called Latin, which Tommy would soon be learning even though it was 'dead' and nobody ever spoke it.

On to every item of clothing his mother had stitched a small tape that said *BEDFORD. T.* Tommy had never seen his name written like that. It was painted the same way on the big black trunk and the wooden 'tuck box' that both stood, gradually being filled, on the floor beside the bed. It seemed strange to be going to live in a place where nobody cared what your first name was. But in just two days' time that was where he would be.

Exactly why his parents were sending him away to boarding school, he still couldn't understand. When they'd broken the news, he thought he must have done something wrong and they didn't want him around any longer. He knew Diane was against the idea. He'd heard her arguing with them about it downstairs one night last winter after he'd gone to bed. She'd been sent away herself when she was eleven to a grim place called Elmshurst in the Malvern Hills and hated it so much she ran away three times. The last time, about a year before Tommy was born, she'd apparently been delivered home in a police car. So, knowing how

20

awful it was, why would his parents want to do the same to him?

Diane never held back when it came to family arguments and it generally wasn't long before she would start shouting. At which point his mother would storm out of the room, usually slamming the door, while his father would stick his pipe in his mouth, hoist his newspaper and pretend he wasn't listening, which was a sure way to make Diane even angrier. Among his mumbled replies to her attack that particular night about boarding school, all Tommy could make out were phrases like *do the boy good, toughen him up a bit, make a man of him*. Tommy had always been in a hurry to grow up, but even so, eight did seem a little early for manhood.

He'd never dared ask his father to explain what precisely the process might involve but his mother assured him that going off to boarding school was simply what all boys from respectable families did. Anyway, she said, he should count himself lucky because some children were sent away when they were only six. What was more, as Tommy had heard her telling Auntie Vera (and anyone else who'd listen), Ashlawn Preparatory School for Boys was considered to be one of the best in Worcestershire. Its list of famous *old boys* included a man who had once played rugby for England, another who'd helped design the Mini and an army major who had won the Victoria Cross fighting the Japanese.

'What did he do?'

'I've forgotten, but I know he was very brave.'

'Braver than Dad?'

'Of course. All he ever did in the war was get

21

shot.'

His father had fought against the Germans and been shot in the leg which was why he still limped a little. He'd even been a prisoner of war for a while though, rather disappointingly, he hadn't escaped, as they always did in films. Tommy was as keen on bravery as he was on manhood. The two things went together. All those hours watching westerns hadn't been for nothing. He'd wondered lately how Flint McCullough would react to being sent off to boarding school. No tears, for sure. A tilt of the chin, perhaps. A manly nod. Tommy tried but the ball of dread in his stomach didn't seem to want to shift.

At its core was the problem everyone—well, his parents and a long line of doctors—had been trying to solve for as long as he could remember. It was the great shame that blighted their lives and was probably the reason they didn't want him to live with them at home any more.

It didn't happen every night. He could go two or sometimes even three nights in a row and then his mother would get all excited.

'Well done, Tommy, that's it! You've cracked it! Good boy!'

Then, the next night, as if some spiteful goblin inside him were playing tricks with them all, it would happen again: he would wake in the early hours to the silence of the house and that familiar warm wetness between his thighs. And he would lie there, cursing and hating himself and silently sobbing with rage and self-pity.

Nobody seemed to be sure why he wet the bed. His mother claimed it was the result of a bad attack of mumps at the age of three. This, she maintained, had weakened his *waterworks*. One doctor, the one Diane called The Trick Cyclist, said that Tommy was doing it on purpose, just to get attention. He prescribed a routine of reward and punishment. And for about a month, they had put it to the test. A dry night and Tommy was allowed to stay up for an extra half hour. A wet one and he wasn't allowed to watch television or have any ice cream or chocolates. It was soon clear that the only effect of this routine was to make everybody miserable and bad tempered and, like all the previous remedies, it was eventually dumped and off they trooped to see another doctor, then another.

The one they went to see in Harley Street provided them with a special new kind of rubber undersheet. It had already proved, he told them, a great success in America and was fitted with electric sensors and a length of black rubber cable that you had to plug in to the wall. At the first hint of wetness, even the slightest trickle, it would administer an electric shock—-nothing too severe, the doctor assured Tommy's mother, *just enough to rouse the boy*—and set off an alarm bell. Tommy didn't know how much it cost, but judging by his mother's expression when she saw the invoice, it was obviously a lot.

In the early hours of the first night they tried it, there was a blue flash and a loud bang and Tommy was launched out of bed like a space rocket. He landed on the floor with a burn on his bottom that took two weeks to heal.

These last few months, with the date of his departure to the brave and manly world of Ashlawn Preparatory creeping ever closer, the hunt for a cure had escalated to a kind of frenzy. And the more they all talked about it, the less control he seemed to have over his bladder.

All summer long he had been taking some little yellow pills, which were supposed to make him sleep so lightly that he would wake when he had to pee. They didn't succeed in waking him but all day long he felt like a different person, like some crazed character from a cartoon. He'd never had more energy in his life, was unable to sit still, not even for a minute, and was so noisy and frantic that a few days ago his mother couldn't bear it any longer and flushed the remaining pills down the toilet.

The latest—and what would probably be the last—attempt to stop his bed-wetting was to prop the foot of his bed up on two stout logs. His mother had read about it in a magazine. The idea, she explained, was to relieve the pressure on his bladder by *harnessing the force of gravity*. This meant that Tommy had to sleep with his feet at an angle of about thirty degrees to the floor. So far he had wet the bed every night and woken each morning crumpled against the wall with a stiff neck.

By the time his father arrived home, Tommy was in bed, trying to banish thoughts of boarding school by reading one of his collection of Illustrated Classics, *Custer's Last Stand*. General Custer was one of Tommy's real-life heroes. There was a full-page picture of him, in his buckskin suit, completely surrounded by bloodthirsty savages, a smoking gun in each hand, his long yellow hair flying in the wind.

Arthur Bedford was an accountant and worked

24

for a company that made parts for motor cars in Birmingham. Tommy didn't really have a clear idea about what this involved except that it meant looking after money and being very good at arithmetic, which was, by a long way, the most horrible subject in the world. The mere word *division* made him shiver. So it seemed only natural that his father came home looking weary and miserable. Though, come to think of it, he nearly always looked that way. This probably had something to do with the fact that he was always being criticized or nagged by Tommy's mother. Whatever the poor man did or failed to do seemed to irritate or annoy her.

The only occasions his father looked happy were when he was in the greenhouse, tending his tomatoes, or in his little workshop at the back of the garage, where he would sit for hours on end with a magnifying glass and a little lamp strapped to his forehead, carefully piecing together broken bits of porcelain. People would send him their smashed vases and plates and cups and saucers to mend. He was very good at it. When he'd mended something you wouldn't guess it had ever been broken.

The most exciting, if slightly puzzling, thing about him was that he belonged to a club so incredibly secret that you weren't allowed to ask him anything about it, nor even mention that you knew about it. They called themselves The Freemasons and held secret meetings once a month on a Thursday evening at a place called The Lodge. They had a special secret handshake so that they would know immediately if you were a real member or a spy trying to infiltrate them.

25

Tommy's father kept all his secret Masonic equipment in a slim brown leather suitcase which he hid on top of the wardrobe in his bedroom. Tommy had once sneaked a look inside it, expecting to find some sort of deadly weapon, like a ray gun or something, but all he found was a little blue-and-white satin apron, some strange-looking medals and badges and a magazine called *Health & Efficiency* which had pictures of naked women in it. He didn't tell anyone, not even Diane. She didn't seem to know any more about The Freemasons than he did, except that at their meetings at The Lodge everybody had to roll up their trouser legs and put hangman's nooses around their necks. She said it probably had something to do with golf because a lot of the men at his father's golf club were Freemasons too.

Tommy heard his father's car now, crunching across the driveway and into the garage. It was a new Rover 105S in two-tone green with beige leather seats and a walnut dashboard and his father treated it as if it had been made personally for him by God. The car door clunked shut and Tommy pictured his father walking slowly around, inspecting the paintwork for any tiny chips. He did this after every trip, however short, then, with a soft cloth and a bottle of methylated spirit, he would clean the squashed insects from the headlamps and the grille.

Arthur Bedford's reaction to his son's bed-wetting was much the same as it was to most things Tommy did. He remained wearily aloof. Cleaning up, changing the sheets and doing the laundry, along with almost everything to do with the children, was women's work. Tommy knew perfectly well however, from the sighs and the occasional overheard remark, that his father saw the problem as part of a general pattern of feminine weakness.

It had only recently begun to dawn on Tommy that his parents were a lot older than those of other children his age. His mother was nearly fifty and his father nearly sixty. People often thought they were his grandparents. His mother had once explained that they had *tried* for many years for a little brother or sister for Diane but that God hadn't wanted it to happen. Then, at last, along came Tommy. He was a *blessing,* she said. What had changed God's mind Tommy didn't know. And he wasn't quite sure about the *blessing* bit either, because he'd once overheard Auntie Vera describe him as an *accident.* Perhaps it was possible to be both.

'Good heavens. Still awake, are we?'

His father was peering in from the landing outside Tommy's bedroom, his unlit pipe sticking like Popeye's from the corner of his mouth. This meant he had to talk with his teeth clenched, which made him sound like a ventriloquist's dummy. The opposite of Tommy's mother in almost every respect, his father was tall and thin, with lots of bony angles to him. His clothes always seemed to have enough room for two of him. His hair was thick and floppy and silvery white except at the front where it was stained yellow by smoke from his pipe.

'*Wagon Train,*' Tommy explained.

'Ah.'

He stood, swaying a little, outside the bedroom door as if he couldn't decide whether to come in or say goodnight from where he was. He made a little jutting movement with his chin.

'That old fellow's going to miss you.'

Tommy didn't know what this meant. He put *Custer's Last Stand* down and watched his father step carefully among all the toy cowboys and Indians who waged constant war across the carpet. He looked as if he wanted to sit down on the bed but then noticed its strange angle and the logs propping it up and decided it was safer to stand. The bedside lamp made his baggy cavalry twill trousers glow while his top half remained in shadow. He plucked the teddy bear from the pillow and Tommy realized that this was the 'old fellow' he'd been talking about.

'Hmm. Poor old chap's looking a bit worse for wear.'

It was true. Old Ted had bald patches and bore the scars of many repairs. He'd once belonged to Diane and had been the victim of countless fantastic misfortunes. He'd been tortured and hanged, burnt at the stake, tossed from windows and subjected to hugely invasive surgery.

'Can't I take him with me?'

His father laughed.

'Teddy bears at prep school? Good heavens, no! What would they think?'

'What would who think?'

'Staff, other boys, everyone.'

'Doesn't everyone have a teddy bear?'

'Only when they're little.'

He ruffled Tommy's hair.

'Don't worry, we'll look after him.'

He tucked the bear back into bed.

'Well, better see what the old girl's done to my

28

supper. Lights out now.'

He bent down and for a moment Tommy thought he was going to kiss him, which he hadn't done for years. But he was just looking for the lamp switch. His tweed jacket smelled of smoke and the whisky he'd been drinking at the golf club.

'Emptied the bilges, have we?'

'Yes.'

'Let's see if we can have a dry night then, hmm?'

'I'll try.'

'That's the spirit. Night-night, old chap.'

'Night.'

Tommy lay on his back, staring at the slice of yellow light that angled across the ceiling from the landing while he performed his nightly ritual, reciting in a whisper one hundred times, *I will not wet the bed, I will not wet the bed, I will not wet the bed . . .*

His parents were watching the TV news in the sitting room. A man was talking about President Eisenhower coming back to London from Scotland where he'd been to visit the queen. His first name was Dwight but everyone called him Ike. He seemed like a nice old man. Tommy had a photo of him shaking hands with John Wayne.

His thoughts drifted back to Flint and how clever he was to have found those hoofprints by the river. He wondered what would have happened to the little girl if she hadn't been rescued from the Indians. Worse than boarding school, for sure. Just two days more at home and that was where he would be. The place had looked pleasant enough in the spring when his mother and father had taken him to see it. Vast rolling lawns and lots of trees. Football pitches. A gym with ropes you could climb. Maybe it wouldn't be too bad after all.

Somewhere in the float of these thoughts, Tommy must have fallen asleep because the next thing he knew was that the house was all quiet and the landing light had been switched off. Someone was stroking his forehead.

'Diane?'

'Hello, my darling,' she whispered.

She was kneeling beside his bed and he had the impression that she'd been there for some time. She leaned closer and kissed his cheek. She was still wearing her raincoat. Her hair smelled of flowers.

'Have you just got here?'

'Yes.'

She kept stroking his forehead. Her hand felt soft and cool. In the dark he couldn't see her face clearly but her smile was sad and somehow he knew she'd been crying.

'What's the matter?'

She put her finger to her lips.

'Sshh. You'll wake them. Nothing's the matter. Just happy to see you, that's all.'

Now it was his eyes that welled with tears.

'Diane?'

'What, darling? What is it?'

'I don't want to go to boarding school.'

He started to cry and that started her off again. She gathered him up in her arms and he buried his face in the warm scented softness of her neck. And they clung to each other and wept.

TWO

Ashlawn Preparatory School for Boys was an imposing Gothic mansion in red brick, complete with ramparts, ornate turrets and various reputed ghosts. It stood on a low hill in twenty acres of parkland planted with oaks and cedars and girdled by a six-foot wall topped with barbed wire of ambiguous purpose. The mansion had been built by a Victorian industrialist who had risen from the slums of Birmingham to make his fortune in the colonies, a fortune which he promptly lost, whereupon the building, intended as a monument to his elevated social standing, became instead, for the next seventy years, a home for the mentally deranged.

During the First World War the clientele was expanded to accommodate a hundred and twenty shell-shocked soldiers and only when the last of them had died or otherwise departed were its decaying corridors and dormitories modestly refurbished as a school. There were smarter, more expensive prep schools in the county to which the sons of established upper- and middle-class families were dispatched. Ashlawn was for the more transitional, both upward and downward, whose social aspirations or pretensions outstretched their means.

For the benefit of the outside world and fee-paying parents, the impressive iron gates, adorned with the school crest and motto, *Semper Fortis*, were regularly repainted and the half-mile meander of driveway rigorously weeded. But in the

31

darker, more remote reaches of the mansion itself, where parents were less likely to stray, little had changed in half a century. The flaking gloss paint, in shades of institutional brown and pale green, remained untouched; the original pipework clanked beneath the worm-ridden floorboards; the iron-framed beds, painted in chipped black enamel, still had slots for the canvas straps that had once restrained the unruly; and the wooden benches of the dank and fetid changing room still bore the etched initials of the demented and the desperate.

For the new arrivals, or *newbugs*, as they were not so affectionately known, fresh faced and swamped by their oversized uniforms, the changing room was one of Ashlawn's most fearful places. One of the first things they discovered was that this was the chamber to which boys were summoned after lights-out for official beatings by the staff and, at almost any other time, for less official but much more inventive torture by the school's many bullies. The walls above the engraved benches were lined with neatly named pegs and wire cages where the boys kept their sports kit. The air was laced with the smell of wet and putrefying socks. Except for a grimy skylight in the adjoining shower room, the only light came from a single bare bulb that dangled from a fraying cord.

It was here that Tommy Bedford, three days and three miraculously dry nights after his arrival, now stood in his baggy knee-length rugby shorts and spotless white shirt, trying to untie the laces of his rugby boots. They had been knotted tightly and intricately to the wire of his cage and his fingernails were bitten too short to free them. His games group was being supervised by the house tutor, Mr Brent, who Tommy already knew was the strictest and meanest of all the masters. The other boys had already set off for the playing fields and, as the echo of their voices faded from the corridor outside, panic was rising in his chest.

'Naughty newbug. Going to be late for games, aren't we?'

Tommy didn't yet know many of the older boys but he knew this one. Everybody knew to steer clear of Critchley. And of his henchman, Judd, whose leering face now appeared in the doorway behind him. They were probably about eleven years old and were in Remove B, otherwise known as Dumbos, the class they put you in if you were stupid or lazy or both.

'Oh, dear. Got our laces in a muddle, have we?' Judd said.

'Yes.'

'What's your name, newbug?'

'Bedford.'

'Oh, you're the Log Boy, aren't you?' Critchley said.

He was tall and sinewy, with flaxen hair that flopped over his forehead. Judd was squat and broad, with a meaty butcher's-boy face. Tommy busied himself with the laces, pretending not to have heard. Nor did he look at them. One of the first things newbugs learned was not to get caught staring at older boys. If you did they would tell you to *face off* and probably punch you or get you in a headlock. From the corner of his eye he could see the two boys sauntering closer.

'Are you deaf as well as stupid, Log Boy?'

33

'No, sir—I mean, no, Critchley.'

'I said, you're the Log Boy, aren't you?'

'What are they for then?' Judd said.

'What are what for?' His voice sounded tiny, crimped with fear.

'The logs, you slimy little turd.'

Matron had been informed about Tommy's bed-wetting but, so far, nobody else knew. He'd already been teased about the logs and, on Diane's advice, had told anyone who asked that he suffered from poor circulation and that sleeping at an angle helped his blood flow better. He started to explain this but didn't get very far. Critchley grabbed hold of his ear and began to twist it.

'Get off!'

He lashed out and knocked the hand away. His knees were shaking and he felt his bladder begin to loosen.

'Oooh, look.' Critchley sneered. 'Log Boy's got a temper.'

Tommy glared at them, his heart thumping.

'Face off!' Critchley yelled.

Tommy looked down and in the same instant, Judd stepped behind him and pinned his arms behind his back. Critchley had hold of both ears now and twisted them until Tommy thought they were going to rip loose from his head. He felt the tears starting to roll down his face and, far worse, a warm trickle down the inside of his thigh. Critchley must have smelled it for he let go of Tommy's ears and stepped back to watch.

'Oh, dearie, dearie me, what's going on here?'

Tommy's long green woollen socks absorbed some of the flow but soon he was standing in a small but spreading puddle. Judd released his arms

34

and stood beside Critchley, their two faces contorting with delight and revulsion.

'Ugh!'

'How dis*gusting*. Log Boy, you are dis*gusting*. What are you?'

Tommy didn't answer. Judd grabbed him by the ear.

'What *are* you?'

'Disgusting,' Tommy said quietly, trying not to whimper.

'That's right. Dis*gusting*.'

There were footsteps coming down the corridor now and from the important click of steel-tipped heels all three boys knew it was one of the masters.

'Tell him we're here, Log Boy, and you're dead meat. Okay?'

Tommy nodded and the two boys darted past him and disappeared into the adjoining shower room. Tommy stood where he was, ears aglow, while the footsteps came closer and stopped. The kind and ruddy face of Mr Lawrence, who taught English and Latin, leaned in around the open door.

'Hello, who have we here?'

'Bedford, sir.'

'Bedford.'

'Yes, sir.'

Mr Lawrence glanced down at the puddle at Tommy's feet.

'Ah. Hard luck, old chap. Let's get you cleaned up, shall we?'

Fifteen minutes later, Mr Lawrence delivered Tommy, in a giant pair of borrowed shorts, down to the muddy plateau of the playing fields. It was starting to rain. Mr Lawrence had a quiet word with Mr Brent, who nodded and snapped at Tommy not to be late again then started yelling at another boy whose shirt wasn't properly tucked in. Tommy must have looked petrified because Mr Lawrence, as he left, put a hand on his shoulder and winked.

'Semper fortis, Bedford,' he said quietly. 'Semper fortis.'

'Sir.'

Mr Brent blew his whistle and, with the icy autumn rain whipping around their knees, Tommy and two dozen other miserable eight-year-olds spent the next ninety minutes running around in the mud and hurting one another and being constantly hectored by Mr Brent.

It seemed more like years than days since he'd stood on the gravel forecourt, waving goodbye to his parents and Diane. He could still see his sister's distraught face looking back at him through the rear window as the Rover pulled away down the driveway. She had been more upset than any of them, even Tommy. The new boys had been told to report to school an hour earlier than the older boys. Tommy had helped his father and Diane haul his trunk and tuck box into the hall, where Mr and Mrs Rawlston, the headmaster and his wife, stood chatting with the other new parents. When it was their turn, his father gave his customary hard handshake (perhaps even a Masonic one) and Tommy noticed Mrs Rawlston wince a little. Diane didn't shake hands because she was crying too much.

'Righty-o then, Tommy,' his father said. 'We'll be off now.'

He held out his hand and Tommy braced

himself for the squeeze. 'Good luck, old chap.'

There were tears in his mother's eyes now too. He'd never seen her cry before. She kissed him on the cheek. Tommy was biting his lip. His father had told him several times that to be seen *blubbing* wasn't a good idea.

'Matron's got the logs,' his mother whispered. 'Don't let her forget.'

'I won't.'

It was the way Diane hugged him that finally put him over the edge and turned on his own tears. She was sobbing and her face was streaked black from her eye make-up.

'Come on, old chap,' his father said, glancing around. 'Let's have none of that.'

When the parents had all gone, the newbugs were shepherded into the dining hall for tea with Matron. There were about twenty of them, some still snivelling, some simply wide-eyed with shock. They were all told to stand around a long table laid with plates of sandwiches and lurid yellow fruitcake. Miss Davies, the matron, was short and wide and wore a blue uniform and round glasses whose lenses were so thick they made her eyes appear huge and fierce. This, along with the starched white wings of her headdress, made her seem like an overweight bird of prey preparing to swoop. She took her place at the head of the table, bowed her head and clasped her hands together. Tommy noticed she had long whiskers on her chin.

'May the Lord make us truly grateful,' she said in a broad Welsh accent. 'Amen.'

One or two of them muttered *Amen*. But clearly not enough for Matron. She made everyone repeat it.

37

'And say it as if you mean it.'

They did and she told them they could be seated.

'Tuck in now, boys.'

There was a choice of water, milk or tea from a huge metal teapot. Tommy chose milk.

For about five minutes nobody, not even Matron, uttered another word. She kept checking the time on the small stainless steel watch pinned to her bosom. Outside in the corridors they could hear the voices of the older boys arriving. They sounded happy to be back, which Tommy found both perplexing and slightly encouraging. He studied his fellow newbugs. Nobody seemed hungry. They were mostly just staring at their plates. The only one still crying was the boy sitting next to him. He had a podgy pink face and dark curly hair and glasses with pink frames in which the left lens was frosted so that you couldn't see his eye. The name tape on his sodden handkerchief said *WADLOW. P.* His crying was so loud and vigorous that it was soon the focus of attention for the entire table.

'Hush now, boy,' Matron chided gently. 'That's enough. Eat your sandwich.'

Wadlow obeyed but it didn't stop his crying, merely modified its tone. Tommy noticed the boy sitting opposite him was grinning. He had freckles and a shock of dark red hair and was the only one at the table who seemed to be enjoying himself. He was by now on his fourth sandwich. He gave Tommy a wink and Tommy, who had never been able to master the art of winking, gave him a forced little smile instead. He was just starting to think he might have found a friend, when Wadlow

38

started to make a strange gurgling sound, leaned forward and threw up, spectacularly, all over the table. A dozen other boys promptly burst into tears.

The red-haired boy was called Dickie Jessop and Tommy was pleased to find they were in the same dormitory and in the same class. Over the next couple of days the two of them became friends. Dickie's parents lived in Hong Kong and he only saw them once a year when he flew out there for the summer. He had been at various boarding schools since he was five years old and after just one day told Tommy that Ashlawn wasn't half as bad as others he'd known. He was funny and was always cracking jokes and didn't seem afraid of anyone or anything. He was cheeky with some of the teachers and the older boys but did it with such charm that they didn't seem to mind. Best of all, he adored westerns and knew almost as much about them as Tommy did. Tommy asked him who his number one cowboy was and without a moment's hesitation Dickie said it was Flint McCullough from *Wagon Train*. They shook on it.

At teatime on that third day, after rugby, Tommy told him quietly about his encounter with Critchley and Judd in the changing room, though he left out the part about wetting his pants and pretended to have acted rather more courageously than in fact he had.

Dickie heard him out then nodded gravely.

'We'll get 'em,' he said.

'I don't think that's a good idea.'

'Don't worry. You don't have to. I will.'

Tommy was dry again that night. That made four nights in a row. He'd never gone that long

39

before and felt cautiously elated. He had upped his nightly recitation of *I will not wet the bed* to two hundred times and it seemed to be working. After breakfast, when he went to Matron's room for his daily spoonful of cod liver oil, she almost smiled at him.

'Well done, boy,' she mouthed. 'Keep it up.'

One week. If he could go one week, he'd beat it forever. But take it a night at a time, he told himself.

Some of the boys in his dorm made remarks about the logs that propped up his bed. And on one occasion, in the bathroom, a boy called Pettifer, who seemed to be jealous of Tommy's friendship with Dickie, called him *Log Boy*. Dickie grabbed him by the throat, pinned him against the wall and threatened blood-curdling consequences if he ever said it again.

Their dorm was long and narrow with sixteen metal beds, eight each side, all with identical scarlet wool blankets. Every boy had a peg for his dressing gown and a metal chair on which to put his neatly folded clothes. Tommy's bed was the nearest to the door and this position carried with it the duty of keeping *cave* (which was apparently Latin for *beware* and was pronounced *KV*) and sounding the alarm at the approach along the corridor of Matron or 'Whippet' Brent.

All the staff had nicknames: Mr Rawlston, the headmaster, was Charlie Chin because he didn't have one; Matron, being Welsh and fierce, was The Dragon; and Mr Lawrence was Ducky or The Duck, for reasons Tommy had yet to discover. Nobody however needed to explain Mr Brent's nickname. It referred both to his pointed canine

40

features and to his reputation for administering the most ferocious beatings. His instrument of choice was a red leather, hard-heeled slipper, which left bruises known to last two weeks. Every night, at eight o'clock, when he came to turn off the lights, he would creep along the corridor in the hope of catching boys in the act of some beatable offence, like pillow fighting or reading a comic or an unsuitable book.

It was on the fifth evening that Tommy was to discover the burden of responsibility that his post as dormitory lookout truly entailed.

The boys had all returned to the dorm, scrubbed and energized, from the bathroom and Dickie Jessop was holding court. He had a seemingly endless repertoire of dirty jokes and rhymes. Few, if any, of his audience understood the sexual references, but they all laughed loudly to pretend they did. Displaying ignorance in these matters could transform you in a moment into a target for derision.

Except for Wadlow and a few others, too shy or unusual—and thus already excluded from the pack to be prey for the likes of Critchley and Judd— they were huddled on and around Dickie's bed, listening to a recital of rude limericks.

'Here's another,' he said.

'A lesbian once in Khartoum
Took a nancy boy back to her room.
As they climbed into bed
The nancy boy said
Who does what and with what and to whom?'

Tommy didn't understand this one at all but he

41

roared with the rest of them. Nobody seemed to have noticed that it was drawing close to eight o'clock. He was sitting alongside Dickie, basking in reflected glory. They were now generally considered to be best friends. Both had their backs to the door.

'Okay,' Dickie said, holding up his hands for quiet. 'Here's one I made up. How about this…

'There once was a Whippet called Brent
Whose cock was exceedingly bent…'

It was at this moment that Tommy noticed the grins beginning to vanish from the faces of the boys sitting opposite, the ones who had sight of the door. He turned to see what they were looking at. Standing just inside the doorway, leaning against the wall, was Mr Brent. He had his arms folded and a strange half-smile on his face. Everyone had seen him now. Except Dickie. He was too carried away by his own brilliance to have noticed the sudden chilling of the air.

'… To save Matron trouble,
He stuffed it in double
So rather than coming, he went!'

He laughed proudly and rocked back on the bed and it was only when he became aware that this one didn't seem to have gone down so well that he looked at the faces around him and then turned to see what they were all staring at.

Mr Brent unfolded his arms and gave three slow claps.

'Very good, Jessop. Quite the poet, I see.'

42

There was a ripple of nervous laughter and Tommy thought for a moment that it was all going to be treated as a joke. Mr Brent still had that odd little smile on his lips. Then suddenly it was gone.

'All right,' he snapped. 'Into bed, everyone.'

He watched them scatter like mice to their holes and when all was still, all eyes upon him, his finger poised on the light switch, he added quietly:

'I'll be seeing you later, Jessop. Lights out now! No talking.'

He flicked the switch and they all lay frozen with fear in the darkness until his footsteps had faded along the corridor.

'You were supposed to be keeping *cave*, Bedford,' Pettifer whispered from the other side of the room.

'I know,' Tommy said. 'Sorry, Jessop.'

Dickie didn't answer. It was about half an hour before Mr Brent appeared in the doorway again and told him quietly to put on his dressing gown and slippers and to report downstairs to the changing room.

'Good luck, Dickie,' Tommy whispered as Jessop shuffled past his bed. But again he didn't answer. For a long while nobody dared speak. Like Tommy, they were probably all imagining the scene. They knew the routine from the older boys, who always enjoyed scaring the newbugs. Dickie would be told to remove his dressing gown and bend over the wooden bench so that his nose was touching the wire mesh of one of the cages. And Mr Brent, in his shirtsleeves, would first slap the heel of the red leather slipper in the palm of his hand to give your imagination a little taste of what was to come. You never knew until the last

43

moment how many strokes to expect. It was usually three, four or six, depending on the severity of the offence.

The silence that now hung over the upstairs of the school seemed to hum with fear and fascination. Every boy in every dormitory was listening. They all heard the distant dull clunk of the changing-room door being shut. Tommy held his breath. There was a long pause. Then the first muted thwack. And in the grateful safety of their beds, the whole school winced and silently began to count.

One, two ...

Sometimes, if the victim was young or insufficiently brave, you would hear him cry out. But not tonight.

Three, four ...

Tommy didn't know if there was a God, but in case there was, he began to pray. And not just for Dickie, that he might bear the pain, but also that he would forgive him and still be his friend.

Five, six ...

Then silence. The listeners began to breathe again.

Now Dickie would be putting his dressing gown back on and then suffering the final humiliation of having to shake Whippet's hand. To absolve him, to thank him for his trouble.

When he came back to the dormitory, Dickie didn't say a word. There were a few whispered *hard luck*s and *well done*s and one idiot even asked him how it had felt. But Dickie didn't answer, just climbed back into bed, turned on his side and pulled the sheet and blanket up above his ears. Tommy couldn't tell if he was crying. For a long time nobody spoke. Then, across the darkness from the other side of the room, he heard Pettifer's venomous whisper:

'Should have been you down there, Log Boy.'

Tommy wet the bed that night. It was just after three in the morning and he lay weeping in the soggy warmth, wondering what to do. As quietly as he could, he pulled off the bottom sheet and tiptoed with it to the bathroom, wincing at every creak of the floorboards. Not daring to switch on the light, he sluiced the sheet in one of the big cast-iron baths then did the same with his pyjama bottoms, wringing them out as best he could. Then he tiptoed back to the dormitory and remade the bed, freezing whenever anyone shifted in his sleep, hardly daring to breathe, scanning the other beds in case someone was awake and watching him in the dark. He climbed back into bed and spent the rest of the night shivering and wet, his head churning with fear. Perhaps no one would notice.

Routine required that the boys strip back their top sheets before breakfast to let the beds air. And the yellow wet stain on Tommy's was as plain to see and almost as fascinating to his peers as the dried blood on the seat of Dickie Jessop's pyjamas. Dickie's stain was a badge of heroism, Tommy's of undiluted shame. Pettifer was the first to notice. He held his nose as he walked past.

'Bloody hell, Log Boy, what a stink! How revolting.'

Tommy wet the bed again the following night and every night for a week. No one called him Log Boy any more, though not for fear of reprisals from Dickie Jessop, who now mostly ignored him. It was simply that someone had come up with a

45

better nickname, the obvious one. He found it painted on his tuck box one morning in a sniggering amendment to his proper name.

To all of Ashlawn, from now on, he was no longer Bedford, but *Bedwetter*.

THREE

Tom regretted coming almost as soon as he got there. He'd never much liked the man and liked even less the twist of jealousy that seeing him always inspired. Some people just brought out the worst in you. Truscott Hooper, known to friends and sycophants alike—both well represented here this evening—simply as Troop, was sitting at a little table in the far corner of the crowded college hall, signing copies of his book. There was a long line of adoring fans, some of whom Tom recognized. They should have known better.

Troop was on tour, publicizing his new bestseller, a thriller set in postinvasion Iraq. He was on the cover of this week's *People* magazine and Tom had seen him on the *Today* show. The book was already being made into a movie. It featured the same hero as the last three books, finely tailored to the spirit of the age (former Special Forces operative Brad Bannerman, dangerous but with the heart of a poet, wrongly disgraced for a misunderstood act of bravery, et cetera). Tom hadn't read any of them. It was hard enough to watch them sit gloatingly at the top of the bestseller lists without running the risk of discovering they were also actually rather good.

That was what the critics said anyhow. There was nothing more galling than a fellow writer who managed to sell millions of books *and* get good reviews. It stole all legitimate grounds for contempt.

No sane New York publisher would include Montana on a book tour for an author as big as Troop. Fewer than a million people lived there and most of them had better things to do than read books. No, Troop's presence here this evening, the return of the famous author to the bosom of his alma mater, the University of Montana, Missoula (to which he had already apparently made a lavish donation—you could almost hear the library sprouting new wings), had nothing to do with selling books. It was, it had to be—in Tom's view— simply an act of patronizing vanity.

Troop was, by a long way, the most successful novelist ever produced by the UM creative-writing program. When Tom enrolled, in the mid- seventies, Troop was in his third year and already a star. He'd sold short stories to *The New Yorker* and was about to have his first novel published. At six- feet-five, he was literally, as well as professionally, head and shoulders above everyone else. He was dressed tonight, as always, entirely in black. It was a kind of trademark. The black beard and flowing black hair were grizzled now, but this—Tom had to concede—only gave him an even greater gravitas. They were both in their mid-fifties but Tom was the only one who looked it.

Troop's handsome face had been on posters all over town for weeks and this evening's talk in the university's largest auditorium had been a sellout. There were even people standing at the back. The speech had been infuriatingly witty and modest and interesting and the applause at the end had made the windows rattle. Admission to this champagne reception afterward was strictly by ticket only.

Just as Tom was looking for somewhere convenient to park his glass so he could leave, he became aware of a young woman hovering in front of him. She was smiling a little tentatively and had clearly been trying to attract his attention while he'd been scowling at Troop.

'You're Thomas Bedford, right?'

'Yes, I am. I'm sorry, I...'

She held out her hand and he shook it, a little too hard. His five-year-old documentary series on the history and culture of the Blackfeet had recently aired again on PBS and Tom imagined she must have recognized him from that. Or maybe she'd been to one of his occasional lectures here at UM. She was good-looking in an unflashy kind of way. Late twenties, he guessed, maybe thirty. Fair skinned and freckly, thick auburn hair bundled up in a green silk scarf. Tom pulled in his stomach and smiled.

'Karen O'Keefe,' she said. 'We have the same dentist. I saw you there a couple of weeks ago.'

'Ah.'

He tried not to look crestfallen. There was an awkward pause.

'Did you enjoy the talk?' she said.

'Oh, Troop always puts on a good show.'

'You're friends?'

'Not exactly. We were on the writers' program here together. He was a couple of years ahead of me,' he couldn't resist adding.

48

'I wanted to kick him.'

Now Tom was interested. He laughed.

'Really? Why was that?'

'Oh, I don't know. All that phony modesty, when you can see from a hundred miles he's got an ego the size of Everest. If he could write a decent sentence, I might feel more charitable.'

Tom smiled, trying not to look too pleased.

'Are you a writer?' he asked.

'A filmmaker. Like you. Except you're a filmmaker *and* a writer. And I'm not suggesting I'm on anything like your level. I really enjoyed seeing your Blackfeet series again, by the way. And I loved the book. Great piece of work. Kind of definitive. I must have given it to a dozen people.'

'Thank you. That accounts for about half the total sales.'

A fan. Tom wasn't used to it. He got the occasional letter, of course, but it had been years since he'd had an encounter like this. He was almost lost for words.

'How come an Englishman has this great passion for the West?' she said, filling the pause.

'Oh, that's a long story.'

But it didn't stop him telling it. He had it perfectly honed: the childhood obsession with cowboys and Indians; how he'd grown up in *little* countryside and how, when he came to live in the States, the sheer scale of the real thing had blown him away; then his fascination at discovering the brutal truth behind all that myth and legend.

'You mean, like, the *true* story of the West.'

'Yes. I remember that first time I went to Little Bighorn—'

'Tommy!'

49

A hand clamped his shoulder and as he turned, Troop locked him in a bear hug that squashed Tom's glasses into one eye. Luckily he'd finished his drink or it would have soaked them both. The *Tommy* had given him a shock. He thought he'd lost that name forever at boarding school. Along with his innocence and much else besides.

'Hello, Troop,' he said. 'How're you doing?'

'Good, man. Good! And all the better for seeing you.'

Troop partially released him but was still gripping Tom's upper arms with his massive, hairy hands so that he could inspect him.

'You're looking good, man. You must work out?'

'No. Never have, never will.'

'How's that gorgeous wife of yours—Jan, right?'

'Gina. We split up fifteen years ago.'

'Shit. I'm sorry. You had a daughter, right?'

'A son. Daniel.'

'Daniel. How's he doing?'

'Okay, I think. I don't see a whole lot of him. He's in Iraq at the moment.'

'Jeez. A journalist?'

'No, he's with the Marines.'

'An officer.'

'Corporal.'

'Well, I'll be damned.'

'Won't we all.'

Tom turned to Karen O'Keefe, who was watching them with a wry little smile. He introduced them and noted the way Troop fixed her with his dark eyes and gripped her arm while he shook her hand, holding it a few moments longer than was necessary. Tom had seen Bill Clinton do the same many times on TV.

50

'Karen is one of your greatest fans,' Tom said.

'There's no accounting for taste,' Troop said.

'Actually, I've never read a word you've written,' Karen O'Keefe said. Tom was getting to like her more each moment.

'Well, that's okay too.'

'Too drenched in testosterone, I'm afraid.'

'And you know that even though you've never read a word I've written.'

'You'd probably call it female intuition.'

Troop smiled but his eyes had already hardened.

'Would I?'

He turned to Tom.

'Still living in Missoula?'

'Don't seem to be able to escape.'

'It's a great part of the world. I just bought a place down in the Bitterroots.'

'Great.'

'It's just a cabin, really. But I figure on spending more time up here. LA gets a little frantic sometimes. Well, listen, I'd better—what do they call it?—*circulate* a little. Catch you later, Tom.'

'You bet.'

Troop nodded at Karen O'Keefe and she gave him a smile that somehow managed to be both courteous and insolent.

'What a jerk,' she said when he was barely out of earshot.

'Remind me to stay on the right side of you.'

She laughed and put her hand on his arm, letting it stay there for a moment.

They swapped numbers and e-mail addresses and went their separate ways. When Tom left she was talking with a cruelly handsome guy her own age. It had been a long time since he'd let himself

51

feel attracted to a woman in that way. But he probably wouldn't call her. Since Gina left he'd had two or three romantic skirmishes but nothing that had lasted. He lived alone with his dog and that was how he liked it. He got lonely sometimes and missed the companionship, the physical intimacy, not that there had been much of either with Gina at the end.

The house they had built together sat in the bend of a creek about a mile east of town. As he came around the last corner his headlights found a small herd of deer holding a meeting in the middle of the road and he slowed and stopped and sat watching them until they melted into the trees. It was early spring and there was no moon and when he got out of his car, he stood for a long time in the driveway, staring at the stars and listening to the rush of the creek.

Makwi was there, as she always was, to greet him when he came in through the front door. She was a mongrel mix of deerhound, greyhound and collie, what in England or Ireland they would call a lurcher. She had a rough brindle coat and the biggest heart of any dog he'd known. He knelt and let her nuzzle his face while he rubbed her neck and her ears and told her he'd take her out for a walk in just a moment. She followed him into the kitchen and stood watching while he poured himself a glass of milk. The answering machine on the divider was flashing red, telling him there were four messages. He hit the play button and, as he waited for the tape to rewind, pulled out his cell phone. He'd switched it off for Troop's talk and forgotten to switch it back on. There were two voice mails.

All six messages were from Gina. They hadn't talked in more than a year. Her voice sounded strained and increasingly anxious at not being able to get hold of him. She didn't say why she needed to talk with him so urgently, but there was no need. He knew there could be only one reason. Danny. Something must have happened to Danny.

FOUR

The cast stood in line with their hands still joined, the crimson velvet curtain in front of them masking for a moment the glare of the lights. It was their fourth curtain call and the applause seemed to be growing with each one. Diane's chest was heaving with pure exhilaration. She could feel the adrenalin coursing through her veins. She was dizzy, her body alight. She glanced at Gerald to her right and he grinned at her and squeezed her hand and at that moment the curtain began to lift again and she turned to face the dazzle of the footlights and the vague impression of the audience beyond.

They were cheering now, calling *bravo!* And even through the glare she could see that people in the stalls and the dress circle were getting to their feet and holding up their hands to clap above their heads. She waited for Gerald, from whom the cast took their lead, to step forward. Only this time, he released her hand and started to clap and so did the rest of the cast and Diane realized that they were applauding her, that this call was for her, just her. It was the first time it had happened. She stepped hesitantly forward and for a moment just stood there with her hands at her side, beaming and glowing and almost in tears. Then she bowed and curtsied and the audience roared.

Fortune's Fool was only in its second week and she still couldn't quite believe the reception it was getting. None of them could, not even Gerald who had a string of West End hits to his name and every night had a crowd of fans at the stage door, begging for his autograph. The run was completely sold out and the critics had been little short of ecstatic. Even that notorious old curmudgeon Harold Hobson liked it. Most of all, they liked Diane. 'In her West End debut as a leading lady,' Kenneth Tynan wrote in *The Observer*, 'Diane Reed is little short of electrifying . . . a presence so luminous, it almost threatens to eclipse her fine fellow players.'

John, the playwright, a walking redefinition of misanthropy who, in rehearsal, had never once smiled nor barely addressed a word to her, had sent her the most extravagant bunch of roses she'd ever seen. With it came a slightly worrying note saying he was already at work on a new piece that Diane had *inspired* in him, with a part only she could play.

Gerald, who was supposed to be the star of the show, had reacted to her theft of his limelight with remarkably good grace and a noticeable stepping-up of his month-long campaign to gain access to her knickers. Perhaps he felt she owed him it.

It had become a ritual that he came to her dressing room after every performance with a half-bottle of chilled champagne and two glasses. And that was where he was now, still in his make-up, his ample backside propped against the edge of her dressing table, while he watched her remove her make-up. They had both shed their costumes and were now in bathrobes, his by far the more sumptuous—burgundy satin, piped in black, tailor-made for him at some extortionate shop in Jermyn Street.

Her dressing room was tiny and crammed with flowers, and this, along with the face-flattering glow of the light bulbs around the mirror and the many cards from friends and well-wishers, managed to disguise the fact that the walls hadn't seen a paintbrush in twenty years. The room was also, currently, full of smoke because Gerald was trying to look like Noel Coward, puffing one of his ghastly Turkish cigarettes in a little tortoiseshell-and-silver holder.

'You were astonishing tonight,' he said.

'Was I?'

'You know you were.'

He was using that deep, husky voice, a kind of gruff whisper, which he obviously thought was seductive. On stage or off, the only effect it ever had on Diane was to make her want to giggle. He took a sip of champagne and came to stand behind her, lowering his head to put it beside hers so that he could admire their joint reflection in the mirror.

'God, you're gorgeous.'

She wasn't sure which of them he was talking to.

'Don't be silly.'

'I've booked a table at Luigi's,' he said, sniffing her hair. Soon he would be nuzzling her neck. It was time to get rid of him.

'Darling, I told you, I can't. I've got to have

dinner with these Hollywood people. They've come over specially.'

'Let's all eat together then.'

Diane stood up and gave him a sisterly peck on the cheek.

'No.'

He held her by the hips and moved in for what was clearly intended to be a different kind of kiss. Diane put her hands on his chest to keep him at bay.

'I have to hurry. They'll be waiting for me downstairs.'

'You're driving me insane.'

'Then we'll just have to lock you away somewhere.'

There was a timely knock at the door and Wilfred, the veteran stage door Cerberus, announced that her agent was in the lobby with 'two American gentlemen'. Diane called out that she would be down in a few moments. Gerald showed no sign of going. He was clearly hoping she might disrobe and dress in front of him, so she went to the door and sweetly held it open for him and, reluctantly, with the face of a lovelorn spaniel, he left.

She hadn't met either of the men Julian Baverstock, her agent, had brought along to see tonight's performance. But she'd certainly heard of them. Everybody had. Herb Kanter was one of the most powerful producers in Hollywood. His films were both critical and commercial successes. And Terence Redfield was one of the new generation of directors that everyone was talking about. He was only in his thirties but had already done pictures starring Cary Grant, Marilyn Monroe and

Marlon Brando. They were looking for someone to play opposite Gary Cooper in a movie for Paramount called *Remorseless*. It was scheduled to shoot next autumn. Diane's hands were trembling so much with excitement, she could hardly fasten her dress.

She had borrowed it specially for the occasion from a friend who was a model and was given clothes by some of the top Parisian fashion houses. This one was in dark green silk and cut perilously low. It fitted her as if she had been decanted into it. She'd borrowed a necklace too, a single strand of real pearls. By the time she was dressed and had done her face, her hair and a few assessing twirls in front of the mirror, she concluded that everything about the way she looked—the hair, the necklace, even the dress—was wrong. They would never offer her the part. Not in a million years.

But as soon as she saw them standing there, watching her come down the dingy staircase with her fur coat over one arm, she knew she was being too hard on herself. Herb Kanter's jaw visibly dropped. He was short and sleek and reminded her of one of the sea lions at London Zoo, except for the heavy black-framed glasses that seemed to steam up a little when he shook her hand. And unless Terence Redfield, who was tall and thin and had a droopy ginger moustache, gave that kind of look to every woman he met (which was, of course, more than possible), Diane guessed she was at least in with a chance.

Julian, looking extremely pleased with himself, introduced them and just as they headed out to the waiting taxi, with immaculate timing, Gerald appeared. He was no doubt still hoping to join

57

them for dinner. He put a proprietorial arm around Diane's shoulders but wilted a little when Mr Kanter got his name wrong and called him Jeremy. It provided just enough distraction for Julian to tell Diane quietly that the movie part was virtually hers for the taking.

'In the bag, darling,' he whispered. 'They're absolutely smitten.'

It was true. They left poor Gerald skulking off into the night and drove across town to The Mirabelle in Curzon Street, where, at the best table, Diane pulled off her second bravura performance of the evening. It was what friends called her Audrey Hepburn impression. This involved appearing, at the same time, to be both confident and self-deprecating, intelligent but endearingly scatty, graceful but subversively earthy, attentive but not overly flirtatious except for the occasional and seemingly unconscious touch of a hand or an arm while laughing at some witty remark. Men, she knew, invariably adored being touched. Above all, she needed to appear *modern*, not stuffy and haughty and English. And, of course, she had to seem appropriately flattered, though not overwhelmed, by their interest.

Three hours later, sitting cross-legged on her bed in Paddington, she relived the dinner in front of her equally rapt flatmates, Helen, Molly and Sylvia, who had waited up in their sensible flannel nightdresses to hear all about it.

'Gary Cooper!' Helen said. 'Is it a western?'

'No, it's a psychological thriller.'

'He must be about a hundred and three,' Molly said.

'At least. I read in a magazine that he's had

58

plastic surgery and doesn't look anything like Gary Cooper any more.'

'I don't care who he looks like,' Diane said.

'I can't believe it!' Sylvia said. 'You're going to be a real movie star!'

'I know!'

'Have you told Tommy yet?'

'Give me a chance; it's two in the morning. I'll write to him tomorrow.'

'He's going to be so excited.'

It was one of the many things, and by a long way the most important, that hadn't yet dawned on Diane: how Tommy would react to the news that she might be going off to Hollywood. She was far too stirred up to sleep and long after the other girls had gone to bed, she lay, as she so often did, thinking about him.

His first few letters from Ashlawn had revealed almost nothing about how he was getting along. Diane remembered from her own boarding school how the new girls' letters were carefully monitored, so that parents wouldn't panic. You weren't allowed to say how miserable you were, how foul the food was, how horribly the teachers and the older girls treated you. Tommy's early letters from Ashlawn had the whiff of exactly that sort of censorship:

Dear Diane,

I hope you are well. I am fine. Today we played rugger. It was good fun. The food is okay [this last word crossed out and replaced, no doubt by decree, with all right]. Please ask Mum to send me some more 'Wagon Wheels' and 'Smarties' with as many different coloured tops

59

*as possible because we are all collecting them.
Blue ones are best. I hope your rehearsals are
going well.
Love, Tommy*

But the letter that had arrived two days ago was altogether different. The writing was scrawled, almost desperate, and the message chillingly brief.

*Dear Diane,
    Please, <u>PLEASE</u> get Mum and Dad to take
me away from here. I carnt stand it any longer.
They are bullying me. <u>PLEASE</u>.
Love, Tommy*

She knew he must somehow have managed to smuggle it out. Diane remembered bribing one of the school gardeners with a kiss to do the same. When Tommy's letter arrived, she had immediately phoned her mother and the conversation escalated in a matter of moments, as it usually did nowadays, into a shouting match.

'As always, Diane, you're being overdramatic. Do you have any idea how much it's costing your father to send Tommy to Ashlawn?'

'I know precisely how much, Mother. You've told me a hundred times.'

'It's always the same. Your father and I try to do what we think is right, looking after him and paying all the bills, and you do nothing but criticize. Miss High-and-Mighty, living the fancy life in London and telling everyone what they can and can't do. Honestly, I've had enough of it.'

'And so have I!' Diane yelled and slammed down the receiver.

Normally she would wait an hour then phone back to apologize. But not this time. If the Americans offered her the part, as it seemed almost certain they would, she would be going to Hollywood. And if things went well and her film career took off, perhaps she would want to stay there. At least for a while. For many months now she had been trying to find the courage to do something about Tommy. She still hadn't decided what, but she knew the time was almost at hand.

FIVE

They mostly left him alone nowadays and it was better that way. There were still, every day, random acts of cruelty, a sly punch or poke in the ribs, a foot stuck out to trip him in the playground, chewing gum placed on his chair, Kick Me notes stuck to his back. But Tommy had learned that if you kept quiet, tried to look as if none of this bothered you, steered clear of those shadowy corners where the worst predators lurked, then life could be just about bearable. There wasn't, he had discovered, nearly so much fun to be had from torturing someone who didn't appear to mind.

For this important lesson in survival, Tommy had to thank the unfortunate Piggy Wadlow. Piggy provided sport of an altogether more gratifying nature. When a tormentor snatched his glasses or tweaked his folds of fat in the showers or threw water bombs at him over the cubicle door when he was sitting on the toilet, he would rise like a fleshy tornado and roar after them, even with his shorts

61

and underpants flapping around his plump, pink thighs, his arms scything the air while he screamed retribution and occasionally managed to inflict it. Which, naturally, made such pursuits and endless variations of them all the more enjoyable.

There were certain measures which Tommy, now in his second term at Ashlawn, routinely took to protect himself. He always, for example, checked his bed before he climbed into it and he never put on a shoe or a boot or a slipper without first making certain it was empty. By so doing he had avoided sticking his toes into items of rotting fruit, dried dog turds and on one occasion, a dead mouse. At mealtimes he was careful never to take his eyes off his plate as it was passed from boy to boy along the table in case one of them chose to spit or shovel salt or something worse on to his food. He kept an obsessive eye on all that belonged to him and knew at a glance if anything had been taken or tampered with. And he never forgot to lock his tuck box, from which the painted alteration to his name had been removed with turpentine, leaving a white smudge just as eloquent.

The fact that his bed-wetting had become less frequent and that the logs had long ago been dispensed with seemed to make no difference. The nickname and reputation had passed into legend. His tormentors-in-chief were still Critchley and Judd, with their new apprentice Pettifer coming a close third. But at least Tommy knew what to expect from them and in their presence could steel himself. Much more upsetting were the many minor insults and injuries from boys who weren't really bullies at all, who were often actually quite decent when you found yourself alone with them, but who, in public, seemed obliged to be cruel.

Tommy knew, as much from instinct as experience, that to seek protection or justice from the staff, even from sympathetic masters like Ducky Lawrence, was counterproductive. Boys on whom you informed inevitably took their revenge, usually after lights-out or at morning break, in the toilets. He had seen it happen almost daily with Piggy, who would go screaming and sobbing to the first available master. And as the weeks and months went by, there had been a change in the way the masters listened to him. What had once been genuine concern and compassion had become a kind of weary contempt. Only yesterday, after someone pushed him over in the playground, Piggy had run howling to Charlie Chin who, quietly but sharply, told him not to tell tales, not to be *such a cissy*.

For two and a half terms, nearly nine whole months, without any real friend, Tommy had increasingly sought the solace of his fictional one. Denied his regular Monday evening dose of *Wagon Train* (television was, naturally, banned at Ashlawn, along with all other inventions that threatened to make life in any way enjoyable), he now had to make do with the photograph of Flint McCullough that he had taped inside the lid of his tuck box. There were pictures of his parents there too, as well as his favourite one of Diane outside the Café Royal. But it was Flint who held pride of place.

The tuck boxes were stored on slatted wooden shelves along a corridor to which the boys were allowed access only after meals. But at those times it was always too crowded and noisy, so Tommy had developed the habit of sneaking in illicitly when he might have the place to himself. It was, like most other minor transgressions, a beatable offence, but he was careful and hadn't yet been caught. His black lace-ups had rubber soles which meant he could move silently on the tiled floors and at any sound he would freeze and wait in the shadows until the danger had passed. When he got to his tuck box he would unlock it with the key he kept on a cord looped to the belt of his shorts. And as he gently lifted the lid, Flint's face would slowly be revealed, staring at him with that slightly sad yet comforting little half-smile, as if he'd been expecting him.

Tommy was aware that treating his tuck box like a shrine and standing before it in communion with a cowboy actor teetered on, if not over, the brink of weirdness. In fact sometimes he wondered if he might be going a little mad. He never spoke out loud to the picture and would have fled in terror had those famous McCullough lips so much as twitched in response. But in his head, Flint's voice rang as clear as if he were there in person.

'How'd you get on last night?'

'I wet the bed, darn it. I'd been dry for nearly three weeks.'

'Hard luck, son. But you're doing fine. How many *I will not*s are we saying now before we go to sleep?'

'Three hundred.'

'Let's try upping it to four.'

'Okay.'

'And that thing Pettifer said to you after breakfast. About your mother having square tits.

Don't let it get to you. He's just an idiot.'

'I know he is.'

'That's probably what his mother's look like.'

'Yeah. Saggy too I should think.'

'Real saggy.'

'Thanks, Flint.'

'You're welcome, Tommy.'

'I'd better go now. I'll see you later. Okay?'

'You bet. You take care now.'

'You too. Bye.'

The only person who came anywhere close to being a mentor in real life was The Duck. Mr Lawrence was an old man—well, probably about the same age as Tommy's father—and wore tweed jackets with leather pads on the elbows. He had little whiskery patches on his neck that he missed while shaving and he smelled comfortingly of pipe smoke like Tommy's father. Some of the older boys said he must be a *homo* because (a) he wasn't married and (b) his first name was Evelyn which was apparently a girl's name. Tommy didn't care. He was kind and funny and full of fascinating stories. He was the master in charge of Tommy's class, 2B, and whenever he came into the room he would say, *Ah, Two B or not Two B, that is the question* and they would all groan. Best of all, he had an infectious passion for books.

When he discovered how keen Tommy was on westerns, he gave him a copy of *Riders of the Purple Sage* and then a collection of short stories by Jack London. Tommy was immediately hooked and was soon reading almost anything he could lay his hands on. The school library was small and meanly stocked. But every Wednesday, after tea, The Duck escorted into town any boys who wanted to go to the public library where they were allowed to take out three books. It was the highlight of Tommy's week.

The walk into town was a winding descent of about a mile and, even in the rain, the sense of freedom as they stepped out of the school gates was thrilling. It wasn't advisable to be seen talking too much to masters in case you got accused of *sucking up* or, worse—when it happened to be Ducky Lawrence—of being a homo. Nevertheless, either on the way there or the way back, Tommy usually managed to have a chat with him. The Duck always had some new book or writer to suggest.

'Been thinking about you, Bedford.'

'Sir?'

'Have you read any Fenimore Cooper?'

'No, sir. Never heard of him.'

'*Last of the Mohicans*?'

'You mean Hawkeye? I've seen it on the telly. It's great.'

'The book's even better. Let's see if we can find it for you.'

By now Tommy had read every western the library had. The nice old woman behind the desk always made a point of telling him when a new one had arrived and even ordered special transfers for him from other libraries. While he waited, with The Duck's guidance, Tommy tried other writers, such as Agatha Christie, P. G. Wodehouse and the most frightening ghost story writer in the whole world, M. R. James. But The Duck's best suggestion by far was Rudyard Kipling. Tommy found himself transported to places that were thrilling and exotic yet somehow reassuringly ordered. Where there was danger, even wickedness, but where truth and decency finally prevailed.

It was on one such Wednesday evening, in the middle of a damp and dismal June, that Tommy found himself, to his surprise and cautious delight, reacquainted with Dickie Jessop. Dickie preferred illegal comics and magazines to books and rarely came on these trips to the town library. They had just walked back through the school gates and Tommy was trailing a few yards behind the rest of the group, partly through self-protective habit but also because he had his nose buried in the new Zane Grey novel he'd just borrowed. It was called *The Arizona Clan* and he was so absorbed he hadn't noticed Dickie had dropped back to walk beside him.

'What did you get?'

Tommy showed him.

'I thought Zane Grey was dead.'

'He is, but he wrote a lot, so the books keep coming out.'

'You read more than anyone I ever met.'

Tommy shrugged.

'I just like it.'

'Is it true your sister's going to be in a film with Gary Cooper?'

If anyone else had asked this, Tommy would have sensed a trap and denied it. Any item of personal information usually got twisted around and used against you. He would be accused of lying or boasting or they would call Diane a tart or make some insulting remark about her looks. But Dickie wasn't like the others.

'Yes,' he replied, simply.

Dickie nodded thoughtfully but said nothing. Tommy couldn't tell if he was impressed or not. So, trying to sound casual, he went on.

'She's over in Hollywood at the moment, actually.'

Dickie still didn't say anything. He just nodded again and stared away across the playing fields that had been transformed by weeks of unremitting rain into an ocean of mud. A watery sun flashed for a moment on the driveway puddles.

'How did you know? I mean, about the Gary Cooper thing.'

Dickie kicked a stone into a puddle.

'I dunno. Someone saw it in a magazine or something.'

Tommy guessed that getting confirmation of this story was probably the only reason Dickie had come back to walk with him. But having got it, he didn't seem in a hurry to go. His silence was more unsettling than it was surprising. Dickie Jessop had changed almost beyond recognition since those first few days when Tommy thought they were best friends. Not that he had become one of Tommy's tormentors. He never called him *Bedwetter*, just ignored him. And Tommy didn't take this personally because Dickie now ignored nearly everyone. In his own, more powerful way, he had become as much of a loner as Tommy. All the early cheek and sparkle and mischief had literally been beaten out of him.

The Whippet had made it a personal mission. There had been weeks when he'd summoned Dickie down to the changing room every single night. Dickie seemed to take it as a challenge and would break rules deliberately right under The

68

Whippet's long and twitching nose. On bath nights and in the showers after games, boys would gape at the bruises. His buttocks were an abstract painting of black and blue and purple and yellow, a work in progress that didn't get a chance to heal. Yet never once had anyone seen him cry. All that happened was that with each beating he had become a little quieter, a shade more serious, retreating one small step further into himself. It was like watching the slow yet steady dimming of a light.

They were trudging up the last stretch of driveway now and it was starting to rain again. As the school building loomed over them, Tommy felt a surge of desperation that he was about to lose a second chance of being Dickie's friend.

'Want to see something?' he said.

'What?'

'You have to promise not to tell anyone.'

Dickie shrugged.

'Okay.'

'Say *I promise.*'

'I promise.'

A few minutes later they were tiptoeing along the corridor to Tommy's tuck box. The time when it was permitted to be there had passed. They were supposed to be in their classrooms getting ready for prep. The corridor was dark but they didn't switch on the light. Tommy unlocked his tuck box and lifted the lid.

'Nice pictures.'

'That's Diane, my sister.'

Dickie nodded his approval then glanced at the picture of Flint.

'And you know who that is.'

''Course I do. Is that all you wanted to show

69

me?'

Tommy shook his head and reached down into the tuck box and carefully lifted out a large manila envelope.

'Look,' he said, pointing at the postmark.

'Hollywood, California.'

'It arrived this morning.'

Tommy glanced over his shoulder to make sure they were still alone. Then he opened the envelope and gently pulled out a large black-and-white photograph.

'See? It's Red McGraw from *Sliprock*,' he said proudly.

'Bedford, I *know* who it is, for heaven's sake.'

'Yes, but look what he's put on it.'

Dickie peered at the large, loopy handwriting.

To Tommy Bedford,
The Quickest Draw in England.
See ya along the trail!
Red

'Did he do this specially for you?'

' 'Course he did.'

'Wow.'

'And you know what?'

'What?'

'Promise you won't tell anyone.'

'Bedford!'

'Cross your heart and hope to die.'

Dickie wearily obeyed.

'They had a *date*.'

'What?'

'Diane and Red—well, he's not really called Red. His real name is Ray. Ray Montane. A *date* is

70

when—'

'Bedford, I know what a date is.'

Dickie stared at the picture for a moment. Tommy could tell he was impressed.

'So is she his girlfriend?'

'I don't know. I think so. They had dinner together, I know that. And she says he's really nice.'

'Wow.'

Suddenly the corridor lights went on.

'What do you two think you're doing in here?'

Charlie Chin was peering at them from the far end of the corridor. Tommy quickly slipped the photo and envelope back into his tuck box.

'Who is it? Speak up, boy!'

'Jessop, sir,' Dickie said. 'And Bedford. Just putting our library books away, sir.'

'You know you're not allowed in here, don't you? Well?'

'Yes, sir,' they said in unison.

'I'll see you both later. Now get along to your classrooms. Go!'

Two hours later, they were standing outside the changing room in their dressing gowns. It was only the second time Tommy had been beaten. The first was when The Whippet had slippered the whole dorm for talking after lights-out. But Charlie always used the cane. Tommy's knees had gone wobbly with fear. He didn't want to cry or, heaven forbid, wet himself. Not in front of Dickie. He tried to think of Flint but it wasn't much help.

'You'll be all right,' Dickie whispered. 'The first one hurts a bit but then it's okay. Just grip the bench and grit your teeth.'

Tommy didn't trust his voice so he just nodded.

71

The door opened and the headmaster stood there for a moment looking down at them. He had taken off his jacket and rolled up his sleeves. In his right hand was a thin bamboo cane, about three feet long.

'You first, Bedford.'

He stepped aside to let Tommy enter then shut the door behind him.

'Well, Bedford. Jessop leading you astray, is he?'

'Sir?'

'Teaching you some of his bad habits.'

'No, sir. It was my idea to go in there, not his.'

'I see. Anything more to say for yourself?'

'No, sir.'

'Very well. Since this is your first offence, I'm going to give you three.'

Tommy swallowed and nodded.

'Take off your dressing gown and bend over that bench.'

Tommy's lip began to quiver and he bit it hard. He laid his dressing gown on the bench and turned his back on Mr Rawlston and bent over until his head was inside one of the wire cages. He gripped the edge of the bench as hard as he could. For a moment all went still. Then the sound of Mr Rawlston taking a step forward and the swish of the cane as it whipped through the air and in the next instant a searing white slash of pain as it cut into his buttocks. Tommy whimpered and at the second stroke cried out. Then he remembered Dickie outside and how all the boys upstairs would be listening and he clenched his teeth and held hard to the bench and on the third stroke kept silent. But he couldn't stop the tears. Slowly he straightened himself and stood for a moment, facing the cage, trying to control himself. He felt humiliated and small and wretched and angry.

'Put your dressing gown on.'

Without looking at him, Tommy did so. He was about to head for the door when he realized Mr Rawlston was holding out a hand. Tommy had forgotten this part of the ritual. The man was actually smiling. Tommy shook his hand.

'It's customary to say *thank you*, Bedford.'

'Thank you, sir.'

'Good. Off to bed now.'

'Sir.'

As he came out Dickie smiled at him and whispered *well done*. Tommy's buttocks were on fire and as he walked along the cold corridor he put a hand inside his pyjama bottoms and gingerly felt the damage. He could trace the three welts but when he checked his fingers there was no blood. He made his way up the creaking wooden staircase and as he reached the top heard the first slash of the cane. He stood there and began to count. Two, three, four, five, six.

Tommy knew he was supposed to go directly back to his dormitory but instead he decided to wait for Dickie. They would return together. And as the thought occurred, standing at the top of the stairs, he began to feel something shift inside him. He wasn't crying any longer. He didn't feel ashamed or even sorry for himself. It was as if the glow of his backside were spreading and filling him with a kind of heroic pride. And now here came Dickie, grinning at him as he bounded up the stairs.

'Six!' Tommy whispered.

'Yeah. Pathetic.'

73

Tommy smiled.

'I heard what you told him, about it being your fault. Thanks.'

He put a hand on Tommy's shoulder and left it there a moment.

'Come on, better get to bed.'

They set off along the corridor. Side by side, like brothers in arms.

SIX

He hadn't seen Gina for nearly five years and he was struck by how little she had aged. She'd put on a few pounds but they looked good on her and so did the little smile lines around those dark brown eyes. Her hair was cut short which suited her too. To read the menu she needed to put on glasses, narrow square ones with glossy black frames that made her look both scholarly and sexy. Life knew no justice. Approaching her mid-fifties, she was every bit as beautiful as the day Tom had first laid eyes on her.

It was she who had chosen the restaurant. It was airy and ruthlessly minimalist. The waiters all wore black and there was an open stainless steel kitchen in the middle so you could watch your food being prepared. Everything on the menu seemed to be *seared* or *drizzled*. They were the only customers and had been given a table right in the window which felt a little like being in a zoo. Gina had already apologized twice, saying the place was new and that she had no idea if it was any good. Tom didn't come to Great Falls nowadays unless he absolutely had to. The east side of the mountains held too many memories and he didn't want to risk bumping into her. It was funny how you could fool yourself that you were over somebody. Watching her now across the table while she chewed her lip, deciding what to order, he knew he wasn't and probably never would be.

The waiter, who looked about fourteen, was hovering to hear what they wanted.

'I'll have the linguini,' Gina said. 'Then the tuna. Rare.'

'Excellent choice. You, sir?'

'Is it locally caught?'

'The tuna?'

'The linguini.'

'Ah—'

'Just kidding. I'll have the same.'

Gina was giving him that weary smile she always put on when he tried to be funny. Maybe she thought, given what had happened to Danny, that lightheartedness of any kind was inappropriate. She was right, of course. He'd allowed his pleasure at seeing her to get the better of him.

They had spoken on the phone almost every day since the news came through and Tom had foolishly allowed himself to enjoy being in touch with her again, almost as if he nurtured hopes. The waiter asked him if they wanted to see the wine list and Tom noticed how the question tightened Gina's attention. She was clearly interested to learn if he was still clean. He was and had been for eight years and he found it faintly insulting that she should doubt it. He ordered a bottle of mineral water.

It was almost a week since they had first found

out about Danny and they still had only a vague notion of what he was supposed to have done. All the military was saying, officially, was that an incident had taken place in which there had been an 'as yet unspecified number of civilian fatalities'. The Naval Criminal Investigative Service had been called in to establish what had happened. All the men involved, including Danny, had been suspended from active duty and were confined to their camp in a deserted factory outside of Baghdad. Danny had called and e-mailed Gina a few times but said he had been advised by his lawyer, provided by the military to represent him, not to discuss the incident with anybody.

'Dutch managed to get hold of his friend in Naval Intelligence last night,' Gina said quietly, leaning forward so as not to be overheard. *Dutch* (even the name made Tom bristle) was her husband. The ex-Marine she'd left him for and who had become stepfather, hero and role-model-in-chief to Danny.

'Does he know anything?'

'More than he was ready to tell.'

The waiter was back with the water and they watched in silence while he filled their glasses. When he'd gone Gina leaned forward again.

'Seems Danny's platoon was out on a routine patrol when they came under attack. One of their vehicles was blown up by a roadside bomb. One guy killed and two badly injured. Danny and the others went after the terrorists and killed them. Apparently there were some civilians killed in the cross fire. That's all the guy would say. He told Dutch we shouldn't worry too much. The investigation's just routine. He said it happens all

76

the time. It's just that after Haditha, the top brass are paranoid about the media accusing them of a cover-up.'

'Did he have any idea how long this investigation's going to take?'

'No.'

'We've got to get him a proper lawyer.'

'What do you mean, a *proper lawyer*? He's got one.'

'No he hasn't. He's got some military gofer they've foisted on him. Whose side's *he* going to be on, for heaven's sake? He'll just be covering their ass for them.'

'Dutch says these military attorneys are completely independent.'

'Oh, really. That's what Dutch says.'

Gina sighed and looked away and Tom silently rebuked himself for the knee-jerk sarcasm her husband's name always triggered.

'Have you heard from Danny?' she asked.

'No.'

She didn't need to ask and he knew it was simply her way of getting back at him. Until the unanswered e-mail Tom had sent last week, there had been no contact between them in years. Not since their scorching argument over the boy's decision to follow his stepfather into the Marines. It struck Tom as odd that only now, when something had gone wrong, was he apparently allowed—or supposed—to be involved again in his son's life. For this he felt both grateful and slightly resentful.

He had failed at many things, but his failure to forge an enduring relationship with his only child was the one for which he most blamed himself.

Even more than his failure to forge one with the boy's mother, though the two issues were difficult to disentangle. Danny's view of him, Tom guessed, was probably much the same as Gina's: that he was a dysfunctional drunk, a spineless, guilt-ridden liberal, a tribeless Englishman who had long ago slipped between the tectonic plates of two continents and never managed to clamber out. Who could blame the boy for wanting to define himself in as stark a contrast as possible to all that?

Tom used to give himself a hard time wondering whether it might all have been different if he hadn't pressured Gina all those years ago into moving to Missoula. She was a rancher's daughter and towns of any kind made her claustrophobic. Although their first years there, when they were building the house on the creek and she was pregnant with Danny, were probably—or so he now believed—among their happiest. The irony was that at the time Tom hadn't even been sure himself about the move. It had been more an act of wishful thinking. He had fooled himself into believing that at last he'd found somewhere he belonged, whereas in fact it was simply a place he wanted to belong.

The two of them had met in the summer of '78, Tom's first year on the UM creative-writing program. He was spending his vacation doing volunteer work on a federally funded program on the Blackfeet reservation in Browning. The idea was to help rekindle young people's interest in their tribal history and culture, a subject that had been his passion for many years. He and one of the tribal elders, who was a friend, were hiking with a group of Blackfeet teenagers along the Front Range and had made camp on what they'd wrongly believed to be public land. They'd lit a fire and were just starting to cook supper when up rode this fantasy figure of a cowgirl on a big black horse. She told them in no uncertain terms that this was her father's summer pasture and they were trespassing. She was wearing a white T-shirt, a black hat and a red bandanna around her neck. The horse was fiery and wouldn't keep still as she issued her reprimand. It was hard to figure out which of them looked the more scary and gorgeous.

Tom apologized and explained who they were and what they were doing and fifteen minutes later she was sitting next to him beside the campfire cooking burgers. She took off her hat and shook out a tumble of hair as black and lustrous as her horse. He was sure he had once seen a movie where something similar happened, some cattle baron's arrogant and beautiful daughter (probably played by Barbara Stanwyck) riding up in a cloud of dust and yelling at the leading man (probably Jimmy Stewart). Tom couldn't remember the title but he knew such first encounters generally had but one outcome.

She asked him if he lived around those parts and Tom told her that he once had, in his early teens, on a small ranch outside of Choteau. And after a few more questions, she announced that she knew exactly who he was and that they had been at high school together.

'I think I'd remember,' Tom said. He meant it as a compliment—hers wasn't the kind of face a man would likely forget—but she seemed to take it instead as a challenge and soon proved she was right. Her name was Gina Laidlaw and she was two years younger than he was. They had indeed overlapped, briefly, at junior high.

'The English boy,' she said. 'Everybody knew who you were. We used to try and copy the way you talked. *The rain in Spain stays mainly in the plain.* You don't sound like that anymore. It's such a pity.'

'Well, dash it all, m'dear, I can still do it when called for.'

She put her head back and laughed. The mouth was more Jane Russell than Barbara Stanwyck. Tom was already lost.

'In the end you just get fed up with people not understanding you,' he said. 'Going *Huh? Excuse me?* I remember telling somebody I'd had to queue for the lift and getting this blank look. Like the one you're giving me now.'

'Queue for the lift?'

'See what I mean? Wait in line for the elevator.'

She laughed again and so did the others who'd been listening. They all started teasing him and talking with English accents and Tom pretended to get haughty and cross and enjoyed every moment.

She only stayed about an hour but it was long enough for him to find out that she was finishing a master's in agribusiness at Montana State, was spending the summer working on the ranch and didn't, so far as he could ascertain, have a current boyfriend. He walked with her to where she'd tethered her horse and asked her whom he should call if they ever wanted to ask permission to camp here again. She swung herself up into the saddle and he could see from the way she was grinning down at him that she knew what he was really asking.

'Hmm. Let me think,' she said. 'Well, I guess you could always call me.'

It turned out to be the best summer of his life. Just sixteen months later, in a little white clapboard chapel, with her father's cattle grazing the sun-bleached grass for miles around and snow already capping the mountains beyond, they were married.

'So, folks, how was it?'

The black-shirted waiter was staring at their plates, both still heaped with food. He seemed to be taking it personally.

'Didn't we like it?'

'We liked it very much,' Tom said. 'I guess we're just not as hungry as we thought.'

Gina gave the boy a guilty smile.

'Sorry,' she said.

'No problem. Can I tell you about our dessert specials?'

'I don't think so, thanks. Maybe some coffee. Regular.'

'Me too.'

'You got it.'

They sat in silence for a while, both staring out at the street. It was a fitful spring day, scudding clouds and sudden, glaring bursts of sunshine that hurt Tom's eyes. He asked about Kelly, Danny's girlfriend. They'd been seeing each other for more than two years and Tom had never met her. Gina said the poor girl was having a hard time, that all she wanted was for Danny to come home.

'When will that be?'

'Dutch says they'll probably all get flown down

81

to the Gulf first. They like to get them out of the combat zone as soon as they can.'

'Do we know any more about who they're supposed to have killed?'

Gina swallowed and stared down at the table.

'There were some women,' she said quietly. 'And children.'

'Oh, boy.'

She was trying hard not to cry but at last a tear rolled down one cheek and she fisted it briskly away. Tom wanted to reach out to take her hand, but didn't. He could see she was angry with herself and would probably spurn any offer of comfort.

'I definitely think we should get him an outside lawyer,' he said, stupidly.

'Damn it, Tom! You don't know about these things, okay? Why can't you just leave it to those who do?'

The waiter reappeared with their coffees. Tom was bracing himself for some cheery, inane comment but the boy had read the atmosphere and was keeping his head down. Tom asked for the check.

'I'm sorry,' Gina murmured.

'It's okay. Just let me know if there's anything I can do.'

He walked her to her car, neither of them talking. Halfway along the street she tucked her arm into his and the gesture brought tears to his own eyes but she didn't seem to notice and he quickly controlled himself.

After they parted he walked on up 13th Street to the Charlie Russell Museum, the shadows of clouds bowling past him along the sidewalk. He hadn't been to see the Russell paintings in a long while. The last time was with Danny when the boy was three years old. In Tom's view no painter had ever captured the spirit of the American West better than Russell. He remembered how Danny had been transfixed by the pictures of cowboys and Indians, of their wild-eyed horses, of the buffalo hunters, chasing and swirling across those vast red dust and sagebrush landscapes. Tom had picked the boy up and held him in his arms so he could get a better look. Every painting had a story and the two of them talked in whispers about what was going on, who had shot first, what were those Indians on the hilltop pointing at, why those men had killed the wolf, what was going to happen next.

By that time things had already started going wrong with Gina. Their early arguments had been mostly about her family. Her father had never taken to Tom nor tried too hard to conceal his opinion that his 'princess', his beloved only daughter, could have done a lot better. C. J. Laidlaw was a bull of a man, tall and wide shouldered, with an ego and temperament to match. His views on almost everything, especially politics, were the polar opposite of Tom's. He liked to goad Tom, trying to flush out some liberal opinion that he could then shoot down. He had a disdainful way of asking about Tom's work, his early and largely unpublished efforts as a writer, and especially his interest in the Blackfeet. He clearly thought his new son-in-law ought to go out and get a proper job.

For the first few years of the marriage, Tom would smile and try not to be drawn, but after Danny was born, he started standing up for himself. At a Thanksgiving dinner just after

Danny's third birthday, he and C.J. had had a blistering fight about Reagan's foreign policy. Gina, tellingly, sided with her father. After that things were never quite the same.

It was around that time that Tom's drinking began to get out of control. Even after years of therapy and analysis and AA meetings, he still wasn't sure why it had happened. There were simply too many reasons to choose from.

The pattern was that he and Gina would fight, usually about something to do with Danny. He hadn't been the easiest of babies. He had colic and for the first two years of his life barely stopped crying. Tom and Gina grew ragged from lack of sleep. Sometimes it felt as if they were hanging on to sanity by their fingernails. She would get angry and tell him he was no good as a father, that he left her to do all the hard stuff, that he put his work before his responsibilities to her and his son. She said she hated Missoula and blamed Tom for dragging her away from her family and friends on the other side of the mountains.

The problem was, though he never admitted it to her, Tom thought she was right. He felt they had made a big mistake in having a baby. And he came to believe that his own unhappy childhood meant he simply wasn't qualified to be a parent. He began to speculate that because everyone he'd ever loved and been loved by had died or deserted him, perhaps he'd grown too thick a carapace and was incapable of love. When Gina attacked him, instead of fighting back, he just took it and apologized and this only seemed to make her more angry. Tom had retreated into his work, finding excuses to go into town. Another trip to the UM library, he would tell her. Research.

And in a way, that's what it was. He was plumbing new, dark depths of himself. He would spend long afternoons and, as the months went by, longer evenings too, in various dingy downtown bars with other refugees from life, each with his or her own set of sorrows but all bonded by the same self-pity.

Tom guessed that in most marriage breakdowns there was a point of no return, when apology and forgiveness lose any meaning and it becomes clear to both parties that this is how it's going to be. That point, for Gina, was the canoe trip he took with Danny, just the two of them, a few days before the boy's fifth birthday.

Tom had by then taken his drinking to a new level. He'd started sneaking a swig or two in the mornings and increased the number of bottles he hid around the house: behind books on his study shelves, in his old cowboy boots in the closet, even out in the woodshed. The canoe trip had been canceled twice already because of the weather and although that Sunday morning he had a wicked hangover, he wasn't going to let the boy down again.

It was a clear, cold day in early spring and Danny was fizzing with excitement from the moment he got up. He tried to help Tom load the old green Coleman canoe onto the car roof but kept getting in the way and Tom told him, too sharply, to be careful. Gina must have heard because she came out and stood watching, with her arms folded and that expression on her face, a sort of weary, critical resignation, a look more powerful than any words. Danny went to stand beside her.

'Are we sure this is a good idea?' she said.

'C'mon, we're going to have a great time, aren't we, Danny?'

Danny nodded but didn't look convinced.

An hour later they were on the river and all was perfect: the sun dancing in diamonds on the water, the cottonwoods along the banks wearing their first haze of green. Tom's head had started to clear. Danny, in his yellow life vest and his red-and-white beanie, was grinning and whooping.

Tom had done the run a dozen times but never with Danny. It was nothing too taxing, just a few stretches of mild white water. Gina was going to meet them downstream with the car in two hours' time. They stopped in a sunny meadow to eat the sandwiches she'd made for them and then stood throwing pebbles across the water.

'Dad, can we do this again?'

'Whenever you want.'

They put their life vests back on and clambered again into the canoe. Danny was sitting in the forward seat with his little paddle. He hadn't quite gotten the hang of it but it didn't matter. It was only when the river narrowed and they reached the top of the last stretch of rapids that Tom realized there was more water in the river than he'd thought. There was a loud rushing sound. Diagonal waves were bouncing back from both banks. Tom told Danny to put his paddle on the floor and to hold on to the gunwales with both hands. The boy must have heard the edge in his voice for he suddenly looked scared.

Quite how it happened, Tom would never be sure. They had shipped a fair amount of water in the first hundred yards of the rapids and with every

86

tilt of the canoe it rushed from side to side and over their feet, making everything unstable. And because there was more water in the river than on the other occasions he'd paddled there, Tom couldn't figure out what route to take through the rocks. Suddenly one of the waves rebounding from the right-hand bank slammed against the bows and the canoe swung wildly around.

'Daddy!' Danny screamed.

'Hold tight! It's okay.'

But it wasn't okay. Before Tom could correct it, the canoe got sucked backward into a fast-flowing channel between the rocks. Tom had to look over his shoulder to see what lay ahead. When he glanced back at Danny, he saw plain terror on the boy's face.

'It's okay, son. It's okay.'

Ahead of them were two large boulders with a narrow gushing gap between them, the water spouting in a huge silver arc down to a pool beyond. If the canoe had entered the gap straight they might have been lucky and not capsized. But the rear end crashed against the right-hand rock and there was a crunching sound and the whole boat lurched as it squeezed through the gap and a moment later it flipped over completely and they were both under water.

Tom could remember the sudden silence, the green gray slabs of rock on the riverbed below him, the swirl of bubbles, his floating paddle and the upturned canoe above him. The water was so cold it hurt his head. He struck out for the surface, his clothes dragging heavily and his lungs fit to burst. Even as he gulped the air he was looking for Danny. But there was no sign of him. Tom thrashed around in circles.

'Danny! Danny!'

Then he saw the red-and-white beanie bob to the surface and a moment later the wide-eyed face of his son, gasping, gulping the air. Tom swam heavily toward him.

'Daddy, are you all right?'

'Yes. Are you?'

Danny nodded. He was clutching his paddle. The pool was calm and Tom managed to haul Danny to the bank then went back to get the upturned canoe. They hadn't brought a change of clothes and by the time they'd paddled on down to the place where they'd arranged to meet Gina, Danny was quaking with cold, his teeth chattering. When he saw his mother standing on the bank he started to cry.

'What happened?'

'We had a bit of an accident,' Tom said.

'Jesus, Tom.'

She carried Danny to the car and stripped off his wet clothes and wrapped him in her sweater and coat and sat in the passenger seat, cuddling and soothing him while Tom loaded the canoe onto the roof. They drove home in a silence colder than the river. When Tom dared glance at her, she was staring straight ahead, tears running down her cheeks.

For about a month, whenever he closed his eyes, Tom replayed the scene of their capsize. The bubbles, the upturned canoe, his little boy bobbing to the surface. *Daddy, are you all right?* Gina didn't say a word about it, even when he begged her to let him talk about it. She didn't need to. And there was probably nothing he could say that would have changed her mind. His drinking was to blame and there was to be no redemption. He wasn't fit to be a father.

Tom had the museum almost to himself this afternoon. The soles of his shoes squeaked loudly on the polished floor as he walked from room to room, trying to find his favorite paintings. He stood for a long time in front of the picture that had once so enthralled Danny. It was called *The Fireboat* and showed four Indian braves on the top of a rocky cliff, a wondrous evening sky of purple blue behind them. They were on horseback and staring with bemused expressions at a steamboat making its way up the river far below them.

'Who's on the boat?' Danny had asked.

'White men.'

'What do they want?'

'They want the Indians' land.'

'Do they get it?'

'Oh, yes. They promised they wouldn't take it, but they did.'

Tom tried to summon the feelings he'd had that day with Danny but he couldn't even find an echo. Only the hollowing memory of his long-lost son and his own lost self.

SEVEN

Tommy and Dickie sat on the vast cream leather back seat of the Bentley, looking out of the open rear window at the crowd of Ashlawn boys that still engulfed Ray Montane and Diane. The boys were jostling one another to get autographs and they kept shouting out *Red! Red!* and making guns with their fingers and thumbs then blowing the smoke off the end of the barrel which was a sort of trademark thing that Red McGraw did in *Sliprock*, like the way he said *See ya along the trail* at the end of every episode.

Ray had long ago run out of the Red McGraw photos that he had brought with him and instead was autographing Speech Day programmes and any other scrap of paper that was thrust in front of him. Diane, at his side, was being kept almost as busy. The photographer from the local newspaper, a rumpled little man whose red cheeks now glistened with sweat, had taken about a hundred pictures of them already but was still snapping away.

'Red! Red! Sign this!' the boys called out. 'Please! Diane! You too!'

Charlie Chin Rawlston was standing by, trying to look important and making sure things didn't get too out of hand. He had been smarming up to Ray and Diane ever since they arrived two hours ago, though Dickie said somebody must have first had to explain to the old fool who they were.

Tommy still couldn't quite believe they were here. In her last letter, his mother had told him she and his father wouldn't be coming to the school's summer Speech Day and that Diane would be there instead. But there had been no mention of Ray Montane coming too. Perhaps they'd wanted it to be a surprise.

And it certainly had been. In fact their appearance was probably the biggest sensation Ashlawn had known since one of the chimneys got struck by lightning and crashed down on Matron's

Morris Minor (unfortunately she hadn't been in it at the time). Their arrival had been perfectly timed. Parents and boys had all gathered down at the sports field, eating their picnic lunches and watching the cricket team get its annual thrashing from the fathers. The parents' cars, whose make and age announced precisely the social status of their owners, were parked side by side around the boundary, plaid rugs and picnic hampers laid between them on the soggy grass.

Gloomy and famished, Tommy and Dickie sat watching from the steps of the pavilion. Because Dickie's parents were in Hong Kong and never came to any school events, Tommy had invited him to share the picnic Diane was supposed to be bringing. She was already two hours late and Tommy was mortified. And the sight of everyone tucking into their cucumber sandwiches, pork pies and chicken legs was almost unbearable. He was about to apologize for the tenth time when in through the school gates purred a big white Bentley.

It had darkened windows and by the time it had glided across the grass and pulled up some distance from the other cars, at least three hundred pairs of eyes were upon it. There was a hush of anticipation and for a long while, nothing happened. The car just stood there. By now the cricket match itself had come to a halt. Every player, even the umpires in their white coats and panama hats, stood waiting to see who was going to emerge.

'Look,' Dickie said.

The driver's-side door of the Bentley was opening. A chauffeur in a dark blue cap and uniform got out and opened the rear door.

'You know who it is, don't you?' Dickie whispered.

' 'Course I don't.'

'It's your sister, dumbo. Look!'

And there she was, stepping gracefully out of the car, laughing at something as she smoothed her dress and adjusted her sunglasses.

'Crikey, just look at her,' Dickie murmured in wonder.

'And look who's with her!'

Except for the white Stetson, Ray Montane was dressed entirely in black. He was wearing a bootlace tie and a belt with a big silver buckle shaped like a coiled rattlesnake. His boots had silver tips and his shirt was studded with what looked like diamonds, though Dickie said they were probably only rhinestones which weren't so precious. The only thing missing was his gun belt.

Oddly, he didn't really look too out of place because everybody seemed to dress up strangely for Speech Day. Charlie Chin and Ducky Lawrence and some of the other masters were wearing their college gowns, voluminous black capes with giant hoods, trimmed with red or purple satin or white fur, that flopped down their backs. All the boys and staff had flowers with sprigs of fern pinned to their lapels and some of the fathers were wearing gaudily striped blazers. Most of the mothers and older sisters had hats with flowers or feathers in them.

But not Diane. Her hair fell loose in thick, gleaming swirls that bounced as she walked. She was still tanned from her trip to California and was wearing high-heeled sandals and a pink dress that showed her shoulders and enough bosom to have all the boys and most of the fathers transfixed.

In front of everyone she gave Tommy a hug that seemed to go on forever and squeezed all the air from his lungs. Then she said hello to Dickie and made him blush by kissing him on the cheek. Ray shook hands with them both, telling Tommy he'd heard all about him. Tommy hoped that didn't include the bed-wetting. He had the bluest eyes Tommy had ever seen. In the back of the Bentley was a wickerwork picnic hamper at least three times the size of anyone else's. It had a giant F&M on the lid which Diane said stood for the famous shop where they'd bought it. It had all kinds of strange things in it, like pâté made from goose liver and black fish eggs called caviar, which Dickie loved but Tommy thought were disgusting. The chauffeur laid rugs on the grass and the two boys sat down and stuffed themselves until they felt sick.

Charlie Chin was supposed to be entertaining the red-faced colonel who had earlier dished out the school prizes and sent everyone to sleep with a long speech about the importance of being a team player, but you could tell he was itching to meet Diane and Ray and eventually he managed to and insisted on giving them a tour of the school. Tommy went with them and soon wished he hadn't because the headmaster kept patting him on the back and sharing little jokes with him as if they were the best of friends. The hypocrisy was sickening. As they walked past the changing room Tommy wanted to say *and here's where this slimy creep enjoys thrashing the living daylights out of us.*

But something even better happened. Just when

they were having tea outside the cricket pavilion, Tommy spotted Whippet Brent talking to the colonel's little ferret-faced wife and whispered to Diane that he was the most savage and sadistic beater of them all. Ray Montane overheard.

'Did he ever beat you, Tommy?'

'Loads of times. He beats Dickie almost every night.'

'He's a real pervert,' Dickie said.

Ray gave a thoughtful nod.

'What's his name?'

'Mr Brent. We call him The Whippet.'

Before anyone thought to stop him, Ray walked straight over and tapped The Whippet gently on the shoulder.

'Excuse me, ma'am,' he said, touching the brim of his Stetson to the ferret. 'I just need a quiet word with this gentleman. We'll only be a moment.'

Brent frowned but allowed himself to be steered aside. Ray leaned in close and talked quietly to him for a few moments. Then he put a hand on Brent's shoulder, smiled sweetly at him and walked back to join Tommy and Diane. The Whippet looked as if he'd just seen his own ghost.

'What on earth did you say to him?' Diane whispered.

'I told him if he ever laid a finger on either of you again, I'd come back and shove his whippety pervert nose right up his ass.'

Now, as the afternoon drew to a close and Ray and Diane were standing by the car, signing the last few autographs, Charlie Chin moved in again.

'All right, boys, that's enough now. No more autographs. Mr Montane and Miss Reed have got a very busy schedule, I'm sure.'

'Hell, Charlie, I was figuring on staying all day,' Ray said.

The headmaster threw back his head and brayed with laughter as if this were the funniest remark he'd ever heard. Ray looked into the car and gave Tommy a sly sideways wink from under the brim of his Stetson. Tommy already liked him, though he still couldn't get used to the idea that this huge star, Red McGraw from *Sliprock*, was now his sister's boyfriend. It was almost as amazing as if she had come home from Hollywood on the arm of Flint McCullough. Ray looked quite a bit older than he did on TV—and certainly a lot older than Diane—but that was probably because he spent so much time out in the sun, riding the range.

'Well, I certainly hope you'll come and see us again,' the headmaster went on, his eyes darting furtively to Diane's breasts. 'Both of you. I mean ...Um, in fact, Mr Montane, perhaps you would like to come and be our guest speaker at next year's Speech Day?'

'Well, Charlie, that's real—'

'You don't have to answer now. I know in the glittery world of show business one has to speak to one's agent and all that malarkey.' He laughed loudly at his own worldly wit.

It was six o'clock now and Speech Day was officially over. The boys were allowed to go home until the same time the following evening. And then just five more days and it would be the end of term and home for two whole months. Tommy quietly asked Diane if Dickie could come home with them because he had nowhere else to go but she said no, perhaps some other time. There were *important family matters* they had to discuss, she said. There was an odd, almost nervous look in her eyes.

'What do you mean?'

'I'll explain later, darling.'

'It doesn't matter,' Dickie said. 'This dump's okay when there's nobody here.'

He climbed out of the car and said goodbye and after more gushing from Charlie Chin, the chauffeur ushered Ray and Diane into the back seat, either side of Tommy, and off they went. A posse of boys ran alongside the car all the way to the school gates, waving and cheering and shouting *See ya along the trail.*

Then there was silence. Ray took two cigarettes from a silver case, lit them both and passed one to Diane. For a long time nobody spoke.

'Is Ray coming home with us?' Tommy whispered.

'Yes, but he's not going to stay. He's got to get back to London. He's flying home tomorrow morning.'

'All the way to California?'

'That's right, son,' Ray said.

'That's a shame.'

'Yep, it sure is. But you know what, Tommy? I reckon pretty soon the two of us will be seeing a whole lot more of each other.'

'Oh.'

Ray glanced at Diane and Tommy turned to look at her too and saw that same odd look in her eyes. She tried to smile then turned away and stared out of the window. And although Ray and Tommy chatted about all kinds of things throughout the journey home, she didn't say another word.

Tommy hadn't been allowed home from school for many weeks and so when the Bentley pulled into the driveway he was expecting his parents might come out to greet him. But they didn't. And Ray didn't even come into the house. They all got out of the car and the chauffeur put Diane's leather suitcase down on the gravel beside her. Ray shook Tommy firmly by the hand.

'Look after my gal for me, okay, pardner?'

'Okay.'

Ray grinned and did the little smoking gun thing with his fingers and thumb and Tommy did it back to him. Then Ray put his arms around Diane and kissed her full on the lips.

'Good luck, sugar,' he said. 'You'll see. It's gonna work out fine.'

Diane didn't say anything, just nodded. Then Ray got back into the car and the chauffeur shut the door and Tommy and Diane stood and watched as the Bentley turned in the tiny driveway then purred off down the lane. Diane put an arm around Tommy's shoulders.

'Come on,' she said. 'We'd better go inside.'

*   *   *

She had rehearsed the speech a hundred times in her head, even done it aloud in front of the mirror, as she did when she was learning her lines for a new play. But it didn't seem to help. She felt more nervous than she'd ever felt on stage, even on a first night in the West End. Plays were just make-believe but this was real life. What was more, she already knew the audience was going to be hostile.

97

Her parents were waiting for them in the lounge. The cricket scores were being read out on the television but nobody was paying any attention. Her father was sitting in his usual armchair, smoking his pipe and reading his newspaper. Her mother was at one end of the sofa with a half-empty glass of gin and tonic in her hand. You could tell from her eyes and the flush in her cheeks that it wasn't her first. As Diane and Tommy came into the room she leaned forward and stubbed out her cigarette in the ashtray.

'Hello, Tommy,' she said wearily.

'Hello.'

Tommy walked over to her and she turned her cheek so that he could kiss it. Diane could tell from his frown that he already sensed something was wrong. Her father cleared his throat and gave him an awkward, forced smile.

'Hello, old chap. How was Speech Day?'

'It was fine. What's the matter?'

Diane's parents were both looking at her, waiting for her to speak. Her father looked sad and weary and suddenly very old. Her mother's eyes glinted with a cold and barely contained anger. After all that had been said during the past week, the shouting and threats and recrimination, it was all Diane could expect. They had spent three whole days and nights arguing before she had finally stormed out and gone back to London to be with Ray at his hotel. He was the only one who understood. Without him she wouldn't have been able to summon the courage.

But this wasn't how she had planned it. Last night on the phone, her father had begged her again, for the last time, not to go ahead with it.

And when she said she wasn't going to change her mind, reluctantly, they had agreed that when she brought Tommy home from school, they would first have a family supper and then, as gently and lovingly as possible, tell him. But the air was already bristling. She had to do it now. She was still standing by the door. They were all staring at her. On the television the cricket scores droned on.

'What is it?' Tommy said. 'What's wrong with everybody?'

'For heaven's sake, Diane,' her mother said. 'Just get it over with.'

Diane walked stiffly across to the television and switched it off. Then she came back to the sofa and sat down at the opposite end from her mother. She tried to smile but it felt as phoney as it must have looked. It was as if all her acting skills had suddenly deserted her. She patted the cushion beside her.

'Tommy, darling. Come and sit here. There's something I've got to tell you.'

'What?'

Instead of simply puzzled, he now looked frightened. Warily watching her, he came and sat down next to her. Diane took his hand in both of hers.

'Tommy, this is something I've wanted to tell you for a very long time. In fact, all of your life. But I've never been brave enough.'

She glanced at her parents. Her mother shook her head and sighed and looked away.

'All these years, darling, you've thought that I was your sister. Well. I'm not.'

'What?'

'Tommy ... I'm your mother.'

Tommy gave a confused little laugh.

'Is this a joke or a trick or something?'

He looked around and saw from their pained faces that it wasn't.

'I was very young when I ... when you were born. Only just sixteen. And we all decided that it would be better, at least for the time being, if everyone thought that I wasn't your mother but ... your sister, instead.'

She couldn't believe what a wretched job she was making of it. She never normally forgot her lines. But now, when it really counted, she could hardly remember a single word of what she had prepared.

'Why?' Tommy said. 'I don't understand.'

Diane looked again at her mother, this time out of some desperate, instinctive hope that she might come to the rescue. But the face showed no mercy, just a stony disapproval, distorted by drink. Her father looked desolate, his forehead now propped by one hand so that she couldn't see his eyes.

'Tommy, I was so young. I was still at school. Girls that age, if they get pregnant, usually have—'

'Diane, really,' her mother said. 'He's just a boy. Surely you don't have to go into all that.'

Diane ignored her.

'Sometimes, Tommy, when women get pregnant but don't want to have the baby, they can ... Doctors can do an operation so that the baby doesn't get born. But I didn't want to do that. I wanted to have you. I ...'

The tears ambushed her, suddenly, out of nowhere. And the last thing she wanted to do was cry. She wanted to be strong, and loving. Like a mother should be for her child. She angrily wiped her eyes.

'I'm sorry. It's just...'

Tommy put his arms around her and clung to her and, of course, that made it so much worse. She was sobbing and couldn't help herself. She put her arms around him and now he was crying too. It was all going wrong. She had completely messed it up. Through her tears she saw her mother get up, snatch her empty glass from the coffee table and walk from the room.

'Joan, dear, please,' her father called after her.

'I'm sorry, I can't listen to this.'

'Joan...'

He got up and hurried after her. It was probably better that way, Diane thought. It had seemed the right thing to do, to tell Tommy when all three of them were there to reassure him and make him feel everything was all right. But she'd been foolish to imagine it could work. Her mother's resentment could never be put neatly to one side. Diane hugged Tommy even more tightly, then held him away from her so that she could look at him. Her son. The poor darling. He was still crying. His face had gone all red and blotchy. Maybe she had made a terrible mistake.

'I know it's an awful shock, darling. But we're all still the same people. We all still love you.'

'Why are you telling me this?' He sniffed. 'Why now?'

'Because I love you. And I'm proud of you. And I want everyone to know I'm your mother.'

'So, Mum and Dad, I mean, aren't...'

'They're your grandparents, sweetheart.'

'You all said I didn't have any grandparents.

101

That they were dead.'

'Well, it's true, in a way. Their parents, my grandparents, are dead.'

He looked so unhappy and confused. He kept rubbing away the tears which, like her own, didn't seem to want to stop.

'So, who's my father?'

Diane had known, of course, that this would come. And for the first time she could remember what she had prepared. It was the truth, after all. She took a breath and spoke as calmly as she could.

'He was at the boys' school down the road from mine. He was called David. His parents lived abroad. I've never seen him again. I heard he got married to someone else.'

Tommy's face contorted and creased up and he wailed and turned away from her. She still had her hands on his arms but he broke loose and ran for the door.

'Tommy! Please!'

She went after him into the kitchen but he ran for the stairs, yelling at her through his tears to leave him alone. Diane stopped and clasped her head between her hands. The slamming of his bedroom door made the whole house shudder. Her mother was slicing some tomatoes, a cigarette hanging from her lips. There was no sign of her father. He'd probably fled out to his workshop. Her mother didn't look at her, just took a long puff of her cigarette and put it down in an ashtray.

'Well,' she said. 'I hope you're satisfied.'

EIGHT

She had only done it for a dare. At least, that was the glibber version of the truth that Diane had settled on. It had a sort of ironic resonance that now, nearly a decade after the trauma of Tommy's conception, she had come to find appealing. Life, after all, was so damnably dark and cruel that if you didn't laugh in its face, it just grabbed you by the throat and swallowed you. Naturally, the notion that her son was simply the result of a dare neither adequately explained nor justified what had happened.

David Willis had been one of a group of boys from St Edward's whom Diane, along with her best friend, Katie Bingham, and a few other Elmshurst rebels, used to sneak out to meet on those long summer evenings when her head felt it might implode from boredom. The two boarding schools had adjoining sports fields and there was a narrow, tunnel-like lane, overhung with sycamore and hawthorn, behind the sheds where the groundsmen kept their lawnmowers and rollers. The boys would always be there, waiting for them with packs of cheap cigarettes in their blazer pockets. Occasionally there would be alcohol too, though rarely anything more potent than a bottle of cider.

Most of the boys were either show-offs or stupid or both, but David Willis was different. He hung back a little, not exactly shy or aloof, just slightly disengaged, as if unsure that he wanted to be there. Diane would often catch him staring at her

103

but he always looked away. She had never been able to resist a challenge, and one evening she smiled at him and he blushed and gave her a crooked little grin.

From then on he was the only boy she could be bothered with during these clandestine nicotine assignations. His father was in the Royal Air Force and every two years was posted somewhere else so the whole family would have to pack up and move. At fifteen, David had lived in half a dozen different countries and this, to Diane, immediately put him in a league far more exotic than all the other boys. His mother and father were currently based in Kenya and the stories he told her about going on safari and seeing lions and elephants and crocodiles made him seem almost impossibly romantic.

On Sundays, the pupils of both schools were allowed out for afternoon walks—though, of course, not together, for to consort with members of the opposite sex was a dire offence at both establishments. At Elmshurst these walks were the subject of strict rules of conduct: a minimum of four girls per walking group; school uniform to be worn at all times, including hats (hideous straw boaters whose sides the rebels would wet and bend to give them a racy, cowgirl look); walking was permitted only on certain designated lanes and footpaths; and, most important of all, absolutely no straying up into the rolling, bracken-clad hills that loomed wickedly beyond.

Upon diehard rebels like Diane and Katie, this last injunction naturally had an effect entirely opposite from the one intended. That nature should be deemed *out of bounds* served only to heighten its allure. And it was thus that on a sultry afternoon in late June, having abandoned, as well as hats and cardigans, their two complicit classmates, they found themselves strolling along one of the grassy trails that wound through the ferns with David and his friend Henry Littlemore, a shambling, acne-smitten creature for whom Katie had developed an unaccountable passion. It was Henry who had provided the cigarettes, some lethally strong, untipped Player's at which they were all bravely puffing and trying not to choke. The boys were walking some ten yards ahead of the girls and were talking about cricket, specifically whether England's Denis Compton could be compared with the legendary Australian batsman Donald Bradman.

No destination had been mentioned for the walk. But despite the temporary distance between them, no one had any doubts about its purpose, which laced the air as blatantly as the musky, moist smell of the bracken. Neither girl could be considered a novice. Their Sunday afternoon walks that summer had already seen much tumbling and fumbling in the ferns, sprigs of which they would later scrupulously pluck from each other's hair. Katie (or so Diane believed) was a lot more advanced in these matters, claiming to have done things with Henry Littlemore that Diane had difficulty even imagining.

The boys were still locked in discussion ahead of them, when out of the blue Katie asked her if she and David had *done it* yet.

'Katie! Sshh!'

'Oh, they're not listening. Have you?'

'No, of course not!'

'Why *of course* not? We have.'

'You haven't!'

'Well, more or less.'

'I didn't think there was a more or less when it comes to . . . you know.'

Katie dropped her cigarette end and squashed it into the grass with her heel. Far below them a patchwork of hayfields stretched away into the distance, shimmering in the heat. The still air trilled with the song of skylarks.

'I dare you.'

Diane laughed.

'Or are you *saving* yourself for the man you marry?'

The mocking tone made the idea sound so boring and bourgeois that Diane couldn't possibly admit that this was, in fact, precisely what she had in mind.

'It wouldn't be the first time for David,' she said instead.

'How do you know? Boys always lie and pretend they've done it.'

'I believe him. He did it last summer in Kenya. With a native girl.'

'Crikey.'

'I know.'

'I *dare* you.'

The odd thing was, Diane wasn't one of those slightly unhinged girls (of which, at Elmshurst, there were several) who found it hard to resist a dare. She would always weigh the fun against the consequences of being caught. But that afternoon, for some reason, she didn't. And half an hour later, when they'd reached a suitably deserted spot and gone their separate ways, each couple wandering off to make its own discreet nest among the ferns, Diane found herself lying on her back while this virtual stranger rummaged inside her clothes and kissed her nipples and slid a hand slowly up her thigh.

That was when she should have stopped him. But she didn't. She even helped him pull down her sensible school underpants then watched while he fumbled with his buttons and pulled down his own. She'd seen artistic depictions of penises, of course, but not one in earnest and the sight was so comical she almost giggled. His face was clouded and flushed and he wouldn't look her in the eye, just lowered himself upon her and, tentatively, as if at any moment he expected to be scolded, found his way into her.

She'd been told that it would hurt but it wasn't as bad as she had expected. The pushing was more painful than the sudden fleshy shock as she gave way. And it was over almost as soon as it had begun. He gasped and twitched and she felt the spurt of him inside and then he rolled off and flopped beside her on the crushed ferns. And he looked so worried and wretched and ashamed that she smiled and stroked his face and gave him a little kiss on his forehead. And then she lay there, gazing at the motionless clouds and listening to the incessant twitter of the skylarks and wondered why this curiously disappointing act was invested with such mystique and importance.

It was almost three months before she knew the answer. Her mother, never overly tolerant with illness of any kind (except, of course, her own) clearly suspected her daughter's morning bouts of nausea were part of a cunning plot to delay going

107

back to school. And only in September, when the family doctor was at last summoned to deal with what they all, Diane included, believed to be an unusually persistent strain of gastric 'flu, did reality finally dawn.

Dr Henderson was a Scotsman with gingery bristles sprouting from his nose and ears and a pair of half-moon glasses which made him seem in a state of permanent surprise. He played golf with Diane's father and belonged to the same Masonic Lodge. He sat that morning on her bed and made her stick out her tongue, then told her to cough while he held the cold plate of his stethoscope to her chest and her back. Finally, in answer to some increasingly intimate questions that seemed to embarrass him rather more than her, Diane disclosed that she had missed two periods, a fact to which she had perhaps surprisingly attached little significance. Dr Henderson made a strange guttural sound, as if he had swallowed a fish bone, and left the room to confer with her mother. And a few moments later, the more or less comfortable world of the Bedford family exploded.

With the help of Dr Henderson's red leather pocket diary, while her mother wailed the scandalous news to her father over the phone downstairs, Diane was able to pinpoint the Sunday afternoon when her morals had so shockingly deserted her. Dr Henderson made the interesting observation that this was the very same day that North Korea had invaded the South, an event that still looked likely to provoke a third world war, for which Diane would no doubt also be held responsible.

Tests confirmed the venerable doctor's diagnosis

and there was so much hysteria during the following days and weeks that Diane's recollection of them, a decade later, was little more than a series of blurred images. Her mother crying uncontrollably in the kitchen, pouring yet another gin and tonic, howling on about the shame of it all, the shame; her father hunched over the telephone every evening, conducting hushed conversations, making arrangements of which Diane as yet had no inkling, then retreating to his workshop to piece together the porcelain fragments of someone else's shattered happiness.

Diane had, some time ago, gathered that her parents had tried for years for another child, and she wondered if her mother's self-pitying rage was somehow tinged with jealousy that her daughter had succeeded where she had failed. Whether or not this was so, she left Diane in no doubt about what now must happen. Auntie Vera had a friend, she said, who knew a man in Birmingham who *dealt* with things like this. It took Diane a little while to understand what her mother meant by this, but when she did, she was outraged. She never had the remotest doubt that the baby would be born and her intransigence on the issue surprised even herself.

Her mother begged and bullied her to reveal who the baby's father was, but made the tactical error of saying that what he'd done, to a girl of only fifteen, was against the law and that men went to prison for such things. Diane had a vision of David behind bars in striped fatigues, a ball and chain shackled to his ankle. She wasn't going to do that to him. In any case, she didn't want him to find out. It had been her decision to allow him to

109

do to her what he had, so it was her responsibility to cope with the consequences. Had anyone dared suggest that in some sly corner of her mind, she saw motherhood as a means of escaping the prison of Elmshurst, she would have reacted with fierce indignation. The idea had not, however, entirely passed her by.

With abortion deleted from the list of options, attention moved on to another *A* word: the baby would be given up for adoption. But Diane announced that she wasn't going to let that happen either. At which point her mother lost what sliver of patience she'd managed to retain. Auntie Vera was summoned to talk some sense into the girl.

Auntie Vera wasn't family. The Bedfords had no family. Both sets of grandparents were dead and Diane's father was an only child. Her mother had a somewhat dissolute brother called Ted who had emigrated to Australia before the war and all but disappeared. Once every four or five years a postcard would arrive from some new and unpronounceable place to prove he was still alive. Vera Dutton was simply her mother's best friend. They had once worked in the same typing pool and shared a more or less misanthropic view of the world as well as a penchant for gin. Every Tuesday afternoon they played whist with two other friends and on Fridays went into Birmingham to do some shopping and have their perms tweaked. Auntie Vera was even shorter than Diane's mother and always wore pale blue and a thick layer of orange-tinted make-up. She had no children of her own and was married to a bank manager called Reggie who was almost as irritating and snobbish as she was. Apart from Dr Henderson, Auntie Vera was the only outsider who knew about the Bedfords' new and shaming secret.

'Your mother's *so* worried, dear,' she said.

They were sitting, just the two of them, on the little white wooden bench under the cherry tree on the front lawn, sipping tea from willow-patterned china cups, the ones that were only brought out for special occasions. Diane's mother was pretending to be busy in the kitchen.

'I know.'

'She only wants what's best for you, you know.'

'I know.'

'And they'll find it a lovely home—'

'*It?*'

'The baby. A family who really want it.'

'I really want it.'

'You may think you do now, dear. But you're only young.'

'And too stupid to know what I want.'

Auntie Vera's face hardened.

'You know perfectly well that wasn't what I meant.'

She stared into the distance in an irritated way and took a long puff at her cigarette. When she blinked, Diane noticed that her eyelids were painted the same powder blue as her dress.

'Is this boy going to marry you?'

Diane laughed and this seemed to annoy Auntie Vera even more.

'Of course not.'

'It doesn't concern you what people will say?'

'No, not really.'

'You won't mind them calling your baby a bastard?'

Diane wasn't going to give the woman the

satisfaction of seeing that, at last, this had touched a nerve. She simply shook her head, trying to look nonchalant.

'They can say what they like.'

Auntie Vera sighed and flicked her cigarette end into the hydrangeas.

'Well, it's your life, dear. If you want to ruin it, I suppose it's up to you.'

'Is that why you never had children? In case it ruined your life?'

It was the last conversation of any length they would ever have. But the issue of adoption remained unresolved for at least another three months. Diane did not, of course, return to Elmshurst. Instead, the school was informed that during the summer, she had developed a pulmonary condition that required specialist medical attention and prolonged convalescence in a healthier climate. In late October when the pregnancy became difficult to conceal, accompanied by her mother, she was dispatched, by ferry and overnight train, to a little town in the Swiss Alps. Everything had been arranged through a discreet chain of Masonic contacts. For the remaining months of her pregnancy, Diane would be confined, along with two other young Englishwomen in a similar predicament, to the home of a rotund and rosy-cheeked widow called Frau Müller.

Her mother stayed long enough to satisfy herself that the medical and educational conditions were satisfactory and the scope for mischief strictly limited. She needn't have worried. Behind the benign smiles, Frau Müller, in her high-necked black gown and tightly coiled tresses, was a stern

112

custodian. And the town, which nestled hygienic and wholesome beside a lake, was as boring as it was beautiful.

A suitably lugubrious doctor from the local hospital came to visit the girls once a week. They were tutored by an arthritic retired schoolmaster called Herr Schneider in English, French and German and by Frau Müller herself in the more vital arts of needlework and etiquette. Diane soon knew the correct way to leave a room of mixed company (head for door, turn only upon opening it, smile, exit) as well as how to get in and out of a motor vehicle without revealing inappropriate amounts of leg (in: knees together, lower backside on to seat, swing legs; out: knees together, swing legs, gracefully raise backside).

In the two weeks she stayed, her mother seemed to soften. The weather was still and sunny and unseasonably warm, the lake a mirror to the pine trees and the snowy peaks beyond. They took afternoon walks together along the shore and, in a little timber-walled café in the town square, feasted on apple strudel and glasses of hot chocolate topped with swirls of whipped cream.

On one such afternoon, her mother asked her what she might have wanted to do with her life, had she not fallen pregnant. And Diane heard herself admitting for the first time that all she'd ever wanted to do was act. The only things she had enjoyed about school were the plays they staged. She was nearly always given one of the major roles and everyone, even the teachers, used to say how good she was. Her mother smiled wistfully and nodded.

'You could have gone to one of those wonderful

drama schools,' she said and took a sip of chocolate. 'In London. Ah, well.'

She didn't rub it in, simply left the thought floating there so that Diane could fill in the subtext for herself. The implication was obviously that if she would agree to adoption, this dream might yet come true. It was a different and far shrewder tack from those initial hostile challenges about how would she and the baby survive the ignominy, where would they live and who did she think was going to pay the bills. A new, more subtle seed had been planted. And after her mother left and the snow began to fall and the weeks drifted by, so it slowly took root.

Her two fellow inmates, both Catholics—Angela, from Bristol, who never stopped crying, and Pam, a much more worldly girl from North London—were both giving up their babies for adoption. It was apparently all part of the package provided by Frau Müller in association with the local Sisters of Mercy, whose convent perched piously upon a little hill outside the town.

In the evenings, after supper, the girls generally retired to their own parlour to read. It was a cosy room with a woodstove and blighted only by an infuriatingly raucous cuckoo clock. On this particular evening, with the smell of boiled ham and cabbage still hanging in the air, Diane and Pam were sitting either side of the stove, trying to learn a passage of Goethe's *Egmont*, which they were expected to recite the following day to Herr Schneider. Angela had already retired and was no doubt already drenching her pillow. Pam, whose pregnancy was a month more advanced than Diane's, suddenly gave a startled little cry and laid

114

both hands on her belly. Diane asked what was wrong.

'It kicked! Oooh. And again.'

Diane got up from her armchair and knelt beside her.

'Can I feel?'

Pam took her hands and guided them to the right place and they waited.

'There! Did you feel it?'

'Golly! What does it feel like?'

'Like, a sort of ... fluttering, I suppose.'

'Does it hurt?'

'No. It's quite nice, actually.'

When the gymnastics were over, Diane went back to her chair.

'Did you ever think of keeping it?'

'The baby? Good gracious, no! I'd have had an abortion but my parents are strict Catholics and think it's a mortal sin.'

'What's a *mortal* sin?'

'I don't know. One that's more fun, I suppose.'

Diane laughed.

'Don't you want to have children?' she asked.

'Of course I do. But not now. I want to have a life first. Get a job, *do* something. And then have children properly with someone I'm married to and love.'

'You didn't love the father then?'

'Lord, no. He's an absolute bounder.'

There was a long silence during which they both went back to *Egmont*. But Diane couldn't concentrate.

'Do they let you see the baby? I mean, when it's born?'

'I don't think so. They just whisk it off. You

know, so you don't get all mumsy about it.'

The prospect didn't seem to bother Pam at all. But Diane couldn't imagine allowing such a thing to happen to her baby. The cuckoo erupted from its little door to tell them it was nine o'clock.

'So help me,' Pam said. 'I'll strangle that bloody thing one day.'

Diane hardly slept that night. And the following day, even after a stern reprimand from Herr Schneider for her slaughtering of Goethe, all she could think of was that there had to be some way of achieving both the things she wanted. The baby and, as Pam so succinctly put it, *a life*.

It was, perhaps fittingly, at Christmas that the plan was broached. And all these years later, Diane still didn't know what was the more astonishing: that she had come up with the idea or that her parents had gone along with it.

They had come out to Switzerland to spend Christmas with her and see in the new year. Diane had prepared the ground well. She had found lodging for them in a pretty little *Gasthof* just along the street from Frau Müller's and had spent a long time (and too much of her modest allowance) finding the right presents for them. She gave her father a finely carved meerschaum pipe and a green felt trilby with a sprig of feathers on the side. For her mother she had found a black velvet waistcoat, prettily embroidered with alpine flowers. And from the moment she met them at the railway station, she had been sweetness and light.

Her mother, she could see, smelled a rat. But Diane's resolute good spirits, her enthusiastic efforts to show them around and introduce them

116

to those in the town with whom she had made friends, seemed to work. Her father, particularly, was unusually affectionate and solicitous, sometimes even putting his arm around her on their walks.

The town had an ancient tradition on New Year's Eve, in which men and boys, all dressed in black, their hands and faces blackened too, and each carrying an appropriately sized cow bell, did a tour of the town. They processed along the streets in single file, clanging their bells, snaking in and out of the hotels and restaurants and the grander houses. The sight was macabre and the sound both thrilling and disturbing, like the gates of hell banging in the wind. When the procession arrived at the *Gasthof* where Diane's parents were staying, dinner was still being served, and everyone sat at their tables and watched, some—including her mother—covering their ears. When it had passed through, they all cheered and laughed and raised their glasses to toast the coming year.

Diane had been waiting for the right moment to make her radical proposal and this seemed about as right as it might get. Quietly and calmly she told them that she had been giving a lot of thought to what would happen after the baby was born. She saw her mother stiffen. Diane told them that she still couldn't bear the idea of giving the baby away. She was his mother, she said (there was no doubt in her mind about the child's gender) and nothing could change that. The idea of losing him forever was too terrible to bear. But...and here her mother's chin and eyebrows lifted a little. Diane had never seen her on such tenterhooks. But, she continued, she understood the shame they would feel at having an illegitimate child in the family. Loving them as she did, she could not bring that shame upon them.

She let that settle in for a moment. The nervousness that she had feared might wreck her performance had curiously evaporated. In fact, the sight of them in such suspense, waiting for her next words, made her feel empowered. Smiling sweetly, with just the right tinge of sadness, she went on.

'I know how much you wanted to have another child. And you know how I'd have loved a little brother or sister. So...' This was the moment. She swallowed. 'Why don't we all treat him as if that's ...who he is.'

She smiled again. They were both staring at her. Her father cleared his throat.

'I'm not sure I quite—'

'You mean, pretend *we're* the baby's parents?' her mother cut in.

Diane nodded.

'I've never heard anything so ridiculous in all my life.'

'Why? What's ridiculous about it? You've always wanted another baby.'

Her mother frowned and looked around, clearly concerned about being overheard. Diane leaned forward and went on more quietly.

'Who'll know? You haven't got any friends—I'm sorry, that sounds awful, but it's true, isn't it? Only Auntie Vera and she knows already. You could tell everyone else that you've been to see some wonderful doctor here in Switzerland and he helped you have a baby.'

'Good Lord, you really have given this a lot of thought.'

118

'Yes, *of course* I have, Mother. I've done this dreadful thing to you and I feel so ashamed and... I've been racking my brains trying to think of a way to make it all work.'

Up until now it had felt like a performance but suddenly it was real—although she would later discover, on stage, that these two things were often hard to distinguish. She began to cry. And her father reached out across the table and held her hand. Her mother glanced around again to see if anyone was watching.

'Please, Diane, don't make a scene,' she whispered.

Her father dug into his pocket and gave her his handkerchief.

'It's all right, dear,' he said. 'Don't cry. It's all right.'

'I'm sorry. I just thought...'

And that was where they left it. At least, for the time being. Back in her bed at Frau Müller's, she realized that she hadn't even mentioned the bit about wanting to *have a life* as well as the baby. Perhaps it was just as well. If she'd gone on to talk about going to drama school, her mother would probably have erupted and denounced it all as another typically selfish ploy.

The following morning the three of them took a horse-drawn sleigh to the station through the softly falling snow. They stood in awkward silence on the platform amid the steam and bustle while the luggage was loaded into the *couchette*. Her father was wearing his new hat and her mother a look of nervous distraction. When the guard's whistle finally blew, Diane asked if they had thought any further about her proposal. Her father

119

gave his unlit meerschaum a thoughtful suck then removed it and cleared his throat.

'Well,' he said. 'We'll obviously have to move. You know, make a new start somewhere. Don't worry, old girl. We'll make a go of it.'

NINE

Tom's study was at the rear of the house, his desk shunted up against the window that overlooked the creek. Sometimes when he glanced up from his computer he would see deer foraging in the dappled shade of the cottonwoods. In spring a few years ago he had sat for half an hour watching a black bear and her two cubs splashing and chasing one another through the shallows. There was an old joke about why writers never stared out the window in the morning (answer: because then they'd have nothing to do all afternoon) and Tom knew he would be more productive if he denied himself the view and put the desk against one of the walls. But they were all lined with bookshelves, so overloaded that they seemed in constant danger of collapse and though the idea of a writer dying in an avalanche of books had a certain appeal, he preferred to leave things as they were.

He had long ago run out of shelf space and so the bare cedar floor, scattered with Indian rugs, had been colonized in every possible place with precarious towers of books and box files, papers and magazines. There was a hide-covered couch draped with an old buffalo wool blanket where Makwi sprawled asleep for most of the day, her

120

paws twitching as she chased squirrels in her dreams. Behind the couch stood a large chest of drawers, painted the same duck egg blue as the walls and shelves, its top cluttered with framed photographs. Only two were of Tom: one of him posing formally with some important Blackfeet elders and the other of him receiving an award for his TV series at a film festival in Canada. The others were all of Danny and Gina, pictures taken on various vacations—hiking in the Bob Marshall Wilderness, skiing at Big Sky, a summer canoe trip along the Missouri, where they'd camped in constant fear of rattlesnakes.

All the photographs that, for several different reasons, didn't qualify for framing, Tom kept in large manila envelopes, each carefully marked and dated, in the chest's bottom drawer. He hadn't dared look at them in a long time. It was something he used to do on those blurred, maudlin evenings after Gina left, when his drinking was at its most epic.

He would sit on the floor with a quart of Jack Daniel's and sift through them, trying to make sense of what had happened and in the process managing only to make himself more unhappy and confused and thirsty for oblivion. In a moment of clarity one night it had occurred to him how rarely he figured in any of the pictures that lay scattered around him on the floor. He was always the invisible one behind the camera. It was as though, in documenting their marriage and the first eight years of Danny's life, he had rendered himself invisible, edited himself out. Occasionally Gina used to admonish him, telling him to put the damned camera down and just *be* with them. At an

AA meeting a few years later someone had pointed out that it was much the same way with liquor. It helped you edit yourself out of your own life.

The process of editing was, of course, second nature to Tom. He'd learned how to do it from the age of thirteen after Diane died. That shaming year he'd spent in junior high in LA when she was on death row had taught him the cost of other people knowing the truth: that his mother had gone to the gas chamber, a convicted murderer. The edited version of his life, in which the illusion was restored of Diane being his sister and Joan and Arthur his parents, made things a lot easier. In this edited version—the version believed by those closest to him, even by Gina and Danny—Diane had died in a car accident in England.

It was strange how a lie much told could acquire a kind of solidity. In the telling it became, in one's own mind, as strong and comforting as the truth. Tom had sometimes wondered, after Gina left, whether things might have been different had he told her the truth about Diane. Perhaps it would have helped her understand his failings as husband and father. Or perhaps it would only have made her pity him. And pity, for Tom, was something worse than shame.

It was after Gina's phone call last night, telling him that Danny was back from Iraq, that he had decided to brace himself and have another look at some of his old photographs. He'd risen, as he always did these days, at around six and gone for a run with Makwi up along the creek. His knees weren't so good anymore, so in truth it was more of an ambling jog and no more than a brisk walk for Makwi. But it always cleared his head and got his blood moving, helped him plan the day ahead.

It was a clear May morning and the meadow and the banks of the creek were greening up fast. He lost Makwi for about ten minutes when she took off into the forest after some creature he didn't even get a glimpse of and all he could do was call and whistle and hope that it was only a squirrel or at worst a deer and not a bear or a mountain lion. The dog was notoriously accident prone and at least once every couple of months came back bleeding from some new wound that would have to be stitched up. He'd gotten her for free from the pound but paid for her a thousand times over in vets' bills. As he waited for her to reappear, he thought about Danny and whether there would be any response to the message he'd asked Gina to give him when she saw him today.

The boy still hadn't called him or replied to the e-mails Tom had sent him. Gina said he shouldn't make too much of this. Danny was getting about a hundred e-mails a day, she said, from strangers who wished him well and others who had already condemned him and wished him dead. She and Dutch had flown down to San Diego yesterday and were seeing Danny at Camp Pendleton later this morning.

'Maybe I should fly down too,' Tom had suggested, though he knew what she'd say.

'I don't think that's such a good idea. Leave it awhile.'

'He is my son too, you know.'

'Tom, please. Don't start.'

'I just feel so, I don't know, so helpless.'

'I know.'

123

'Will you send him my love? Ask him to call?'

'Of course I will.'

'Or tell me when I can call him. Does he have a new cell phone number?'

'Yes.'

There was a pause.

'Did he tell you not to give me the number?'

'Tom, you've got to remember, there's a lot of history here. I mean, between you and Danny.'

'Did he?'

'Yes.'

The history was right there in front of him now, on his desk, inside the manila envelope he'd laid there last night after Gina's call. It was marked *Danny '93 thru . . .* He hadn't felt strong enough to look at the pictures last night but now, with the resolve of the new day, he was ready. He'd showered after his run, fed Makwi (still panting and wired but otherwise unscathed) and had some breakfast himself, while he skimmed the *Missoulian*. Then he'd carried his coffee into the study and sat down at his desk. He stared at the envelope for a while then gently shook the photos from it. The ones that charted the rest of the boy's childhood, his teens and transition into manhood.

Some of these Tom had taken himself on those increasingly awkward weekends when Danny used to come to stay. The smiles more and more forced, the eyes less and less readable. His own son slowly becoming a stranger. There were others, from later, after Danny had said he didn't want to come to stay anymore, photos Gina had sent in an effort to retain at least some strand of a link between the two of them. Danny in the football squad, with girlfriends Tom had never met, his high school graduation picture, the head freshly shaven. It had been taken only a few months after their argument.

Even now, five years later, Tom could remember almost every word, every moment of it. Danny had called to say he was coming over to Missoula and asked if he could drop by around lunchtime. It was the first time they had been in touch since Christmas and from the tone of his son's voice Tom sensed that this was going to be more than just a casual visit. There was something important the boy wanted—or, more likely, had been cajoled by his mother—to discuss.

Danny arrived at midday, driving a big black pickup with a lot of chrome and lamps up front and flames painted along the sides. He said it belonged to Dutch, which didn't surprise Tom in the least. Makwi made a big fuss of the boy, which helped break the ice a little. While Tom cooked them a cheese-and-tomato omelet and put together a salad, Danny slouched against the divider, looking awkward and asking polite questions about Tom's work in which he'd never before expressed the slightest interest. His head was still shaved, except for a little buzz-cut patch on the top. It made Tom, with his thinning, grizzled mane curling over his collar, feel like an old hippie. He nearly made a joke about it but decided not to.

'So, what's up?' he said at last when they'd sat down to eat.

'I'm going to enlist.'

Danny said it without looking up from his food.

'I just wanted, you know, to let you know.'

'In the Marines.'

'Yeah.'

'Of course. You mean, after college.'

'No. I'm not going to college. Not now, anyhow.'

'I thought that was the plan. Montana State, then decide after you graduate.'

'I already decided.'

'But, without a degree, that means you go in as a ... what is it?'

Danny gave a derisive little laugh, as if only a moron would have to ask what enlisting meant.

'A private.'

'I thought you wanted to be an officer.'

'I still can be. Later though.'

'But—'

'Dad, the country's at war! I've waited long enough already.'

'Well, it's a war that some of us—'

'I know what you feel about the war. And I don't care, I just—'

'How? How do you know what I feel about the war? I don't recall our ever having discussed it.'

'I just know, okay?'

Tom took a deep breath and for a few moments the only sound was the clack of their cutlery. The omelet suddenly tasted like glue. He silently cursed himself for not having seen this coming. Thanks to Dutch, joining the military had always been in the cards. But as an officer, with a college degree under his belt. And four years of college, Tom had naively hoped, might well change the boy's mind, make him want to do something else with his life.

'So, did you come here today to tell me or to ask my opinion?'

Danny still didn't look up.

126

'Mom said I should come tell you.'

'Well, thank you. So she's all for this, then, I take it.'

'Of course she is.'

'Why *of course*? It's not every mother who'd be happy to see her only son go off to war. Especially a war that a lot of people think we shouldn't be fighting in the first place.'

Tom regretted saying this before it was even out of his mouth. Danny looked away, gave a small, disdainful shake of his head.

'That may be what people like you think, but—'

'Sorry, hold on a moment. What does that mean? *People like me.*'

'People who are prepared to stand by and watch our country be attacked and do nothing to fight back.'

The boy's eyes were on him now and the contempt in them was so shocking that Tom had to swallow before he could speak again.

'Attacked? You mean nine-eleven?'

'Of course I mean nine-eleven, for godsake.'

'They weren't from Iraq, Danny. They had no connection with Iraq. Everybody knows that now.'

Danny pushed his plate away and stood up, his chair grating on the floor.

'Danny, please . . .'

'Forget it.'

'Listen, I'm sorry. Please, sit down.'

'Why the hell do you liberals always want to make excuses for those who want to kill us?'

'Danny—'

'Don't you *get* it? You don't, do you? You just don't get it.'

He was at the door now. Tom stood up and

127

opened his arms.

'Please, Danny. Don't just walk out.'

But he was out of the house, Makwi running after him, barking, clearly thinking this was some new kind of game. Danny got into the truck and slammed the door with its painted flames. And by the time Tom got there, the boy had fired the engine and rammed it into reverse, the wheels ripping furrows in the gravel, while Makwi went on barking. Tom reached for the door handle.

'Danny, please!'

But it was too late. The truck lurched out of the driveway and roared off down the road.

Tom had revisited these moments a thousand times, plotting the points at which he might have reacted differently instead of letting his ego do yet more damage to their fragile relationship. Rather than listening, he had immediately challenged. Rather than offering respect and support, he had chosen to undermine the boy's beliefs. Even a moment's reflection would have told him that the only possible outcome would be anger and resentment. In that brief exchange they had both lived up to the caricatures each had fashioned of the other.

What made it so idiotic was that Tom, truly, had no aversion to the military or to those who served in it. On the contrary, he had only respect and sympathy for the young men and women who had been sent to fight in Iraq and Afghanistan. It was little different from how he had felt about those who had risked and lost their lives in Vietnam three decades before. The aversion was only to the men in suits, safely ensconced in Washington and London, who for suspect reasons had sent them there.

He realized too that the argument with Danny had nothing to do with the military or with politics. It was personal. About Tom's self-pity and jealousy at having been ousted by another man, replaced as a father. And now that he could view the world more clearly, instead of through the wobbling haze of liquor, he knew he should be grateful that the boy had found a father figure with values he could admire.

At his desk, he had been staring at Danny's high school yearbook picture for a long time. And now he turned it over to see the last photograph in the file. It had been taken at the recruit-training depot north of San Diego, on the day Danny was awarded his eagle, globe and anchor, the emblem that showed he had finally become a US Marine. Tom hadn't, of course, been invited to the ceremony. Gina had sent him the photo that fall, as if daring him not to be proud. But it had only served to confirm that the process of separation was complete. It had been like looking at a stranger. And, much as he wanted it to be otherwise, it still felt the same.

That lunchtime, however, he took the picture into town and in a little gift store on North Higgins found an appropriately elegant frame for it. When he came home he didn't put it with the other framed pictures on top of the chest but placed it instead on the windowsill in front of his desk. And while he got on with his work and waited for Gina or—hope beyond hope—for Danny to call, whenever he looked up from his computer screen, he would see his stranger son staring back at him.

Tom was writing a piece for the *Missoulian*

about a Jesuit boarding school for Blackfeet children that had been set up in the late 1890s along the Two Medicine River near Browning. It was called the Holy Family Mission and it lasted for more than forty years. Tom had devoted a chapter to it in his book and in the course of his research recorded interviews with some of the old-timers who had attended it. To refresh his memory, he had listened to the tapes again and was as moved by their testimony as he had been the first time.

The purpose of the place, naturally, had been to civilize the savages and save their souls from eternal damnation. Many of the early pupils were taken by force and in tears from their homes on the reservation. Their braids were cut off and their buckskin clothes and moccasins taken away to be replaced with the kind of clothes the white folk wore. If they ran away, as many tried to, their families' rations, supplied by the Government Agency, in many cases the only source of food, were cut off. Once captured or returned, the absconders were soundly whipped, as indeed they were for many other sins, such as speaking in their native tongue.

The discovery that had moved Tom most was how few of those he interviewed seemed to bear any sort of grudge. In fact some, while embracing Christianity, had later been among the most diligent defenders and sustainers of what survived of the Blackfeet culture and language. The capacity to forgive was one of life's most mysterious miracles. Tom only wished he could find more of it in his own heart, for grievances infinitely more trivial.

He turned off his computer around six when the shadows of the cottonwoods were reaching out across the meadow and the light had gone golden and hazy. Danny, in his smart uniform, was still staring at him from the windowsill. And Gina still hadn't called.

He took Makwi along the trail that curled up through the forest on the other side of the road and watched her weaving through the glades of Douglas fir and ponderosa. The air was warm and smelled strongly of resin and the undergrowth was coming so fast you could almost hear it unfurl. They walked up to the foot of the rocky cliff where the ravens were already building their nests and while he watched them Makwi stood a little way off, panting from her patrol. When they got back to the house she went down through the meadow and took a stately bath in the creek, then lay on the grass and rubbed her back and sides.

He switched on the TV in the kitchen and watched CNN while he made Makwi's supper, then cooked some pasta and beans for himself. Two American soldiers had been killed by a roadside bomb south of Baghdad; fifteen Iraqi civilians dead or injured in a suicide bomb attack in a marketplace in Basra. Tom had just sat down to eat, was barely concentrating anymore, was just about to take a mouthful of pasta, when the next item froze his hand in midair.

'And back home, at Camp Pendleton in California, two US Marines have been charged with premeditated murder following an incident, January twenty-four, in which seven Iraqi civilians were killed...'

And there was Danny, 'Lance Corporal Daniel

131

Bedford', his photo alongside that of the other boy accused. There were no police mug shot numbers hanging from their necks nor matching profiles but there might as well have been. On TV and in the eyes of the millions who watched, you were guilty until proven innocent. The report was agonizingly short. There was no account of what had happened. All it said was that the accused were not in custody but had been flown back to Camp Pendleton where they were on restricted duties, 'pending Article Thirty-two hearings'. If found guilty as charged, the piece concluded, both men could face the death penalty.

Tom dumped his supper in the sink and went directly to his office to phone Gina on her cell. His heart was beating hard and his hand shaking so badly that he had to dial the number twice. He didn't know if his anger had more to do with what he'd just learned or with how he'd come to learn it. He stood tapping his desk, staring at Danny's picture, while he waited for her to answer.

'Gina?'

'Tom, I can't really talk right now.'

'Did you see the news?'

'Yes. Listen, I'll—'

'Have you seen Danny?'

'Yes, we're with him now.'

'Don't you think you could have called me?'

'I'm sorry. It's been quite a day—'

'Christ, Gina. I mean—'

'Tom, I'm going to have to call you back, okay? I have to go now. Bye.'

And the connection went dead.

TEN

Tommy gripped the pistol with both hands and squinted along the barrel, trying to keep it steady while he waited for the Indian to rear up again from behind the rock. It was a nickel-finished single-action Colt .45 with a seven-inch barrel and engraved ivory grips—the most beautiful thing he'd ever had in his hands. It was heavy and hard to hold steady. He'd already fired five rounds and missed every time.

'Spread your feet a little more,' Ray Montane said. 'And don't hold your breath, just take the air in real slow and deep. That's the way. You'll get him now, son. Aim for the chest where he's good and wide and don't forget, gentle on that trigger. Are you ready?'

Tommy nodded.

'Okay. So let's cock that hammer again.'

Tommy clicked it back. From the edge of his vision he saw Ray once more take hold of the steel lever.

'One, two, three...'

Ray thrust the lever forward and there was a creaking sound as the cable tightened and then up came the Indian again behind the rock, pointing his rifle at them, as if about to shoot. Tommy took a last deep breath and squeezed the trigger. The jolt and the bang still made him jump and he was sure he'd missed again but there was a different sound this time, a loud clang. Ray and Diane whooped.

'There you go, pardner, you got him!'

Diane had been sitting in a wide-armed wooden chair up on the deck behind them. But she was on her feet now clapping and Tommy turned, still holding the gun, and grinned at her.

'Whoa there, cowboy,' Ray said. 'Careful where you're pointing.'

'It's empty.'

'I know. But you always have to check.'

Ray took the gun from him and ejected the spent cartridges and placed it on the table alongside the tall cocktail glasses and the ashtray where Diane's cigarette lay discarded, smoke curling in the hot still air. Then the three of them set off along the strip of sunbaked sand to check out the Indian.

Tommy's spurs clinked as he walked, his eyes locked on his own shadow. The brim of his hat was perhaps a little too big but the general effect was still impressive. A real cowboy's shadow. He was wearing the outfit Ray had given him the morning after they'd arrived in LA. It was a perfect junior version of the one Red McGraw wore on *Sliprock*. Ray said he'd had it specially made at the studio and that it was much better than the ones they sold in the toy stores. The jacket and chaps were made out of genuine fringed buckskin and the leather gun belt had a silver buckle and silver-painted bullets all the way around that looked completely real. The gun that went with it wasn't real, of course, not like Ray's, the one he'd just been shooting, but it had the same ivory grips and six chambers with bullets that came apart so you could put caps in them. The bang was so loud it hurt your ears. Ray had also given him a Daisy BB gun that looked like a real Winchester rifle. It had a lever action and shot red pellets that Ray said could actually kill birds and little animals like chipmunks. Tommy had tried a few times but hadn't yet managed to hit anything.

'Hey, good shootin', son. Look, you got him plumb in the neck.'

Ray unclipped the painted cardboard Indian from its metal frame and held it so they could all have a closer look. The face, above the bullet hole, was striped with war paint and had a wicked scowl.

'You just notched up your first Injun.'

Ray held out his hand and Tommy, grinning and flushed with pride, shook it firmly.

'Now it's Mom's turn.'

Diane laughed.

'Oh, no. I don't think so.'

'Come on, sugar. You've got to learn sometime. What's old Gary Cooper going to think when he finds his leading lady can't handle a gun?'

'I play a teacher not a gunslinger and I don't think he'll give two hoots one way or the other.'

Ray put his arm around her waist and pulled her close.

'What do you say, Tommy? Don't you think she should have a go?'

'Yeah! Come on, Diane!'

He hadn't yet called her *Mum* or *Mom* or anything other than what he'd always called her. And he couldn't imagine ever doing so. It was hard enough to get used to the idea that she wasn't his big sister anymore. It was like playing a game in which suddenly all the rules had been changed and everybody was having to guess what they were.

It wasn't scary or even upsetting, except, of course, that terrible evening when everything got

135

turned upside down. He'd never forget the look on his mother's—or, rather, his grandmother's—face when Diane broke the news. Or how his father-grandfather had looked when they said goodbye at the departure gate at the airport. His face was pale and haggard and his eyes suddenly went all watery. As they walked away Tommy had looked back and waved and was shocked by how old and frail the man looked, how his bony body seemed to be crumpling inside his coat.

Tommy didn't know what he should call them either. Diane said he could call them *Grandma* and *Grandpa* or even Joan and Arthur. But neither of these seemed right. When they had spoken on the telephone a few days ago he'd managed not to call them anything at all, just told them about the flight from London and how hot and sunny it was here in LA and how he would soon be starting at his new school which he and Diane had been to see. It was called Carl Curtis and everybody seemed really nice and friendly, he told them, even the teachers. He couldn't hear them very well because the line was all crackly and they kept cutting each other off when they spoke, but even so he thought they'd both sounded sad.

Tommy worried that maybe he ought to be feeling sad too but he didn't. It was strange suddenly not to have a father. Sometimes, before he went to sleep at night, he would lie there thinking about David, the schoolboy who was his real father. He wondered where he lived and what he might be like. Maybe he had other children by now, children who would be Tommy's half brothers and sisters. This didn't exactly make him feel jealous; it was more like missing someone. But then how could you miss people you'd never even met? Or feel jealous of people who might not even exist?

No, what had happened was certainly pretty weird but there was no point in getting upset about it. As Diane kept saying, they were still the same people after all. Anyway, Ray was going to be his dad now and who could want a better one than that? And how could he possibly feel sad about not ever having to go back to Ashlawn and about moving to Hollywood and being here, right now, shooting Indians with real guns in Red McGraw's garden?

It was almost two weeks since Tommy and Diane had arrived. They had rented a little apartment just off Wilshire Boulevard but hadn't spent more than the occasional night there because they'd been living up here at Ray's. Tommy's bedroom was about ten times as big as his old one and every morning when he woke up he would lie there with his eyes closed and wonder if it would all still be there when he opened them. Then he'd get out of bed and tiptoe to the shuttered doors and step out onto his very own balcony, the decking hot beneath the soles of his bare feet. And the sky was always blue and the sun was warm on his skin and the strange new birds were singing in the trees. And he would walk to the balustrade and lean there looking down at the swimming pool and the palm trees and beyond to the city far below, with its vast grid of straight streets and palm trees, stretching away into the haze. Miguel, the gardener, would be mowing the grass or watering the flower beds or scooping leaves from the pool and he'd look up and see

137

Tommy and wave and shout *Good morning, Mister Tommy! How are you today?*

The house was gorgeous. It had a roof of red tiles and the rough whitewashed walls were smothered in creepers with pink and purple flowers. In the middle of the red brick driveway there was a bronze statue of a rearing horse. The inside walls were made of swirling whitewashed adobe and hung with the stuffed heads of deer and elk and buffalo as well as lots of western paintings each with its own brass light. The downstairs floors were polished stone and scattered with cowhides and Indian rugs and in the living room there were chairs whose arms were made of real saddles with silver studs. The TV set was about three times the size of any he'd seen in England and the leather sofa he sat on to watch it was so enormous he felt like Alice in Wonderland after she'd drunk that magic shrinking potion.

Ray now tugged a fresh Indian from the stack that leaned against the wall of the shooting range and fixed it to the frame and when he'd done it the three of them walked back to the deck, Ray in the middle with his arms around both of them. He let Tommy reload the Colt with bullets from the cardboard box on the table and Tommy did it just as he'd been taught, clicking the cylinder back into position and checking the safety before offering the gun, grips first, to Diane.

'Okay, Annie's got her gun,' Ray said. 'Let's see her handle it.'

He showed her how to hold it and raise it into position and then stood behind her, holding her shoulders, and told her all the things he'd told Tommy. She missed with her first shot but then hit the Indian five times in a row through his head and chest. Tommy felt jealous and proud in about equal measure. Ray lifted her off her feet and swung her around in a big circle and then he hugged her and kissed her for a long time on the lips. They did this sort of thing a lot, which Tommy found a bit embarrassing. He generally just looked away or pretended to be busy doing something.

When they'd finished, Ray said he was so hungry he could eat a horse so the three of them set off back up to the house. It was a steep and winding climb, forty-two steps and then a narrow gravel path through the palms and eucalyptus trees and some spiked bushes that Miguel said were called *yuckers*. Little greeny brown lizards scurried everywhere and Ray said you had to keep your eyes open because sometimes there were rattlesnakes too. Up on the lawn the sprinklers were on, making rainbows, and Ray dared him to run through them so he did and got half soaked but it didn't matter because it made everybody laugh and the sun was so warm he'd be dry again in minutes.

They walked up the final few steps from the lawn and around the swimming pool to the white marble terrace where Dolores, the housekeeper and cook, had lunch all laid out ready for them. There were plates of ham and turkey and cold roast beef and shrimps and lots of other things, including the best potato salad Tommy had ever tasted. The table was decorated with pink and white flowers and stood in the shade of a big old pine tree that had hundreds of fairy lights hidden in it which were turned on every evening when it got dark, along with the underwater lights in the swimming pool and the waterfall that trickled into it like a real mountain stream. It wasn't so much a house as a palace.

Tommy didn't know if this was how all the stars in Hollywood lived because he hadn't so far been to anybody else's house. But he had seen some stars. During the flight on the Britannia jet from London to New York (which, along with shooting a real Colt .45, was probably the most exciting thing he'd done in his entire life), the air hostess had taken him up to the cockpit where he met the captain and copilot who explained about all the dials and switches and even let him steer for a while. And on the way back to his seat, Tommy recognized Charlton Heston. He was sitting just two rows in front of them. It was funny seeing him in a sports coat instead of the leather skirt and toga he wore in *Ben-Hur*. He gave Tommy a big smile. Diane kept nagging at him to go and ask Mr Heston for an autograph but he was too shy, even to let her do it for him, and had regretted it ever since.

Once they were over their jet lag, Ray had taken them for a drive around Hollywood in his car. It was a pale blue convertible Cadillac Eldorado with rocketship taillights and massive fins and white leather seats with enough room up front for all three of them. Tommy sat in the middle and wondered where the gear stick was until Ray explained the car was an automatic and changed gears all by itself. Ray switched on the radio and tuned it to a station that played all the latest hits and they drove east along Hollywood Boulevard with the Everly Brothers singing 'Cathy's Clown' so loudly that everyone turned to stare at them.

They stopped at the forecourt of Grauman's Chinese Theater where film stars left their hand- and footprints in wet cement and then had a look at the new Walk of Fame where pink and gold stars were being set into the pavement—or *sidewalk* as Tommy had to get used to calling it—each with a famous name on it. Ray hadn't been given one yet but he said this was only because they were doing all the *old-timers* first.

While they were there a group of girls and boys came up and asked Ray for his autograph and he chatted with them and signed pictures of himself which he always carried with him just in case. One of the kids asked Diane if she was famous too and before she could answer Ray said she was soon going to be bigger than Marilyn Monroe, so they all asked her for her autograph too. Tommy felt really important.

They got back into the car and drove slowly past the Max Factor building which Ray said was Hollywood's first skyscraper and had only just been built. It had black glass windows which Tommy thought made it look a little scary. They drove past the famous gates of Paramount Studios where Diane was soon going to have her very own dressing room and then they headed back up onto Sunset Strip and stopped at a place called Schwab's drugstore, which Ray said was where lots of movie stars liked to *hang out*. There wasn't anybody famous hanging out there at that particular moment but Tommy had an ice cream float at the soda fountain counter so he didn't mind. Then, just as they were leaving, an open silver car shaped like a space rocket roared up and squealed to a halt and out jumped the driver over

141

the side. He had short blond hair and was wearing sunglasses and a white T-shirt and blue jeans and he grinned and waved at them.

'Hey, Ray! How're you doing?'

'Okay. How about you?'

'Not bad.'

They shook hands. The man nodded at Diane and Tommy and gave them a nice smile but Ray didn't seem to want to introduce them.

'Heard they let you do that picture down in Mexico after all,' Ray said. 'How'd it go?'

'Oh, you know. Got a little edgy now and then.'

'When are they releasing it?'

'Pretty soon. I haven't seen it yet but Sturges seems happy, so...' He shrugged. 'How're things going with you? More *Sliprock*?'

'Uh-huh. Couple of movies coming up too.'

'No rest for the wicked.'

'Guess so.'

There was an awkward pause. The man looked at Diane again and smiled.

'Hi.'

'Hello.'

'Well, we gotta be going,' Ray said.

'Me too. Just getting some smokes. See you around.'

'You bet.'

The man tilted his head to peer over his sunglasses at Tommy. His eyes were even bluer than Ray's. He grinned and winked then went off into the store.

'Asshole,' Ray muttered.

As they walked to the Cadillac, Diane asked who the man was and Ray said his name was Steve McQueen. He was in a TV show called *Wanted:*

142

Dead or Alive which Tommy had heard about but never seen. Ray said it was a crock of shit and Diane told him off for using those words in front of Tommy. Ray said sorry but it was true because the guy couldn't act his way out of a wet paper bag. The movie he'd just done was sure to be another crock of shit.

'It's just a remake of some two-bit Japanese picture,' he said. 'They offered it to me, but I turned it down.'

Tommy asked what it was called and Ray said the script was so bad he'd forgotten. All he could remember was that it was about seven gunslingers rescuing a Mexican village from some corny bunch of bandits.

Tommy had already noticed that Ray didn't seem to like many other westerns or the actors who were in them—apart from a few, like John Wayne and James Stewart and, of course, Gary Cooper. Tommy had asked him early on whether he'd ever met Robert Horton, the actor who played Flint McCullough, and Ray said he hadn't but that, for a wagon train scout, Flint always seemed *kind of faggoty*, which Tommy didn't understand except that it probably wasn't a compliment.

They'd already seen the famous Hollywood sign from a distance, but on the way back to the house, Ray took them up a winding canyon where they parked and walked along a trail to get a better look. The letters were enormous. Ray said they were fifty feet tall and that the sign used to say *HOLLYWOODLAND* until someone decided to take away the last four letters. Somehow, up close, there was something sad about it. The paint was

143

peeling from the letters and the props behind them were all overgrown and rusty. Ray said that a few years ago a young British actress called Peg Entwistle, who nobody wanted in their movies anymore, had climbed to the top of the letter *H* and jumped off and killed herself.

'Well, Ray, thanks a lot for sharing that with us,' Diane said.

Ray laughed and put his arm around her.

'Sugar, I told you. The whole world's gonna want you.'

Lunch on the terrace was almost over now. Tommy had finished all the potato salad and was on his second helping of chocolate ice cream. Ray and Diane were sitting on the other side of the table smoking their cigarettes and smiling at him.

'Didn't they ever feed you back in England?' Ray said.

'Not like this.'

As usual, after lunch, Diane and Ray disappeared off to Ray's bedroom for what they called a *siesta* and even though he wasn't tired, Tommy was expected to go to his room and have one as well. It was too hot outside to do anything else, so he didn't mind. He lay on his bed and tried to read some more of his book. It was called *White Fang* and it was good but for some reason he couldn't get into it. It had been like that ever since they arrived. His head was always fizzing with too many new things.

The past two weeks had been wonderful, just hanging out with Ray and Diane, having fun. But everything was about to change. Tomorrow was going to be Tommy's first day at Carl Curtis and even though the school had seemed perfectly

144

friendly when he and Diane visited it, he couldn't help feeling nervous. He knew it was silly. He hadn't wet the bed in a long time and, in any case, he wasn't going to be boarding. But he was still afraid that somehow somebody would find out and start calling him Bedwetter again.

That night Diane and Ray were going out to a party being thrown by Herb Kanter, the producer of *Remorseless*. Tommy asked if he could go too but Diane said it wouldn't be starting until after his bedtime and was only for grown-ups. Dolores would be at home to look after him, she said. Tommy liked Dolores. She was little and very pretty and had big dark brown eyes. To begin with, Tommy had assumed she was married to Miguel, but she wasn't. She had a tiny room along the corridor that went between the garage and the kitchen with a lovely picture of Mary and the baby Jesus on her wall, along with photos of her own little son who, oddly, was called Jesus too. Dolores said he lived with his grandparents in Mexico City. Tommy told her that's what he used to do too, only in England.

When it was time for Ray and Diane to leave, he was already in his pajamas and bathrobe, eating his supper from a tray and watching *I Love Lucy* on the huge TV in the living room. He'd seen the show in England and had never found it as funny as the people in the audience obviously did. They screamed with laughter at everything anyone said.

There was a noise in the hallway and through the big double doors he saw Diane and Ray coming down the wide, curving staircase. They looked wonderful. Ray was wearing a black suit with a long jacket and a tie like Bret Maverick's

145

except that it had a silver steer's skull at the knot. His hair was all slicked back. He gave Tommy a little wave and waited in the hallway while Diane came into the living room to say goodbye. She was wearing a strapless silver dress that shimmered as she moved. Her hair was pinned up and her lips were painted bright red. She put her hands on Tommy's shoulders and bent to kiss him.

'Goodnight, sweetheart. Be a good boy.'

'Will there be lots of film stars there?'

'I imagine so.'

'But you'll be the most beautiful.'

Diane laughed and kissed him again.

'You're so sweet. Oh dear, I've put lipstick on you.'

'I don't mind. Have a nice time.'

'Goodnight, darling. Love you to bits.'

'Love you to bits too.'

After the front door had clunked shut, Tommy went to the window. A long black sedan stood waiting for them beside the statue of the rearing horse, a uniformed chauffeur holding the back door open. Diane glanced back at the house as if she knew Tommy was watching and she blew him a kiss and then climbed in. The chauffeur shut the door and got into the front and the car pulled slowly away. Its windows were darkened so he couldn't see them anymore but in case they were still looking he waved again and stood watching until the car had disappeared.

ELEVEN

Diane had always been ambivalent about the effect she had on men. She had long ago discovered that if she looked at a man in a certain way, met his eyes at a particular moment with a kind of knowing intensity, she could walk inside his head and usually, in no time at all, reduce him to a state of quivering and malleable infancy. This wasn't among the tricks of the trade that she had learned at drama school in London or, after that, in repertory where she'd leapfrogged the customary starter parts, those nameless and lineless ladies-in-waiting and girls-in-the-crowd, to be cast, from the outset, in speaking roles. The talent to attract was most likely innate, from some remote ancestor, for she had trouble imagining that it had ever been anything other than latent in her parents.

It took her some years to understand the other side of the contract, namely that heterosexual men, however much they protested that all they desired was friendship, inevitably had sex in mind. And Diane's pleasure in the power this invested in her was tinged only by a weary disappointment that it appeared to be the way of things, that men should be so tragically and predictably primitive.

She was aware that those who thought they knew her, even some of her closest friends in London, believed that because she liked to flirt and relished the effect she had on men, she must therefore be promiscuous. It wasn't so, however. In the five years that followed Tommy's birth, the very thought of repeating with someone else what

147

she had done with David Willis in the musky Malvern bracken had repelled her. This wasn't because the act had proved less than rapturous or because it had become too entwined in her memory with all the consequent trauma. It was more because of a sense of obligation to Tommy, a feeling that, despite the charade that she and her parents had chosen to play for fear of scandal, to allow another man to know her so intimately again would be a betrayal of her responsibilities as a mother. The fact that, to all practical purposes, she had ceded these to her own mother in no way diminished this.

During these years, the men who pursued her— mostly actors, directors and producers but also a few who had no connection with her work— frequently ended up bemused and disgruntled. They found it impossible to fathom how, having seemed so eager for their attentions, when it came to the final act, Diane Reed wasn't prepared to perform. On many occasions these poor, injured creatures (men's pride in these matters, she soon discovered, was quite hilariously fragile), having invested time and emotion and probably several expensive dinners, would accuse her of being frigid or heartless or—what to them was clearly the most damning insult—a *cock teaser*.

When, finally, she did allow herself to *go the whole way* once more with a man, it was more from a casually rekindled curiosity about sex than from passion. She was pleased to discover that disillusion wasn't inevitably part of the package. But neither, it seemed, was love. Perhaps love, she thought, of whatever complexion, was finite, each of us allotted just a certain amount to spend on what or whom we chose.

If so, in Diane's case, all of it was spent on Tommy. She would travel home to see him whenever she could, talk to him on the phone even before he had uttered his first words. When she was on tour, in some far-flung provincial town, she would hurry to the station after the Saturday night performance and catch the last train so that she might spend even just a day with him.

Pretending that she was simply his loving older sister became harder with the passing of each year. And watching the weary way her mother treated the boy, as if everything she had to do for him was a burden, made Diane feel ever more guilty and wretched. If she dared voice so much as a minor criticism, her mother would point out that the charade had been of Diane's own making. And this would usually be garnished with some snide reference to the carefree, hedonistic, even decadent life that their arrangement had liberated her to lead.

The fact that Tommy was turning out to be what even a doting, albeit clandestine, mother had to admit was an unusual, if not slightly odd, child only served to deepen the guilt. His every foible—the bed-wetting, the tireless obsession with cowboys and Indians, the way he whimpered in his sleep and woke up screaming and often talked out loud to himself and to his pictures of Flint McCullough, the bullying at Ashlawn—all this and more she attributed to her absence and to the face-saving lie in which she had conspired. And, gradually, this had come to cast a shadow on her success.

She loved the adulation, of course, the standing ovations, the glowing reviews, the stage door

149

scuttle and bustle and pop of the flashbulbs. But part of her stood to one side, watching it with what almost amounted to derision. And this tendency to disengage worried her because sometimes it happened on stage. When *Fortune's Fool* was the hottest show in London and the whole world seemed to be talking about it, she would find herself, even in the play's most dramatic moments, thinking how ridiculous it all was. All these grown-up human beings *pretending*.

Oddly, this never seemed to affect her performance. Or rather, nobody ever seemed to notice. And, of course, she never dared mention it to anyone because nowadays real acting was about *being*, not pretending. The Old School of Fakery was closing down, the grand thespians—Gielgud, Redgrave, even Olivier—with their knighthoods and mannerisms and tremulous intonations mocked as ailing dinosaurs. All the young directors and actors were talking about Stanislavsky and Lee Strasberg and *the Method* and about how the only route to real, honest, meaningful acting was through tapping into some deep and personal emotional memory and reconjuring it in the heart and head of whatever character you had been called upon to inhabit.

Diane had always been as good as any of her peers at doing this. And the emotional memories she tapped into, be they joyful or traumatic, had invariably been connected with Tommy. While many of her peers needed eyedrops or menthol puffed into their eyes, Diane could summon tears at a moment's notice, simply by thinking of her lost son. In the early days of *Fortune's Fool* she had even exploited his unhappiness at Ashlawn, kept

150

his most wretched and despairing letter in her pocket to read in the wings before her final tragic scene. Now, however, just as she was finding fame, the idea of using him as a resource for her own ends made her feel ashamed. The irony was almost laughable. She had succeeded in what she had always wanted: to have a child as well as a career. And yet it now seemed impossible fully to enjoy either.

That the solution to this conundrum might be the love of a good man was not a sudden revelation, for the lack of logic would then have been too blatant. It was more of a slow coalescence of ideas, a sort of sprawling resolve, that if she were to meet a man she could love, who might be ready to share the responsibility, she would then be in a strong enough position to do the right thing: to reclaim her son and thereby, at a stroke, eradicate her guilt and his unhappiness.

Whether there had been something about Ray Montane, when she'd first laid eyes on him, that suggested the moment might be at hand, Diane would never be sure.

They had met in June, on her first trip to Hollywood, after *Fortune's Fool* closed its six-month run in London. Herb Kanter had organized a screen test in London. It was just a formality, he said. The *suits* at Paramount and, just as important, Gary Cooper needed to get an idea of what she was like.

The test, as far as Diane was concerned, was a disaster. She wasn't a complete novice in front of the camera. She'd been in a couple of small, very British, films and some TV plays and knew a little about the difference between stage and screen

151

acting, how intimate the camera was, how much your eyes mattered, how less was invariably more. But on the day of the screen test, all of this seemed to fly from her head.

In a shabby corner of Elstree Studios, where Herb (who in his shiny black jacket that day looked even more like a sea lion) sat watching from behind his glasses, Diane acted out a scene from the screenplay of *Remorseless* with a young actor—clearly hired more for his price than his talent—playing Gary Cooper's part. They did it seven or eight times, each one worse than the last, as Diane got angrier and angrier with herself. When it was over, she managed to laugh about it and stayed for a while to chat and smoke a cigarette. But as soon as she was in the taxi, heading home, she burst into tears and cried all the way back to Paddington. It had been her big break and she'd blown it.

Only later did she find out that Herb had cunningly told the cameraman to keep rolling and that what had clinched it for the *suits* was her natural, riotous, self-deprecating performance after she thought the test had ended. When Gary Cooper saw it, he apparently declared her a *knockout*. Everyone was eager to meet her and as soon as she was free from the play, she was flown out, first class, to Hollywood.

It was a two-week whirlwind of meetings and parties, lunches and dinners. She met managers and agents, publicity people and studio executives. Just about the only person she didn't meet was *Coop*, as everybody seemed to call him. Their planned lunch at the Paramount commissary was canceled because of what Herb said were unexpected and unavoidable family matters. Coop sent his apologies in a sweet handwritten note saying how much he was looking forward to working with her.

Diane was offered a three-picture deal, starting at eight hundred dollars a week which her newly acquired LA agent, Harry Zucker—an elegant little man who wore bow ties and a trademark white gardenia in his buttonhole—managed to hoist to a thousand. Diane would happily have worked for nothing. In celebration, at the end of her first week in Hollywood, Harry held a party for her at the agency offices on Sunset. And in walked Ray Montane.

He hadn't been invited. He just happened that same evening to be visiting his own agent who had brought him along. Diane noticed him as soon as he entered the room. Had he been wearing a cowboy hat, she might have recognized him, for she tried to keep up with Tommy's TV westerns and knew most of his heroes, including Red McGraw, from the pictures on his walls. Tonight, however, Red was out of uniform. All Diane saw was a tall man, lean and tanned, dressed in an open black leather jacket, a white snap-buttoned shirt and black jeans (she couldn't yet see the hand-tooled cowboy boots). His dark hair was cropped short, with long sideburns, and he had the kind of craggy good looks that made his age hard to pinpoint. Somewhere in his mid-thirties, she guessed. What was clear, even across the room, was that he had presence, the kind of easy confidence that Diane had always found attractive.

Harry made a little speech, funny and sweet, saying how thrilled and proud he and everybody at

153

the agency were to be representing England's new and bright young star, Miss *Knockout* (the nickname had already been in the trades), Diane Reed. He toasted her and everyone clapped and Diane said a few suitably modest but charming words—just the way Audrey Hepburn would have done it—and, as she wound up, found herself smiling at the man standing by the door, giving him that knowing look that had launched a thousand ships of frustration back home. Ray Montane returned the smile and raised his glass in an intimate toast of his own and Diane shocked herself by blushing, something she hadn't done since she was twelve years old.

By the end of the following week, after a series of long, late dinners at Ciro's and Romanoff's, walks along the beach, dancing at the Mocambo, her room at the Beverly Wilshire so full of Ray Montane's flowers that it looked like a greenhouse, England's newest and brightest young star found herself, for the first time in her life, in love.

He had a sort of old-fashioned and irresistible cowboy charm and at the same time was hip enough to know about the latest rock-and-roll bands. In fact he knew and hung out with some of them. He even knew Jack Kerouac. And he was kind and attentive and interesting and, most important of all, he made her laugh. He was also the most confident and accomplished lover she had known. In their lovemaking there was sometimes a frisson of danger that Diane, to her surprise, found herself excited by.

On her last evening in Hollywood, on the terrace of his sumptuous house in the hills, under a tree of fairy lights, Ray Montane asked her to marry him. And she said no.

'Is that no as in never?'

'No. Just no as in now.'

They were sitting side by side and she took his hand and held it in both of hers and said she had something important to say. And she told him about Tommy. He listened without once taking his eyes off her. And as she finished—by now, naturally, in tears—saying it was her dream that one day, one day soon, she could be a proper mother to the boy, be openly his mother, for all the world to see, and do for him what she should have been doing all these years, Ray held her face in his big brown hands and kissed her tears and looked her in the eyes and said simply:

'What's stopping you? Let's do it. Do it right now.'

He told her that he had been married once before but was now divorced. His wife, an actress called Cheryl, had suffered from acute depression. He had longed for kids, he said, but she hadn't wanted them. She'd remarried, found a good psychiatrist and now lived, more or less happily, in Oregon.

In the two and a half months that followed Diane's revelation to Tommy that she was his mother, Ray had been calm and strong. He flew back from LA and they rented a cottage in the countryside near Pinewood Studios. The three of them lived there in a kind of limbo between bliss and pain while all the arrangements were made for their move to California. Diane's mother made everything as difficult and acrimonious as possible. But with the help of some expensive London

155

lawyers and Ray's dogged diplomacy, they managed. Signed statements were made so that Tommy's birth certificate could be officially altered. They got him a passport and organized an American visa. Ray insisted on paying all the bills.

What clinched it for Diane was seeing how good he was with Tommy, how patient and caring and full of fun. And once the boy was over his shyness and the shock of living with one of his TV heroes, he began to blossom. Watching the two of them from the cottage window, laughing and joking and chasing each other around the garden, was sometimes almost too much for Diane to bear and she would well up with tears. This was what she had longed for. They were a real family. Always one to examine the cloud around any silver lining, she asked herself whether she'd been too hasty, whether her guilt and desire to make things right for Tommy had made her commit to this man too deeply and too soon. But all the evidence spoke only of how fortunate she was to have found him.

Julian, her London agent, was deluged with offers. Every producer in England seemed to be after her. But Diane turned every one of them down. The only role she wanted, until *Remorseless* started shooting in December, was to be a proper, full-time mother to her son. She would be there for him whenever he needed her, play with him, cook for him, take him to his new school and pick him up again in the afternoons, do all the things forbidden by those long years of deceit.

Ray had to fly back to Los Angeles for some meetings two weeks before Diane and Tommy were due to leave. She ached inside, almost made herself sick, from missing him. On their first

156

evening together, back on his terrace in the hills, LA twinkling below them like a million promises, Tommy asleep in his new bedroom, Ray pulled a little suede box from his pocket and handed it to her. The ring was in rose gold with an entwined *D&R* in sapphires set in a square bed of diamonds. The fit was perfect. They planned to be married at Christmas.

TWELVE

Herb and Ellie Kanter's house was of the sort that struck envy in the hearts of all but their most generous or myopic guests. It sat upon a rocky elbow of one of the most exclusive glens in Beverly Hills, looking out over groves of olive and lemon trees. In its four acres of garden, designed by a renowned Tuscan architect and manicured by a small army of men in green uniforms, were a helicopter pad, tennis court and croquet lawn and two cottages for guests, each with its own steam room, pool and hot tub.

The reception rooms of the main house were spacious and exquisitely lit, the floors of polished limestone, the walls hung with Herb Kanter's famous collection of paintings. There were Monets and Gauguins in the living room, Cézannes and Picassos in the hallway. Only his lawyer and his accountant knew that these were all, in fact, perfect copies and that the originals were stored in a steel-walled, air-conditioned, fireproof vault sunk into bedrock below the basement garage.

This same combination of refinement and

financial prudence had been the hallmark of Herb's career. As well as doing excellent business at the box office, his movies almost invariably won wagonloads of Oscars in all departments, including three for Best Picture, which were tucked away modestly (though unmissably lit) in his den. He was known to be ruthless and tightfisted but as honest as the business allowed.

Above all, Herb was well connected. He and Ellie had become members of the young and glamorous new presidential candidate John F. Kennedy's Hollywood inner circle. During the Democratic Convention in LA that same summer, they had dined with Jack and Jackie in booth number one at La Scala, where a special presidential phone was later installed. When Jack and Bobby helicoptered in for lunch with the Lawfords at Louis B. Mayer's old beachside house in Santa Monica, Herb and Ellie would be there along with the great and the gorgeous. And if either brother needed somewhere for assignations of a more carnal kind, Herb would discreetly make one of his garden cottages available.

To be invited to a party at the Kanters' was thus to be ushered into the Hollywood hallows, to mingle with the gods and goddesses who supped at the summit of the A-list. Diane Reed, of course, wasn't yet on any list. For the moment she had that most thrilling, if precarious, of passes that gave access to all areas: potential.

For the past few months, Herb had been doing what he most enjoyed: spreading the word. Over dinner at the Bistro, cocktails at the Polo Lounge, lunch at the Brown Derby and the Paramount commissary, he had been telling those who would be sure to pass it on most effectively that he had discovered the *Next Big Thing*.

Diane Reed, he would quietly confide, was the new Liz Taylor; she was like Marilyn, only smarter and saner; like Audrey Hepburn, but with tits, of the kind that would give the Hays Office censors a collective heart attack. Herb didn't want too much publicity too soon, just the right kind of snippets in the right kind of places. And it was already working. Only last week those archrival queens of Tinseltown tittle-tattle, Hedda Hopper and Louella Parsons, had both mentioned her—and *Remorseless*, of course—in their columns.

Sitting back in the plush hush of the sedan as it slid through the gates and began to wind its way up the Kanters' driveway, Ray Montane was feeling a lot less at ease than he appeared. He was holding Diane's hand but they were both lost in thought, gazing out at the torches that flamed among the thicket of palms and shrubs on either side. It was like the set of a Tarzan movie.

Ray wasn't looking forward to the party at all. It was the kind of fancy do he never normally got invited to. He was only here because of Diane and everybody would know it. Though he pretended not to be bothered with such trivia, Ray knew he wasn't A-list. In fact, he was barely B.

Anyhow, the whole list thing was just bullshit. He was more famous than nearly all the jumped-up little jerks who'd be there tonight. More people watched *Sliprock* than watched all of their goddamn movies put together. Walk down any street in any town in America and Ray Montane would get mobbed. At a supermarket opening in Fresno just three weeks ago, nearly a thousand

159

people had shown up to see him cut the ribbon. Even with their names printed on their foreheads, some of these so-called movie stars never got recognized by anyone. In any case, everybody knew that movies were in trouble. TV had the studios on the skids; they just didn't know what to do anymore. Except throw away more and more money making bigger and bigger turkeys. Wider screens, Cinerama, movies in 3-D, hell, they were so goddamn desperate they were even making movies you could smell. Yet, in his less acrimonious moments, Ray knew that TV was and always would be the poor relation. In Hollywood all that truly mattered was movies.

Not that he hadn't had his chance. He'd done a dozen pictures, probably more. But never one that had hit the mark. They were all B pictures, the kind that kids went to watch on Saturday afternoons at the Hitching Post. He'd told Enid, his agent, a hundred times that he wanted to break out of playing cowboys, that she should put him up for other kinds of movies, modern movies like Brando did or Jimmy Dean used to do. Ray had that same kind of moody charisma, for heaven's sake. The camera loved him. But nothing ever came through. He'd said the same as many times to the suits at Warners and they said *Sure, Ray, that's a great idea, let's look for something*. But it was all bullshit. All they ever really wanted was another season of *Sliprock*.

A couple of years ago, he'd gotten within an inch of landing the big one, of joining the guys who always worked for Jack Ford, the so-called Stock Company—Duke Wayne and Ward Bond, Ben Johnson, Dobe Carey, that gang. Ray knew them all, got drunk with them sometimes, was as good an actor as any of them—well, maybe not Duke, but as good as the others for sure, better even.

At the time, Ford had been casting *The Horse Soldiers* and sent word for Ray to drop by his office. It was a done deal, Enid said. Ray thought the meeting went pretty well but the guy never called back. Then he heard on the grapevine that Ford hadn't liked his attitude, thought he was too full of himself or something. Next time they met, Ray cut the grouchy old buzzard dead. The picture turned out to be a crock of shit anyhow, so he was probably well out of it.

A glimpse of these grouchy reflections must have shown on his face because Diane squeezed his hand. She was staring at him. He told himself to snap out of it, not to spoil her big night. The car was on its final approach now, cruising in under the marble porch that jutted out like some movie-set Greek temple over the driveway, valets in red-and-yellow-striped vests scampering like squirrels down the steps to open the car doors. He smiled at Diane and she smiled back. She looked so goddamn sexy it was all he could do to keep his hands off her. The most wondrous piece of ass he'd ever had. He should count his blessings.

'Are you okay?' she said.

'Are you kidding?'

'What were you thinking about?'

The valets had both the rear doors open now.

'That I must be the luckiest guy alive.'

He leaned close and kissed her lightly on the lips.

'Knock 'em out, kid.'

161

It probably had something to do with the endless flow of champagne, but Diane felt as if gravity had somehow taken the evening off and that she was floating a foot above the ground, gliding from room to room, lips locked in a smile of barely suppressed ecstasy.

There were more famous faces than she'd ever seen gathered in one place and Herb had introduced her to almost all of them. At dinner on the torchlit terrace, the scent of jasmine wafting in over the treetops, she'd been placed between Billy Wilder and David Selznick. Across the table, Ray hadn't done so badly either, Jennifer Jones on one side and Merle Oberon on the other. William Holden was there, Natalie Wood, John Huston. Even Frank Sinatra had dropped by but he had some other commitment so hadn't been able to stay for dinner. When Herb led her up to meet him, Sinatra had held on to her hand and fixed those blue eyes on her and said he'd heard all about her. It was clearly a lie but Diane didn't care. The only one missing was Gary Cooper, who she still hadn't met. He was in England shooting a movie with Deborah Kerr called *The Naked Edge*.

There were other faces, less famous but a lot more important, big-shot agents like Lew Wasserman from MCA, who Herb said was probably the most powerful man in Hollywood. While she was speaking with him, Diane noticed dear Harry Zucker, with his white gardenia buttonhole, hovering nervously nearby, pretending he wasn't trying to eavesdrop.

After dinner Connie Francis sang some songs

beside a white grand piano that had been wheeled out by the swimming pool upon which floated hundreds of white and gold balloons. Then there was dancing. Diane did the twist with Bill Holden and by the end of the song she was laughing so much she almost fell backward into the pool and he put his arm around her and steered her over to the bar. Ray was there on his own, with a glass of straight bourbon in his hand and he didn't seem too happy. She introduced him to Bill Holden and the two of them shook hands. Ray didn't manage so much as a smile and Holden soon got the message and moved away.

'Are you having a good time?' Diane said.

Ray shrugged.

'Sure. You obviously are.'

'I'm having the time of my life.'

'Great.'

At that moment Herb appeared with a young writer called Steve Shelby who'd apparently been wanting to meet Ray all evening. He had a tangled mop of curly hair and looked about fourteen years old.

'Sir, this is such a privilege,' Steve said, shaking his hand. 'I'm a big fan.'

It was the first time Diane had seen Ray smile since they'd arrived and while the two of them got talking, Herb led her to one side.

'I didn't know you had a son,' he said quietly.

'Yes. Tommy. He's the light of my life.'

'That's wonderful. How old?'

'He's nine.'

'We kept trying for a boy. Got three girls and gave up.'

'I bet you wouldn't change them for the world.'

163

'You're absolutely right.'

They were silent for a few moments. The band was playing one of Tommy's favorite songs, the one about Running Bear and Little White Dove.

'So, Diane. Forgive me. You're divorced or . . .'

'Oh, no. I was never married. Tommy was, well . . . I was very young.'

'I understand.'

They strolled over to the balustrade. There was a sudden breeze, the tops of the trees swaying and rustling below them in the darkness. Diane shivered.

'You know, Diane, this is a funny kind of town. On one level everything seems easy and modern, as if anything goes. But there's an underside. People talk and the talk gets picked up by those who make a living from it. Sometimes the studios can get a little, well, edgy about things.'

It took Diane a moment to understand what he meant by this.

'Forgive my asking, but do you and Ray plan on getting married?'

She showed him the ring and Herb smiled.

'We're hoping to do it at Christmas.'

'Well, congratulations. I'm happy for you—and for Tommy. Even so, there's someone I'd like you to meet. Would you mind?'

Ray was still talking to the earnest young writer and looked a lot happier now, so Diane took Herb's arm and they walked around the pool and through clusters of guests then up some wide stone steps and into the house. On the way Herb explained that the man he wanted her to meet was called Vernon Drewe. He was an attorney but also the best public relations guy in town.

They found him beside one of the Gauguins in the long living room, talking with Herb's wife. He was a tall, elegant man, probably in his early fifties, with a voice so soft you had to lean in close to hear. He said he had been looking forward to meeting Diane and after they'd chatted for a while he said that if he could ever be of any service, he'd be only too delighted. She had the impression that Herb had already told him a lot about her, that things had been discussed and arranged. Vernon handed her his business card and she promised to call.

*   *   *

They left a little after midnight, the stripe-vested valets summoning the sedan from the shadows to take them home. Once they were in the car, Ray told her about Steve Shelby and the screenplay he'd written with Ray in mind for the lead. It was a kind of modern-day western, a little like *The Misfits*, the one Gable and Marilyn had just shot. Shelby was clearly going places, Ray said. He was sending the script over in the morning.

'That's great,' Diane said.

'Yeah, well. We'll see.'

'*We'll see*. Come on, it's great.'

He put his arm around her and she snuggled in close.

'I'm sorry if I was a little, I don't know, moody earlier on.'

'You looked like you were at a funeral.'

He laughed. He almost told her the truth, that he got jealous as a jilted skunk when he saw her enjoying herself with another man. Especially

165

some big-time womanizer like Bill Holden. It was a whole new experience for Ray. He'd never felt that way about any woman. *They* were the ones who got jealous, for godsake, never him. In fact that was how things always ended, in some great, violent bust-up, with ranting and tears and more often than not a flying fist or two, when he paid too much attention to some new gal who happened to catch his eye.

But Diane was different. Four months and still there wasn't a moment in the day when he didn't want to fuck her. And she obviously felt the same way. It was like some kind of hungry sickness that had gotten hold of both of them. The idea of any other man doing it with her, even thinking of her in that way, stirred dark feelings in him.

He kissed her neck and breathed the warm smell of her, sweat from her dancing mingled with her perfume. The kind of scent money couldn't buy, the kind that went straight to a man's loins. She sensed it and put her hand right on it. Lord have mercy.

Dolores was watching TV in the living room and when Diane asked her, in a perfectly friendly way, if Tommy had been okay, she replied without smiling that of course he had, as if the question carried some kind of criticism. The poor gal still had a thing about him and kept giving Diane the evil eye. Ray had already had to have a word with her, telling her to be nicer. He wished, as he often had in the past, that he hadn't been quite so free with his affections. He'd fucked her no more than three or four times. Why the hell did women have to take these things so seriously? As she walked past him, heading off to her room, Dolores gave him a private look with those big sad eyes. Maybe he'd have to get rid of her.

He unzipped Diane's dress as she walked up the stairs in front of him and she stopped and leaned back into him and he slid his hands inside her dress and held her breasts and she swiveled her neck and kissed him.

'I have to go and check Tommy,' she whispered. 'I won't be long.'

Ray went to the bedroom and threw his jacket and shirt over the back of a chair then walked through to the bathroom and had a look at himself in the mirror. It wasn't a pretty sight. His head was blurred from too much Jim Beam and the joint he'd smoked down by the Kanters' croquet lawn. He switched off the light and went and sat on the bed and pulled off his boots. Candles, she always liked candles. He opened the drawer in the nightstand and fumbled to find some matches, pushing aside the bag of grass and the snub-nosed Smith & Wesson .38, both of which Diane gave him a hard time for keeping there.

He lit the candles on both sides of the bed then collapsed onto the bed, lying on his back with his chest heaving a little. He closed his eyes and fought the drink as it tried to swirl him back through his own head. Where the hell was she? He'd been hard as a gun barrel back on the stairs and now he was starting to wilt. What the hell. There was always tomorrow. He thought about the nice things that young writer had said. Someone, at last, who *got* him, knew how great he might be, given half a chance. And the kid sure knew his stuff. He was a Stanford graduate, for godsake, knew all about French movies and all that fancy art

167

house stuff.

And the belle of the ball, the woman every man at the party had been drooling over, was going to be his wife. Hell, weren't they going to be some couple? Burton and Taylor, Bogey and Bacall. Montane and Reed. He'd show the bastards. Goddamn it, he'd show them.

THIRTEEN

Tom saw the cat a couple of seconds before Makwi did. They were walking up through the woods and there it was, sitting on a fallen tree on the uphill side of the trail. In the dappled light he thought at first it was a squirrel, then he saw the collar and the shiny metal tag and in that same moment Makwi saw it too or got a whiff of it and was off like a Tomahawk missile. Tom yelled and yelled but it did no good. The crocodile brain had clicked in and the dog might as well have been deaf.

Tom had never much cared for cats. He'd watched enough wildlife films on TV to know that the only difference between a tiger and a pet tabby cat was size. One was big enough to kill you and the other wasn't but would if it could. You could see it in their eyes: basically you were prey and that was all there was to it. Had this one been smarter, it might have stood a chance. But it wasted too long lowering its head and bushing its tail and by the time it got the message and jumped off the tree, the story was pretty well over. Mercifully, Tom didn't see the moment of its demise. He scrambled through the undergrowth after them, sliding and hollering and once taking a heavy fall that knocked all the wind out of him. He found them down by the creek, Makwi standing over the kill with a kind of tentative pride.

'Damn it, Makwi. Couldn't you see the collar? That means *no*, okay?'

It wasn't just any old cat, it was one of those fancy breeds, a Siamese or Burmese or something and had clearly cost someone a small fortune. Tom picked it up. There wasn't even a drop of blood. The dog must have simply snapped its neck. He looked at the tag. It was engraved with the name *O'Keefe* and a phone number. He carried the cat home, feeling the warmth ebbing out of it, with Makwi contrite at his heels.

There was no answer from the number, just a machine. Tom thought it best not to mince words. With what he hoped was an appropriate tone he said he was really sorry but his dog had killed a cat in the woods and the collar had this number on it. He left his name and number and hung up, then stared at the body lying on the kitchen table, wondering what the hell he was going to do with it.

First thing tomorrow he was setting off for California. His friend Liz was coming to mind the house and Makwi, so if the cat's owner didn't call tonight, at least there would be somebody here. The weather was hot. Maybe he should put the corpse in the freezer. Then again, the owner might not appreciate getting his or her beloved pet back all stiff and frozen.

Tom emptied some postcards from an old shoe box and lined it with a hand towel then laid the cat inside. He stood there a moment staring down at the animal. The tilt of its head propped on the red

169

towel gave it a kind of comic grandeur, like some embalmed feline pharaoh. Tom put on the lid and went off to shower.

He was going down to California to see Danny. Not that Danny had invited him or seemed at all keen on the idea. But at least he hadn't said no. Gina had at last let him have the boy's new cell phone number and two nights ago, after many hours spent summoning the courage and planning what he might say, Tom had called. The conversation was about as stilted as it could be and still qualify as one. Danny's voice was more guarded than hostile but it still made Tom feel like a cold-calling salesman. Which, when he came to think about it, was pretty much what he was, pitching reconciliation to someone who had many more pressing things on his mind.

Tom had decided it might sound better if he didn't make too big a deal of it, so he lied and said he had some meetings in LA and would be renting a car anyway and it wasn't too much of a drive down to Camp Pendleton. Maybe they could have lunch or something? It all came out wrong, as if he wouldn't dream of making a special trip just to see his son and didn't much care one way or the other.

'Lunch? Why?'

'Or something, I don't know. Danny, I'd really like to see you. I've missed you.'

There was a long silence. Tom heard him take a deep breath.

'Listen, I don't know if it's a good idea—'

'Please, Danny.'

Ever since, Tom had been expecting him to phone back and cancel. More likely he'd do it via Gina. But when she did call it wasn't to cancel, just to ask him to go easy, not to lecture Danny or criticize him.

'Gina, do you honestly think I'm that dumb?'

'No, of course not. I'm sorry. He's just so fragile at the moment.'

'Oh, really? I'm so glad you told me.'

'Tom, don't be like that. The desk job they've given him is driving him crazy and so are the lawyers.'

Tom nearly raised the issue again of whether they should get him an independent lawyer, but decided not to. He'd talk to Danny about it instead.

He watched the news while he had his supper but there was nothing about Danny. There hadn't been for days, only the usual tally of suicide and roadside bombs, the random loss and ruin of anonymous lives. He was about to turn in when the phone rang.

'Is that Tom Bedford?'

It was a woman's voice and somehow familiar.

'Yes.'

'This is Karen O'Keefe.'

He hesitated. The name didn't mean a thing.

'Ah...'

'We met at your friend Troop's book party?'

Tom remembered. He even felt a flutter of flattered excitement.

'I'm sorry. Of course. How are you?'

'Fine. Your dog just killed my cat.'

She didn't sound so much upset as intrigued that he should be the killer's owner. Then she explained that, actually, the cat didn't belong to her but to her mother who lived on the other side of the hill. Karen O'Keefe was staying with her for

171

the summer. She asked where the body was.

'It's in a box on the kitchen table.'

'I'll come and get him.'

'What, now?'

'Is that okay?'

He told her the address and how to find the house then went to his bedroom and put on a smarter shirt and checked himself out in the mirror. Within twenty minutes the headlights of a car panned into the driveway.

Tom went out to meet her and they shook hands and he ushered her into the kitchen. He'd forgotten how striking she was. The thick pre-Raphaelite hair, those green eyes, the freckled skin that gave her a kind of glow. She was wearing a short red skirt and a cropped pink T-shirt that showed her navel. She caught him sneaking a look. Makwi greeted her rather too intimately, sticking a wet nose up her skirt. Tom pulled the dog away.

'So this is the murderer, huh?'

'Yep.'

'And this is . . .'

'I'm afraid so.'

He lifted the lid of the shoe box and stepped back so that she was slightly in front of him. They stood in silence for a few moments, looking down at the cat.

'I'm so sorry,' he said.

She nodded and then her shoulders started to shake. Tom didn't know if he should put a consoling arm around her but decided not to. Then he realized she wasn't crying but laughing. She put her hands up to her mouth but couldn't stop herself. He didn't know what to say.

'I'm sorry,' she said. 'This is so inappropriate.'

She controlled herself for a few moments and adjusted her face to a suitable expression of concern, but that just made her burst out laughing again and it was so infectious and bizarre that Tom couldn't help joining in. Then she started to cough and he went to the sink and got her a glass of water and after a couple of sips and one more eruption of laughter, she managed to stop.

'I'm not normally so heartless,' she said. 'It's that red towel. He looks so grand, like Lenin or Chairman Mao or something. To be honest, I'm more of a dog person.'

'What was his name?'

'Maurice.'

This started her off again, but she quickly contained herself and took another drink of water.

'Do you have anything a little stronger?'

He always kept a couple of bottles of wine in the cupboard, strictly for visitors. It made him feel stronger to have alcohol in the house and not be tempted. She chose the pinot noir and he opened it and poured her a glass, then poured himself a glass of water. While he did this she put the lid back on Maurice's casket and told him that what had happened actually solved a problem. Her mother's boyfriend had run off earlier in the year and her mom was planning a major life change which apparently involved moving to France. The only thing stopping her was not knowing what to do with Maurice. Now she'd have no excuse, Karen said.

They went out and sat on the deck overlooking the creek and Tom lit the candles that stood on the rail in little glass jars and they talked for more than an hour. About her parents, her work, what she'd been doing lately. In all of it, he noticed, there was no mention of a boyfriend. She'd seen the piece he'd written for the *Missoulian* about the Holy Family Mission and she said how much it had moved her.

'I know you already touched on it in the TV series,' she said. 'But it would make a great film on its own.'

'You think?'

'Definitely.'

'I've got a lot of stuff on tape I've never used. Maybe we should do it.'

'I'd like that.'

He said he would call her when he got back from LA. He didn't mention Danny or the true purpose of his visit. It would impress her more, he thought, if he told her the same lie he'd told his son, that he had a couple of meetings down there. He didn't elaborate, just let it hang in the air with its implication of movie deals and schmoozing with Hollywood hotshots. It was so pathetic, it made him cringe as he heard himself. He thought about her as he lay in bed that night and the next day on the flight to LA. It was ridiculous, of course. He was old enough to be her father.

*   *   *

Danny had let it be known—as usual, through Gina—that he didn't want Tom to come to the base. They were to meet at the Fisherman's Restaurant in San Clemente. The flight got in ahead of schedule and even with the heavy traffic on Interstate 5, Tom arrived half an hour early. The restaurant stood on stilts above the beach. It

174

had a bleached wooden deck with tables under blue umbrellas. There were palm trees behind and a long pier in front reaching out over the water. The ocean was flat and glassy and overhung with a pinkish haze.

Tom strolled out along the pier, seagulls wheeling and squawking over him. A group of boys were fishing over the rail near the bait store, their brown bodies streaked with salt. They were making a lot of noise, much to the annoyance of a few old-timers who didn't seem to be having nearly so much luck. One of the kids hauled out a big silver fish that looked like some sort of tuna and there was pandemonium while the others tried to hold it still so he could take the hook from its mouth. Then one of them plunged a knife into the top of its head and it flipped and flopped and thrashed around a little more then lay still, blood spreading in a gleaming crimson plate around it. One of the boys put his hand in the blood and made a palm print on the bare back of another who yelled and chased after him.

When Tom got back to the restaurant Danny was already there, sitting on his own at a table in the far corner of the deck. Tom had expected him to be in uniform but he was wearing jeans and a white short-sleeved shirt and a pair of aviator shades. When he saw his father, he stood up but didn't come to meet him, just waited. Tom took off his sunglasses but Danny didn't.

'Danny, hi!'

'Hi.'

He'd been planning to give his son a hug but the body language suggested this maybe wasn't such a good idea, so he held out a hand instead and

175

Danny shook it with a brief, almost formal smile.

'Sorry,' Tom said. 'I got here early and walked out along—'

'Yeah, I saw you.'

His head was shaved and his skin looked as if he had been living under a rock. He was thinner than Tom had ever seen him. He had a US Marine Corps tattoo on his forearm which he saw Tom notice. Danny gave a little shrug and almost smiled but didn't say anything about it. He had a glass of iced tea in front of him. Tom caught the waitress's eye and ordered the same.

'So,' he said, sitting back and trying to look relaxed. 'What's new?'

It was a stupid remark and deserved the smirk it got.

'What's *new*? Well, let me think...'

'I'm sorry. Danny, I—'

'Would you mind not calling me that?'

'I'm sorry. Dan. Your mom told me.'

It wasn't a great start. Tom wanted to ask him to take off the sunglasses, so they could at least see each other's eyes. There were enough barriers between them already. But he didn't feel he had the right. That he had any rights, come to that.

'How's Kelly?'

'Okay. She was here all last week.'

'So I heard. She sounds like a great girl.'

'She is.'

'Be good to meet her sometime.'

'Yeah.'

There was a short silence. Tom's heart was already sinking. Out on the pier an old woman was throwing scraps to a raucous squall of gulls.

'So, how did the meetings go?'

176

The tone was a fraction short of sarcastic and for a moment Tom didn't know what Danny meant.

'In LA. You said you had to come down for some meetings.'

'Oh, yeah. They went well. Thanks.'

'Great.'

Tom swallowed. He wanted to tell the truth, that there hadn't been any meetings. It now seemed dumb to have lied. But something stopped him. He leaned forward.

'Son, I just wanted to say how bad I feel about what happened between us. There hasn't been a day gone by that I haven't thought about you. And wondered how to make things right again.'

Danny shifted his shoulders and looked away. Tom could see the tension in the muscles of his neck. The boy seemed to be at the edge of himself, waiting for some excuse to erupt or pounce. The waitress arrived with his iced tea and the menus and told them about the day's specials as though she were auditioning for a part in a sitcom. At one point Tom thought she was even going to pirouette. Danny ordered the grilled lobster and because he didn't want to think about it, Tom said he'd have the same. When she'd left he went on. Quietly, in what he hoped was a measured tone, he said how much he regretted his remarks on that last occasion they'd seen each other, when Danny had told him he was going to enlist. How he'd had no right to be so judgmental and should simply have offered his support.

And all the while Danny made no attempt to speak, just sat there behind his sunglasses, like a screened priest at confession. His mouth set tight, not so much as a flicker changing his expression as he listened. Tom felt a surge of desperation and, simply to get a reaction, whatever it might be, pressed on.

'The fact is, son, I was jealous. I've always been jealous.'

'What? Jealous of what?'

'Of your stepfather. Dutch has been more of a father to you than I ever was. Or maybe ever could be. And there you were, following in his footsteps.' He laughed. 'Not that I'd left too many worth following. Only thing I could ever have taught you was to drink.'

Even as he heard himself say it, he knew he'd gone too far. What had started off as an apology had morphed into mawkish self-pity. And Danny reacted accordingly. He shook his head and sat back.

'Dad, I can't do this right now.'

'What do you mean?'

'I mean I can't handle us going into all this history and stuff. I've just got too much going on right now.'

'I know. I'm sorry, I just wanted—'

'No! I mean it. No more!'

He held up both hands. It was a command. People were looking at them. Tom nodded and at that moment the waitress arrived with the lobsters. She clearly sensed the tension because the grin rapidly vanished and she went about her business with hardly a word. Tom stared out across the ocean. The haze had thinned a little. On the horizon, the silhouette of a vast tanker was surging south.

'Maybe this wasn't such a good idea,' Danny

said.

His eyes were fixed on the enormous lobster in front of him and for a foolish moment Tom thought he meant he'd chosen the wrong dish.

'Mom kept on at me about it, how I ought to see you, but—'

'Danny, Dan, please. Can't we just try to move on?'

'Sure, whatever.'

The sarcasm made Tom wince and Danny saw it and seemed to realize how harsh he had sounded.

'Listen,' he said more gently. 'I've just got a lot on my plate at the moment and...'

He looked down again at the lobster who seemed to be staring lugubriously back at him and, despite himself, he smiled. Then he began to laugh. And suddenly Tom got a glimpse of the boy he'd once known and he too started to laugh. And for maybe as long as a minute the two of them sat there rocking with laughter over their lobsters. People at nearby tables were turning again to look at them. It was going to be all right, Tom thought. Everything would be all right again. Then he noticed that although Danny's shoulders were still shaking, he wasn't laughing anymore but crying. And soon the boy was sobbing uncontrollably, his whole body convulsing. Tom reached out and touched his shoulder.

'Son...'

Danny pulled away and sat back in his chair but still couldn't stop crying. Then he stood up, shaking his head, and walked quickly across the deck and out of the restaurant and Tom got up to follow then realized he couldn't leave without paying, so he pulled out his wallet and tucked a hundred-dollar bill under a glass on the table and hurried after Danny.

When he came out of the restaurant there was no sign of the boy. He ran toward the parking lot but Danny wasn't there either. There hadn't been time enough for him to drive away and anyway, surely, he wouldn't just go like that, would he? Then he saw a figure in a white shirt, running away along the beach. Tom set off in pursuit, calling after him but Danny neither turned nor stopped. The sand was soft and heavy going and soon Tom was gasping.

'Danny! Danny, please! Son!'

At last the boy stopped. He didn't turn, just stood at the water's edge, clasping his face in his palms. By the time he caught up, Tom had no breath left to speak. Danny was still facing away from him so he tentatively put his hands on his son's broad shoulders, half expecting to be shrugged off. But instead Danny turned and crumpled into his arms, still sobbing. And the two of them stood there, clinging to each other, while the water flooded and foamed over their shoes.

FOURTEEN

Carl Curtis, Tommy's new school, was at the eastern edge of Beverly Hills, next door to a little park and zoo where you could go for pony rides and pet other equally miserable animals that lived there. The school wasn't nearly as big or as splendid as Ashlawn. It was just half an acre with seven classrooms, an asphalt yard and a swimming pool.

To Tommy, it didn't really feel like a school at all. There wasn't even a proper uniform, just blue sweatshirts with the school's name on the front. What made it so different was that there were girls as well as boys and that everyone was friendly, even the staff.

All except two of the teachers were women. The headmaster, Mr Curtis, had black hair and glasses and a very white face and stood every morning at the gate to say hello to all the children as they arrived. Then there was Mr Badham, who everybody called Baddy, who was always cracking jokes and having fun, like trying to cadge your sandwiches at lunchtime. Baddy organized all the sport and there was a lot of it. This, at first, had made Tommy nervous because at Ashlawn sport had simply been an excuse for the bullies to beat you up without getting into trouble. But, thanks to Baddy, everybody at Carl Curtis actually enjoyed it and there didn't seem to be any bullies anyway.

There was PE and trampolining and basketball and, twice a week, everybody got to go swimming. The boys even did boxing which—probably because he'd spent so much time defending himself at Ashlawn—Tommy found he was rather good at. In his first bout he actually gave a boy called Wally Freeman a bloody nose. Wally didn't seem to mind too much and afterward nicknamed him Floyd, after Floyd Patterson, the heavyweight champion of the world.

The day always began with Flag Salute. They all gathered in the yard and put their hands on their hearts and recited the Pledge of Allegiance. At first Tommy, being British, didn't know whether

181

he ought to do this. But he'd always loved the Stars and Stripes and didn't like being the odd one out and was soon joining in as if he were a real American. Which was what he'd always wanted to be. It just seemed more modern—*cooler*, as Wally would say—than being English. You only had to look at the new president they'd just elected. He was young and always smiling and had little kids and a beautiful wife, while the British prime minister, funny old Mr Macmillan, was about a hundred years old and looked like a walrus who'd lost his tusks.

At Carl Curtis they held their own election, with two sixth-grade boys pretending to be the candidates, and on election day everybody got to vote. The one who was Senator Kennedy won by a mile, which didn't please some of the teachers, who were mostly Republicans. The result of the real election didn't please Ray either because he was a Republican too and couldn't stand Senator Kennedy. He said he was a disaster waiting to happen and too young to know anything about anything. Worst of all, he was a *pinko* which meant he wouldn't stand up to the Russians who had hundreds of giant rockets with atom bombs on them, all pointing at America. Along the street from the school there was an air raid siren that was tested every month just to make sure it would work when the Russians attacked. Wally said this would most likely happen at night when everybody was asleep.

The subject Tommy liked best was English. Mrs Hancock, the teacher, was impressed by the number of books he'd read and got him to tell the class about some of them. She didn't seem to mind when he got American spelling wrong or said *trousers* instead of *pants*. Some of the kids teased him about his accent but the girls really seemed to like it. One of them, Wendy Carter, kept concocting weird things for him to say, like *tomatoes can't dance*. And because she had a long blond ponytail and was probably the prettiest girl in the whole school Tommy would oblige and put on his plummiest English accent and say *tom-ahr-toes cahrn't dahrnce* which made her squeal with laughter and try to imitate him.

He enjoyed history too. It wasn't like Ashlawn, where they had to recite boring lists of dates and all the kings and queens of England. In fact the only king Mrs Hancock ever mentioned was George III who she called the king who lost his marbles as well as his colonies. Soon they were going to be learning about how the West was won and the railroads were built and how the Indians were beaten and civilized. Tommy could hardly wait.

Meanwhile Diane was busy preparing for *Remorseless* which was due to start shooting in just a few weeks. She was having acting lessons at Paramount and having lots of meetings with costume and makeup and publicity people. When filming started Miguel was going to have to ferry him to and from school, but so far it was always Diane who did it. Usually after school they would drive out to Warner Brothers to see Ray who was hard at work shooting the new season of *Sliprock*.

Being on set and watching a real movie—or, at least, a TV show—being made was nowhere near as exciting as Tommy had imagined. In fact, after a while it was downright boring. There was too much waiting around while they fiddled with the lights and touched up the actors' makeup. And then they had to film the same thing again and again and again. It took three whole days to film a show that lasted less than half an hour. Tommy couldn't really understand why it took so long but Ray said that compared with proper movies, this was quick.

Ray always made a big fuss when they arrived on set. On their first visit he took Tommy around and introduced him to all the other actors and the people who worked behind the scenes. The director lifted Tommy up so he could peer through the camera and the cameraman explained how you could fix it so that even when the sun was shining everything looked like nighttime. This was called *day for night*. A lot of the scenes that looked as if they were done outside were actually done indoors in the studio. There was even a man whose job it was to hide behind the bushes and move them so that it looked as if it were windy.

Today, however, they weren't going to the studio. They were going to drive out of town to the ranch where all the exciting action scenes were shot. Tommy had been looking forward to it all day.

He always felt proud when he saw Diane sitting there waiting for him in the new car Ray had bought her. It was a pale yellow Ford Galaxie convertible with black leather seats. There were lots of kids at Carl Curtis who had moms or dads who were in the movies but none as glamorous as Diane. Wally Freeman said she was a *doll* and today she really looked it. She was wearing a blue-and-white polka-dot dress and those big sunglasses with the white frames. Her hair was tied up in a pale pink scarf. Tommy climbed in and gave her a kiss and, while they drove up onto Sunset, he changed into the clothes she'd brought along for him. He liked to look the part when he went on set. On his first visit he'd worn his Red McGraw cowboy outfit but it made him feel a bit silly, so now he mostly just wore a plaid shirt and his new jeans which Dolores had washed about a dozen times to make them look faded and worn, just like Ray's.

Soon they were turning off the main highway and onto the little road that wound up into the hills. The air was warm and smelled sweet and there were cactus plants and lizards sunbathing on great slabs of pink rock that shimmered in the heat. Tommy had been telling her about his day and how he'd won again at boxing. He'd been so busy talking that he hadn't noticed until now that Diane wasn't asking him questions the way she usually did. She didn't even really seem to be listening.

'Are you okay?'

She brightened.

'Me? Of course. Sorry, darling. I'm just a little tired.'

They reached the ranch and parked the car with all the film crew's trucks. One of the assistant directors sent word to let Ray know they'd arrived and in a few minutes he came to meet them, grinning and giving them his usual big welcome. They headed out along a dusty path to where the filming was going on, Ray walking between them with his arms draped around their shoulders. This always gave Tommy a kind of glow inside, made him feel safe and normal. Life was so good and

185

happy and packed with excitement that he sometimes worried that it couldn't possibly last.

Ray explained that they were doing a scene in which Red McGraw had been ambushed by some outlaws and was holed up in a clump of rocks while they all shot at one another. Then he had to whistle for Amigo, his famous white horse, and jump onto him as he ran past. They'd already done the close-ups of Ray shooting and whistling and getting ready to jump and now they were filming Cal Matthieson actually doing the jump.

Tommy had heard about Cal and was excited to meet him, not just because he was the head wrangler but also because he was half Blackfeet Indian. Tommy had never met a real Indian and he could remember reading somewhere that the Blackfeet had been one of the most ferocious and terrifying tribes of all. Cal wasn't only in charge of the horses, he was also Ray's stunt double which meant he had to pretend to be Red McGraw when there was a fight or when Red had to jump off a horse or a roof or do anything else that was too dangerous for Ray to do. Ray said he could easily have done these things himself but the studio insurance people wouldn't let him.

Now they were almost ready to shoot. Dressed in an outfit identical to Ray's, Cal Matthieson was squatting on top of the rock, giving some final instructions to the wrangler below him who was holding Amigo. From the top of the rock to the horse's saddle was a drop of about ten feet. The wrangler nodded and led Amigo to a place about a hundred yards away where they turned and waited. Cal went back into the rocks and crouched down. When everyone was ready the first assistant

186

director called for quiet and then the director, who was up beside the camera, yelled *Roll 'em!* and *Action!*

Cal whistled and Amigo pricked his ears and started to run. By the time he reached the rocks he was almost at a gallop and Cal ran across the rock and leaped into the air and landed right in the saddle and Amigo didn't even flinch, just kept on running.

'Wow!' Tommy called out. Everybody turned to look at him and he remembered how you were supposed to keep quiet and he felt stupid and started to blush. It didn't seem to matter too much though. Ray just laughed and slapped him on the back and anyway everybody was now clapping and cheering Cal Matthieson for doing the stunt so well in a single take.

'It's kind of easy, once you know how,' Ray said.

The sun was getting low and the light was going all golden. Ray said this was called *magic hour*, the time directors loved best because it made everything look so pretty on film. He had to do one more scene and while he went off to the makeup trailer Tommy and Diane walked over to the corral and leaned on the rail watching the horses. A few minutes after they got there, Cal Matthieson arrived with Amigo. He smiled and said hello and touched the brim of his hat to Diane.

'That was really impressive,' Diane said.

'Thanks, but it's this fella here who deserves the praise.'

He rubbed Amigo on the neck and the horse snorted and tossed his head as if he agreed.

'See? He even speaks English.'

They laughed and Cal climbed down and shook hands with them both.

'I'm Diane and this is Tommy.'

'I know. Good to meet you, Tommy. I've heard a lot about you.'

He had shiny black hair and kind brown eyes with little creases at the sides. Tommy knew Indians didn't really have red skin but Cal's wasn't even brown. He just looked as if he had a bit of a tan like everyone else. It was funny seeing him in Ray's clothes.

'So, young man. Do you know how to ride yet?'

'I've been on pony rides at the zoo but that's all.'

'Want to have a go?'

'You mean on Amigo? Really?'

'Sure. If it's okay with Mom.'

Tommy looked at Diane and saw that it was. Cal shortened the stirrups then hoisted him into the saddle.

'How does that feel?'

'Great.'

'Okay, now gallop over there and jump that rail,' he said.

'Oh, I don't think...' Diane began then realized he was only kidding and laughed.

Cal showed Tommy how to sit properly and how to hold the reins then how to let the horse know that he wanted him to move out. And as Amigo stepped forward, Cal walked beside him, not holding on to anything, just keeping a little to one side so that Tommy felt in control.

'He's beautiful,' Tommy said.

'He is. Best Amigo of 'em all.'

'You mean there's more than one?'

'Four. The others are good at different things,

188

falling, jumping, having guns go off by their ears. This fella can do it all. Move your hips a little so you get his rhythm. That's it. That's good. Now you're riding. Try taking him around that tree and back on your own.'

*   *   *

Diane was starting to breathe more freely. The air up here in the hills was clean and fresh and, now that the sun was getting low, the world seemed more benign again. Seeing Tommy so happy always lifted her spirits. He was riding away toward the tree on the beautiful white horse, their joined shadow long on the dusty red earth. With her arms folded, she walked slowly up to stand beside Cal Matthieson and he turned briefly and smiled. Tommy had reached the tree now and was bringing the horse around. It was as if he'd ridden all his life.

When Ray had come to meet them, all smiles and kisses and hugs, it had taken great self-restraint not to make a scene. Throughout the day she'd been itching to fly at him, scream at him, strangle the lying bastard. Now all she wanted was to talk and find out the truth.

Perhaps it was just a misunderstanding.

The phone had rung that morning just as she was walking out to the car that had come to take her to the studio. Dolores had answered in the hallway and called out *Miss Diane!* from the front door, only a shade more politely than if she were summoning a dog.

'It's Louella Parsons.'

'For Ray?'

189

'For you.'

Diane had never met nor spoken with the woman and had a sudden flutter of nerves. Like most people in Hollywood, she often read the famous column in the *Examiner* and she had felt flattered by the positive snippets it had carried about her. Louella Parsons was in her late seventies and her influence was waning, but a few casually poisonous words in her column could still kill a career. For her to call Diane at Ray's and at such an hour meant she obviously knew they were living together.

'Diane, my dear. So glad to find you in. I hear such marvelous things about you.'

The voice was sickly sweet, almost a caricature of falseness. Diane had an image of a fat and fluffy pink spider.

'Really? That's nice.'

'Ye-es. Dear Herb is so, so clever, don't you think? And such a darling. You and Coop. I just can't wait. It's going to be like Vivien Leigh and Clark Gable all over again. Dear, dear Clark, God rest his soul. What a terrible loss to us all. Did you know him?'

Clark Gable had died of a heart attack just two weeks earlier. Hollywood was still in mourning.

'No, I—'

'Such a marvelous man. He was *always* on my radio show.'

'Yes, I—'

'Anyway, my dear. Back to business. I hear on the grapevine that you and Ray are to be married?'

'Well, we—'

'Oh, come along, dear. Don't be coy. You can tell Louella.'

'We hope to get married at Christmas.'

'How lovely. Congratulations. Ray is *such* a charmer, isn't he? And I'm sure it's going to be a case of third time lucky for him. Matter of fact, I didn't know his divorce had come through.'

Diane froze.

'Diane? Hello?'

'Well, actually, I—'

'You did know he was married?'

'Yes, of course I did. Louella, I'm sorry but I'm running a little late for a meeting. Can I call you later?'

'Of course, my dear. Just one more thing. Your son, um...'

'Tommy.'

'Tommy! Silly me. Just so I don't make a mistake, who is his daddy?'

For this, at least, thanks to the good offices of Herb Kanter and Vernon Drewe, Diane was prepared. They had worked out a story for exactly this sort of occasion.

'He died. Shortly after Tommy was born.'

'I'm so sorry. How terrible.'

'Yes.'

'Of what?'

'Excuse me?'

'Of what did he die?'

'TB.'

'Terrible. You must have been devastated.'

'Yes.'

'And what was his name, dear?'

'Louella, do you have to write about this? I don't want to upset Tommy.'

'Of course, dear. But just for background, what was the father's name?'

191

'David.'

'David Reed.'

'David Willis.'

She hung up and, as soon as she could gather her wits a little and breathe again, called Vernon Drewe and told him all about it. He tried to calm her, said she'd handled it perfectly and there was nothing to worry about. He knew Louella well and would call her, he added, just in case there were any misunderstandings. Diane didn't mention Louella's comment about Ray's divorce. She had to ask Ray about it first, but he'd been working out here at the ranch all day and they hadn't yet been able to talk.

Tommy was walking Amigo back now, the sky glowing pink and orange behind them.

'The boy's a natural,' Cal Matthieson said.

'I think Amigo's looking after him.'

'Well, that's true.'

'Does he belong to you?'

'He kind of belongs to himself but I was there when he was born. Hell, I was even there when he was made.'

'And all the other horses? Are they yours too?'

'Some are but they mostly belong to my partner, Don Maxwell. Not that you can really call it a partnership. Don owns all the real estate and I get to do all the work.'

'Do you live up here?'

'Uh-huh. Little place just around the hill there. It's about as close to a city as I like to get.'

He looked at her and they both smiled. For a moment neither of them seemed to know what to say next.

'I hear you're going to be doing a movie with

Gary Cooper.'

'Yes. We start shooting next month.'

'He's the best.'

'So everybody says. I haven't even met him yet.'

'A real nice guy. Born in Montana, so it figures.'

'That's where you come from too?'

'How'd you guess?'

Diane laughed. Tommy was coming close now and Cal Matthieson told him to sit back in the saddle and tighten the reins a little and the horse came to a halt directly in front of them.

'Tommy, were you kidding me when you said you hadn't ridden before?'

'No, honestly, I haven't.'

'Well, I was going to say, if it was okay with your mom, you might care to come up here for a lesson sometime, but you seem to have it all pretty much figured out already.'

'Could I? Could I really come up here and ride?'

'You'll have to ask your mom.'

'Of course you can,' Diane said. 'If Mr Matthieson doesn't mind.'

'Mr Matthieson doesn't. It's Cal, by the way.'

It was dark by the time they wrapped. Ray let the studio car and driver go and drove them home himself in Diane's Galaxie. They came back beside the ocean and Tommy fell asleep between them with his head on Diane's shoulder. She put her arm around him and stared out at the horizon and watched a thin band of crimson turn to purple and black.

Ray was going on about the director, how slow and useless he was, how he always managed to put the camera in the wrong place. And Diane half listened and murmured brief replies when he started asking her about her day until eventually he gave up and there was silence between them, just the rush of the wind and the whoosh of passing cars.

'Are you okay?' Ray said.

'I'm fine.'

'No, you're not. What is it?'

'Not now. I'll tell you later.'

'Come on, sugar, tell me.'

'Not now!'

When they reached home Miguel came out to greet them then drove the car off to the garage. Ray carried Tommy cradled asleep in his arms into the house and upstairs to his room and laid him on the bed and left him alone with Diane. Tommy stirred a little as she undressed him and hauled his slack and skinny limbs into his pajamas. There was a film of red dust on his face and hands but she didn't have the heart to wake him and make him take a bath, so she wet a sponge with warm water and wiped away the worst. Then she gently pushed him under the covers and sat on the bed beside him, staring down at him. She stroked the hair from his forehead. He was growing so fast, the face getting leaner, somehow less vulnerable. She turned off the bedside light and leaned forward and kissed his cheek. He smelled of horses. Sometimes the love she felt for him was like a pain in her chest.

When she came downstairs Ray had two margaritas waiting for them in the living room. Dolores was on her knees, putting a match to the fire she'd laid in the enormous cast-iron grate. She stood and smoothed her apron then walked past Diane without a greeting or a smile, just a sideways glance.

'Goodnight,' Diane said.

Dolores muttered something and was gone.

'What is it with that woman? What have I done?'

'Nothing,' Ray said, walking over to her. 'It's just territorial, I guess. I'll have another word with her.'

He put his arms around her and Diane kept still.

'More to the point,' he said, 'what have *I* done?'

Diane hesitated. She didn't want to sound ridiculous or neurotic. He was holding her by the shoulders now, peering into her eyes for a clue.

'Come on,' he said. 'Tell me.'

'Ray, are you still married?'

'What?'

'You told me you were divorced. Are you?'

'Sugar, who have you been talking with?'

'Oh, only Louella Parsons.'

'Jesus Christ! What's that goddamn bitch been saying? Diane, listen—'

'Are you divorced, Ray? Yes or no? Tell me!'

'Technically, not quite, but—'

'So you lied to me.'

She was trying to tug the engagement ring off her finger but the damn thing wouldn't budge.

'Diane—'

'You lied! And can we just be clear *which* divorce we're talking about here? Is it wife number one or wife number two?'

'Diane, for heaven's sake. Just let me explain.'

The ring was off now and she slammed it down on the glass top of the table, making the margarita glasses tremble and spill.

'You'd better have that back.'

She was about to walk away but he grabbed her by the wrist.

'Diane, listen, please.'

'I'm listening.'

'The papers are due any day. Everything's settled. All I have to do is sign. In a week or two it'll be—'

'You said you were divorced and you're not.'

'I know, I'm sorry. But it's only a formality—'

'Oh, really? And the other marriage? The one you somehow forgot to tell me about, was that a formality too?'

'Diane, we were just kids. It lasted ten months.'

'And that's why you didn't think to mention it?'

'Well, I—'

'And how about number two, was that a little longer? Eleven months or did you make a year?'

'Sugar, don't do this.'

'Don't *sugar* me!'

He took her other arm now and held her in front of him so that she couldn't move.

'Let go of me!'

'Diane, look at me. Look at me!'

From the flash in his eyes, for a moment she thought he was going to hit her.

'I love you more than anyone or anything I've ever known. You and Tommy are my life now. We're not all as perfect as you. I've made a lot of mistakes in my life, things I wish I could undo. But I know about you and me, how good we are together, how we're meant to be together. Sweetheart, I'd do anything for you. And for Tommy. Jesus, Diane, I'd die for you both.'

Those were the words that clinched it, though she was still too proud and angry to let him see the effect they had on her. If he'd spoken merely of his love for her, she might have let him suffer much longer. She might even (indeed, the idea had already occurred to her) have gathered Tommy from his bed and left for good. But the fact that, in his corny B movie declaration of love, he had included her son seemed to crack her resolve. And this in turn made her angry, not with him but with herself. She slapped him hard across the face.

He took it without flinching, as if it was only what he deserved, and as she saw the reddening mark she had made on his cheek she bent her head and began to cry and he held her and kissed her forehead. He gently helped her sit on the edge of the couch and sat beside her in silence with his arms around her while she wept.

And when she could speak again he answered her cold questions about his marriages and kept saying how sorry he was that he hadn't been honest with her and that the only reason was his fear of losing what he now knew for sure to be the love of his life. An hour later he led her to the stairs and up to their room and took off her clothes and kissed her neck and her breasts while she stood stony and proud and confused and not yet forgiving before him. And during what followed, into the darkest hours, she punished him for his lies.

Their lovemaking, from the outset, had always carried the hint of violence, like some sleeping feral creature whose potential and containment excited them both. But that night Diane opened the cage. She struck him and gouged his skin with her nails until he bled and wrenched his hair and bent him at his root until he cried out in pain. And the dormant creature, the one that would ultimately devour them, was roused and loose and on the prowl.

FIFTEEN

Ray had been waiting for more than half an hour and was mad as a jilted rattlesnake. He hadn't had a one-on-one with the Colonel for nearly two years and it wasn't the kind of opportunity you blew by losing your temper. The whole idea was to intimidate you, make you feel you were nothing, so it was best to try to stay cool, pretend you didn't give a damn.

The self-important grandeur these studio bosses liked to surround themselves with would have been scary if it wasn't so ridiculous. The sweeping circular driveway, the stately trees and lawns, the imperial staircase, the acre of reception where, in a reverential hush, a tight-haired dragon in a suit and schoolmarm glasses sat guard at her desk. Coming to see Jack Warner was like having an audience with Mussolini.

Ray was sitting on one of the big couches, thumbing through the trade papers, doing his best to look relaxed. Every so often the intercom on the dragon's desk would buzz and she would pick up the phone and say *Yes, Mr Warner, of course, Mr Warner*. Then once in a while the door to the inner sanctum would open and out would trip one of the Colonel's luscious, tight-skirted secretaries to hand a package to the dragon. One of them, a blonde with big tits that the old devil had doubtless already had his hands on, flashed Ray a smile as she went back in. Jack Warner was pushing seventy but still chased almost any skirt that rustled. Word had it there was a secret door and staircase in his office so that aspiring young actresses could aspire more discreetly.

The dragon's buzzer sounded again and she picked up the phone.

'Yes, Mr Warner, he is. I'll tell him.'

She got up and walked over to Ray.

'Mr Warner says to apologize, but his ten o'clock is running a little late. I'm sure they'll soon be through. Can I get you more coffee?'

'No, I'm good, thanks. Nice glasses.'

'Thank you.'

He tossed his paper onto the coffee table in front of him and picked up the glossy book of photographs he'd been trying to resist looking at. It had full-page pictures of Warner Brothers' stars, Bogart and Bergman, Jimmy Cagney, Errol Flynn, Henry Fonda, even some the studio had fallen out with and would happily have murdered, like Bette Davis. Toward the back was a thinner section devoted to TV stars, two per page, Clint Walker, James Garner, Ty *Bronco* Hardin, Will Hutchins from *Sugarfoot*. Ray thumbed on through it, with a knot slowly twisting in his gut. He couldn't believe it. The bastards had left him out. But no, at last, there he was. Tucked away at the back, after Rin Tin Tin.

He shut the book and tossed it back onto the table then went to the restroom to take a leak. He was still sore down there, where Diane had bent him. He washed his hands and checked himself in the mirror. Luckily, most of the damage she'd done didn't show, though one of her scratch marks was just visible above his collar. Jesus, he thought. What a night. He walked back to the lobby and sat down again to wait.

He hadn't intended to lie to her. No more than he ever intended to lie to anyone. It was just second nature. He'd lied so long and so often that he didn't realize anymore when he was doing it. For most people lies had consequences that made them wary about telling them, or telling too many of them. But for Ray it was the other way around. It was the truth that had always landed him in trouble. He'd never understood what the big deal was about telling the truth anyhow. People got enough of it in their everyday lives. It was what made them so goddamn miserable most of the time. What they really wanted was lies. That was what Hollywood was all about. It peddled lies that fed people's fantasies and made them feel better.

It wasn't just the movies themselves. Almost everybody involved in making them had to tell lies of various kinds. It was part of the job. The best liars of all were the producers. To get a movie going you had to lie to absolutely everybody, juggle five lies in the air so that everybody believed everybody else was in on a good thing and then, with luck, the lies all became true and stayed up there.

Actors generally only lied because the studios and the producers wanted them to. If your name didn't sound good enough, they just made up another one for you. There was nothing bad about it. They had to. Who the hell would ever have heard of John Wayne and Cary Grant if they were still called Marion Morrison and Archibald Leach?

Who'd have ever hired poor old Ty Hardin if he'd stuck with Orison Whipple Hungerford Jr. ?

Ray's own real name was Lennie Gulewicz but nobody knew it. And when journalists asked about his early life, he would paint a picture of what he wished it had been, the kind of picture the world had once wanted of its cowboy heroes. Of sitting on his daddy's knee on the porch of their little ranch in west Texas, of helping his mommy cook the cornbread and churn the butter, of learning how to rope and brand steers when he was just five years old. He'd told it so often, he'd good as forgotten it hadn't happened.

Like all the best lies, there had to be a smidgen of truth in it. He had indeed lived in Texas, though never on a ranch. He'd busted his ass drilling wells and hauling pipes for various oil companies, until he got smart and landed a job as a bouncer at a nightclub in Houston. Getting physical with someone on the door one night, he was spotted by a young photographer who was about to shoot a cigarette ad. He asked him if he could ride and Ray said sure, he'd been born on a horse, and got offered the job. He had a hard time learning to ride and as a result had never much liked the animals since and it was mutual. But the ad got him noticed. Within six months he'd moved to LA and found himself an agent and the two of them came up with the name Ray Montane and a more appropriate life story.

Remembering his true life story now required real effort. How, forty-two years ago—some eight years more than he ever admitted to—little Lennie Gulewicz had been born in the sulfurous shadow of a Pennsylvania smelting plant; how the only

201

time he'd ever been on his daddy's knee was when the murderous bastard thrashed him half senseless with a belt or an ax shaft or whatever else came to hand; how his mommy was mostly too drunk or beat up or too busy in the back bedroom screwing some stranger to make so much as a cup of coffee; how, as soon as he could, little Lennie had upped and run away and spent his teens in and out of the reformatory, mostly for thieving except for the time he knifed and nearly killed some little fuck who'd ratted on him.

The funny thing was, there were young actors in Hollywood nowadays who would pay good money for that kind of background. Kids who'd been brought up in decent homes in nice neighborhoods with loving moms and dads and nannies and puppies and new bicycles every goddamn Christmas. And these same kids were now busy making up fake histories of suffering and all kinds of cruel deprivation because this was now considered *cool* and might make the public think they were the new Marlon Brando or Jimmy Dean, all moody and mean, all tortured and twisted and sexy.

Not that Ray blamed them. Hell, if he were twenty years younger he wouldn't have to lie at all. And then he wouldn't have gotten stuck in the rut he was stuck in now, pretending to be the man in the white hat, the wholesome hero he'd come to despise. Movies had already gotten the message, that it was okay to have stars with dirty faces and dirtier pasts. But TV was in a time warp and still seemed to think America wanted these laughable Mr Clean cardboard cutouts, heroes who never broke wind or went to the bathroom.

Given all this, he still couldn't quite believe that he'd managed to find himself—and, so far, hold on to—a woman as classy as Diane. She was young and gorgeous and talented enough to have anyone she wanted. Such as that arrogant little fuck McQueen who'd given her the eye that day outside Schwab's and whose crappy movie *The Magnificent Assholes* was apparently doing infuriatingly good business all over the world. At the Kanters' party, at every party they went to, guys were falling over themselves to get at her. And yet, until that meddling cow Louella Parsons had poked her fat nose in, Diane only seemed to have eyes for him. Hell, she even wanted to marry him.

Ray wasn't dumb. He'd figured out pretty early on that the way to her heart was through Tommy. She was so flooded with guilt for having pretended to be the boy's sister all those years that she wanted to give him everything she could to make up for it. From the first time he saw the two of them together, at the school Speech Day, Ray had noticed how her eyes went all mushy whenever he made a fuss over Tommy. And soon afterward he'd sensed in her a kind of desperation to find the boy a father and give him a proper family life. And the kid was nuts about cowboys, so what better candidate for the job could there be than good ol' Ray Montane?

Putting it that way made it sound too calculated, as if taking on the kid was the price he'd had to pay for getting Diane. And it wasn't like that. Of course, Ray had often wished—and still mostly did—that it was just the two of them, just him and Diane, with no baggage attached. But over the past few months he'd actually come to like the kid.

203

Okay, he was a little weird, but he learned fast and wasn't anything like as wimpy as he'd first seemed. In fact, he was turning out to be quite a tough little sonofabitch.

Ray was still dazed by what had happened last night and even more by what had happened this morning. The sex had been something else, the best they'd ever had. And after a night like that, he'd kind of assumed he was forgiven and that everything would be all right again. But this morning she'd packed their things and told him she and Tommy were moving out and going to live in her little apartment. As she left she said, all cold and sarcastic, that maybe he'd let her know when he wasn't still married to somebody else. What she told Tommy, Ray didn't have any idea, but the poor kid sure didn't look happy when they drove off.

During the interrogation last night, Ray had answered her questions more or less truthfully. And if she'd asked some better ones he'd probably have told her a whole lot more. He might even have owned up to having a daughter. Maybe he should have volunteered it, just to get it out of the way. Or maybe not. Most likely, it would have been the final straw. Anyhow, there was no danger of Diane finding out. He hardly knew the kid, hadn't seen her in years. Hell, he wouldn't even recognize her if he bumped into her in the street. And she'd know better, from that bitch of a mother of hers, than to come calling or give him any trouble.

The door to the Colonel's office was opening now and there was a burst of laughter. An agent whose name Ray could never remember, one of Lew Wasserman's MCA foot soldiers, was coming out with a pretty young broad in a yellow dress and too much red lipstick. Some young actress who'd just been signed and would doubtless soon be making her way up that secret staircase. Jack Warner had his arms around their shoulders. They all looked so damn pleased with themselves, it made you want to puke.

With little waves and meaningful glances, the agent and the actress went off down the staircase and Warner straightened his blue silk tie and walked toward Ray. The old bastard looked as dapper as ever. The tailored gray suit, the perfect triangle of pale blue silk poking from the breast pocket. Hair slicked back, eyebrows cocked sardonically, the pencil-thin mustache above that toothy smile.

'Ray! Sorry you've had to wait so long.'

Ray stood up and shook his hand.

'No problem, Colonel. Good to see you.'

'You bet. Come on in.'

Ray gathered up his briefcase and followed him past the dragon and into the outer office where blondie flashed another smile and then on and through and into the great man's office with its imperial desk and casting couch. Colonel Jack settled back in his throne behind the desk and Ray sat in front of it on one much lower. It was all part of the same bullshit game, to make you feel small and insecure.

The meeting had been scheduled a month ago when they'd bumped into each other one lunchtime in the commissary. Ray had said it would be good to have a chat sometime, about the future and all that, and the Colonel said he agreed and had been meaning to get in touch for a while.

Ray had taken this as a hint that, at long last, thank the Lord, the old bastard was going to see sense and let him do a proper movie.

Ray had come prepared. He'd brought along the script he'd been sent by Steve Shelby, the young writer he'd met at the Kanters' place. Ray's part needed a lot of work to build it up, but for a first draft it was pretty good. He slipped it out of his briefcase and put it on the desk. Jack Warner was leaning back staring at him, his fingertips delicately pressed together.

'So how're ya doing, Colonel?'

'Oh, you know. Uneasy lies the head that wears the toilet seat.'

Ray had heard it before but dutifully smiled. Warner looked at his watch and sat up a little.

'Ray, I have to be at a board meeting at half past, so we better cut to the chase.'

'Okay. Well, I've got one or two—'

'We're going to drop *Sliprock*.'

Ray stared at him for a moment.

'You're what?'

'You know as well as I do it's not getting the audience it used to. The network isn't happy.'

'Well, Colonel, the latest figures I saw weren't—'

'It's not your fault. The show's just too old-fashioned.'

'Well, that's exactly what I've been saying for a long time. I've been telling the idiots to—'

'Which idiots? Dan and Lew are fine producers.'

'I know, I'm sorry. But I've been telling them we've got to get with it. Get some grittier scripts. All you gotta do is watch shows like *Wagon Train*. Get some of the guys who write that stuff. And get someone under the age of sixty to direct now and then. Some of these younger guys around town are hot stuff. And they don't cost so much either. Colonel, believe me, I've been saying these things till I'm blue in the face—'

'Ray, listen to me. The show is sinking. When a ship is sinking you don't fuck around with the furniture.'

Ray couldn't believe this was happening.

'The western's had its day.'

'Oh, Colonel, I don't think that'll ever—'

'I tell you. People don't want them anymore. Don't get me wrong, it's not going to happen tomorrow. The good ones—your *Wagon Trains* and *Bonanzas*—they'll roll on for a while. But in ten years' time there won't be a single western left. Mark my words. Maybe the odd movie, but on TV? Not one.'

There was a long pause. Ray shook his head.

'I don't know what to say. But, hell, you know, maybe it's an opportunity. Tell you the truth, that's what I came along here today to talk about. You know I've been itching to do a movie. I don't mean some Saturday afternoon Hitching Post deal, I mean a real movie...'

The Colonel gave a little sigh and looked down at his fingertips. Ray picked up the screenplay. His hand was shaking. He suddenly felt desperate, like some sniveling little kid.

'...and I've got some great ideas. In fact, I've brought this script along that might just fit the bill—'

'I'll have someone take a look.'

'The kid who wrote it, Steve Shelby, I tell ya, Colonel, he's really something. Herb Kanter reckons he's some kind of genius—'

'Sure, sure. We'll take a look. But I have to tell you, Ray, leaving that aside, after this current season, we'll be terminating your contract.'

SIXTEEN

The snow had been falling since dawn. There was almost a foot of it by now, enough to deaden all sound except the shuffle of their feet as they followed the coffin out of the church and into the graveyard. There was no wind and the flakes settled fat and feathery on the bare heads and on the shoulders of the bearers in their black overcoats. The funeral director was at the door, handing out black umbrellas.

As the procession wove its way through the gravestones, one of the bearers slipped and the coffin lurched and for a moment Tommy thought it was going to crash to the ground and spill his grandmother's body on to the snow. But the other bearers deftly braced and he righted himself and all that fell was one wreath of roses, a splash of red in a world of white and black.

It was the church where Tommy had been christened. It was six hundred years old and some of the gravestones tilted precariously and were so overgrown with moss and lichen that you couldn't read what was written on them any more. His grandmother had never believed in God. She used to say it was all *stuff and nonsense* and never came here with them at Christmas or Easter. But, for some reason, this was where she was to be buried. The grave that had been dug for her was close to

208

an old yew tree, its sprawl of branches bending under the weight of the snow. Tommy remembered reading somewhere that yews were witches' trees.

The bearers put the coffin down on some canvas straps that had been laid ready beside the grave and then, using these, they lifted it again and lowered it slowly between the sliced walls of frozen earth.

There had been no more than a dozen people at the service in the church and fewer still had stayed on for the burial. The only people Tommy recognized across the grave were Dr Henderson and Uncle Reggie and Auntie Vera, who'd cried loudly all through the church service and was still crying now. Nobody else was. But then they were mostly men and men weren't supposed to cry. Tommy felt too empty and numb to cry. And much too cold. His feet felt like clumps of frozen rock. He was wearing his old Ashlawn school suit and wished he'd put on a thicker sweater.

Diane was still wearing her sunglasses. Perhaps she didn't want people to see whether or not she was crying. Tommy was close enough to know she wasn't. She was standing beside him, trying to shelter both him and her father under her umbrella which was difficult because the old man seemed to be off in a world of his own and kept swaying out to stare at the sky with a kind of weary surprise, blinking whenever a snowflake landed on his eyes.

The umbrellas looked like igloos. The old rector's nose had gone purple with cold and his breath made clouds in the air as he hurried through what he had to say. Dust to dust, ashes to ashes. The handful of frozen soil rattled on the coffin lid.

The telegram had been delivered to the apartment in LA on Sunday morning, just over a week before Christmas, telling Diane to phone home urgently. It was Auntie Vera who answered. She said Joan had died of a massive heart attack. Arthur had found her lying on the kitchen floor when he came home from work.

Ray drove them out to the airport that same afternoon. They hardly saw him any more though he still phoned every day. Tommy missed him a lot and felt sorry for him too because the studio was going to stop making *Sliprock*. Diane was still being horrible to him after their argument. She wouldn't tell Tommy what it had been about. She said he was too young to understand which was one of the most maddening things a grown-up could ever say. On the way to the airport, Ray was really sweet. He looked sad and sheepish and somehow smaller than he used to. Diane hardly spoke to him, just sat there, staring out of the window while Ray and Tommy did all the talking. On the plane, after they'd had supper and the lights had all been turned down, Tommy asked her why she had to go on being so unfriendly to Ray.

'He didn't tell me the truth about something. Something very important.'

'What?'

Diane sighed.

'He didn't tell me that he'd been married before.'

'Even I knew that.'

'Twice.'

'What's so bad about that?'

210

'*And* that he's not yet properly divorced from his last wife.'

'Maybe he forgot.'

She laughed.

'You don't forget about something like that.'

Tommy thought for a while.

'What's different about him not telling you about that and you not telling me all those years that you were my real mother?'

Diane didn't reply for a moment, just looked at him with a sad smile.

'How come you're so darned clever? Come on, let's get some sleep.'

The rector had stopped talking now and everyone piled back into their cars and drove home to eat all the food that Auntie Vera and Diane had prepared. Tommy helped hand out the sandwiches and soup and then walked around with a jug of steaming fruit punch into which Uncle Reggie had poured everything alcoholic he could find in the house. The cold seemed to have made everybody very thirsty. They all asked him about living in California and Uncle Reggie, who'd clearly already had too much punch, kept putting on an American accent and saying *howdy, pardner* whenever Tommy walked past.

It had been strange to see all his grandmother's things around the house when they arrived two days ago. It was as if she'd just nipped out to the shops. Her apron hanging by the kitchen door, her slippers on the floor by the doormat, her cigarettes and lighter on the sideboard where she always kept them. Diane had cleared a lot of it away and they had gone out and bought a Christmas tree and tried to make the house look a little more cheerful.

But the decorations only seemed to make the place seem sadder still. There was another big difference which, for a long time, he couldn't put his finger on. Then he realized it was simply the silence. Joan had always had the radio on.

As the big bowl of rum punch slowly emptied, the voices got rowdier. And when he could do so without being noticed, Tommy slipped away upstairs. His old room had been redecorated as a guest room with green floral wallpaper and a sickly yellow carpet. He stood by the window, staring out at the back garden. The light was fading fast. He remembered how excited he always used to be when it snowed but today everything just looked flat and dull. It didn't seem like home any more. He no longer knew where home was.

*   *   *

Diane thought they were never going to leave. And even when at last they did, Auntie Vera insisted on staying on to clear up. Tommy and Uncle Reggie were in the sitting room, watching TV. Diane's father had long ago quietly escaped to his little workshop.

'So, whatever happened to that film you were supposed to be doing with Gary Cooper? What was it called?'

Vera was at the kitchen sink, washing the last of the dishes. Diane was standing beside her drying them and longing to smash them over the woman's head. She hadn't stopped yakking all afternoon and everything she said was snide or scornful. Diane took a deep breath.

'*Remorseless*. It's been delayed.'

212

'Again?'

'It happens all the time.'

'Oh, really? Must cost a lot. More money than sense, I suppose, these film people.'

Diane wasn't going to give the woman the satisfaction of knowing that the movie would now, in all probability, never be made. Herb Kanter had told her only last week that Gary Cooper had cancer and had been given only a few months to live. Herb asked her to keep this news to herself for the moment because only a few people knew. He claimed he was confident they would be able to recast, but Diane didn't really believe it.

There was a long pause, just the clack of the dishes in the sink and laughter from the TV in the next room.

'Of course, she never got over it,' Vera said.

'Sorry, who never got over what?'

'Your mother. When you told Tommy about . . . you know. It broke her heart.'

'Why don't you just say it?'

Auntie Vera turned to stare at her. Her face was flushed with drink.

'Say what?'

'That I killed her. It's obviously what you think.'

'Don't be so melodramatic.'

'Get out,' Diane said quietly.

'What?'

'Put your coat on, take that drunken old fool of a husband with you and just go. Now!'

Not another word was said. When they'd gone, Diane went into the sitting room and slumped on the sofa beside Tommy.

'What happened with Auntie Vera? I heard you arguing.'

213

'Oh, nothing really. I just lost my temper.'

'I'm glad they've gone.'

'Me too. Give me a hug.'

She put her arm around him and he snuggled in close.

'I love you,' she whispered.

'I love you too.'

For a long time they sat there, staring at the TV. It was some kind of variety show, full of forced Christmas cheer, two men in reindeer suits doing a comic dance routine. It was so alien to how Diane was feeling that it could have been a broadcast from Mars.

The satisfaction of throwing Auntie Vera out of the house was giving way to guilt. But at least the anger had been reassuring. It was the first genuine emotion Diane had felt since learning of her mother's death. All there had been was a vaguely aching void. She hadn't managed to shed a single tear. She tried to tell herself that this was perfectly normal, that she was simply in shock. But she wasn't convinced. The truth that she was slowly being forced to confront was that she had never really loved her mother nor felt loved by her. All she had ever been to the woman was a tiresome problem.

Diane sometimes worried about how this might have affected her. Could an unloved child, she wondered, ever know how to love a child of her own? Perhaps she had been forced to become so intensely selfish, obsessed with her own survival and desire to prove herself of value, that she was incapable of loving. She was certain (or as certain as she imagined one could be in such matters) that what she felt for this other being that she had created, now nestling against her, nine years old but still so small and vulnerable, was a love as true and vivid as any parent could ever feel. Sometimes it was almost too painful to bear. But perhaps that pain was merely guilt dressed in other clothes. Guilt and—the idea so appalled her she could barely name it to herself—pity.

The phone was ringing now in the hallway and she kissed Tommy on the forehead and went out to answer it. The operator asked for her by name and said she had a long-distance call from the United States.

It was Ray. He asked how the funeral had gone and how she was and how Tommy and her father were doing. For weeks, ever since she and Tommy moved out, she had been cold and ungiving with him whenever he called. And he had simply taken it and never complained or stopped calling. But with all that had happened, continuing to punish him seemed petty and wrong. He seemed to sense a thawing.

She told him about their day and realized as she did so how comforting it was to talk with him, to have someone who knew her and listened and supported her. When she told him about throwing Vera out, he laughed.

'That's my girl,' he said.

The phrase hung in the ether between them.

'I'd better go,' she said at last.

'Okay.'

For a moment neither of them spoke.

'I miss you, sugar.'

She didn't reply.

'I love you so much.'

'Oh, Ray—'

'It's okay. You don't have to say a thing. I just wanted to tell you...The divorce papers came through.'

She didn't know what to say.

'You asked me to let you know,' he said, bridging the silence.

'Thank you.'

'So, there you go. Say hi to Tommy. And give my condolences to your daddy.'

'I will.'

She lit a cigarette and stood alone in the kitchen, thinking about Ray. Then she stubbed it out and put on her coat and walked across the back yard to the garage to find her father. The snow had stopped and it was freezing hard. The sky was thick with stars.

He was hunched in a little pool of light over his workbench at the end of the cold, dark tunnel of a garage. He was wearing his headlamp, a magnifying glass clenched in one eye while he delicately painted over the final join of a blue-and-white porcelain vase. She stood beside him, watching, hugging herself against the cold.

'Everybody gone?' he said, without looking up.

'Yes.'

'Thank God for that.'

It had been years since she'd watched him work. She'd forgotten how nimble his fingers were. He put down the brush and gently revolved the vase to inspect it. You wouldn't know it had ever been broken.

'That looks good.'

'Hmm. Not too bad. It was in seven pieces.'

'Daddy?'

He took off his magnifying glass, looked up at

216

her for the first time and saw the tears sliding down her cheeks. He reached out and patted her arm.

'Come on, old girl. No need for that.'

'I'm so sorry.'

'What on earth for?'

She wiped her eyes but the tears wouldn't stop.

'I don't know. Everything.'

He got to his feet and put the headlamp down on the bench then awkwardly took her in his arms. The smell of him, that blend of smoke and soap and mothballed tweed, made her feel like a child again, only deepened the sadness. She sobbed into his shoulder.

'I ruined her life,' she said.

'No, no.'

He was stroking her hair. His voice a rasping whisper.

'I did.'

'No, you didn't. She did that all by herself.'

SEVENTEEN

'It was a Thursday night,' Danny said.

'Things had been kind of quiet for a few days. There'd been a couple of mortar attacks on the base but nothing serious, nobody hurt. It was one of the guys' birthday and his buddy in the kitchen had made this killer chocolate cake shaped like a Humvee. By the time we had to go out on patrol we were all feeling stuffed and happy.'

He paused for a moment, staring out at the ocean. The waves were bigger now. A hot wind

217

had risen and was shifting what was left of the haze and filling the air with a salty tang. Tom and Danny were sitting on the sand in the shade of some tilting palms, their shoes, father's and son's, drying side by side before them in the sun. Danny had rolled the wet bottoms of his pants up to his knees and was idly brushing the sand from his legs. Tom waited for him to go on.

At first he'd found the way Danny talked difficult to understand. He used so much military slang and jargon, so many wry euphemisms and acronyms, that it was sometimes like listening to a foreign language. Tom knew his NCOs from his RPGs but had to interrupt to ask about IEDs (improvised explosive devices) and NVGs (night-vision goggles), QRFs (quick-reaction forces) and SAWs (squad automatic weapons—M249 light machine guns). Danny had laughed when Tom asked what WTF meant (what the fuck) and again when he asked how many had been in the Hummer.

'What's so funny?'

'We call them Humvees, Dad. Hummer means blow job.'

That was when Tom decided to stop butting in and just listen to the boy's story.

Danny's company had been based some forty miles north of Baghdad in a derelict food-processing plant that had been converted into a fortress. It was infested with rats and roaches and smelled evil which was probably why its first occupants had nicknamed it *Mordor*. The land around was mostly farmland, vineyards and orchards, crisscrossed with irrigation canals and unmapped roads and scattered with sprawling little

218

towns and villages.

As in most other parts of the country, the local people had originally welcomed their liberating invaders with open arms, Danny said. But now they expressed their feelings with nightly mortar and rocket attacks on the base and ever-more-inventive roadside bombs. These were usually made from 155 mm artillery shells buried in the dirt shoulder or a hidden culvert but sometimes they were packed into the carcass of a dead dog or goat and triggered remotely by cell phone.

'The one that got us that night was stuffed into a dead donkey,' Danny said. 'Can you imagine doing that? Jeez. If we'd just used our noses we could probably have smelled the damn thing a hundred yards away.'

They were a QRF of three Humvees. Danny was in the third. Those in the lead vehicle should have seen the bomb and probably would have seen it had there not been a near to full moon that night. It had risen late and huge, Danny said, casting stark shadows. And in one of these shadows, beneath a tree at the edge of a scrawny orchard, lay the donkey. In the moonlit green world of their night-vision goggles it looked like nothing more than another shaded undulation of the earth.

'I just happened to be looking ahead when the bomb went off. There was this incredible white flash and the lead Humvee bucked into the air like a rodeo bull or something. The blast knocked me off my seat. For a moment I thought we'd been hit too, but we hadn't. And when the smoke and all the debris cleared we saw the hit vehicle was nose down in the gully on the other side of the road. Rear wheels spinning in the air. The whole lower

219

part of its right side had been ripped open. The steel all peeled back like the petals of some weird kind of flower.'

Danny shook his head and stopped talking for a few moments.

'Then there was, like, nothing. Just this spooky stillness. You know, everybody just stunned, thinking, shit, has this really happened? Am I still here? And then, as if somebody's pressed the play button again, slowly everybody comes to life. People hollering and swearing, shouting out each other's names. And then all the radio babble, everybody asking what's happened, giving positions, calling in support.'

Danny turned and looked at Tom earnestly, as if he really wanted him to understand.

'It's not panic. It's like a kind of controlled frenzy, you know? Everybody knows what to do. You're trained for it. But you're just so shocked and pumped with adrenaline and your head's still all blurred and ringing from the blast that it takes a while to claw your way through and remember. And that's the really dangerous moment, because while you're still stunned and trying to piece it all together, the motherfuckers who've planted the bomb and watched all the fun will usually start to shoot the hell out of you.'

And that was exactly what happened next, Danny said. As they scrambled out of the other two Humvees (though scramble, Danny said, wasn't quite the word when you were each hauling a hundred pounds of gear, weaponry and Kevlar body armor), they heard the crackle and ricochet whine of incoming fire. Then the mortars started.

Luckily, Danny said, the insurgents rarely

seemed to know how to aim mortars with any consistent accuracy. It was hard to tell how many were out there firing at them. They seemed to be laid up somewhere in a thick wall of reeds that ran along a canal about two hundred yards away across the orchard. Though not for long because the turret gunners of the two functioning Humvees swung around and opened up with their .50 cals and everybody on the ground did the same with their M16s, laying down a wall of suppressive fire and decorating the night with tracers.

'Like, within a minute the reeds were shredded and the trees in the orchard shot to hell. All ragged and splintered. And the bastards were either dead or shitting themselves and saving their asses, because the incoming completely stopped.'

The driver of the bombed Humvee was dead and probably never knew much about it. Both of his legs were missing. Two other guys were badly wounded and one of these turned out to be Danny's best friend, Ricky Peters. He was from Pasadena and had just turned twenty. He was one of the funniest people on earth, Danny said, adored by everyone who knew him.

By the time Danny was able to scuttle across the road and down into the cover of the wrecked Humvee, someone already had an IV rigged up and a needle into Ricky's arm and he was drifting off on a cloud of morphine. A jagged slice of steel had been driven up into his groin and his legs were bloody, like butchered meat.

'He had this weird little smile on his face,' Danny said quietly. 'He kept trying to say something and I couldn't make it out. It was some kind of sick wisecrack about his balls. All I could do was hold him and stroke his forehead.'

Danny swallowed and stared at the sand for a while. This is my son, Tom thought, my little boy. That he should have seen such horrors was almost impossible to imagine. Tom put a hand on his shoulder. And Danny composed himself and went on.

The medevac Black Hawk touched down within minutes. They all scoured the ground and found one of the driver's missing legs but couldn't find the other. For the sake of the bereaved, Danny explained, corpses were always sent home as complete as they could be. The medevac guys were supposed to take only the wounded, not the dead, but this time they did and once they were loaded up, the Black Hawk hoisted itself into the air and veered away across the moon.

Danny's squad regrouped. The job now was to find the motherfuckers who'd done this. Roadside bombs were often triggered by cell phone, but this one had been detonated with wires. One of the QRF squad leaders, a sergeant called Marty Delgado, told Danny to come with him and the two of them followed the wires in the green moonlight across the orchard while an Apache helicopter crossed and recrossed ahead of them, panning the reeds and canals with its searchlight.

Danny and Delgado didn't get along. At least, not anymore. All Marines by definition were hard-core, but Delgado took it to a whole new level, Danny said. He was titanium-grade hard-core and never missed an opportunity to let the world know.

'All rippling muscle and tough-guy tattoos,' Danny said. 'Always checking himself out in the mirror. And he carries all this extra gear in his pack, in case he suddenly has to climb Everest or something or go scuba diving.'

Anyhow, Danny went on, a couple of weeks earlier, at the base, after Delgado had been banging on about how many superhero bench presses he could do, Danny and Ricky had been in the latrines and they were joking about it, imitating him. Not in any mean kind of way, just having a laugh, the two of them. Or so they thought.

Danny happened to mention the size of the Delgado dick (which, he added, for the record, was uncommonly small), when who should walk around the corner but its owner. Danny felt sick to his stomach, prayed the guy hadn't heard. But it soon became clear that he had because from that moment on, Delgado was on his case, finding fault with everything Danny did. Calling him clumsy and putting him down in front of everyone in the platoon.

What really sucked, Danny said, was that on this particular night, the night of the donkey bomb, the mean bastard had good cause. After they'd found the place where the bomber had laid up (he'd made himself a cozy nest in the reeds and left the wires still attached to a twelve-volt car battery), Danny tripped and found himself slithering on his back down the side of an irrigation canal. The cement was smooth and covered in slime and there was nothing to grab hold of. He ended up chest deep in the foul-smelling water.

'I tried to climb out but, what with the slime and the weight of the body armor, there was no way. I just kept sliding back. All I could do was stand there looking dumb. Delgado stared down at me and didn't say a word, just shook his head like I was some kind of imbecile. Then he took a rope from his pack and threw me one end and hauled me out.'

Danny had been furious with himself and muttered something vivid and profane about what he was going to do to that little *hajji* fuck of a bomber when they found him. Delgado told him sharply to get ahold of himself.

There was a path through the reeds that had no doubt been used for the getaway and as they were following it—Danny dripping like a fruit strainer, stinking to high hell, boots squelching all the way—they heard over the radio that a man in a camouflage jacket and white pants (which sounded a pretty weird combination, Danny said, kind of *see me, don't see me*) had been sighted running toward some farm buildings just a few hundred yards ahead of them. Delgado replied that they were after him.

There was a narrow wooden bridge over the canal and they ran across and at the edge of the reeds got their first glimpse of the farm, a cluster of ramshackle sheds and block-built barns, roofed with rusted iron sheets and beyond them the taller white walls of the main building. A dog came rushing out at them, barking loudly, and Delgado shot it stone dead with a single round from his M16.

They headed toward the buildings and were about fifty yards short when someone opened up at them with an AK. The terrain was scrubby and scattered with derelict pieces of farm machinery, so there was cover enough. They returned fire and made a series of runs to the shelter of the first barn and, just as they got there, saw the man in the cammie jacket, carrying an AK, dashing from behind a shed then disappearing around a corner of the farmhouse. It was all in an instant. They fired but he was gone.

Of course, Danny said, there was no sign of him when they came around the corner themselves. What they found instead was a group of maybe a dozen women and children and a few men, mostly old guys, standing there all huddled together in this shitty little whitewashed courtyard, dogs barking and chickens skittering and squawking around them. All terrified out of their minds.

'Two of the women were holding babies. And all of them were screaming and hollering and holding up their hands. It was weird, but my goggles made them look scary. Their eyes were all white. Like they were ghosts or something. Like a gang of wailing zombies.'

A moment later, four other guys from the QRF burst in through the other entrance to the courtyard and then the Apache suddenly slid in over the rooftop and hung overhead, shining its searchlight directly down on them all, which immediately ratcheted up the screaming and hollering from frantic to full-blown hysterical. Where the hell the guy with the AK had vanished to was anyone's guess.

Danny paused and swallowed again. He was sitting with his knees bunched up in front of him and he lowered his head onto them for a moment, as if summoning the strength to go on. Tom put his hand on his shoulder again and waited. A young woman was standing at the water's edge flinging a stick into the surf for a big black dog. The wind

225

had grown stronger and shifted onshore and the waves were big now and, again and again, the dog got tumbled like laundry in the foam but always came back with the stick to ask for more.

When Danny resumed, his voice was quieter and Tom had to lean in close to hear. He said maybe it was hard for Tom to understand how hyped they'd all been that night. He said he couldn't get the image of his blood-soaked friend out of his head. Of Ricky, lying there smiling, trying to crack some dark joke about his balls being blown off. And the women wailing and screaming just made it worse. Danny was so churning with hate and fear and God knew what else that he felt as if his head were going to explode.

Then Delgado ordered him and a young private called Eldon Harker to stand guard over the crowd in the courtyard while he and the other three Marines searched the house. Danny challenged this because he'd seen the guy who'd shot at them and it seemed only sensible that he should take part in the search. But Delgado told him to shut the fuck up and do as he was told. Harker was from Cleveland and had only just arrived on his first tour of duty. Danny barely knew him. The poor guy looked scared out of his mind.

Delgado led the others into the house and left the two of them in the courtyard and they'd only been standing there a few moments when the Apache above them tilted and swerved off and Danny made the mistake of looking up at it and was dazzled by the beam of its searchlight. In that same instant there was some shouting from inside the farmhouse and a crash of breaking glass and then a burst of gunfire.

When he looked again at his wretched band of captives, his sight still half blitzed by the searchlight, something or someone moved behind one of the women holding a baby. It was a man, a little younger than the others, and Danny was sure—almost sure—that he hadn't been there the moment before.

'He was wearing a white shirt and white pants and he looked me right in the eye and I suddenly thought, holy shit, that's him, that's the guy we've been chasing. The little motherfucker has simply dumped the cammie jacket and joined the crowd, trying to act all innocent. Then Harker hollers, so I figure he must be thinking the same.'

This all happened in a matter of a few short seconds, Danny said. Less than that. It was like one extended moment. You could see in the guy's eyes that he knew he'd been rumbled. He was shaking, bobbing, as if he were about to run. Then, all of a sudden, he bent down and Harker hollered again and one of the women shrieked and Danny heard—he definitely, distinctly heard—the clicking sound of what was obviously a weapon being racked. And then he saw it.

'There it was, the glint of a barrel behind the woman's hip. The little fuck has picked up his AK and is getting ready to fire.'

And Danny yelled and both he and Harker opened up with their M16s.

Seven dead. An old man, three women, a five-year-old girl and a baby boy. And the younger man who'd reached for his weapon. Except there was no weapon. Only an alloy crutch. The guy was an invalid, only had one leg.

The little girl and the baby lay side by side, their

227

bodies bloody and ripped open by the bullets but their faces untouched. The girl's eyes were still open. The image had engraved itself in Danny's head.

'I see her face every night,' Danny whispered. 'Every time I close my eyes, there she is, staring at me.'

Tom put his arm around his son's shoulders and pulled him closer. It was a long while before either of them spoke again. They listened to the rush and draw of the waves and watched the sun sink, ragged and shimmering, into the ocean.

'They're going to hang me out to dry, Dad. They're going to let me hang there and twist in the wind.'

EIGHTEEN

Tom's flight home from LA wasn't until the following afternoon so he'd booked a room at a hotel called the W in Westwood. The room was chic and luxurious and about as big as a closet. He was tired but his head was churning too much for sleep, so he went down to the lounge. It was all darkened mirrors and low lighting and everyone there seemed to be half his age and impossibly good-looking. He sat at the bar and ordered a mineral water and, for the first time in many years, yearned for something stronger.

Back in his room he lay on the bed still half-dressed and watched Jay Leno interviewing some young stubble-faced actor Tom didn't recognize. He tried to concentrate but couldn't. All he could think about was Danny and what was going to happen to him. The thoughts transmuted into anxious, half-awake dreams in which he was hunting through a swamp of tall reeds, parting them with his hands and calling Danny's name again and again until he found himself at the rim of a dark pool. He looked down and saw his son covered in slime and calling for help, stretching his arms up. Tom would wake in a sweat and open his eyes wide and rub his face and try to shrug the dream out of his head but as soon as he closed his eyes again he was back there. Danny's face below him, pale and ghostly and full of fear. Tom lay on the bank and reached down to try to haul the boy out but it was too far. Their outstretched hands just wouldn't touch. And then he saw that Danny wasn't the only one down there and that the water around him was full of floating bodies.

He got up around six and showered and checked out. He hadn't been to LA for many years. There were too many ghosts. The streets were almost empty. He drove across to West Hollywood, cruising past places he remembered as a boy. But everything had changed. Carl Curtis School had long ago relocated, the little park with its petting zoo now built over. He drove up La Cienega then along Sunset and up into the hills, the way Diane used to drive him back to Ray's place. But when he came around the last corner he saw that the gates had changed and the red roof beyond was gone. The house had been knocked down and replaced with a sleek palace of glass and cement.

He drove back down the canyon and headed east and then north on the freeway to the crematorium where they had held Diane's funeral.

In those days the place had been surrounded by open land but now every available acre seemed to have been built on and it took him a long time to find it.

The cemetery was much smaller than he remembered. There was no grave nor gravestone. Because of all the shame that surrounded her death and probably because of something he had read, as a boy, Tom had believed that this was because convicted murderers weren't allowed proper graves. But he'd later learned that this was how Diane had wanted it. Her ashes had simply been scattered in what was called the Garden of Remembrance. Tom found it and walked slowly among the flower beds under the hot morning sun. There was a stone bench set in a bower of white and pink roses. The smell of roses had always reminded him of Diane and he sat there for a while with his eyes closed, thinking about her and trying to picture her. The image that always came first was of that last time he'd seen her. Dressed all in white, standing in the sunlight in the prison cell. How he wished he'd been kinder to her that day.

He drove out to LAX, returned the rental car and checked in early for his flight. While he waited he read all the newspapers and weeklies. They were full of stories about Iraq but there was nothing about Danny in any of them. The media seemed to have lost interest. At the outset, Tom had expected TV crews showing up on his doorstep but it hadn't happened. The only reporter who'd called him was a friend who worked on the *Missoulian* and all she wrote was a small piece tucked away on an inside page, with no mention of Tom's name.

It had been a lot worse for Gina. A week of reporters foraging for family reaction and background, but Dutch had soon seen them off. There was a fair amount about the case on the Internet but you had to search hard for it and it was nothing compared to all there had been about Haditha. Maybe it was a simple matter of arithmetic. In Haditha Marines had killed twenty-four civilians. A mere seven dead maybe didn't rate anymore.

They landed on schedule and the Missoula air smelled good and clean and cooler than the air had in LA. Tom found his car and headed east toward town then crossed the Clark Fork to the Good Food Store on 3rd Street to pick up something for his supper. He was going through one of his healthy-eating phases (they usually lasted about a week) and as he was busy loading his cart with organic oranges his cell phone rang. It was a woman's voice and she didn't say who she was, just jumped straight in as if he should know.

'Hi,' she said. 'How'd it go?'

Tom hadn't any idea who it was or what she was asking about. So he just said *hi* and *oh, not bad* and then, thank heaven, some elusive synapse clicked in and he knew he was talking with Karen O'Keefe.

'So, did you get that big movie deal?'

He remembered the lie he'd told her about his meetings in LA.

'Oh, no. Well, things aren't quite at that stage yet.'

'Oh.'

'I just got back, as a matter of fact.'

231

'Oh, I'm sorry.'

'No, no. It's good. How've you been? How's your mom been? I mean, about her cat... What was his name?'

'Maurice. Couldn't be happier. That makes her sound mean, doesn't it? But she's thrilled. You know, in a kind of guilty way. She wants to meet you. Do you want to have dinner?'

'What, with your mom?'

Karen O'Keefe laughed. He liked her laugh a lot.

'No, with me. I can bring my mom if you like.'

'Another time maybe. Look, I could get us something. I'm right here in the food store—'

'Me too.'

'What?'

'Right here in the store. Look to your right.'

And there she was, just twenty yards away, grinning at him. She snapped her phone shut and walked toward him. He felt a little flutter in his chest and told himself again not to be a fool.

'First the cat, now this,' she said. 'You must think I'm stalking you.'

'Be my guest.'

She said her intention was to buy him dinner but Tom said here they were, surrounded by all this fabulous produce and he loved to cook, so why not eat at his place? She shrugged and said *sure* and transferred the few things she had in her cart into his and they set off around the store, deciding what they would eat.

Tom pushed the cart and watched her while she did the research, picking things up to inspect them, feeling the fruit to see how ripe it was, checking out the labels. He liked the way she bit her lip

232

while she concentrated, liked the little frown on the freckled forehead, the way she kept tucking her hair behind her ears. In fact, he liked everything about her. Most of all he liked the idea that anyone looking at them might assume they were a couple. He'd forgotten how pleasant that felt.

They bought steak and salad and some exotic French cheeses and fresh raspberries and some gourmet ice cream Tom had never heard of but which she said was the most delicious in all the world. To hell with the diet. She wanted to pay but he wouldn't let her.

She followed him home in her dusty old yellow Volvo station wagon and when they arrived Makwi came bounding out and made a big fuss of him as if he'd been gone for years. Tom's house-and-dog-sitter friend Liz was in a hurry to get away so he thanked her and paid her and then he and Karen took Makwi for a walk up through the forest to the raven rocks.

Tom normally went only to the foot of the cliff but this evening they climbed around and up along the edge to reach the top. The last hundred yards were steep and strewn with loose stone and twice he had to give her his hand and haul her up behind him and when they reached the top she was short of breath and they sat side by side on a platform of rock and stared down over the treetops.

You couldn't quite see Tom's house from here, just the bend of the creek a little farther downstream and the cottonwoods that grew beside it and the meadow where Gina used to keep the horses. The fading light was soft and tinged with blue and, as the sun went down, a tide of shadow

233

rose on the far side of the valley. During the walk they'd hardly stopped talking but now a comfortable silence fell between them. A pair of ravens were mobbing a hawk that had probably flown too close to their young. The raucous calls echoed down the valley.

They had been talking about her parents, how her father had been much older than her mother and had been dead now for many years. She said she never really knew him. Now it was her turn to ask the questions and she asked Tom about his parents and he told her that he too had never known his father. That, in fact, he'd never even met him and didn't know whether he was alive or dead.

'Aren't you curious?'

'A little. But not enough to find out.'

'Do you know where he lives?'

'I know where he lived thirty years ago. I saw him once.'

He paused. Those green eyes were fixed on him, waiting for him to go on. Gina was the only person he'd ever told. Karen O'Keefe suddenly seemed to sense that the subject was delicate.

'I'm sorry. It's none of my business.'

'No. It's fine.'

And he told her about Diane getting pregnant at fifteen and how his grandparents had pretended to be his parents and how, many years later, when he was in his early twenties, he had gone in search of his father and, with surprising ease, had managed to find his address. David Willis was by then in his late thirties and living in a town called Tunbridge Wells in the southeast of England. Tom had considered writing a letter but could imagine the poor man's shock at opening it. Diane, after all, had never even informed him that she was pregnant.

So, on one of his rare trips to England, Tom had rented a car and driven down to Tunbridge Wells and found the house on a leafy suburban street.

'It was a sunny Sunday morning. People were out in their gardens and mowing their lawns and I drove slowly past the house and there was this man, washing his car in the little driveway. It was a Volvo, just like yours, only a lot cleaner.'

Karen O'Keefe laughed her lovely laugh.

'What did he look like?'

'Tall, slim, good-looking. I got all those genes, obviously.'

'And then?'

'I drove on past, turned around, came slowly back and parked up under some trees, just across the street from the house. And I sat there for a while. And watched him. And then a little girl, maybe five or six years old, came out of the front door and he pretended to point the hose at her and she giggled and squealed, sort of daring him to drench her. And then he lifted her up and put her on his shoulders while he finished hosing the car down.'

'Your little sister.'

'I guess. Half sister, anyhow.'

'Go on.'

'And then I just started the engine and drove away.'

'And never got in touch?'

Tom smiled and shook his head.

'Why?'

'What would I have said? *Hi, I'm Tom, the son*
235

you never knew you had. It seemed to me that, to do that to him, to drop that bomb into his life, I needed a reason. I mean a good reason, not just curiosity. Which, when it came down to it, was really all I felt. There was no . . . connection.'

They were silent for a moment.

'And what about your mother? Is she still alive?'

'Oh, no. She died a long time ago.'

'Brothers and sisters?'

'A sister. She died in a car accident when I was thirteen.'

'That's tough.'

'Yeah. It was.'

The lie seemed tired and worn. It was a long time since he'd heard himself tell it and he had a sudden urge to confess how Diane had really died. But how could he tell this virtual stranger what he'd never managed to tell anyone? Not even in therapy, not even Gina. It would be too great a betrayal. That was the thing with lies. Like the gnarled and twisted pine trees that grew along the Front Range, the longer they lived the stronger they became. One of the ravens swerved in front of them on a gust of warm wind and it gave Tom the chance to end the conversation. He stood up.

'I'm getting hungry, how about you?'

'Sure.'

He called Makwi and she came trotting out of the trees, panting after what had obviously been another hectic hunt.

'Do we have to go look for a body?' Karen said.

'Did your mother get another cat?'

They walked back down the trail and hardly spoke until they reached the house. Tom poured her a glass of red wine and a soda for himself and

236

then set about cooking the steaks. Karen O'Keefe lit the candles out on the deck then came back in and sat at the kitchen table and put the salad together.

The last time they'd seen each other, he'd given her the tapes of the interviews he'd recorded with the old Blackfeet about the Holy Family Mission. She was buzzing with ideas about how they might be used in the film she was determined the two of them would make. He leaned against the divider and watched her ripping up the lettuce as she went on about it. He liked the way she talked. It was a kind of western drawl, both nonchalant and earnest at the same time.

The steaks were good. And while they ate he got her talking about herself. About going to college in Boulder, then after that to UCLA film school, about some of the documentary films she'd made since. The subjects were mostly social and environmental issues and sounded quite radical both in style and content. One she'd made, about a coyote-killing contest in a small town in Wyoming, had won an award the previous year at Sundance. One of the hunters had sent her a note saying if she ever dared show her face there again, she'd get the same welcome they extended to coyotes. The film she was working on at the moment, she said, was about Iraq war veterans.

Tom took a sip of soda.

'Oh, really?'

'Yeah. I'm going to call it *Walking Wounded.* It's about how everybody thinks the casualties of the war are the ones who get injured and killed, which on one level is true, of course. But the *real* casualties are the hidden ones, all these young

237

guys—and women too—who come home so fucked up by what they've seen and what they've done that their whole lives are ruined—not to mention the lives of those they come back to.'

She paused. She was clearly waiting for him to say something.

'Sounds interesting.'

Tom's spirits were sinking fast. So this was what it was all about. He felt dumb to have been so blinded by his own vanity, to have imagined that she'd called because she was attracted to him. He was simply her conduit to Danny.

'You've gone all quiet on me,' she said.

'I'm sorry.'

'No, I'm sorry. I heard about your son. I should have said something.'

'No. Why should you?'

'Because now you're thinking that's the only reason I'm here.'

'It had crossed my mind.'

'Shit.'

She got up and walked to the rail and stood there staring down at the creek, hugging herself as if against the cold. Somewhere down in the cottonwoods an owl called. The candles were guttering in their glass jars. The light wobbled and flickered on her dress. Tom could see how upset and embarrassed she was and he suddenly felt mean. What the hell did it matter why she was here? Whatever her motives, he enjoyed her company and that was all that should count. In her position he would probably have done the same. He told himself to grow up.

'Karen?'

She turned to look at him and he saw she was

close to tears.

'I'm so sorry if that's what you think,' she said.

'I don't. Please come and sit down.'

'Because it isn't true.'

'Please.'

She walked slowly back to the table and sat down, her arms still tightly folded.

'Shall we have some of the world's best ice cream?' he said.

'No, thanks. I couldn't.'

'I want to tell you about Danny.'

'Please, Tom. You don't have to.'

'I want to. Honestly I do.'

He filled her glass with wine and then leaned back in his chair and began. He spoke, briefly, of his divorce and the gradual estrangement from his son. Of how jealous he'd been of Dutch. About the resentment and guilt and the shocking argument they'd had over Danny's enlisting. Then he confessed the true purpose of his visit to California and gave her Danny's account of what had happened on the night of the killings. And she listened without once interrupting and when he had finished he could see she was moved. She reached out across the table and took his hand and they sat like that for what seemed a long time, neither of them speaking. All but one of the candles had gone out.

'Thank you,' she said quietly.

Tom nodded and smiled.

'Does he have a good lawyer?'

'Just the one the military gave him. I said from the start he ought to have someone independent. But Gina and Dutch won't hear of it.'

'What does Danny think?'

239

'To begin with he agreed with them. But now he thinks he's being made a scapegoat, he's not so sure anymore. We've got to find him someone good.'

She was still holding his hand. Tom gently disengaged.

'It's getting cold,' he said.

Despite his protests she insisted on clearing the table and carrying the dishes back into the kitchen. She even loaded them into the dishwasher for him.

'The vacuum cleaner's over there in the closet when you're done,' he said.

She laughed and turned to face him and they stood for a moment looking at each other. It was only fleeting but he knew from the look in her eyes that if he were to step toward her and kiss her, there would be no rejection. What stopped him he wasn't sure. Maybe it was simply the difference in their ages or else some lingering doubt about her motives.

'Your mom will be wondering where you are.'

It was such a crass remark he cursed himself even as he uttered it.

'Wow, yeah. Don't want to get grounded.'

'I'm sorry. I didn't mean—'

'No, you're right. It's time I was going.'

He walked out with her to her car and she thanked him for dinner and said she'd enjoyed herself. Makwi had come out with them and Karen O'Keefe stroked her and said goodbye then gave him a chaste kiss on the cheek. Tom stood and watched her drive away until the taillights vanished and the silence slowly reconfigured. He glanced down and saw Makwi staring despondently up at him. You blew it, the dog was telling him.

'What are you looking at?'
And they walked back into the house.

NINETEEN

The trail stretched away ahead of them along the flank of the ridge, a ribbon of red dust winding north among the silver green sage. There were boulders on either side, one as big as a house that jutted out over the trail so that they had to duck down beside the necks of their horses. On the slope below them was a grove of oaks whose leaves rustled and clattered in the breeze and through them every so often came a glimpse of brighter green where the valley bottomed out by a creek and turned to grass.

It was the end of May and the weather was getting a little hotter every day. Not that there really was what you'd call *weather* in LA. It was always sunny and warm. The only thing you ever heard anybody complain about was the smog.

Tommy was leading on Chester, the sure-footed little paint pony he always rode. Cal was behind him on Amigo. Tommy liked it when it was just the two of them though it was fun too when Diane rode with them, which she had been doing a lot lately. She had to know how to ride for the movie she and Ray were going to be doing and, thanks to Cal, she was already pretty good. She would have come with them this afternoon but the studio had called her in for some last-minute hair and makeup tests.

Just three more days of school and at the

weekend they would be heading off to Arizona to start filming. Tommy was so excited that for the past few days he'd hardly been able to think or talk about anything else. For two whole months they were going to be *on location*. Ray said they'd be able to go and see Monument Valley where all those great John Ford movies were made. And Cal was coming too, to look after the horses and be Ray's stunt double.

Suddenly Chester skittered sideways and reared and Tommy just managed to grab the horn of the saddle to save himself from falling off. Cal rode up alongside and soon had the horse calm again.

'Why did he do that?'

Cal pointed up the slope and Tommy saw a black-and-white snake slithering into a crack in the rocks.

'Wow, is it a rattlesnake?'

'California king snake.'

'Are they poisonous?'

'No. The rattler's the only poisonous one around here. Hey, Tom, you did well to stay on board then.'

Tommy liked the way he called him Tom. In fact he liked everything about Cal. He knew the name of every plant and tree and bird and animal. Tommy pestered him with questions and tried not to forget anything he was told. He knew that in California there were seven different kinds of hawk, eight kinds of lizard and eighteen kinds of snake, though he'd seen hardly any of them. He only wished he hadn't boasted, on one of their early rides together, about shooting birds with his BB gun in Ray's garden. Cal had frowned.

'Do you kill them to eat them?'

'Of course not.'

'So why would you want to kill them?'

Tommy hadn't known what to say. He nearly blamed it all on Ray who'd shown him how to do it. But that wouldn't have been fair because the truth was he enjoyed doing it, enjoyed the stalking and being a good-enough shot to hit them. Wally Freeman liked doing it too when he came back to the house after school sometimes. The two of them would dress up and pretend to be Hawkeye and Chingachgook hunting in the forest.

Cal's question had made him feel ashamed. And later when he thought about it Tommy realized the answer was that he was simply curious. The birds were so free and quick-witted that you could never get near them. But if you shot them you could actually get to touch them and hold them and see how beautiful they were. Though when the thrill of the kill was over and he held the limp and lifeless little body in his hands and felt the warmth fading from it, he always felt a pang of remorse. After that conversation with Cal, he had vowed to himself that he would never again shoot any living creature.

Cal said there used to be a lot more wildlife up here in the hills but the way the city was starting to spread was driving the animals away. Only last week the two of them had ridden out the other way from the ranch, up onto a hill where they'd stood the horses and looked down on the bulldozers that were stirring great clouds of dust as they cleared the land for a new freeway. Cal said Mr Maxwell, who owned the ranch, had been offered a lot of money by a real estate company that wanted to build houses on the land. Every time he turned

243

them down, they offered more, Cal said. It was only a matter of time.

That same day they'd seen mule deer and gophers and a coyote. Most exciting of all, in a patch of dried mud beside a creek, they'd come across the tracks of a mountain lion. The paw marks were enormous. Cal said there were lots of mountain lions around but you rarely got to see them unless one jumped down from a tree and bit the top of your head off, which was how they liked to attack. Since then Tommy had scanned every tree they rode under. Cal said there were lots of mountain lions back home in Montana. And lots of grizzly bears as well which were even more dangerous, especially if you came across a mother with a cub. There used to be wolves too but they'd all been trapped or shot.

Tommy loved to get Cal talking about growing up in Montana. His mother was full-blood Blackfeet born on the reservation near a town called Browning which Cal said was a pretty dismal place. His father was a white man and they lived on a little ranch farther south on the Front Range of the Rocky Mountains. His great-grandfather on his mother's side of the family was almost a hundred years old and could remember the days when they used to hunt buffalo. There were once enormous herds of them, Cal said. So many that the land sometimes looked black. But then the railroad came and they all got shot too. Fifty million of them in little more than ten years.

'So, did they give you a part in the movie yet?' Cal said.

Tommy laughed.

'Not yet. Ray says he's working on it.'

'We'll have to figure something out. Maybe I'll just have to give you a job as a wrangler.'

The movie was called *The Forsaken*. Everybody said the script was brilliant. Tommy had tried reading it but all the scene numbers and camera directions—exteriors and interiors and fades and pans and tracking shots, all that sort of stuff—got in the way and he couldn't really tell what was going on. But Diane had told him the story. It wasn't exactly a western, at least not the sort of western Tommy liked. There were cars and planes in it and people talking on the telephone and not a single Indian.

It was more of a love story than anything. Diane was to play an Englishwoman called Helen who was married to a rich man called Dexter Dearborn. They lived on a beautiful ranch at the edge of the desert but Dexter wasn't at all nice to her or to anybody else for that matter. He owned an oil company and was always away on business or sneaking off to town to visit his girlfriend, so Helen got really sad and bored and lonely. Until Dexter's brother Harry came to stay.

This was Ray's part. Harry had once been a famous rodeo rider but had been badly injured and forced to retire and was now broke and sad and lonely and drank too much, but was basically a really nice guy. To help him out, Dexter had given him the job of looking after the ranch. Of course, this being a movie, Helen and Harry had to fall in love and for a while everything, as Diane said, was lovey-dovey and hunky-dory. But not for long. One night Dexter arrived home unexpectedly and caught them kissing and started hitting Helen. So Harry went to the rescue and in the fight that followed killed Dexter and got sent to the electric chair, so it all ended in tears. Nobody seemed to know why the movie was called *The Forsaken*, but Ray said that didn't matter, it was just a good title.

The fact that it was going ahead seemed to have made everybody happy again after all the bad things that had happened at the end of last year. Along with the wedding of course.

Ray and Diane had married last month on the day after the Russians sent Yuri Gagarin up into space (though Ray said this hadn't actually happened and was all faked in a TV studio and that the Americans got there first when they sent Alan Shepard into space three weeks later).

Ray had been keen to make the wedding a big event and invite lots of people but Diane hadn't wanted that so in the end it was just the three of them. They drove to Las Vegas in the open Cadillac and stayed in an enormous suite in a wonderful new hotel called the Tropicana. They were treated like royalty and were even given a chauffeur-driven Rolls-Royce to ride around in. The next morning they got up before dawn and drove for hours across the desert to see the Grand Canyon which was so vast and strange it was like being on the moon or Mars or somewhere.

The following evening, back in Vegas, Ray and Diane got married in a little chapel that was decorated with thousands of fairy lights. Diane looked amazing. Her dress was made of white satin covered in rhinestones and she had white lilies in her hair. Tommy wore a white suit that had been made specially for him by one of the costume designers at Paramount. Ray was in a white suit too and they had matching white Stetsons and

246

bootlace ties. The priest had black hair all slicked back like Elvis and for a moment Tommy thought that's who he actually was.

The wedding was supposed to be a secret but somebody must have tipped off the newspapers because when they came outside there were lots of photographers and the three of them had to stand there on the steps smiling blindly at the popping flashbulbs while everybody shouted *Diane! Ray! Over here! Diane!* One of them even called out *Tommy!* It was the first time in his life he had ever felt famous. The following day they flew to Hawaii for the honeymoon and there were photographers there too and a picture of the three of them with garlands around their necks was on the front page of the local newspaper.

'Okay, Tom, shall we let these guys have a run?'

By now he and Cal had ridden down through the oaks and into the valley where the ground was flatter and greener and the air smelled warm and sweet. Tommy gently pressed his heels into Chester's sides the way Cal had shown him and the little paint launched himself forward. They loped along the creek and for the final few hundred yards took the horses up to a gallop. Tommy loved the thundering thump of the hooves and the rush of warm wind in his face. His hat blew off but Cal leaned out of his saddle and plucked it off the ground and handed it back to him when they slowed back to a walk. They rode up out of the valley and along the narrow dirt trail that skirted the final hill and then they saw the corrals and Cal's little house below them and Diane waiting for them beside the yellow Galaxie. She waved.

'How's my star pupil?' Cal said as they rode up.

247

'Hey, I thought I was your star pupil,' Tommy said.

They laughed.

'That's what he tells all his pupils,' Diane said. 'Wish I could have come with you fellas. How was the ride?'

'We saw a California king snake.'

'You did?'

'They're not poisonous though. The rattler's the only poisonous one around here. Chester spooked but I stayed on, didn't I, Cal?'

'You sure did. Stuck there like glue. He did good. I'll be out of a job if he gets any better.'

They got off the horses and led them to the corral. Tommy unhitched Chester's cinch and lifted off the saddle and hung it over the rail then rubbed the horse's back where he was all sweaty. Cal said they loved this. Then Tommy led both horses to the water tank and stood watching them drink while Cal and Diane chatted by the car. Since Diane started riding, the two of them had become really good friends.

On the way home Tommy asked her why someone as nice as Cal didn't have a wife and Diane said sometimes it took a long time to meet the right person and anyhow not everybody wanted to get married. Some people just liked it better living on their own.

'If you'd met Cal before you met Ray, would you have wanted to marry him?'

Diane laughed.

'What's so funny about that?'

'Nothing. Just you and your questions.'

*   *   *

248

They flew to Arizona in Herb's Lockheed Lodestar, watching its shadow slide below them. The mountains were pink and corrugate and gashed with dried-out riverbeds and secret lakes that flashed the lowering sun at them. Tommy got a second chance to see the Grand Canyon and they gazed down on it trying to figure out where they'd stood the previous month but the scale was too immense to make sense of. A little later Herb told the pilot to make a detour so they could take a look at Monument Valley and they flew in low with tilted wings and circled among the towers that blazed red and vast like the fiery citadels of some wasted race of giants, their eastern walls shadowed and purple against an orange sky.

Herb was sitting beside Tommy at the window and he kept pointing out the landmarks, places where Ford had shot famous scenes for *The Searchers* and *Stagecoach*. Tommy watched wide-eyed and even though Ray had seen the place before, he too felt a kind of childlike awe. He put his arm around Diane and she smiled and nuzzled against his neck and kissed him.

Ray had never believed in fate or destiny or whatever else people liked to thank or blame for what befell them. If everything was preordained, etched in the sky by some invisible, almighty hand, leaving no scope for choice or change, what the hell was the point of being here? His philosophy was rather that life was like a mean cop who, given half a chance, would kick you in the balls. Sometimes, though, the sonofabitch got bored and looked away and that was when you had to grab all you could, like a shoplifter, stuff your pockets full

249

before he turned his evil eye back upon you. Survival was merely a matter of low cunning and had nothing whatsoever to do with luck. He had to concede however that during the past few months the cop seemed to have been more than usually distracted.

Just when Ray thought he'd lost it all—career, fiancée, self-esteem, the whole damn shooting match—suddenly here he was, flying high with one of Hollywood's big-shot producers, married to the woman of his dreams and about to become what he'd always known he could be and should be: a real movie star.

He'd never heard back from Jack Warner about what he thought of *The Forsaken*. The idiot had probably filed the script in the garbage the moment the meeting was over. This was, after all, the same genius who'd turned down *Gone with the Wind*, saying nobody would want to go see a picture about the Civil War. It gave Ray a twinge of vindictive pleasure to think that the old bastard would doubtless know by now that *The Forsaken* was happening without him at another studio.

That this should be so was entirely thanks to Herb Kanter and his unwavering belief (and considerable investment) in Diane. It had been the quickest deal Ray had ever known. Once she'd flown back after Christmas and forgiven him and everything between them was okay again, Diane had at last read Steve Shelby's script. She loved it and agreed there was a great part for her. She showed it to Herb who read it that same night and said he loved it too. He got Terence Redfield on board to direct, pitched it to Paramount and bingo: the following day the suits gave them the green

250

light.

Almost the entire crew who'd been geared up for the Gary Cooper picture were simply going to move across to *The Forsaken*. Poor old Coop had finally pegged out just a couple of weeks ago. Along with the rest of the nation, Ray had mouthed all the right sentiments, of course: what a tragedy, what a terrible loss it was et cetera. But secretly he saw the great man's demise as a blessing, a useful narrowing of the competition.

He later learned that Redfield, the sneaky little shit, had tried to get Steve McQueen or Bill Holden to play Harry—even though the part, the whole movie, for christsake, had been written with Ray in mind. Luckily both these assholes were tied up with other projects and Herb managed to convince Redfield that casting the former Red McGraw as a washed-up rodeo star had the kind of resonance the public loved. Added to which there was great publicity to be had from Ray and Diane being a real-life couple. In this, Herb had already been proved right. Both Louella Parsons and Hedda Hopper had written about it and every paper and magazine that printed their wedding pictures had also mentioned the movie by name. Tipping off those snappers in Las Vegas was the best stroke Ray had pulled in a long time.

The downside was that his fee for the movie was peanuts and the budget and shooting schedule were tight as a rat's ass. This was because there were no big-name stars involved and because Paramount's financial woes were getting worse by the day. For sure, making *The Forsaken* was going to be tough. But what the hell. It was a movie, a real big-screen movie. Montane and Reed, up

251

there together at last. The thought of it almost gave him a hard-on.

By the time they reached Medicine Springs the sun had gone down and the airstrip was but a dim black scar on the fading red of the desert. As the Lodestar touched down it caught a gust of wind and bounced and lurched sideways and everyone gasped then laughed when it steadied. They climbed out and the air was still hot and Diane stood with her eyes closed, breathing in deeply and saying how she loved the smell of the desert. Ray pretended to agree but in truth it carried too many memories of his drilling days, backbreaking work and eating dirt on some godforsaken Texan plain.

Frank Dawson, the line producer, was waiting to meet them with his assistant and a couple of brand-new Chevy trucks. Ray had never worked with the guy but had heard only good things about him, that he was tough but fair. He was six-foot-six with the chest of a bull wrestler. They all shook hands and Frank put their bags in the back of one of the trucks. Herb had to go straight into a series of meetings and went off with the assistant, saying he'd see them in a couple of hours at the little get-together he'd arranged at the Hungry Horse. Frank would drive them to the motel.

Medicine Springs was a one-street town that squatted forlornly below a dome of red sandstone that Frank Dawson said was a thousand feet tall and was once some kind of sacred place for Indians. There were apparently some ancient rock paintings at the top of it, he said. The town had a hardware store, a Laundromat, a grocery store, a gas station, four bars (including the Hungry Horse) and, by the look of it as they drove

252

through, a world record for the number of mangy dogs. Three times Dawson had to stop and hoot the horn to get the varmints to move out of the road. There were groups of young Indian guys hanging around on the sidewalk, smoking cigarettes. They turned and watched without a flicker of a smile as the movie stars drove by in their gleaming vehicle.

'Are they Indians?' Tommy asked.

'Navajo,' Dawson said.

'They don't look very happy.'

'They sure don't.'

The production had booked every room in town. There were two motels and Dawson assured them they were staying in the nicer one, though this wasn't a word that sprang readily to mind when they pulled up outside. It stood on slightly raised ground at the southern edge of town. There was a big plastic cactus outside and a red neon sign that said *Motel Casa Rosa*. The last two letters were faulty and kept fizzing and flickering out.

The reception area was about ten feet square, painted a pale green and lit from the ceiling by a single fluorescent box. There was a small Mexican woman with sad eyes behind the desk. She nodded and smiled when Dawson introduced Ray and Diane, saying they were the movie's main stars who'd just flown in from Hollywood.

'Jesus, Frank,' Ray whispered while she turned to get the keys. 'This is the *nice* place?'

'I think I said *nicer*. You should see where I'm staying.'

They were in rooms six and seven, the woman told them as she led them around to the rear of the building, the best rooms they had, with a linking

253

door and *mountain views*. There was also a view of a rusty yellow bulldozer standing in a deep pit, piled around with earth. The woman announced proudly that this was to be the swimming pool.

'Terrific,' Ray said.

Something scuffled as the woman opened the door. The room was small and hot and dingy, the screens at the window torn. On a midget-sized table stood a big bouquet of flowers and a basket of fruit. There was a card from Herb, wishing them luck for the shoot.

'That's so sweet,' Diane said. 'Thank you.'

A cockroach scurried out from the fruit and disappeared over the edge of the table. Diane didn't notice but Tommy did and gave Ray a look.

'Frank,' Ray said. 'Can I have a word? Diane, why don't you show Tommy his room?'

Dawson followed him outside again and the two of them stood facing each other at the edge of the pit. Ray lit a cigarette and didn't offer one.

'Did I get the date wrong? Is it April first?'

'I'm sorry?'

'Is this some kind of joke? What are you doing, putting us in a shit-hole like this?'

'Ray, this is the best accommodation available. Sometimes it can be a little basic when you're on location. You have to make allowances.'

'Allowances! We've got a kid with us, for christsake! Did you see that roach? The goddamn place ought to be condemned. And don't tell me what it's like being on location, as if I'm some kind of wet-eared kid.'

For a long moment the two men stood staring at each other. The motel woman was watching. Dawson was the first to blink.

254

'I'll have a word with Herb.'

'Yeah. You do that, pal. We're not staying here, okay? You got that?'

Diane said that he'd been too harsh, but Ray told her she didn't understand how the movie business worked. These guys were paid to squeeze every goddamn cent and did this kind of thing to test you, to see what they could get away with. If you didn't stand up to them they walked all over you. You had to show them right from the start that they needed to treat you with respect.

Sure enough, within twenty minutes, Herb Kanter was on the phone saying he was sorry and that he was already trying to sort out somewhere better for them. A car for their personal use was on its way to them and would it be okay if Leanne, the girl they'd hired to be Tommy's nanny, came to see them first thing in the morning?

'Anything you need, Ray, please don't hesitate. Just call me.'

'See what I mean?' Ray said when he hung up.

TWENTY

The Hungry Horse stood on its own halfway along Main Street. Its front was coated with whitewashed adobe and it had slatted swing doors like a Wild West saloon. The interior was gloomy and smelled of spilled beer and smoke with undertones of things it was best not to think about but out the back was a pleasant enough courtyard with a jacaranda tree and long wooden tables and benches and strings of colored lights. The food was basic—steaks and ribs and burgers and a chili con carne hot enough to make smoke come out of your ears.

Presiding over this from his bar stool throne beside the jukebox that stood on the back porch was a cadaverous Norwegian who, for unknown reasons, called himself Chico and everybody else either *hombre* or *señorita*. There were signed pictures on the walls of him embracing various uncomfortable-looking minor celebrities. Palpably thrilled that, for the first time in years, a movie had come to town, Chico made everyone on *The Forsaken* feel welcome. And as there was no real competition for fifty miles or more, the Hungry Horse had quickly become the main social haunt for cast and crew.

It was here that Herb had hosted the party that first weekend. Ray and Diane had been toasted and feted and Terry Redfield had made a short but generous speech, welcoming everybody and telling them what a privilege it was to be working with such talent. Ray, after too many tequilas, had responded in kind but at much greater length and Diane had needed to tug his coattail to get him to sit down.

Now, a week later, the photograph of Ray and Diane with Chico already in pride of place behind the bar, everyone was here again. Tomorrow was a rest day and the mood was both lively and relaxed. Chuck and Tony, two of Cal's wranglers, had brought along their guitars and were playing country songs and the latest rock-and-roll hits. They'd even played 'Running Bear' for Tommy before he slumped against Diane's shoulder and fell asleep. Leanne had just taken him back to the house. The boy had been spending every day with Cal and the wranglers, helping out with the horses. He was having the time of his life and came home so blissfully tired he could barely stay awake for his supper.

The house Herb had found for them was just along the road from the ranch that was the movie's main location and where most of the shooting was taking place. It was small and spartan but a much better place for them to be than the Casa Rosa. Herb himself was staying in a smaller house half a mile down the road. Both of the houses and the ranch too belonged to some property tycoon from Flagstaff, who was no doubt as happy as Chico that Hollywood had come to town.

Diane was happy too. She'd only had two beers but they'd gone straight to her head. It was good to be working again and she'd had a great week. Apart from the heat. It was hotter here than any place she'd ever been, well over a hundred degrees by midmorning. The house had no air-conditioning and if you stepped out without shoes, the soles of your feet almost sizzled like steaks. But at least it was a dry kind of heat and in the evenings there was generally a breeze.

She was sitting at the end of one of the long tables with Herb and John Grayling who was playing her husband in the movie. He was blond and handsome, like an old-fashioned matinee idol which was probably why Ray had taken against him. Diane liked him a lot. He was always friendly and funny and had an endless supply of indiscreet stories about the stars he'd worked with. He'd just had them in fits with one about the day he got trapped wearing only a towel in a hotel elevator with Lana Turner and an amorous chimpanzee.

Scurrilous stories aside, Johnny Grayling was a fine actor. He and Diane had already done two important scenes together and there had been a palpable charge between them. Diane hadn't seen the dailies but Terry Redfield and Herb were thrilled. Sadly, there was nothing like the same enthusiasm for Ray's work.

They weren't happy with anything he did. Terry demanded take after take of almost every shot. Only this evening poor Ray had again come home in a rage, saying if it went on much longer he'd end up strangling the guy. Diane hugged him and tried to soothe him, telling him it was early days and it would all work out but this only seemed to make him madder.

The two of them had been so very happy these past months, happier than they'd ever been. But for the past two days he'd been sullen and brooding and had barely spoken to her or to Tommy. And last night, when she said she was too tired to make love, he'd stormed out of the house in a fury and didn't come back until just before dawn. She had no idea where he'd gone.

'Come on, Diane, let's dance.'

Chuck and Tony had started to play 'Let's Twist Again' and Johnny was on his feet beside her, holding out his hand. Diane laughed and got up and he led her out onto the little patch of baked earth that passed for a dance floor. They were the first couple out there but soon four or five others took the cue and joined them. Johnny wasn't much of a dancer and pretended to be even worse, just to make her laugh.

Diane looked around for Ray but couldn't see

258

him anywhere. He'd already had a lot to drink and had been getting loud. She could also tell from his eyes that he was more than a little stoned. He knew how much she hated him smoking pot and he'd promised many times to stop. Instead he just sneaked out and did it on the quiet. Which was probably what he was doing right now. He had a brown paper bag of the stuff hidden in his suitcase under the bed along with the snub-nosed revolver that for some reason he always traveled with too, even on their marriage trip to Vegas. He said you never knew what might happen.

She spotted him now, coming into the yard through the gate that led to the parking lot. He was with Denny, his new best buddy, one of the construction crew, a young guy with straggly hair and a leather vest, who never seemed to take off his sunglasses. It wasn't hard to guess that they'd been smoking. Ray saw her dancing with Johnny and she waved but he looked away without a smile. Instead he walked over and said something to Tony and Chuck and they stopped what they were playing and started up again with 'Johnny B. Goode.' It might have been funny were it not for that mean look in his eyes. Johnny just smiled.

'Do I detect some kind of message from the master?'

'I can't think what you mean.'

It was just like that night at Herb's when he'd been jealous of her dancing with Bill Holden. But she was damned if she was going to let herself be bullied out of having a good time. She took hold of Johnny's hands and they started to jive. He was a lot better at this than he was at the twist and soon they had all the moves going and people noticed and started to clap and whoop.

Diane knew Ray was watching but she didn't care.

*   *   *

'And ... action!'

Ray came out of the barn carrying the saddle and walked over to the corral with the camera tracking along beside him, just a few feet away. The horse was tied to the rail and when he got there he had to swing the saddle over its back. That was when Diane's character, Helen Dearborn, called out his name and he had to turn and look at her. It was an important moment in the story, the first time Harry laid eyes on the woman he was going to fall in love with. And it was Ray's first big close-up. Diane was standing off camera, ready to deliver the line—again. This was the fifth take.

'And cue Helen.'

'You must be Harry,' Diane said.

Ray turned and gave her the look, tightening his jaw muscles and slightly lifting an eyebrow. He'd seen Gary Cooper do it many times. Cary Grant too. It wasn't quite a double take, more a slow registering of what a beautiful woman his brother was married to.

'And cut,' Terence Redfield said.

He stepped out from behind the camera.

'Once more, please, folks.'

The makeup woman stepped in again to dab the sweat from Ray's face but Redfield asked her to give them a minute. He put his arm around Ray's shoulders and led him aside a few paces so that

260

nobody else could hear. Ray was seething but trying not to show it. This was the first scene he and Diane had done together and this jumped-up little shit was clearly out to humiliate him in front of her. Redfield still had his arm around him, like he was some goddamn father figure or mentor.

'Ray, that was better, but—'

'It's okay, you told me a hundred times already. *Less is more*, right?'

'It's not just that. All I want is for you to be yourself. She's a stunning, beautiful woman. The look you're giving her is maybe a little, well . . .'

'A little what?'

'Well, maybe just . . . a little too much.'

'Right. *Less is more*.'

Over Redfield's shoulder Ray could see everyone, including Diane, pretending not to look, chatting as if nothing special were going on here, studiously ignoring them. Even Tommy, who was helping Cal with the horse, was avoiding his eyes. But the air around them hummed with tension.

'The thing is, Ray. You've got such a powerful, expressive face; all you—'

'Don't give me that bullshit.'

'I'm sorry. All I'm trying to say is—'

'Listen, I'm not some fucking kid, okay?'

'Don't be like that, Ray.'

'Don't be like what? You've been on my back ever since we started. All that patronizing shit about how this isn't TV. I mean, who do you think you are, Cecil fucking B. DeMille?'

'I'm sorry you feel that way, Ray.'

'Listen, pal. I know you didn't want me in the first place—'

'That's not—'

'I *know*, okay? But at least you could try just treating me with a little respect.'

Nobody was pretending not to look anymore. The whole unit was openly staring. Ray felt like he was in high school. Redfield turned and quietly summoned Joel Davis, the first assistant director, who walked toward them.

'Joel, let's take an early lunch, okay?'

'Yes, sir.'

Joel called the break and told everyone to be back on set in an hour.

'Let's both cool down and talk about this later,' Redfield said.

'Whatever you say.'

'Ray, trust me. It'll be okay.'

'Yeah, sure.'

Redfield walked away and Ray stood for a moment with his head down, glaring at his boots and at his shadow on the red dust. Then he swung a leg and kicked a rock that went skidding off across the corral.

His trailer was hot as hell and he took off his shirt and lay on his back on the couch and stared for a long time at the ceiling. One of the catering girls knocked on the open door and came in with his usual steak and salad and a glass of orange juice and Ray thanked her and said just to leave it, he wasn't hungry.

He couldn't take much more of this shit. Maybe he should just walk, tell them he quit. Over the years he'd worked with scores of directors, some good, some bad and some downright hopeless. He'd gotten along with nearly all of them. He wasn't what people liked to call *difficult*. He could take direction. In fact he'd always been open to suggestion, welcomed it even, was always happy to take good advice on board. But never, not in all those years, had any of them gone so far as to challenge his talent or undermine his technique like this little fuck seemed set on doing.

There was clearly some other agenda and Ray couldn't figure out what it might be. Maybe it was something to do with Diane. They all had the hots for her, the riggers, the wranglers, that little faggot Grayling who couldn't keep his hands off her last night. Even Herb Kanter. Every goddamn one of them. You could see their tongues hanging out every time she breezed by. Maybe that was what Redfield was up to. Directors always wanted to screw their leading ladies, after all, and often did. If the male lead hadn't got there first. The little shit probably figured if he could get Ray out of the way, make life so unpleasant for him that he walked, he might be in with a chance. Well, fuck him. Walk? The hell he would.

'Ray?'

It was Tommy at the door.

'Hi, son. Come on in.'

He swung his legs off the couch and sat up. The boy had quite a tan. Ray patted the couch and Tommy came and sat down beside him.

'How're you doing? Got those horses sorted out?'

'Yes.'

'How's that Leanne girl shaping up?'

'She's okay. She's nice.'

'What with you spending all day with Cal, I guess she doesn't have a whole lot to do, huh?'

'I suppose not. Are you all right?'

'Yeah, sure. Why?'

263

'I don't know. You didn't look very happy just now. With Mr Redfield.'

'Oh, I'm okay, buddy. Sometimes people have different ideas and things can get a little tense. It'll all sort itself out. Where's your mom?'

'Having something to eat with Mr Redfield. She said to tell you she'd be coming over in a minute.'

'Oh. Well, thanks for doing that.'

They were silent for a moment, Tommy staring into space, kicking the heels of his new cowboy boots against the couch. Ray suddenly felt bad about not having paid the kid much attention these past days.

'How about the three of us taking a ride this evening?'

'Cal and I are going up the mountain to see the rock paintings.'

'Oh, okay.'

'I'm sure he wouldn't mind if you came too.'

'We'll see.'

'I'd better go now.'

The boy went and Ray stood up and stretched then went to stand in front of the long mirror on the closet door, wiping the sweat off his chest. His face was drawn and tense around the eyes. God, he was starting to look old. He turned sideways and tried to shift his mind into character. Tending the saddle, Helen coming up unseen beside him. *You must be Harry.* He turned and looked into the mirror again. A little less tightening of the jaw, maybe. Lose the lifted eyebrow. Do it with the eyes, just the eyes. Real intense, seeing her, knowing her. That was it. That was good.

Diane suddenly appeared in the corner of the mirror. She was in the doorway behind him.

'Hi.'

'Hi.'

'Can I come in?'

'Sure.'

She walked toward him, tentatively, as if unsure what kind of welcome to expect. The sight prompted in him both anger and desire. They hadn't spoken since last night. She had left the party before him and was asleep when he got back. Her call this morning had been earlier than his and when he woke she'd already gone. They hadn't made love for a week.

She stopped in front of him and laid her hands on his bare chest.

'Where have you gone?' she said quietly.

'What do you mean?'

'You know what I mean. You've gone all cold and distant.'

'I'm right here.'

She tilted her face and hesitantly kissed him on the lips. For a moment, ridiculously, childishly, he didn't respond but then he opened his mouth and kissed her. He put his hands on her hips then slid them under her shirt and slowly up following the curve of her body until he was holding her breasts.

'I want to fuck you,' he whispered.

'Darling, not now.'

'Come on.'

'Later.'

'Forget it.'

He shoved her away and she fell back against the table and the tray with his lunch and the glass of orange juice went crashing and spilling onto the floor.

'For godsake, Ray. What the hell's wrong with

you?'

'Just get out of here.'

*   *   *

They reached the top of the dome a little before five, the horses' hooves clacking and scraping on the hot sandstone. In the west the sky was stacking itself with bulbous, flat-bottomed clouds. There was no horse work in any of the scenes being shot that afternoon, nor any involving Diane, and since Ray didn't seem to want her support she'd decided to join Cal and Tommy on their ride. She wanted the company but still felt too hurt to talk so she let the two of them ride ahead. Tommy turned around twice to ask her if she was okay and she told him she was fine and to stop fussing. He and Cal hadn't stopped talking all the way. Thank God, she thought, that the boy had at least one man in his life who was sane and stable.

Cal had found an old Navajo in Medicine Springs who'd told him where they could find the rock paintings but it still took them a long time. At last they found the gully the old man had described. It ran north to south down one side of the dome like a knife crack in the top of a boiled egg. They left the horses to graze among the sage and scrambled down into the shadow and cool of the gully. In places the walls grew steep and there were crude steps and footholds carved in the sandstone and some had crumbled or been worn away so that Cal had to lift and lower Tommy and do almost as much for Diane.

Along one side of the gully ran a shelf some six feet wide where the rock had been scooped out to

266

make shallow caves. Cal said people used to live in these, people now known as the Anasazi, though this probably wasn't their real name. It was an old Navajo word for enemy.

'Just like what you told me about the Sioux,' Tommy said. 'How that was what their enemies called them.'

'That's right. The Oglala and Lakota and the others never called themselves the Sioux.'

'What happened to the people who lived here?' Diane asked.

'Nobody knows. They just vanished. About a thousand years ago.'

'Maybe they were their own worst enemies,' Diane said.

'It can happen.'

'It sure can.'

Cal looked at her and gave her a sympathetic smile and she could tell he knew the reference was to Ray.

They found the paintings in an overhang at the far end of the shelf. Only twenty yards farther the gully tilted into a dizzying chute down which you could see the outskirts of the town a thousand feet below. Cal found them a safe place to stand and the three of them stood staring up at the paintings. Diane remembered once seeing photographs of some cave paintings in France that showed hunting scenes, stick figures throwing spears and shooting arrows at running animals. But what was depicted here was quite different and it took her a while to work it out. There was a row of what looked at first like vases or bottles, each about six or seven feet tall. Some were in groups, others on their own, all a deep bloodred against the ochre of the rock. Then she realized that they were figures, silhouetted heads and shoulders, tapering to their base. They appeared to be cloaked or shrouded for there were no visible arms or legs. It was like some silent convocation of ghosts, watching and waiting. Diane shivered.

There was one among them that was larger and seemed to have wings and Tommy asked Cal what it was but he didn't know. Maybe it was some sort of eagle god or shaman, he said. He had seen figures like it once in a canyon in Utah a hundred miles farther north.

'Some of the rock paintings in this part of the world are thousands of years old,' he said.

'It's like they're telling us to go away,' Tommy said.

'Then maybe we should.'

They climbed out of the gully and sat on a shallow bench of stone and watched the shadows of the clouds pass across the mellowing red of the plain far below them. Tommy said the flat-bottomed clouds looked like ice cream floats. The ones over the mountains were starting to tinge with pink. Diane's horse, a stocky bay mare, had strayed a little and Tommy waded off through the sage to fetch her, leaving Cal and Diane alone. For a while neither of them spoke, just sat there gazing out at the mountains.

'Cal, how long have you known Ray?'

'Ten, twelve years, maybe.'

'Have you ever seen him upset like this before?'

He didn't answer for a moment. He picked up a stem of sage and began stripping off the leaves.

'I'm sorry. I shouldn't ask.'

'No, it's okay. He's having a hard time and this

picture means more to him than anything he's done. It's like what you said. Sometimes Ray can be his own worst enemy. Forgets who his friends are.'

'He doesn't seem to have any friends.'

'I guess he is kind of a loner.'

He was about to go on but then seemed to think better of it.

'What were you going to say?'

'Nothing much. Just that, with my kind of work, if something goes wrong, you just fix it, make sure you do it better the next time. But with acting, there are no mistakes. It's just you. Do something wrong, it goes right to the heart of who you are. Sorry, I don't know how to explain what I mean.'

'I understand.'

'I'm not saying there's no skill or technique involved. Of course there is. You gotta hit your marks, know what the camera's seeing, all that stuff. But when it all boils down, it's just you and what you are. And if someone rejects that, says that's no good, it's not your work they're rejecting, it's you. That's hard for anyone to take. But for actors it's even harder because . . . Hell, I shouldn't be talking to you like this.'

'Please, go on.'

'Well, because they're generally so darned insecure. They want approval. They want to be loved. We all do, of course, but with some actors it's like a hunger. And if they don't get it, they can fall apart.'

'Oh, come on, Cal. There are harder ways to make a living.'

'Not many that can do that kind of damage to a man's self-esteem. Please, don't get me wrong. I

269

think what you guys do is a kind of magic. Especially you. I've watched you and that's exactly what it is. You have a great gift.'

Tommy was tramping toward them now, leading Diane's horse. Cal stood up.

'Good work, Tom. We better be moving. It'll be getting dark.'

The three of them barely spoke on the way down. Diane listened to the clatter of the horses' feet and the skitter of broken rock and breathed the scent of the sage and piñon and juniper and watched the clouds go red and purple and darkness unfold itself across the plain and one by one the pinprick lights of the town below begin to glimmer. And she thought about what Cal had said and about the life she had made for herself and for her son, this blossoming child who rode between them. And about those watchful, waiting figures painted on the mountain.

TWENTY-ONE

It had been Karen O'Keefe's idea to contact Troop. She couldn't stand the guy or his macho books but said Tom had to admit it made sense. With all his military contacts Troop was better placed than anyone to help find a good civilian attorney to defend Danny. Tom needed a lot of persuasion. He hated asking favors even of friends and Troop would have been last on any list.

'Listen, the guy could be useful in all kinds of ways,' Karen said. 'I googled him. He's the US armed forces' most popular author. Having him on

270

Danny's side might not be such a bad idea. Think of the publicity.'

'That sounds like a good reason *not* to get him involved. He'll probably just turn us all into a novel.'

'Great,' Karen said. 'I'll make the movie.'

'I thought you already were.'

'Ouch.'

When Gina and Dutch had first heard that Tom had Danny's blessing to find a civilian lawyer, they were predictably angry. They clearly felt as if they had been sidelined. But Tom knew he had to deliver—and fast. After a week of research and many abortive phone calls, he ran out of options and concluded that Karen might have a point. Swallowing his pride and the Pavlovian envy any mention of Troop's name inspired, he picked up the phone one last time.

As luck would have it the Famous Author was at his Montana residence, no doubt dashing off another throbbing ten-million-dollar blockbuster. He told Tom to get in the car that very minute and drive down to see him. The *cabin*, as he liked to call it, was five miles outside Hamilton, less than an hour's drive from Missoula and, predictably, turned out to be more of a mansion that just happened to be built out of wood. There were tall metal gates that opened spookily as Tom approached and security cameras whirred as he passed, tracking his progress along the driveway that wound for a mile up through the forest. There was a small black helicopter on the lawn and a glinting ruby-and-chrome Hummer near the front porch with a beautiful young blonde about to leap in. Tom foolishly assumed this had to be Troop's

271

daughter but, of course, it turned out to be his girlfriend. Troop came out to greet him with a brave hug and a look overloaded with sympathy. He introduced him to Krista, who said a sweet hi and bye, kissed Troop lingeringly on the lips then thundered off in the Hummer.

The house had a travel brochure view of the mountains. The interior was lavish western chic, like an updated version of Ray's house only with more taste. It was all polished wood and stone and thick cream-colored rugs. There were elk and buffalo heads on the walls and Wild West paintings, including a Charlie Russell that Tom recognized. Troop's office was a kind of military command center the size of a small football field, with banks of computers and screens and flashing machines that were probably linked directly to the Pentagon. There were pictures of him on the walls with grunts and generals and politicians, including one on the White House lawn with George W. and Laura as well as countless framed bestseller lists with Troop's titles inevitably at number one.

They settled on the leather couch by the window and talked for an hour. Or rather, Tom talked, telling him about Danny and what had happened that night in Iraq. Troop listened, sipping a glass of ginseng tea and gravely stroking his beard.

'There's only one man for this,' he said when Tom had finished.

It sounded like a line from one of his thrillers— or perhaps all of them. Tom almost expected to hear movie music and the thump of chopper blades. Troop went to sit behind his immense desk and picked up one of the half-dozen phones.

The lawyer's name was Brian McKnight. He had

his own law firm in Detroit and specialized in defending cases of alleged military malpractice which, according to Troop, he was rarely known to lose. The two of them chatted and joked for a while and then Troop told him why he was calling and put the phone on speaker and introduced Tom.

McKnight seemed to know a lot about the case already.

'So, you were a Marine too,' he said.

'No, that's Danny's stepfather.'

'And is he okay about you bringing in an independent attorney?'

'Not yet. I guess he thinks it's disloyal or something.'

'That figures. It sometimes takes a while to understand that loyalty has its limits. Cases like this are about politics. But you all need to agree on this.'

'I'm working on it.'

They arranged to speak again in a couple of days when Tom had consulted with Gina and Dutch.

Troop got up from his desk and came to sit on the couch again.

'I watched the DVD of your Blackfeet film the other day,' he said. 'It's a hell of a piece of work.'

'Thank you.'

'I remember once, all those years ago, when we were on the UM writers' program, you reading out a short story you'd written about a young Blackfeet boy living on the reservation. It was the best thing I ever heard. I remember thinking, shit, I wish I was half as good as that.'

Tom laughed. Compliments always made him feel uneasy.

'I'm serious.'

'Well, thanks. We were all completely in awe of you.'

'Did you go on writing fiction?'

'Oh, I've got the usual drawer full of unfinished novels. They all kind of hit a wall halfway through.'

'That's a pity.'

They were silent for a moment.

'Thanks for doing this for us,' Tom said.

'You're welcome. If there's anything else, just let me know.'

* * *

It was easier than Tom had dared expect to persuade Gina that they should at least meet with Brian McKnight. The three of them flew down to San Diego the following week. In all the years since Gina left, Tom and Dutch had never really had a conversation. In fact the only times they'd ever met were when Tom picked Danny up or dropped him back home. Tom remembered the guy being tall and big, like a bear with a buzz cut. But when the three of them met at the airport, Dutch wasn't at all like that. He was shorter than Tom and not remotely like a bear. Tom realized he must have concocted an image of him that fitted the Marine cliché. They shook hands while Gina watched, trying not to look too anxious.

On the plane they sat three in a row with Tom in the middle and it took him a while to get over how strange that felt. Sitting next to the guy he'd hated for years, the one who'd stolen his wife and his only son, whose influence—you could at least argue—had landed Danny where he now was, in the dock. And here they were, eating pretzels and coffee and making polite conversation, while Gina pretended to be engrossed in her book.

McKnight had booked a room for them to meet at a hotel called the Bristol on First Avenue and he was already there with Danny when they arrived. Danny looked as if he'd forgotten how to sleep. There were dark rings under his eyes. The months of waiting were clearly taking their toll. He gave Tom and Dutch exactly the same, carefully measured welcome.

McKnight was a dour ramrod of a man with gold-rimmed glasses and a ginger seventies-style mustache. Over the next two hours, during which time he never once smiled, they discovered that he was a former Marine, an NCIS investigator and attorney and knew every murky corner of the labyrinth in which Danny was currently trapped. He had already read all the paperwork and said he had serious misgivings about the way Danny's defense was being conducted.

All now hinged on the Article 32 hearing, he told them. It was already scheduled for the first week in January. It was on the preparation for this that all their energy needed to be concentrated, McKnight said.

'What is this hearing exactly?' Tom asked.

'It's the military equivalent of a grand jury. Basically it decides whether there's a case to answer.'

'And if it decides there is?'

'Then the case proceeds to a court-martial.'

Gina cleared her throat.

'What's the worst that could happen?' she asked.

'The worst?'

McKnight paused for a moment. He looked at Danny.

'Well, ma'am. Your son already knows this. The US military hasn't passed a death sentence on one of its own in many years. But I have to tell you that the power to do so remains untouched.'

They didn't talk much on the flight back to Montana. When they said goodbye at the airport, Dutch shook Tom's hand and held on to it for a moment.

'Thank you, Tom, for doing this,' he said. 'I was wrong about getting an outside lawyer involved. I still find it hard to believe, but it looks like they were going to let the poor kid take the rap. With this guy McKnight on our side, maybe he stands a chance.'

That night, for the first time in many years, Tom dreamed about Diane. It was a kind of updated version of the dream he'd had again and again during the year before she went to the gas chamber. The one that used to leave him cowering in the corner of his bedroom, shrieking and clutching his head until the whole house was awake. It had never actually been about the moment of execution. The terror had been more insidious, a kind of creeping prelude: sitting with her in a darkened cell, footsteps coming closer down the corridor, a shadow below the door, an eye at the grille, the click of a key in the lock, the door beginning to open.

It was Karen O'Keefe who kept him level as the weeks went by and summer turned to fall. She was often away, doing research or shooting interviews for *Walking Wounded*. But whenever she was in Missoula, staying with her mother, she would drop by two or three times a week. They would have lunch or supper and then spend a couple of hours going through some of the research material for their film about the Holy Family Mission. She had in mind a dramatized documentary and had written an outline that Tom liked a lot. And she had delved around and turned up some interesting new material, including photographs Tom never knew existed. Better still, she had located a journal kept by one of the Italian Jesuit priests who had run the place.

They went for walks with Makwi, who seemed to like her just as much as Tom did. The three of them even occasionally went running together. It was all still strictly platonic, though not without substantial restraint on Tom's part. As for Karen's, he couldn't be sure. She seemed to like him a lot. And by now he knew much more about her. She was thirty-three years old and for the past seven years had been living in Vail, having an affair with a ski instructor who had apparently always kept promising to leave his wife but never did. Finally Karen did the leaving instead.

Tom remained confused about what he felt for her (or, more accurately, what it was appropriate to feel, for lust was an unruly beast and not so readily restrained). But what the hell. They enjoyed each other's company; she was fun to be around and she made him feel younger and more alive than he'd felt in years. The important thing was, he no longer doubted her motives. She made no secret of her continued wish to meet Danny and, should he prove willing, to interview him for *Walking Wounded.*

The opportunity would probably come at

277

Thanksgiving. Danny was flying home to spend the holiday with Gina and Dutch in Great Falls. Relations were now so amicable that Gina, remarkably, had invited Tom to join them for Thanksgiving dinner. He was touched but not sure he was ready for this and had gratefully declined, saying he'd already accepted a previous offer. Danny was going to come over to Missoula at the weekend. Apart from the minor matter of timing, the alternative offer turned out to be real, for the very next day Karen invited him to her mother's Thanksgiving dinner.

'She's been driving me crazy, asking when she's going to get to meet you. She says if you don't show up she'll come by and grab you.'

'I don't know which sounds the more exciting.'

'Dinner, believe me.'

For at least a decade, Tom had treated Thanksgiving and Christmas as if they didn't exist, turning down so many invitations nobody asked him anymore. Had it not come from Karen, he would certainly have turned this one down too. But when the day came he was glad he hadn't.

Lois O'Keefe looked at least five years younger than Tom knew she had to be—and so like her daughter it was uncanny. She had a wicked wit and teased him from the moment he arrived, mostly about the late and, it seemed, not unduly lamented Maurice.

'Tell you the truth, Tom, it was Norm who bought the wretched creature.'

'Norm?'

'My ex-boyfriend. He absolutely doted on him—rather more than he did on me, as it turned out. They even had the same blue eyes. After Norm

278

absconded, I found that a little disconcerting. As if the sonofabitch was still there, staring at me, checking up on me. Are you an absconder, Tom?'

'No, I think I'm technically an abscondee.'

'Ah, well, there we are. We have something in common. Here's to all abscondees.'

Apart from Tom and Karen, the other guests were a charming ragbag of the divorced and the displaced. There was a sweet elderly aunt from Chicago, a heart surgeon from Vancouver who was clearly one of Lois's old flames (according to Karen, there were a fair few of these), a University of Montana botany professor and her hunky but rather slow-witted boyfriend, and a suave, sad-eyed New Yorker called Günter who did something incomprehensible with other people's money and seemed slightly ashamed of it.

Tom sat between Lois and Karen and felt honored. The food was delicious and the conversation fun.

'So, Lois,' he said as she served him a second slice of pumpkin pie. 'I hear you're moving to France.'

'Oh, I don't know.'

'She changes her plans all the time,' Karen said. 'Last week it was Provence. This week it's Tuscany.'

'Ah, Tuscany.' Günter sighed into his glass.

'What's wrong with France?' the heart surgeon said. 'I mean, apart from the French.'

'I *adore* the French,' Lois said.

'They sure don't like us.'

'Nobody likes us. Tom, if you don't mind my asking, I mean, I know you've lived here most of your life, but are you still a Brit or . . . ?'

'Lois, I don't have the faintest idea what I am.'

Everyone laughed.

'I still have the passport, if that's what you mean.'

'But what do you *feel*?'

'You sound like my therapist.' He thought for a moment. 'To be honest, I've never really felt I belonged anywhere or to any country or tribe. Which isn't to say I haven't wanted to belong. Anyhow, nobody likes the Brits either anymore, so we're all in the same sinking boat.'

'Nonsense. I love the Brits,' Lois said decisively. 'Whenever I get the chance.'

'Mother,' Karen groaned.

Lois raised her glass.

'Here's to the good old sangfroid.'

They all dutifully joined in the toast.

'What does *sangfroid* mean?' the professor's hunky boyfriend whispered.

'It's French for cold-blooded,' Tom said. 'Like reptiles.'

'Nonsense,' Lois said. 'It's much stronger and more dignified than that. It means...composure.'

As Tom left, while Karen stood behind her mother, grinning and shaking her head, Lois held on to his hand and gazed into his eyes and said how much she'd enjoyed meeting him.

'We didn't get to talk about your wonderful Indian book and that fabulous film. There was so much I wanted to ask you about. I'm only over the hill—'

'You can say that again,' Karen quipped.

'Ignore my insolent daughter, Tom. Promise me you'll come again when all this noisy rabble isn't here.'

He promised and she put her hands on his shoulders and kissed him on both cheeks.

Danny and Kelly drove over from Great Falls two days later for lunch. He looked less pale and drawn and had put on a few pounds in the month or so since Tom had last seen him. They gave each other a long hug and then Danny introduced Kelly. She was small and pretty and when Tom shook her hand she gave him a shy smile with a look in her eye that showed she knew a lot more about him than he did about her.

The conversation over lunch was a little strained. The court hearing hung unmentioned but defiant in the air around them. Tom asked Kelly about her family and her work. She was the daughter of a Marine Corps sergeant and had some sort of civilian administrative job at Malmstrom Air Force Base and seemed very smart. The two of them clearly adored each other. Every so often, without looking, Kelly would reach out and hold Danny's hand.

Over coffee in the living room Danny cleared his throat and announced that the two of them were engaged to be married. They weren't going to make a big deal of it, he said, just do it quietly, after Christmas. Kelly blushed and Tom said what wonderful news it was and went off to rummage through the kitchen cupboards for a bottle of champagne he knew to be buried there. He found it and put it in the freezer and while it was chilling Karen arrived. Tom had invited her to join them for lunch but she said it might be better if she just dropped by afterward.

She'd brought along a stack of documents about the Holy Family Mission and some tapes for him

281

to watch. This was intended to signal the nature of her relationship with Tom, that it was strictly work, though Tom could see in Danny's eyes that the boy wasn't entirely convinced. The three of them sat chatting while Tom dusted the champagne glasses then they all drank a tepid toast—Tom with soda—to the forthcoming marriage, whose date had yet to be fixed.

As if working to a script, Danny asked Karen what kind of films she made and she told him about one or two of them, playing down the radical element, and finally, ever so casually, mentioned *Walking Wounded*. Tom watched his son carefully—and a little guiltily—to see if he suspected some sort of setup but he didn't appear to. And Kelly, bless her heart, even suggested that Karen should interview Danny for the film.

'Look what they're doing to us all,' she said, taking his hand. 'You risk your life for your country and this is how they treat you.'

Danny patted her knee as if to say that was enough. But when Karen was leaving he asked for her phone number and gave her his.

Defying all protest, Kelly said she'd clear up and wash the dishes. It was obvious she wanted to give father and son some time together so they put on their coats and took Makwi for a walk. They went up into the forest and halfway along the trail Danny asked if Karen was his girlfriend. Tom laughed, a little too loudly, and said absolutely not, they were just working on the mission film together. Danny looked relieved.

'I thought she seemed, well, you know, a bit ... young.'

'Absolutely.'

'I don't mean...'

'It's okay. I agree. Hell, I could be her dad.'

They reached the raven rocks and sat there awhile staring out across the valley. There were ribs of snow along the distant ridge, the blue winter light fading fast. Tom asked about the final preparations for the hearing and Danny said he and McKnight had gone through everything over and over again. They were as well prepared as they could be. He said McKnight was bullish about their chances but that was probably how he always was.

'Well, he doesn't often lose.'

'Dad, the case against me is pretty heavy. When Delgado gets up there on that stand... The guy hates my guts.'

They were silent for a moment. Tom put his arm around the boy's shoulders.

'Just tell the truth, son. It'll be okay.'

Danny nodded.

'There's something else Kelly and I wanted to tell you. I couldn't really say it in front of Karen.'

'Oh?'

'Kelly's going to have a baby.'

Tom didn't know what to say. Danny was watching him carefully.

'Wow. Is this, you know...I mean, was it planned?'

'Yes, of course it was.'

'How many, I mean when is the baby—'

'She's twelve weeks. It'll be early June.'

'Well, that's terrific news, son. Congratulations.'

'Thanks.'

'The timing's kind of interesting.'

'Dad, the timing's what it's all about. If the case

goes to court-martial and they find me guilty, then
...Well, you know what the sentence could be.
Kelly just wants to make sure we—she has some
kind of, you know, someone to...'

Tom pulled his son toward him and hugged him.
Damn it, he was going to cry and he so wanted to
be strong for the boy. He swallowed and managed
to hold back the tears. And then he laughed and
gave Danny a slap on the back.

'Hell,' he said. 'I'm going to be a grandpa.'

*   *   *

It was three weeks later that the Marine Corps
delivered their early Christmas present. Brian
McKnight got a phone call informing him that the
murder charges against the other defendant,
Eldon Harker, were being dropped. There had
been some kind of deal. Harker would be testifying
against Danny. It changed everything. The hearing
was rescheduled for the beginning of May.

TWENTY-TWO

Things got better before they got worse. Though
looking back on it later, after everything exploded,
Tommy would realize that things had never been
right and would blame himself for being stupid
ever to have thought otherwise. He was probably
just blinded by some lingering infatuation with
Red McGraw, the cowboy hero who didn't exist,
who couldn't do his own stunts, couldn't even ride
a horse properly and was as fake and fatuous as his

costume and the six-gun he twiddled on his finger. If only Diane could have met Cal before she met Ray, then everything would have worked out and they could all have been happy.

Tommy wasn't so blind that he hadn't noticed the tension during the first couple of weeks of the shoot. He was aware—the entire crew was aware and talked about it the whole time—that Ray and Mr Redfield weren't seeing eye to eye. And he could sense the tension between Ray and Diane, saw how he looked at her when she was having fun on set with John Grayling and how rude he'd been to Cal that evening when they came back late from their trip to see the rock paintings. The walls of the little house they were staying in were thin and almost every night Tommy could hear Ray and Diane shouting at each other.

But then everything seemed to calm down and for the next few weeks everybody was happier. Mr Redfield didn't make Ray do so many takes anymore and there weren't those long waits while the two of them walked off on their own and everyone had to stand around while they argued. Though once or twice since then Tommy had seen Mr Redfield sigh or give Mr Kanter a secret look that showed he wasn't as pleased as he wanted Ray to think.

Tommy meanwhile was having the time of his life. Every day he learned something new from Cal, whether it was about riding or wrangling or wildlife. Best of all, he liked to get him talking about the Blackfeet and the history of his family, the things they did and believed in, their hunting rituals and their ceremonies, the pipes and medicine bundles, all that kind of stuff. Cal even

285

taught him to speak a few words of the Blackfeet language and sometimes in the evening when they rode out into the desert, just the two of them, to exercise the horses, Tommy would ask Cal to test him.

'Okay, what's the word for mountain lion?'

'Omachk-atayo.'

'And what does it mean?'

'Big howler.'

'Good. Wolf?'

'That's easy. Makwi.'

'Moose?'

'Darn it, I always forget that one.'

'Sounds like a sneeze.'

'Siks-tsisoo!'

'Very good! And what does it mean?'

'Something coming through. Black! Black coming through.'

'Hey, Tom, you're doing real good. What's the word for friend?'

'Nitakau.'

They were riding side by side and Cal reached out and put his hand on Tommy's shoulder and said the word again.

'Nitakau.'

It was after one of these rides, just two weeks before the Arizona shoot was due to end, that Tommy found out about Ray.

It was getting dark and Cal was over at the far side of the corral seeing to one of the horses who'd taken a knock to the leg earlier in the day. Except for the hopeless old security guy a couple of hundred yards away at the ranch gate, there was nobody else around. Or that's how it seemed. Tommy had just put their saddles in the barn and was coming out the door when he heard a woman's laugh then someone hushing her. The sound had come from the roped-off parking lot about twenty yards away where they kept the trucks and actors' trailers. There were no lights on in any of them and Tommy began to think he must have imagined it, that all he'd heard was one of the horses whinnying or an owl or a coyote or something. Then he saw the door of Ray's trailer open and a woman step down from it. He froze. She looked around but didn't see him. Then she hurried off. It was Leanne; there was no mistaking it.

'Okay, young man, let's get you home,' Cal said. 'Your mom'll be wondering what I've done with you.'

Tommy didn't say anything. Cal obviously hadn't seen her. They got into the pickup and Cal started the engine and switched on the lights. As they drove past the trailer, Tommy looked sideways and saw, without any shadow of a doubt, Ray's face peeping out the window.

They caught Leanne in the headlights and she turned and smiled, shielding her eyes. Cal slowed and asked her if she needed a ride and she said thanks but no, she was just out for a walk.

When they reached the house, Diane came out to meet them.

'Don't you two ever get tired of each other?' she said.

Cal laughed and said goodnight and drove away.

Diane had Tommy's bath all run and ready for him and he lay in it worrying over what he'd just witnessed. The scene belonged to a world he wasn't old enough to assess. Maybe he was wrong and there was an innocent explanation. Since he spent most of his time with the wranglers, Leanne didn't have too much to do and had become a kind of assistant—mostly to Diane, but also to Ray. She'd go into town and get things from the store for them, take messages, that kind of thing. Maybe that was all she'd been doing at the trailer. Then he remembered other times he'd seen the two of them together, how Ray was always teasing her and making her giggle, how he'd seen him only yesterday on set, closely examining the palm of her hand, pretending to read her fortune. Sometimes you just knew things by the way people looked at each other. Maybe he should tell Diane. He should definitely tell her. But what if it wasn't true? Sometimes telling her things about Ray only got him into trouble. Like the other day when he'd repeated a joke that he'd overheard Ray telling Denny:

What do you tell a woman who's got two black eyes?

I don't know.

Nothing. She's already been told twice.

Tommy didn't understand it but Denny had laughed loudly so he knew it had to be funny. But when he tried it out on Diane, she got angry and told him never to say it again.

He got out and dried himself and cleaned his teeth at the sink. Diane was sitting on his bed, going on about something funny John Grayling had told her. Tommy pretended he'd been listening. He put on his pajamas and climbed into bed.

'You're very quiet tonight,' she said. 'Are you okay?'

'Just tired, I guess.'

She smiled down at him and stroked his hair.

'Look at you. You've gone completely blond.'

'How much longer are we going to be here?'

'Two more weeks. Then all we have left to do are the interiors, back at the studio. Why? Aren't you having a good time?'

Tommy nodded.

'I'm sleepy now.'

She kissed him on the cheek and told him she loved him and said goodnight.

Not long after she'd gone downstairs, he heard Ray come in and call to Diane that he was going up to take a shower. He peeped into Tommy's room but Tommy pretended to be asleep. Later he heard the two of them laughing in the living room and later still, when they had come upstairs, he heard them in their bedroom, heard the thumping of the bed against the wall, heard Diane cry out and Ray telling her to hush. Just as he'd told Leanne. Tommy blocked his ears and when at last silence fell upon the house, he lay for a long time, staring at the ceiling, hating Ray and feeling foolish for ever having liked him.

*   *   *

It had only lately occurred to Ray that the funny thing about power was that the ones who most flaunted it didn't always have it. These big-shot producers and directors wanted you to think you owed them everything, that you should be down on your knees kissing their goddamn boots for hiring you, that at a moment's notice they could fire you, just on a whim, and get some other sucker instead. But it was all bullshit, because they knew damn well that if they did fire you, they were basically admitting to the fat-assed suits back at the studio that they'd screwed up. And then the trades and the gossip vultures would get a whiff of it (nothing in Hollywood had such a pungent smell as failure) and they'd write it up and, lo and behold, the picture was dead on its feet and being flushed down the john before anybody even had a chance to see it.

The truth was that if you stood up to them, the bastards didn't have any power at all. And, thank God, Ray had understood this just in time. For the first two weeks, he'd allowed that little schmuck Redfield to trample all over him, let him humiliate him in front of everyone, sat across the table from him and Herb Kanter (who was just as bad, but came on like some kind of friendly fucking uncle, making out to be all warm and supportive) and listened to them ripping him apart, basically telling him he was no good, couldn't act to save his life and should have stuck to TV where he belonged. Of course, that wasn't how they'd phrased it. No, it had all been couched in the usual bullshit about the character's *motivation*, the writer's *intention*, the *subtext*. Well, fuck all that. Fuck the lot of them. The *subtext* was that they couldn't fucking fire him or they'd fuck the whole fucking picture.

As soon as he began to stand up for himself, they didn't know how to handle it. If Redfield asked for another take when Ray thought the last one was fine, he didn't let it get to him, just ignored the notes and did it again exactly the same until the little shit gave up. It worked fine. Soon the guy didn't bother. Oh sure, Ray saw him sigh, saw the little looks of resignation, but so what?

He didn't bother to see the dailies anymore, which had no doubt come as a relief to Redfield, but he'd seen enough to know that what he was doing was okay on screen. Hell, it was more than okay. The fight scene with John Grayling was terrific. Ray had failed to pull his punch on the last take and the look of genuine shock on the little faggot's face was priceless. His jaw still showed the bruise. And the love scene in the hay with Diane had nearly set the goddamn barn on fire. He hadn't needed any lectures about *motivation* that day.

How things stood between them in real life was another matter. The one thing he'd never have guessed about Diane was that she'd turn out to be frigid. Things in that department had always been electric. For more than a year they'd hardly been able to keep their hands off each other. She'd always wanted it just as much as he did, if not more. Even better, she wanted it in ways women generally didn't.

The mistake, of course, was getting married. It was so damn predictable. Get hitched and in no time at all sex flew out the window. Oh sure, they still did it now and again. On those rare occasions when she wasn't too tired. But even then it wasn't how it used to be. All he could say was thank the Lord for that wicked little filly Leanne. There was a dark horse if ever there was one. Only eighteen and knew more tricks than a Vegas hooker.

They'd had to be pretty damn careful though. There had been more than a few close shaves. Diane had nearly caught them a couple of times back at the house when he thought she was still on set or gone to a meeting. And then the other

291

evening when Ray didn't know that Tommy and Cal were out with the horses and they rode right in and nearly caught him and Leanne rocking the trailer off its springs. Ray had stuffed a lot of dollars into the pocket of the old drunk who guarded the gate and later gave him a good bawling out for failing to warn him.

As for Tommy's infatuation with Cal, Ray didn't know what to think. To begin with it had gotten on his nerves, even made him feel jealous. But then he only had himself to blame. He'd been so obsessed with his own problems with Redfield that he hadn't been able to pay the kid enough attention. But Cal was a decent enough guy, for a half-breed anyhow, and Tommy was enjoying himself and learning all kinds of new things. And of course the arrangement had the dividend of freeing up the lovely Leanne, so Ray wasn't going to make any kind of fuss about it. Anyhow, it was all soon going to be over. One more week and they'd be wrapping and heading home to LA to shoot the studio stuff.

It was Sunday night and Ray's call wasn't until the following afternoon. Diane's was first thing in the morning and she was already in bed preparing the last scene she had to do with Grayling. Leanne was going to be down at the Hungry Horse and Ray had promised to meet her there. With luck and a little shrewd footwork, maybe they'd be able to slip away down to the trailer. He felt a twitch in his pants at the thought of her. He'd just showered and put on a new white shirt and his black jeans and was giving himself a final scan in the bathroom mirror. Hell, was he one handsome sonofabitch or what?

He switched off the light and went to the bedroom door and stood watching Diane. She was in bed, propped up with pillows, wearing her little reading glasses and scribbling notes in the margins of her script. Like a fucking schoolmarm. She was so goddamn diligent, it was tiring. She looked up and saw him and smiled.

'You're going out?'

'Yeah, it's Denny's birthday. The boys are having a few beers down the double H. I said I'd drop by.'

He kissed her on the forehead.

'I won't be late.'

He parked the car at the end of the street and walked along the sidewalk. He liked to do this because sometimes there were kids who knew him from *Sliprock* and they'd mob him and ask for his autograph. They all knew the little Red McGraw trademark, making guns of their fingers and blowing off the smoke. Tonight they didn't seem to be about. But everyone he passed recognized him and some of them smiled or nodded and he smiled back regally and tipped the brim of his hat.

He was about halfway along the street when he saw the group of young Indian guys. They often hung around outside the double H and clearly thought they were the coolest dudes in town. And here they came, four of them, smoking and slouching along with their hangdog faces. Hell, didn't anyone ever teach these lazy punks how to smile?

It was as if they heard him thinking, for, on cue, they started to smirk at him. They were directly in front of him and blocking the sidewalk and showed no intention of making space for him to pass. One of them muttered something and the others laughed and Ray knew he was the object of some snide joke. But he wasn't going to rise to the bait. He nodded at them and stepped aside and three of them pushed past him. The fourth, however, stood his ground.

'Hey, *Red*,' he said sarcastically.

The others had stopped and turned to watch. One of them sniggered. Ray looked steadily at the one who'd spoken to him and nodded.

'Evening,' he said.

The kid took a last puff of his cigarette and flicked it away into the street. Looking Ray directly in the eye, he slowly lifted his hand and made the Red McGraw gun except that the barrel consisted of only one finger—the middle one. He blew a lungful of smoke at it and grinned. And Ray felled him with a straight left to the chin.

Then it was mayhem, the other three were on him and one of them had a bottle and would have cracked it over Ray's head if he hadn't seen it coming and gotten in first with a good kick in the balls. The kid groaned and doubled up but the other two kept at him and one of them had some muscle and got him in a kind of bear hug from behind while his shitty little Injun friend got a couple of good punches in. Then Chico and Denny and some of the other construction guys came bursting through the swing doors of the double H and set about the little fucks and gave them a damn good hiding, maybe a little too good because when the dust settled one of them was out cold and the other had a broken jaw.

A police car came and hauled off the two still standing and an ambulance took the other two. They wanted to take Ray as well but he told them he was okay. He looked worse than he was. His new white shirt was covered in blood but his nose had stopped bleeding and didn't seem to be broken, just a little tender. The guys took him inside and Chico gave him a bottle of Jim Beam and a Hungry Horse T-shirt to wear and everybody gathered around to hear what had happened. Leanne, the little honey, fetched a bowl of warm water and a towel and cleaned him up.

Someone must have called Herb Kanter because soon he was there too, clucking around like an old mother hen and asking questions everyone already knew the answer to. Ray made him sit down and have a drink and in no time at all everything was fine and calm and cool again. When Herb had gone, Denny and Ray slipped out the back and smoked a joint and by the time they came back inside Leanne had disappeared but so had Ray's inclination and his nose had begun to throb, so he said goodnight and walked unsteadily to his car and drove home.

He was woken earlier than he would have chosen by Diane screaming like a banshee. He'd bled again in the night all over his pillow and she was standing there with Tommy gawping down at him.

'What on earth happened?'

He made light of it and tried to do so again when the young deputy arrived from the county sheriff's office to interview him, accompanied by Herb Kanter. The deputy was young and earnest and very nervous. He claimed to have evidence that Ray had struck the first blow, which Ray naturally denied. Eventually the poor kid seemed to run out of steam and just sat there looking a little sorry for himself. As he walked him out to his truck, Herb put an arm around the boy's shoulders and said something that seemed to cheer him up. He drove away with a smile and a wave. When Herb came back into the house, Ray asked him what he'd said.

'Just promised him a pair of tickets to the premiere.'

Maybe there was something to be said for producers after all.

*   *   *

Cal arrived just twenty minutes before Frank Dawson was due to pick them up and drive them out to the airstrip. Their bags stood ready in the hallway. While she was packing the last few things and tidying the house, Diane had kept looking out the window and wondering whether Cal had forgotten his promise to come say goodbye. Then she saw his truck approaching along the dirt road, a cloud of red dust drifting away behind it.

'Tommy! Cal's here.'

They'd said most of their goodbyes last night at the wrap party. It had been a lot of fun. Even Ray had seemed to enjoy it. He'd danced with her and been kind to her, much more like his old self, though what had gone wrong between him and Tommy she still couldn't fathom. Tommy never spoke to him anymore unless he absolutely had to. Ray was as mystified as she was. But every time she asked Tommy what the matter was he just got moody or cross and said it was nothing, everything was fine.

At the party Diane had handed out the gifts

she'd bought for the crew and the other members of the cast and she was touched by how many she received in return. They all said how much they'd enjoyed working with her and how they would miss Tommy. He'd become a sort of mascot for the production. Herb Kanter presented him with a clapper board with *T. Bedford, Wrangler* written on it.

Tommy had stayed up until after midnight with all the women on the movie vying with one another to dance with him. Where the boy had learned to do the twist like that Diane had no idea. It was a revelation. She'd never seen him so uninhibited. The downside was how hard it had been to get him out of bed this morning. Every time she went up to wake him he just groaned and rolled over. Now at last he was up and (she hoped) getting dressed. Ray had just gone into town saying he had to get some cigarettes. There was a full pack on the sideboard where he always kept them. Somehow he must have missed it.

'Tommy! Did you hear me?'

'Coming.'

Diane opened the front door and the two of them stood shielding their eyes from the glaring sun and watched Cal pull up and get out of the truck. He waved and started walking up the steep path toward the house. He'd been there at the party, of course, along with everybody else. Diane had kept hoping he might ask her to dance but he hadn't. She was going to ask him but the chance never arose. Tommy was going to miss him badly. And so was she.

'Hi. I'm sorry I'm late.'

'We'd almost given up on you.'

He was standing in front of them now. He had a brown paper grocery sack under one arm. He took off his hat and smiled and Diane asked him if he'd like a cup of coffee and he followed them into the house, through the hallway and into the kitchen. He put his hat and the package on the table and sat down while Diane made some fresh coffee.

'Well, Tom, did you enjoy the party? Sure looked that way.'

'It was okay.'

'Okay for you maybe. You were the only guy the gals wanted to dance with.'

'Oh, you didn't seem to be doing so badly yourself,' Diane said. 'Some of us couldn't get a look in.'

'Wranglers don't get to dance with the belle of the ball.'

'Seemed more like the other way around.'

He looked at her and smiled. And for a moment there was a connection between them. In his eyes, a kind of tender sadness that she hadn't before seen. She turned away and busied herself with the coffee.

'So, where's Ray?'

'Gone to get some cigarettes. He'll be back in a minute.'

Tommy asked how long it would take to trailer all the horses back to LA and Cal said they were going to take it easy, over a few days, because of the heat.

'How soon can we start riding up at your place again?'

Cal didn't answer right away and when Diane looked at him she could see something was wrong.

'Cal? What is it?'

'I was going to tell you before. But a couple of days ago I had a phone call from Don Maxwell. He's selling up. He had three people bidding for the land and the price went so high he said only a fool would turn it down. So...that's the end of the ranch.'

'He can't do that!' Tommy said.

'Unfortunately he can, Tom. He owns the whole thing. It was going to happen sometime, we always knew.'

'What will you do?' Diane said. 'Can you find some other place? There are other ranches where they shoot movies, aren't there?'

'Oh, sure. Iverson's, Disney. Thing is, Diane, I'm not sure I want to do this kind of work anymore.'

'What will you do instead?'

'Go back up to Montana. Give my daddy a hand. He and my mom are getting on a little. They could do with the help. And there's a place for me there and plenty of space for the horses.'

Tommy just sat there staring at him. He looked stunned.

'When?'

'When what, son?'

'When will you go away?'

'Oh, I don't know. It'll take a month or so to sort things out. The bulldozers'll be moving in come early fall. I want to be out by then. Not too keen on seeing that happen.'

He smiled at Diane.

'Any danger of that coffee?'

As she poured it they heard Ray's car arrive and a few moments later in he came, all bright and loud and chirpy, slapping Cal on the back and ruffling Tommy's hair. Tommy didn't even acknowledge him.

'Hey, what's up?' Ray said, looking at them all. 'Somebody die?'

'Did you know about Cal's ranch being sold?' Diane said.

'Oh, yeah. I forgot to tell you. Terrible, ain't it? Still, there's other places—'

'He's going back to Montana.'

Ray looked at Cal.

'Really? You didn't tell me that. You mean you're giving up the stunt work and all?'

Cal nodded.

'Who the hell's going to be my stunt double?'

Before he left, Cal gave them what was in the grocery bag. There was a gift for each of them, wrapped in white tissue paper and tied with red string. Tommy asked if he could open his right there and then and Diane said of course. For Ray he'd bought a belt buckle with Medicine Springs on it and for Tommy a Navajo pipe carved from an antler and decorated with fur and feathers and turquoise beads. They both thanked him. Cal said the pipe had been carved by the old man who'd told him how to find the rock paintings.

'Don't you go smoking it, mind, until your mom says you can.'

Diane's gift was a polished red rock with two silhouettes painted on it in a deeper red, exactly like those they had seen on the mountain.

'It's beautiful,' she said simply, turning it in her hands.

She felt foolish tears welling so she put it down on the table and swiftly left the room, calling over her shoulder that they had something for him too. She'd left it with the bags in the hallway and she stood there a moment, rubbing her eyes and telling herself sternly to get a grip.

Diane had taken the photograph herself on one of their late-afternoon rides then had it printed in town and found a frame of gnarled piñon that fit perfectly. The picture showed Tommy and Cal sitting side by side on their horses with the mountains behind them and their faces aglow with the evening sun. They were smiling at the camera and Cal had his hand on Tommy's shoulder.

'It's from us all,' Ray said.

It wasn't true but Diane didn't bother to say so. Cal knew. He stared at it for a long moment then nodded and looked only at her.

'Thank you.'

'No, Cal,' she said quietly. 'Thank *you*.'

Frank Dawson arrived and they loaded the bags and drove to the airstrip, Cal following in his truck with Tommy. Herb was waiting, the Lodestar all ready to go. Cal helped them with the bags and everybody stood by the plane's steps and said goodbye. Cal shook hands with Ray and Tommy who seemed to have lost his voice.

'See you when we get back,' Cal said.

Tommy nodded and stared at the ground. Diane kissed Cal on the cheek. She wished she could store the touch and smell of his skin.

The plane took off to the east and as it banked and circled back toward the west they could see Cal below them walking to his truck. He looked up and stopped and stood there, waving his hat as they flew over. And Tommy at the window gazed down, silent and bereft.

TWENTY-THREE

It was the third week in August and hot and not a whisper of wind to stir the tall eucalyptus trees that grew below the terrace. Between them you could see downtown LA sweltering below a blanket of yellow brown haze. It had been like this ever since they came back from Arizona and even though the air up here in the hills was clearer, Tommy sometimes felt he was going to suffocate.

In the evening the clouds would close in until you could count the seconds before the air exploded. The storms were fast and ferocious and Tommy would get out of bed and stand at the open doors looking out over the balcony and watch the lightning silhouette the trees and listen to the thunder rumbling and rolling down the canyons. The rain was so thick and heavy and sudden that the street at the end of the driveway would flood and soon be rushing like a river.

It wasn't just the weather that made him feel listless. The fun he'd had in Arizona had taken the shine off everything there was to do in LA. He'd had one last, sad ride with Cal but now the ranch was being wound up. Most of the horses had already been sold and the ones that belonged to Cal—including Chester—had been trailered up to Montana. Cal had gone with them. He was coming back to clear his house of all his furniture and belongings. But by the end of October, he'd be gone for good. Tommy missed him so badly he sometimes wished they'd never met.

On top of this, Diane and Ray barely spoke to

each other anymore. All they ever did was shout. They generally didn't do it when Tommy was around, only after he'd gone to bed. The storms inside the house were sometimes worse than those outside. Screaming and shouting, doors being slammed, and one night just after they got back from Arizona, a terrifying crash of breaking glass. The next morning Tommy found Dolores on her knees, picking up the last few pieces of the big living room mirror. Diane said it had blown down in the storm but he knew this wasn't true.

Twice now he had found her crying. The second time, only last week, Tommy had lain in bed listening to the two of them arguing at the dinner table out on the terrace. Then he heard the front door slam and Ray roaring off in the Cadillac. Tommy got out of bed and went to find her. She was lying on her bed sobbing. And when he asked her what was wrong she just said (as if he might not have noticed) that things between her and Ray weren't so good at the moment. This often happened, she said, when people married and were getting used to each other and at the same time working hard. Once they'd finished making *The Forsaken*, she said, everything would settle down and be back to normal.

'Do you still love him?'

Tommy hoped she would say no so that he could tell her at last about Leanne, but she just smiled and told him not to be silly and said of course she still loved him. She gave him a long hug and stroked his hair.

'Everything's all right, sweetheart. Honestly. When the movie's finished we'll be happy again, I know we will. All of us. Maybe we can all go away

303

somewhere. Somewhere lovely, by the seaside. Would you like that?'

'I suppose. Couldn't just the two of us go?'

'Tommy, you've got to stop feeling that way about Ray. He loves you. I can't tell you how upset he is that you don't talk or want to be around him anymore. Darling, why are you like that with him?'

'I told you, he's not nice to you. I don't like him shouting at you.'

'Please try and be friendly. Please. Let's all be happy.'

'Okay.'

As if happiness could simply be switched on like a light. In fact, Tommy rarely saw Ray—or even much of Diane. They were at the studio all day long and Tommy just hung around the house on his own or watched TV or lay on his bed and read. When he got bored of doing all these things he would help Dolores in the kitchen or help Miguel clean the cars or mow the grass or scoop the leaves off the pool. Diane kept saying he should have a friend over to play but all his Carl Curtis friends were still away at camp or on vacation.

Then, two days ago, when Tommy was so bored and miserable he thought he might go crazy, Wally Freeman's mother had called to say Wally was back from camp. Tommy asked Diane if they could have a sleepover and it was all arranged.

Wally had arrived yesterday afternoon and the two of them hadn't stopped laughing and talking ever since. He'd slept in the spare bed in Tommy's room, though *slept* maybe wasn't the right word because they'd talked until two in the morning. Tommy told him all about Arizona and Wally had him in fits with accounts of the mischief he'd made in Oregon, putting frogs in people's beds and stranding the meanest member of staff on an island in a lake where there were known to be bears.

This morning Tommy had been woken by the sound of shouting down in the hallway. It was Dolores yelling at somebody to go away and not come back. Wally slept through it but Tommy got out of bed and when he opened the door of his room he saw Diane in a bathrobe, just out of the shower and plainly as curious as he was. She called down into the hallway and asked Dolores who she'd been shouting at. Dolores answered in her usual unfriendly voice that it was *just some kid, a beggar.*

Diane and Tommy walked across the landing to the tall window that looked out onto the driveway and saw a teenage girl slouching away toward the gate. She had a frizzy blond ponytail and was wearing a yellow dress that was too big for her and needed a wash. She seemed to sense them staring at her because she turned and briefly glowered back at the house. Her face was pinched and angry and wounded. Diane shrugged and they went back into her room and Tommy sat on the bed and told her all about Wally's adventures at camp while she dried her hair and got dressed.

Shortly after that she left for work and Tommy woke Wally and they had breakfast and went for a swim. They spent the rest of the morning playing Indians, stalking and ambushing each other in the garden. Wally wanted to shoot birds again with the BB gun but Tommy said he didn't do that anymore and that it was wrong to kill any creature unless you needed it for food. Wally said this was a load

305

of horsefeathers.

They went for another swim and dived for nickels then sat on the edge of the pool, dangling their feet in the water and debating which of the Three M's—Marilyn Monroe, Jayne Mansfield or Mamie Van Doren—had the best tits. Wally said that when school started again he was definitely going to get a kiss from Wendy Carter and Tommy said she'd probably rather kiss a dog's bottom and this led to a bout of wrestling and ducking and splashing which got so out of hand that Dolores came running from the house and told them to stop.

On Wally's last visit, Ray had proudly shown off his collection of guns and while they were changing out of their swimming things, Wally asked if he could see them again. Tommy said they were all locked away in the basement and that Ray had the only key.

'There is one he doesn't lock up though.'

'There is?'

'I'm not supposed to know. Want to see it?'

'Do bears shit in the woods?'

Tommy led him back into the house and checked that Dolores was busy in the kitchen so she wouldn't be likely to catch them. Then he led Wally up the stairs and they tiptoed like a pair of thieves across the landing and into Diane's bedroom and over to the nightstand on Ray's side of the bed.

'Promise you won't tell anyone.'

'I promise.'

'Because he'd be mad as a rattlesnake if he knew I'd shown you.'

'I told you, I promise.'

'Cross your heart and hope to die.'

'Jeez, Tommy. Okay, cross my heart and hope to die.'

Tommy opened the drawer and they stood side by side staring down at the revolver. It had a dull and mysterious gleam.

'Wow,' Wally said. 'A Smith and Wesson.'

'It's a thirty-eight. Like Sergeant Friday's in *Dragnet*.'

Wally reached out but Tommy told him not to touch it.

'Why not? Who'll know?'

'It's loaded.'

'So what? It's okay. Don't be such a wimp.'

He picked it up and held it carefully in both hands.

'Wow. It's a beauty.'

'Just be careful.'

'Yeah, yeah.'

He closed his right hand around the grips and pointed it at Tommy.

'Okay, mister, stick 'em up.'

'Wally! Don't do that! It's loaded, you idiot!'

'Okay, okay. Don't pee your pants. Anyhow, the safety's on, moron.'

'Put it back. Now!'

Wally sighed but did as he was told.

'Aha! What have we here?'

He picked up the plastic bag that Ray always kept there too.

'It's just tobacco or tea or something.'

'*Tea?* It's pot, you dodo.'

'What?'

'It's a drug. You smoke it. You know Scotty Lewis in sixth grade? His big brother smokes it all the time. It makes your eyes go all pink and funny. Man, your dad could go to jail for having this stuff.'

'He's not my dad. Wally, just put it back, will you!'

'Okay, keep your hair on.'

*   *   *

Hollywood was a place of many illusions and one of these was to do with friendship. Diane had first been alerted to this shortly after she arrived the previous year by Paramount's legendary costume designer Edith Head. She was a woman of startling looks: a helmet of dyed black hair and enormous glasses with round dark blue lenses that she apparently wore to help her know how a costume would look when filmed in black and white. At the age of sixty-four she had seven Oscars to her name and had dressed nearly all the great leading ladies of the century, from Marlene Dietrich and Mae West to Sophia Loren and Grace Kelly. For some reason she had taken an immediate shine to Diane.

'There's not a town in the world where you can make or lose friends faster,' she said.

Diane was standing before her in the red satin ball gown, one of several gorgeous Edith Head creations she never got to wear for the aborted Gary Cooper movie.

'What you have to remember is that in Hollywood everything is about business. Including friendship. It's best not to confuse the two.'

At the time, Diane hadn't quite understood what she meant by this. But now she did. During the year she'd lived here, she'd met plenty of women she liked well enough and was happy to think of as friends. They were all, in one way or another, involved in the movie business or had husbands or boyfriends who were. They would call each other, meet for coffee or lunch, come with their partners for cocktails or dinner. But there wasn't one among them in whom Diane felt able to confide or with whom she could talk candidly about Ray and the problems they were having. It was only in October when her old friends Molly and Helen came to visit that she realized how much she missed their long midnight talks, huddled in their dressing gowns around the gas fire on those freezing London nights.

They were on a two-week trip to California and, because they were trying to cram in as much as possible, could only stay a couple of days. Diane drove them around and showed them the sights, just as Ray had done for her and Tommy a year earlier. They bombarded her with questions about her work and about the people she'd met and Diane did a fine impression of being happy and enthusiastic.

The following day was a Saturday and Tommy persuaded them they couldn't go home without seeing Disneyland. He'd already been there three times but couldn't get enough of it. Ray said he couldn't come, so the four of them drove down to Anaheim and screamed and laughed so much on the rides that by the time they got home they were all aching.

At dinner, Ray was charming and attentive, regaling Helen and Molly with funny, if self-serving, stories about the movie business that

309

Diane had heard a dozen times. She watched her friends getting steadily starstruck. He left the table early, saying he had to go into town to see someone and that he was sure the three of them had a lot of *girl talk* to catch up on. He was scarcely out of earshot when Molly whispered loudly what a *dreamboat* he was. She leaned back in her chair and looked around at the pool and the house and the fairy lights glinting in the tree above and she sighed and shook her head.

'Just look at all this. It's simply heaven. You're so lucky, Diane.'

'I know.'

She smiled and lit another cigarette. And Helen, always the shrewder of the two, must have sensed some wistful reservation.

'But?' she said.

'But nothing.'

'Come on, Di. I know you too well.'

And little by little they coaxed it out of her.

At first Diane made it sound as if her misgivings were to do with Hollywood, how superficial and insincere life here could sometimes be; how, perhaps, it wasn't the best place in the world to bring up a child. She said they, of all people, knew how passionate she'd always been about her work but that, somehow, since taking over responsibility for Tommy, her heart didn't seem to be in it anymore.

Then, with Helen's canny questioning, she started to talk about how things were with Ray. At first she couched it all in the past, made it sound as if things were better now. And, in a way, this was true. The lowest patch had been the weeks after they came back from Arizona and were shooting

310

the studio scenes. Ray had behaved like a spoiled child and at times much worse. That Terry Redfield and Herb Kanter had managed to put up with his tantrums was a minor miracle. And at home there was no restraint at all. The drunken ranting rages, the storming out of the house, the constant jealous sniping at her for being *frigid* or for some affair he fatuously imagined she was having. Diane spared her friends—or perhaps herself—the worst. Such as the night he threw a glass at her and shattered the living room mirror or the dark and vengeful way he now made love to her on those rare occasions when either from pity or guilt she acquiesced. She told them enough however to shake the stardust from their eyes. Told them how mean he could be, how he'd disappear and come back in the early hours, drunk or stoned or both.

'Has he actually hit you?' Helen said.

'God, no,' Diane said.

It was technically true, but only just.

'He's just sometimes, you know, a little... rough.'

It was a subject with which Molly seemed uncomfortable for she swiftly broadened it.

'Mummy says the first year of marriage is always the worst. After marrying Daddy she cried for a whole year. Sobbed her poor little heart out every morning after he left for the office. But she says you just get used to it.'

'What a frightfully depressing idea,' Helen said.

'No, but listen. It was the same for me when they sent me off to boarding school. I cried every night. For months. Then, after that, it was fine. Somehow you do just... get used to it.'

311

'Well, I'm sure those poor people in the war got used to being shut up in concentration camps, but it doesn't make it right.'

'Helen, honestly, you always twist everything I say. All I mean is that marriage isn't easy. You've got to work at it.'

'The thing is, I so want it to work,' Diane said. 'For Tommy's sake more than anyone's. That's partly why I married Ray in the first place, to give Tommy a father, a proper family.'

On that front too things had become a little better. At least the two of them were talking again, though sometimes when Ray snapped at her or was in one of his moods, she noticed the way Tommy glowered at him.

She must have let the sadness show more than she meant to for a moment because Molly and Helen got up and pulled chairs close on either side of her and put their arms around her.

'It'll be all right, Di,' Molly said. 'You wait, when the film comes out and everyone's saying how wonderful you both are, he won't be so anxious and edgy and it'll all be fine. We're so proud of you!'

'Of course we are,' Helen said. 'But don't ever let him hit you. If he does, you go, all right?'

'Oh, Helen, really—'

'Promise me.'

'I promise.'

She hugged them close.

'I miss you.'

'We miss you too.'

The campaign Herb Kanter and the Paramount publicity people had devised for *The Forsaken* was almost as arduous as making the picture itself. The release was scheduled for the end of February, with premieres planned for Hollywood and New York City. And Herb was determined to fill every available moment until then making sure the whole world got to know about the studio's *sensational new star* Diane Reed.

The day after she put Molly and Helen on the train to San Francisco, Diane began a marathon routine of interviews and photo shoots. These generally took place at the studio or in a suite Herb rented for the purpose at the Beverly Hills Hotel. For journalists from the more influential newspapers or magazines, a lunch would be arranged at the Brown Derby or the Bistro. The subject that cropped up more than any other was Diane's on-screen, off-screen relationship with Ray Montane. The questions became relentlessly familiar.

So how did you two meet? Was it love at first sight? What was it like doing the love scenes together?

But she was a skilled performer and always answered as if for the first time. She would flatter the journalists' perspicacity, give that sweet, self-deprecating smile or that little frown while she paused in fake reflection. Modest, professional, sometimes, if appropriate, even a little coquettish, she liked to leave the impression that their incisive skills had coaxed far more from her than she'd intended.

Much more difficult were the interviews she and Ray did together. They would sit side by side on the couch and pretend to all the world that life was bliss and their love undying. Sometimes, in the middle of an interview, Ray—so sweet and caring and gentle that it made her want to gag—would

313

take her hand or put his arm around her or lean in and kiss her on the cheek. And the moment the journalist and the publicist had left the room and it was just the two of them, he would erupt.

'Am I invisible or what? The little prick didn't ask me a goddamn thing. *Tell me, Diane, how has stardom affected you? Do you have a message for all your fans back home in England?* Well, fuck him.'

Diane, with Molly's exhortation to *work at it* echoing in her head, would take a deep breath and kiss and console him. If the press sometimes seemed a little more interested in her than in him, she said sweetly, it was only because she was new. He was already a star. Everybody—the whole world, for heaven's sake—knew about Ray Montane.

On the last Sunday in October Cal Matthieson phoned to say goodbye. He was about to leave for Montana for the final time. Diane drove Tommy up to the ranch and, as soon as she saw the place, wished she hadn't. The bulldozers had torn everything apart. All but a few of the trees had gone. The foundations for hundreds of homes were already laid, the hillside carved into a dirt geometry of streets and sewer ditches. Cal's house stood condemned in an ocean of dried mud, its contents already loaded into the truck that stood by the front porch.

There wasn't much to be said and Tommy said nothing. His eyes kept wandering away to where the corrals had once stood and where now the last of the rails lay charred and smoldering on a bonfire. The smoke drifted away across the hillside like the aftermath of some lost and pointless war.

Cal handed her a piece of paper on which he'd written his address in Montana and the phone number. He told her to call if there was ever anything she needed and made them promise they'd come visit. They were welcome to stay any time, he said, for as long as they liked.

'You know, Tom, that little pony of yours is already getting grouchy on me. You'd better come ride him soon or he'll be heading down here to find you.'

Tommy smiled bravely, then looked away. Cal looked at Diane.

'How're things?'

'Good,' she said brightly. 'Better.'

She could tell he didn't believe her.

'I hear the movie turned out real good.'

'So they say. We haven't seen it yet.'

There was a long silence. She wanted to throw her arms around him, hold him, tell him what she felt for him, that she couldn't bear the idea of his going. But of course it wasn't possible. Tommy was biting his lip.

'I think we'd better go now,' she said quietly. 'Are you leaving today?'

'Yep. Just a couple of things to clear up and I'll be heading off.'

'Well.' She swallowed. 'Go safely.'

'You too.'

TWENTY-FOUR

They walked to the courthouse in the order Brian McKnight had stipulated. Danny's two uniformed military attorneys led the way, with Danny and Kelly, now eight months pregnant, arm in arm behind them. Following closely, dapper in their dark business suits, came McKnight and his assistant attorney, Kevin Nielsen. Then Dutch and Gina, also arm in arm, with Tom bringing up the rear.

Ahead of them the crowd of TV and press reporters was waiting for them in the sunshine. It was the second day of the hearing and Tom had imagined there wouldn't be so many but there seemed to be even more. The security seemed tighter too. Everywhere you looked, even on the rooftops, there were Marine Corps police with M16s, talking to one another on their radios. Tom wondered what they were expecting. There had been many death threats against Danny on the Internet, e-mails that promised obscene and horrific retribution, not just against him but against Kelly too and even their unborn child. Whatever the reason, Camp Pendleton, this hot and cloudless May morning, was again in a state of high alert.

The reporters had spotted Danny and his entourage coming now. Tom saw the crowd ripple with anticipation, the microphones bristling, cameras being hoisted to the ready.

'Okay, folks,' Brian McKnight said quietly. 'Don't forget, just leave the talking to me.'

He had given them all a thorough briefing the day before on how to walk the media gauntlet. They weren't to answer any questions, however friendly or provocative. They weren't to look smug or scared or sour. They should walk at a reasonable pace, neither hurried nor too leisurely, and should hold their heads high, looking calm and modest and confident.

'The impression we want to convey is that we know this fine young soldier is innocent but at the same time we respect the legal and democratic system that has brought him here.'

They had reconvened this morning in the conference room for what they all knew would be a much rougher session. The previous day had been mostly taken up with procedural formalities. Today was when the prosecution would be rolling out its big-gun witnesses. Danny looked paler and more drawn than ever. He had the spectral stare of the sleepless. While he was going through some last-minute briefing with McKnight and the other attorneys, Gina had taken Tom aside and whispered about the twitching muscle in the boy's left cheek.

'Do you think he knows he's doing it?'

'I don't think so. It's okay. He'll settle down.'

'He looks terrible. Have you seen his fingernails?'

They were bitten to the quick. Tom tried to reassure her. He said any judge worth his salt must surely know these things were only the result of nerves and no more a sign of guilt than of innocence. Gina didn't seem convinced.

McKnight had asked that Danny be allowed to wear his *alphas*—the formal Marine uniform with

317

its dark green pants and belted jacket and necktie. But, as expected, the application had been denied. The reason, he'd explained, was that with *alphas* you got to wear your service decorations and the last thing the government wanted was any hint that the guy they'd put in the dock might be some kind of hero. Instead, Danny was wearing the same as all the other military personnel involved—regular digital-pattern cammies.

Tom saw the boy's shoulders stiffen. Their little procession was nearing the courthouse now and on either side of the path, reporters were leaning out over the orange barriers, shouting questions and pointing their microphones and cameras at Danny.

'Corporal Bedford! Are you feeling confident this morning?'

'Daniel, over here, please!'

'Kelly, how are you? When's the baby due?'

'Boy or girl, do you know yet?'

'Ladies and gentlemen, thank you,' McKnight called out as they forged on. 'If you could just let us through here, thank you very much. I'll be happy to answer any questions after the hearing. Thanks a lot.'

At last they were inside the building and out of the heat. Two Marine MPs shut the doors and the hubbub faded to a hum. McKnight plainly enjoyed this part of the process. He was as close to smiling as Tom had yet seen. The guy had better taste than to mention it, but it was obvious he thought Kelly's condition played well with the media. He put his arm around her shoulders.

'Okay, young lady?'

She nodded bravely.

'Come on, you can tell us. Boy or girl?'

318

'Win for Danny and I'll tell ya.'

Two more MPs stood outside the courtroom doing security checks on all who entered. The one with the metal detector smiled when it was Kelly's turn and let her pass unchecked. The room already seemed familiar. It had cream walls and a lot of wood paneling and a low white ceiling with concealed lights. The large red office chairs were comfortable enough to fall asleep in. The government attorneys were already at their table across the aisle and the lead prosecutor, Major Richards, gave McKnight a solemn nod.

Wendell T. Richards was a seriously decorated Gulf War hero, six and a half feet of him, with the kind of stoical, steely gaze Tom remembered from his western comic books. According to McKnight, the guy's nickname was Maximus because he was the government's top legal gladiator.

Tom followed Kelly and Gina and Dutch through to the family's allocated seats behind the defense table, putting a hand on Danny's shoulder as he passed.

'Good luck, son.'

'Thanks, Dad.'

There were only a few seats for the media. Most of the reporters would be watching the proceedings on closed-circuit TV in another building. Apart from them, the only others present were the judge's legal adviser, a stenographer and, for some peculiar reason, a sketch artist. The jury box stood empty. Danny's fate lay in the hands of one man only, the man who now entered the courtroom to take his seat on the wood-paneled podium in the front left-hand corner of the room. Investigating officer Colonel Robert Scrase was a gentle-mannered Texan with impeccable credentials both as a soldier and as a military lawyer. And though both sides had yesterday had the right to challenge his suitability to hear the case, neither had sought to exercise it.

Richards had already called two witnesses the previous afternoon, both members of Danny's company, who had set the scene and described the conditions in which they had been operating in Iraq in the weeks leading to the night of the killings. What they'd said had given Tom a vivid picture of the routine terror that was his son's life for so many months. Apart from a few points that McKnight had sought to clarify, the two soldiers' testimony went uncontested. But now Richards called Sergeant Marty Delgado.

From what Danny had told him about the man, Tom had been expecting horns and a whiff of sulfur. He was broad and pumped and shaven headed but as he settled into the witness box and took the oath, his manner was polite and restrained, almost genial. It was all theater, of course. No doubt the prosecution lawyers were as shrewd as McKnight when it came to coaching credibility. Delgado kept his eyes on Major Richards without so much as a glance at Danny.

Richards spent the first ten or fifteen minutes establishing Delgado's unblemished record as a soldier, what his job involved and the precise nature of the mission that he and his platoon had been on that particular night. Then, step by careful step, he began to take him through the events that led to the killings: the roadside bomb and its bloody aftermath, how he and Danny had found the detonation wires and followed them.

'Whose decision was it that you were accompanied in this by Lance Corporal Bedford?'

'Mine, sir.'

'You chose him to accompany you?'

'Yes, sir.'

'For any particular reason?'

'He was in pretty bad shape after the IED, seeing his friend Private Peters wounded like that, I guess.'

'When you say *in pretty bad shape*, how was he behaving?'

'He seemed angry. Kind of disturbed. I was worried about him.'

'Did he say anything in particular that you recall?'

'Yes, sir. He kept ranting that he was going to get the little *hajji* motherfuckers, kill the *hajji* bastards, that kind of thing.'

'*Hajji*, meaning?'

'It's a kind of insulting word for Iraqis, sir.'

'I see. I imagine after a bomb like that, when fellow Marines have been killed or injured, it must be hard to stay calm and self-controlled.'

'Yes, sir. But that's what we're trained for. Whatever happens, you have to keep your self-control. To be effective.'

'Would you say that Lance Corporal Bedford was able that night to keep his self-control?'

'No, sir. I wouldn't.'

'Did he appear more excited or disturbed than the other men?'

'Yes, sir, he did.'

'And is that why you ordered him to accompany you, so that you could keep an eye on him?'

'Yes, sir. I was concerned about him.'

'Had you ever seen Lance Corporal Bedford react in a similar way on any other occasion?'

'Not that I recall, sir.'

'How would you describe his attitude as a soldier, in general?'

'I'd say his attitude was kind of average, sir.'

'Kind of average.'

'Yes, sir.'

'Had you any recent occasion to find fault with him?'

'Yes, sir, I had. Two, as a matter of fact.'

'Could you describe them for us?'

Delgado and Richards spent the next fifteen or twenty minutes going through the details of the two incidents that were supposed to illustrate Danny's inefficiency. It would have been quicker if McKnight hadn't been constantly bobbing to his feet to object. The first incident involved a search operation carried out in an area where there had been intelligence reports of insurgent bomb making. According to Delgado, Danny had failed to secure two houses properly, potentially endangering the lives of his platoon. The second concerned a failure to file some routine report back at the base in the time that was stipulated. Delgado attempted to spice it up with a generalized smear about Danny and Ricky Peters and the sarcastic banter they sometimes indulged in. Colonel Scrase sustained McKnight's persistent objections to this but overruled most of his earlier ones.

Richards returned to the night of the killings. He had Delgado describe Danny's fall into the canal and how this had seemed to fuel his anger so that Delgado repeatedly had to tell him to calm

322

down and pull himself together and then how they'd come under fire and seen the man in the cammie jacket with the AK-47. The picture Delgado calmly painted was that, by the time they ran into the courtyard of the farm, Danny was in a state of vengeful frenzy. This, Delgado claimed, was why he'd ordered him to stay with Harker, standing guard over the Iraqis in the courtyard, rather than have him join in the search of the house.

During that search, Delgado said, one insurgent had been killed and although he wasn't wearing the camouflage jacket and no such jacket had been found, he did have an AK-47. Delgado believed it to be the same man who had earlier fired on them. Richards asked him what happened next.

'Just as we'd made sure the house was secure, I heard shouting from the courtyard.'

'Do you know who was shouting?'

'Yes, sir. I went to a second-floor window and saw it was Lance Corporal Bedford.'

'And could you hear what he was saying?'

'Yes, sir. He was shouting at the group of Iraqis, telling them to be quiet. Some of them, the women, they were pretty scared and upset, wailing and all. He was telling them to stop.'

'What did he say, precisely?'

Delgado paused for a moment and glanced at Colonel Scrase, as if for permission.

'He kept saying, *you fucking hajji bitches, shut the fuck up.*'

Tom saw Danny, in front of him, shift in his seat as if he were going to say something to contradict this, but McKnight put a restraining hand on his arm and Danny just sat there shaking his head.

Just in case anybody hadn't heard the first time, Richards repeated what Delgado had said. Then he asked the sergeant what Harker was doing during this time and Delgado said he'd heard him twice tell Danny to *cool it*.

'Those were the words he used?'

'Yes, sir. He said *cool it, man*. Then *for christsake, cool it*.'

'Then what did you see?'

'Lance Corporal Bedford seemed to get even more agitated and then he yelled at Harker to use his weapon and opened fire.'

'What exactly did you hear him yell?'

'I believe it was, *use your goddamn weapon*.'

'*Use your goddamn weapon*?'

'Yes, sir.'

'And then he opened fire?'

'Yes, sir.'

'At the crowd, the women and babies, everyone?'

'Yes, sir.'

'And what about Private Harker?'

'He opened fire too, sir.'

'Were you able to see which of them was the first to fire?'

'Yes, sir. It was definitely Lance Corporal Bedford.'

Kelly was sitting between Tom and Gina. She swallowed and looked down and Gina reached out and gripped her hand. Richards only had a few more minor questions, just to clarify the horror for them all, to let the killer punch sink in. Then he courteously handed the witness over for cross-examination and sat down.

McKnight started gently, so gently in fact that for a while Tom wondered what the hell the guy

324

was doing, being so nice. Then, carefully, McKnight began to undermine Delgado's credibility.

'This word *hajji*, Sergeant, the word you say Lance Corporal Bedford used so much. What does it mean?'

'As I think I said, it's an insult word for Iraqis.'

'Yes, I heard you say that. But what does it actually mean?'

'I believe it means someone who has visited Mecca.'

'And that's an insult, is it?'

'Well, literally, maybe not, but—'

'Maybe not. And is Lance Corporal Bedford the only Marine you've heard use this word?'

'No, sir.'

'You've heard others use it.'

'Yes, sir.'

'Is it a word commonly used among US soldiers in Iraq?'

Richards stood up to object but McKnight preempted him.

'Let me rephrase that. Was the word *hajji* commonly used among the Marines you personally worked with?'

'No, sir. I wouldn't say commonly.'

'Occasionally, then?'

'I guess so.'

'Is it a word you personally ever use, Sergeant?'

'No, sir.'

'Never?'

'No, sir. Not that I recall.'

'So you don't recall saying on the night we're discussing, after the IED went off…' McKnight adjusted his glasses and read from the document he had in his hand. *'Let's hunt their hajji asses down and burn them.* You don't recall saying that?'

'No, sir, I do not.'

For the first time, Delgado looked uncomfortable. McKnight moved on, challenging the sergeant's testimony about what had happened on the night of the killings, what he'd allegedly heard Danny say, asking him whether he might have misheard or misinterpreted any of these comments. The intention was obviously to dismantle the impression that Danny had been as out of control as Delgado alleged.

How, for example, could Delgado have considered it unsafe to allow a man so overwrought to search the house but safe enough to have him stand guard over the group in the courtyard? How clearly had Delgado seen what he claimed to have seen from the window? Had he seen, in that crucial moment before they opened fire, one of the deceased, a man with one leg, reach down to pick up his crutch?

To this last question Delgado, of course, said no.

McKnight pressed on. With all the noise going on, the women wailing and screaming both inside the house and outside in the courtyard, how could he have heard so distinctly what Danny had shouted? Could he have been mistaken? For example, might he have misheard what Danny yelled to Harker before opening fire? Instead of *use your goddamn weapon*, might he in fact have been alerting Harker to the one-legged man lifting the crutch and yelled *he's got a goddamn weapon*? Delgado was adamant that what he'd seen and heard was exactly as he'd testified.

There was a long pause.

'Do you have any cause, Sergeant, to dislike Lance Corporal Bedford?'

'Dislike? No, sir.'

'But you weren't friends.'

'No, not exactly.'

'Not exactly. On the afternoon of January tenth, two weeks before the night we've been discussing, do you recall overhearing a conversation between Lance Corporal Bedford and Private Peters in the latrines at the base?'

Delgado frowned and grinned, as if he found the question absurd.

'Why does that amuse you, Sergeant?'

'It doesn't. I mean, I just ... No, sir. I don't recall that.'

'A conversation in which Lance Corporal Bedford made a lighthearted reference to the size of your penis?'

'No, sir.'

'Let me try to refresh your memory. It was shortly after you had been talking, in the company of both these men, about the impressive number of bench presses you can apparently do.'

'I don't remember that.'

'And you don't remember coming across them in the latrines afterward and overhearing Lance Corporal Bedford saying the reason you boasted about such things was that you had a small penis?'

'No, sir.'

'I think the exact words he used were ...' McKnight referred to the document he was holding. '... that it was like *a little acorn*.'

Wendell Richards stood to object. Scrase overruled but told McKnight to move on and that he'd made his point, which prompted a ripple of

327

smiles around the courtroom.

'What I'm suggesting, Sergeant Delgado, is that you did hear Lance Corporal Bedford make this remark and that, because of this, for the next two weeks, up to and including the night of the incident, you constantly attempted to criticize him for almost everything he did. Is that not so?'

'No, sir. It is not. I wouldn't do that kind of thing.'

'You wouldn't.'

'No, sir.'

McKnight took him through the two occasions on which he'd found fault with Danny and managed to cast a layer of doubt (at least, in Tom's unlawyerly reckoning) on both. On the first allegation, the impression was left that Danny had, arguably, done all he reasonably could to secure the houses. And his failure to file the report on time was, by the sergeant's reluctant admission, something that happened routinely. By the time he left the stand, Marty Delgado looked a lot less composed than he had two hours earlier.

They adjourned for lunch and over sandwiches and juice in the conference room, watched themselves on TV, trooping into the courthouse, ignoring the barrage of questions. With a scrupulously straight face, the woman reporter recounted the courtroom exchange about the size of Sergeant Marty Delgado's penis. Tom could imagine the mirth this must have caused in the newsroom.

Danny looked better than he had for days. Even the muscle in his cheek had stopped twitching. Tom watched him across the room, sitting in the corner with Kelly, holding his palms against her

328

bulging belly, the sun shafting in on them from the window. The scene stirred some vague memory but Tom couldn't nail it and knew it was generally safer not to try.

'She's a great girl.'

Tom turned and saw McKnight standing next to him. He was munching on a sandwich and had been watching the young couple too. Tom smiled and nodded.

'She is. You did a good job this morning.'

'I did okay. The other one's going to be a whole lot tougher.'

'You mean Harker?'

'Uh-huh. Ever done any climbing?'

'Rock climbing? A little. Nothing serious.'

'When you climb, sometimes there aren't any ledges or toeholds. So what you look for is cracks. Just a little crack you can squeeze your fingers and toes into. Delgado had cracks. This guy'll have 'em too, for sure. Trouble is, finding them.'

TWENTY-FIVE

They stood there, side by side on the red carpet that had been laid across the sidewalk, smiling at the flashbulbs, their names in huge letters above them on the illuminated front of the theater. Behind the red velvet ropes, the crowd was cheering and calling to them, while the searchlights panned and swerved across the sky.

Diane was in an ice blue strapless satin dress designed for the occasion by Edith Head. A white mink stole fell loosely around her shoulders and

329

ten thousand dollars' worth of diamonds—courtesy of Marcel of Beverly Hills, for one night only—sparkled above her already famous cleavage. Ray had his arm around her waist and as they waved one last time and turned and walked regally into the foyer, keeping up this fine charade of marital and professional bliss, it occurred to him that this was the first time he'd had his hands on her, except in anger or by accident, in at least a month.

And now some jerk of a photographer wanted a picture of them standing next to Kanter and that little fuck Terry Redfield. The two of them were standing there, waiting with their fat and ugly wives.

'Diane, you look stupendous,' Redfield said, kissing her on both cheeks like some faggot French hairdresser. The smile faltered when he turned to Ray. He didn't even offer his hand, just nodded and muttered a token hello. It was understandable, given what had happened the last time they met, at the screening, which was when Ray discovered what they'd done to his performance. Though the bruise on the little bastard's jaw had gone, the memory clearly lingered on.

But neither of them was dumb enough to make a scene at what was now, since New York had been canceled, the only premiere *The Forsaken* would be getting. They all stood there, in front of the palms and the posters, dutifully smiling for the cameras. And soon it was over and they were making their way through to their seats where, for the next ninety-eight minutes, Ray would have to watch the damn picture all over again and pretend how wonderful it was.

Tommy was already sitting there with Leanne and didn't look too happy about it, though he perked up at the sight of his mom. Herb had thoughtfully hired the girl for the evening to look after the kid. Ray hadn't seen her since Arizona and was hoping they might get a few quiet moments at the party afterward so she could tend to his needs too. He managed to wink at her before the house lights went down, but she didn't seem to see him.

The previews in the trades had been damning. The only consistent praise was for Diane who, it seemed, could do no wrong. The critics all said things like *this major new talent deserves a better vehicle* and *against all odds, a star is born*. About Ray, on the other hand, the bastards were a lot less generous. *Variety* suggested he should *stick to the day job* and the smartass headline in the *Hollywood Reporter* said *RED ROPES HIMSELF A TURKEY*.

Ray wondered how they'd managed to form such an opinion because when you looked at the movie (which, as he watched it for the second time now, was even worse than he remembered), he was hardly in the damn thing. Redfield and Kanter, the little shits, had pretty well cut him out of every scene. Talk about a love story. It was like Diane's character was having an affair with the Invisible Man. Even the fucking horses had more close-ups.

Judging by the applause after the credits started to roll, the audience at the premiere seemed to like it enough despite some jerk at the back, cheering at the end of the court scene when the judge announced Ray's death sentence. What the hell did they know, anyhow. Herb Kanter had packed the place with friends and flunkies.

331

The party afterward was almost as bad as the movie. Tommy was tired so Diane had sent him directly home from the theater with Leanne, thus managing to skewer any hope Ray had of a cozy reunion. You could tell from the venue and from the quality of the food and the liquor that Kanter and the studio, the mean sonsofbitches, were already trying to cut their losses. Ray wandered around like a leper, the phony smile slowly sliding from his face. It was like the last night on the fucking *Titanic*. He made his way to the bar and had to wait for a long time to attract the young barman's attention.

'Excuse me?'

The kid seemed to be deliberately ignoring him.

'Do you have a problem with your hearing?'

'No, sir. May I help you?'

'Just give me a bottle of Jim Beam.'

'Sorry, sir. I can give you a glass.'

'Just give me the fucking bottle.'

'Sir—'

'Do you know who I am?'

'Why, have you forgotten?'

Ray grabbed him by the neck and hauled him halfway across the bar, knocking over glasses, liquor splashing everywhere. The kid went red in the face and squealed like a piglet and said he was sorry, he was only kidding, it was just a joke. Everyone around them had stopped talking and were all staring. Some guy in a tuxedo, the party manager or whoever the hell he was, came to the rescue and Ray let the kid go. He got the bottle he'd been after and went off and found a quiet corner and sat there watching the sycophants flutter and fawn around Diane.

Of what happened after that, he had no clear recollection.

*   *   *

Diane slept in Tommy's room nowadays but she still usually heard Ray come home in the early hours. When she'd left the premiere party, a little after midnight, he was still sitting in the corner with a couple of young guys she didn't know. Much later she'd heard the car that dropped him home, heard him fumble with his keys at the front door, bump into the hallway table then stumble up the stairs. He would probably surface sometime around midday with his normal hangover.

The late night had taken its toll on Tommy too. Getting him out of bed this morning had been like prizing a limpet from a rock. There wasn't time for him to sit down for breakfast so she'd made him a bacon sandwich which he could eat in the car while she drove him to school. She was standing in the hallway, waiting for him to come downstairs.

'Tommy! Come on, we'll be late.'

'Okay, okay.'

The phone started to ring and she quickly picked up before Dolores could do so in the kitchen. It was Herb Kanter.

'Diane, thanks so much for all you did last night. You were great.'

'Thank *you*, Herb. It was fun. Did you enjoy yourself?'

'Oh, yes.' He paused for a moment and Diane realized Dolores was listening on the kitchen phone.

'Dolores? I've got it. Would you hang up,

please?'

There was silence then a click.

'Herb?'

'Yes. Diane, we've got a bit of a problem.'

'Oh? Don't tell me, more bad reviews.'

'As a matter of fact, this morning's aren't too bad at all. No, it's more of a personal thing.'

Diane couldn't think what he might mean. She waited for him to go on. Tommy was coming down the stairs now.

'An English newspaper, the *Daily Express*, has run a story today with a lot of ... private things about you and Ray. And about Tommy too, I'm afraid. Of course, it's all a pack of lies. I've already spoken with Vern Drewe and he's on the case. He's had it wired over from London and we'll get a copy over to you as soon as we can.'

Tommy was standing in front of her now. He had his sweater on back to front and still looked half asleep.

'Go brush your hair.'

'Oh—'

'Do as you're told. Now!'

He slouched back up the stairs.

'And hurry up! We're late. Sorry, Herb. I have to go. I'll call you back in twenty minutes. But tell me quickly, what does it say?'

'It's about, well, you know ... About the years when you claimed to be Tommy's sister. And the effect this had on your mother. It suggests that ... well, that it might have played some part in her death.'

'What! Where have they got this from?'

'It quotes someone who claims to be a friend of the family. A Mrs Vera Dutton. She appears to have some kind of grudge against you.'

'I don't believe it.'

'Of course, it might all just blow over. But we've already had a couple of calls from reporters who've picked up on it over here. The studio is, well...getting a little exercised. We need to get together with Vern and sort out a response.'

Tommy had come downstairs again.

'Herb, I'll call you back.'

She hung up. Tommy looked wide awake now and worried.

'What's the matter?'

'Nothing. Just, some of the reviews aren't so good. Come on, let's go. Got your bag? Here's your breakfast.'

Miguel had the Galaxie ready and waiting outside with its roof down. Diane gave him as cheerful a good morning as she could muster.

'How was the premiere, Tommy? Good?'

'It was great.'

'Momma's a big star now, no?'

'Yes.'

Diane was praying there wouldn't be any reporters outside the gates and there weren't. Maybe it wasn't that big a story after all. But there was someone there, waiting under the trees. A young woman with a frizzy ponytail. And as they drove past, Diane recognized her. It was the same girl who had come to the house a few months ago and been so brutally turned away by Dolores.

Diane stopped and put the car into reverse.

'Diane, what are you doing?'

'It's that girl again.'

'What girl? I'll be late for school.'

'It won't take a moment.'

The girl backed away as the car pulled up alongside her.

'Can I help you?' Diane said.

She didn't reply.

'Do you need help? Money or something?'

The girl gave a sort of sneering smile and looked away.

'Diane, please,' Tommy whispered. 'Let's go.'

'Just a moment.'

The girl was looking from one of them to the other. Her face was grimy and it was hard to know whether the look in her eyes was fear or contempt or both. Diane spoke more gently this time.

'Who are you?'

'As if you don't know.'

'I don't. Honestly. Why should I?'

The girl looked away again with that same little sneer.

'Well, most people know their own stepdaughters.'

It took a moment to sink in.

'My God.'

Tommy looked frightened.

'Diane, what is it?'

She had to think quickly. For a moment she almost opened the door and told the poor creature to get in. But there was something about the look of her that made her decide not to. No. Better to drop Tommy off at school and then come back and sort it out. Sort everything out. Diane's heart was thumping.

'Wait here,' she said. Then, more gently: 'Please, wait here. I've just got to take my son to school. I won't be long. Then we can talk. Promise me you won't go away.'

336

The girl shrugged, which was probably as close to a promise as Diane was going to get. As they went down the hill and around the first bend, she saw in the rearview mirror that the girl was still standing there. Tommy kept asking questions to which she had no answers. Eventually she snapped at him and told him to be quiet and eat his sandwich.

When they pulled up outside the school, it took her a few moments to realize something was different. At this time of day the street was always crowded with cars while parents escorted their children to the gates where Carl Curtis stood ready to greet them. But as Tommy was about to climb out of the car, Diane saw a group of men, half a dozen of them, maybe more, running toward them. Some had cameras and were already taking pictures.

'Diane! Good morning! Can we have a word, please?'

'Tommy,' she said, starting up the engine again. 'Get back in the car.'

'What? Why?'

'Just do as I say! Shut the door.'

She pulled away so fast that the tires screeched and if the reporters hadn't been so agile and quick and jumped aside, she would almost certainly have knocked them down.

'What's going on?' Tommy wailed.

'It's all right. Just some silly newspapermen.'

'What about school? I'm late already.'

'You're not going.'

'Why not?'

'Tommy, you've got to help me out here. I'll tell you everything later. Please.'

When they got back to the house, the girl wasn't there anymore. Maybe it was just as well. It wasn't until they were heading up the driveway that Diane decided what she was going to do. As they pulled up outside the house she told Tommy that when they got inside he was to go directly up to his room, get his bag from the closet and pack his things.

'Why? Where are we going?'

'I don't know. We're just going.'

Miguel was heading out of the house to put the car in the garage but she told him as they walked past to leave it where it was, they would soon be going out again. When they came inside, Dolores handed her an envelope that had been delivered and a piece of paper with the numbers of all the people who had called while she'd been out. Diane didn't even bother to look at it. She followed Tommy up the stairs.

'Why is the boy not at school?' Dolores called after her.

'Mind your own damn business.'

She pushed Tommy gently into his room and told him to hurry with his packing. He looked confused and scared.

'It's okay, sweetheart. Really. Just be as quick as you can.'

Ray was sitting naked and hunched on the bed, with his feet on the floor, trying to rub the blur of his hangover from his eyes.

'What's going on?' he said. 'The goddamn phone's been ringing nonstop.'

Diane didn't reply. She headed for the closet and threw her suitcases onto the bed and started to pack.

'Diane, would you mind telling me what the hell you're doing?'

'We're going.'

'You're what?'

'Are you still so drunk you can't hear? I said we're going.'

'Why? What the fuck is this all about?'

She wasn't bothering to fold things, just stuffed whatever came to hand into the suitcases. Forget the dresses. Sweaters and coats, a few T-shirts, that's all she would need. Ray had got up and was standing behind her. From the edge of her vision she saw him reach out to touch her and she turned on him with such ferocity that he stumbled back and sat heavily on the bed. He looked pathetic. His nakedness disgusted her.

'Don't you dare touch me.'

'What the fuck's gotten into you?'

'Ask your daughter. Or maybe you've got more than one. Ask all of them.'

'Oh, Jesus, Diane. What the hell...? Oh, man. Did she show up again? You don't know how long I've wanted to tell you—'

'Is that so?'

'The kid's disturbed.'

'I'm not surprised, the way you get Dolores to chase her away, like she's some sort of beggar.'

That was enough clothes. She packed some shoes and a pair of hiking boots then went into the bathroom and scooped her things into her toilet bag. She knew she should be thinking it all through more carefully but she was too angry, not just at him but at herself for being so damn stupid for so damn long. When she came back into the bedroom he was pulling on a pair of jeans, hopping

339

comically from foot to foot. She walked past him and fastened the suitcases and hauled them off the bed and headed for the door.

'Tommy?'

'I'm coming!'

'Diane, let's just sit down and talk about this. There's so much I need to tell you.'

'I bet there is. Tommy, are you ready?'

She was on the landing now and put down the suitcases while she waited for Tommy. And here he came, struggling out of his room with a bag overflowing with clothes. Ray had followed her and came up behind her. He was still bare chested and she could smell the alcohol sweat on his skin.

'Diane, please.'

'Where are we going?' Tommy said.

'You're not going anywhere, son. Mommy's just a little upset. We're going to sort it out, don't you worry. Go back in your room.'

Diane put a hand on Tommy's shoulder.

'It's okay, Tommy. Let's go.'

'Diane!'

Ray grabbed her arm as she started to pick up the suitcases.

'Let go of me!'

She tried to free herself but couldn't and now, with his other hand, he took hold of her shoulder and she lashed out at him but he caught her hand and slapped her hard across the face. Diane screamed and so did Tommy. She clawed at Ray's face and he shoved her violently back and she tripped and fell and hit her head hard against the wall. Tommy screamed again and Ray just stood there staring down at her, red eyed and clearly shocked by what he'd done, his face creasing in

340

contrition.

He'd cut her lip. She could taste the blood and dabbed it with the back of her hand. She got to her feet and without another word picked up the suitcases and ushered Tommy with his bag down the stairs and past Dolores who was standing in the hallway, no doubt enjoying the show. And then they were outside and throwing the bags into the back of the Galaxie. Miguel came running, asking if everything was all right.

'No, it isn't,' she said.

She opened the door and pushed Tommy across into the passenger seat then got in herself and slammed the door and started the engine. She didn't look back but she knew Ray was standing outside the front door with Dolores behind him and she could picture that proud little smirk on the bitch's face. When they drove out through the gates, she looked to see if the girl was there but she wasn't. Diane pointed the car down the hill and accelerated hard and soon they were around the bend and out of sight of the house and careering down the canyon, the sun strobing in on them through the trees and the glimpsed city shrouded in haze below.

It was a long time before either of them spoke. They were out on the new freeway and heading north, a thousand cars streaming the other way and the sky clearing to a limpid blue. And at last, quietly and without looking at her, Tommy asked where they were going.

'How about Montana?' she said.

TWENTY-SIX

McKnight had been right about Private Eldon Harker. The young man looked as smooth and unassailable as a shoulder of polished granite. Not a crack in sight. From what Danny had said about him, Tom had imagined some furtive, flickery-eyed kid whose self-serving lies would shine out for all to see. Instead, Harker appeared the kind of man the Marine Corps might use in a recruiting commercial. He was straight backed and handsome and his answers sounded confident without a whiff of cockiness. The guy was a natural-born witness and had clearly been well coached.

Richards lobbed him the routine preliminary questions, designed to portray him as the perfect stalwart soldier, then began to talk him through the events that had led to the killings.

'Was there anyone among the crowd in the courtyard who seemed to you in any way suspicious or dangerous?'

'No, sir. They were all too terrified.'

'Were you aware of a man among them who was missing one leg?'

'Yes, sir. I was.'

'You saw him?'

'Yes, sir.'

'When did you first become aware of him?'

'Right from the start, sir.'

'And you noticed then that he had only one leg?'

'No, sir. Not right away. He didn't seem able to keep still, then I realized this was because he had a

342

leg missing and that his crutch was on the ground beside him.'

'You saw quite clearly that this was a crutch and not a weapon of any kind?'

'Yes, sir.'

'Did you point this out to Lance Corporal Bedford?'

'Yes, sir. I tried to tell him but he was shouting so much, he didn't seem to hear me.'

'Who was he shouting at?'

'At the people we were guarding, sir. At the women who were screaming.'

'And what was he shouting?'

'He was kind of swearing at them, telling them to shut up.'

'What precisely did you hear him say?'

'He kept calling them *hajji bitches* and telling them to *shut the fuck up*.'

It went on and only got more depressing. Everything Harker described, each moment, each word and nuance, matched what the hearing had already been told by Delgado. McKnight did his best, jumping up whenever he could to raise objections. Some were sustained but the young soldier's testimony was relentless and damning and his every answer felt like another shovel-load of earth on Danny's coffin. Worse still, in this shoveled earth were seeds of doubt that, try as he might, Tom found hard to dismiss. Maybe Danny had said those things after all. Maybe he had been blinded by rage and desire for revenge.

Tom stared at the back of his son's head, wondering and hating himself for doing so, his heart growing ever more leaden. By the time Richards had finished, you could almost see the

343

cloud hanging over the defending side of the courtroom. Kelly and Gina sat in silence, staring at the floor.

In his cross-examination, McKnight probed and nagged and tried to find some loose thread to tug on, but with little success. He put to Harker the possibility that he had misheard what Danny said, that there had been too much noise and confusion for him to be so adamant, that he himself had been too agitated and fearful to have such clear recollections. But Harker didn't balk or rise to any bait or taunt, just repeated what he had said, calm and dogged and without a single stumble.

Then they moved on to what happened afterward. It had taken nearly forty-eight hours before the NCIS investigators had first interviewed Harker, and McKnight asked him if, during that time or at any later date, he had conferred with Sergeant Delgado. Harker said no. Apart from what had been said in Danny's presence in the immediate aftermath in the courtyard, he and the sergeant hadn't spoken.

'I was told not to, sir. It was an order, so I obeyed it.'

McKnight went to the table and was handed a document by his assistant. He walked slowly back to the stand.

'In your initial statement, Private Harker, you were a lot less specific about what Lance Corporal Bedford said or was shouting before you both opened fire. Why was that?'

'I didn't want to land him in trouble, sir.'

'You didn't want to land him in trouble.'

'No, sir.'

'You said in your statement—and I quote—*there*

344

was too much noise. Everybody was hollering and screaming. Is that right?'

'There was a lot of hollering, sir, but he was hollering louder and I did hear.'

'So in your first statement, you were lying.'

'No, sir. I was trying to protect a fellow soldier.'

'By not telling the truth.'

'By not telling the whole truth, yes, sir.'

'So we're not to believe what you said initially but we *are* to believe what you said later, when the murder charge against you just happened to be dropped—'

Richards was on his feet at once.

'Objection!'

'Sustained.'

McKnight rephrased and went on in the same vein. But it was clear, even to Tom, that he wasn't going to get a lot further. Harker was presenting himself as an honorable man forced to choose between protecting a colleague and telling the whole truth. Again and again, without so much as a blink, he denied that he had at any time conferred or conspired with Sergeant Delgado to bring their stories into line. And, at last, the quibbling, sometimes almost hectoring tone of the interrogation seemed to irritate Colonel Scrase. Several times he intervened to ask McKnight where he was going with a particular line of questioning, urging him to move on. Harker left the stand not only unscathed, but with an air of brave credibility that even Tom found hard to doubt.

The mood over dinner that evening at Marco's, the little Italian restaurant two blocks along the street from their motel, was close to somber. It was

345

just the family, the five of them, Dutch and Gina, Danny and Kelly, and Tom. Nobody talked about the hearing but it had a place of its own at the head of the table.

Dutch did his best to lighten things up with a story about a golfing buddy called Doug who had flown out to Bangkok for a thousand-dollar health screening.

'They send these little cameras inside you,' he said. 'One down your throat and the other up the, you know, the Khyber Pass.'

'Dutch, please,' said Gina. 'We're trying to eat here.'

'It's okay, I'll spare you the detail.'

'Let's hope.'

Kelly asked what the Khyber Pass was and Dutch said it was an English term and invited Tom to explain.

'I believe it's cockney rhyming slang for your backside.'

'Anyhow,' Dutch went on. 'They film your insides and give you the DVD so you can watch it at home afterward. So Doug makes me sit down and watch the darned thing. I tell you, it was amazing. Better than any sci-fi movie you ever saw. Journey to the center of your bowels—'

'Dutch, that's enough already.'

'And the climax is when one of the cameras is traveling along this winding, gooey pink tunnel and comes around the corner and bang! It's face-to-face with the other one.'

Everybody laughed, even Danny. When they came out of the restaurant the sky was a glowing salmon pink, crisscrossed with vapor trails, and the air was balmy and laced with the scent of jasmine planted along the sidewalk. Dutch walked ahead with his arm around Kelly. Tom and Danny walked either side of Gina and she tucked her arms into theirs and pulled them close and none of them spoke. And Tom wondered how life could manage so to conspire that in adversity, among all their confounding woes, this little band of beings should somehow have found a kind of peace. Perhaps there was some innate and inexorable code of forgiveness that determined such things.

These sentimental musings were soon dispelled however when they gathered in Tom's room, some twenty minutes later, to watch the TV news. It wasn't that the report of the hearing was biased. What it said was simply an accurate reflection of the day's events in the courtroom. Eldon Harker's calm and cogent evidence spoke for itself. The reporter described McKnight's cross-examination as *relentlessly aggressive*. As the five of them stood silently watching, Tom knew they were all thinking the same thing: that this day had clinched the prosecution's case.

Perhaps because the producers felt the piece needed some sort of balance, it ended with a clip of the interview they had shot the previous week with Troop—or, as the local NBC news billed him, *bestselling novelist Truscott Hooper, acclaimed for his military thrillers.* Brian McKnight had been keen on getting some positive publicity and they had all been waiting for it to be shown. Karen O'Keefe had done a much longer interview with Troop—and one with Danny—for her *Walking Wounded* film. And now here he was, dear old Troop, flatteringly lit (he would have made sure of that), sitting like a four-star general behind his gleaming desk.

'Daniel Bedford is a fine young man,' he said. 'The very best. The kind of young man this country of ours needs and depends on. War's a dirty and confusing business and when armchair snipers pretend otherwise, it does no service to any of us. To turn on our heroes when the going gets rough, to treat them like common criminals, is something we should be ashamed of.'

'What does he know?' Danny said. 'I've never even met the guy.'

'Honey, he's only trying to help,' Kelly said.

Danny and Kelly and Gina said goodnight and went off to their rooms but Dutch asked if he could stay for a moment to catch the ball game results and Tom said of course he could. It was the first time the two of them had ever been alone together and it felt more than a little odd.

'Can I get you a drink?' Tom asked. 'There's coffee or soda.'

Dutch laughed. 'No, Tom, thanks. I'm good. Listen, I only stayed because I wanted to say thank you.'

Tom frowned.

'For what?'

'For making things so easy—well, that's not the right word. It's not easy for anyone. I mean for being so supportive and all. I can't tell you how much it means to Danny and to Gina. And to me too.'

'You guys have done a lot more than me.'

'No. I know how hard it must have been on you all these years. You and me, well, I guess we're from different tribes, as you might say. I know you weren't keen on Danny enlisting and how that

348

came between you. It was his decision but I can't pretend that I didn't have some influence on him. Now, of course, I feel what's happened is partly my fault.'

Tom didn't know what to say.

'Anyhow. I just wanted to thank you and to tell you that, whatever happened between you and Danny, the boy never stopped loving you.'

Tom smiled and nodded and, a little clumsily, reached out and patted the guy on the shoulder.

'Thanks, Dutch.'

For a moment neither of them spoke and the room was filled with the lilt and blabber of the TV sport report. Tom cleared his throat.

'So, how do you think it's going?'

Dutch sighed and wearily shook his head.

'After today? Not good. But tomorrow we've got Ricky on the stand and that won't do us any harm.'

Tomorrow was the day McKnight would start presenting the case for the defense. Ricky Peters, paralyzed from the waist down, would be wheeled into court to testify. He was their star witness, upon whom everyone's hopes were pinned.

The two men chatted for a while then Dutch said he'd better be going. They shook hands at the door and said goodnight and Dutch went off along the corridor. Tom got undressed and brushed his teeth in the cramped little bathroom, half listening to the TV and trying not to think of what Dutch might be doing now. Climbing into bed with Gina. Lying there with her. The consoling warmth of her body. He hadn't longed for her in such a way for years.

The following day McKnight set to work with a roll call of witnesses who all swore what a great guy and a fine, brave soldier Danny was. Ricky Peters, soft-spoken and frail as a bird with a broken wing, sat hunched in his wheelchair and told the hushed court of two occasions on which his friend had saved his life. He recalled how Danny had held him and comforted him after the bomb exploded and how Marty Delgado's behavior toward the two of them had changed after the incident in the latrines. It was a powerful and moving performance and when they adjourned for lunch, Tom felt more optimistic than he had all week. As they walked to the conference room, he fell into step beside McKnight.

'That seemed to go down pretty well,' he said.

'Who with?'

'Well, everyone.'

'Tom, you've got to understand what's going on here. Ricky did as good a job as anyone could've hoped. If there were a jury, he'd have had them in tears. But there is no jury. Just one man. Scrase is the only guy who matters and he's seen and heard that kind of stuff a hundred times. I don't mean he doesn't care. I'm sure he does. But it's facts he's after, not emotion. Ricky wasn't there that night in the courtyard and didn't see what happened. As far as Scrase is concerned, that's all that counts.'

'You think he'll recommend a court-martial?'

'Right now, short of a miracle, I'd say that's all he can do.'

TWENTY-SEVEN

It took them nine days to drive to Montana, about twice as long as Diane said it might take. They crossed four states and clocked up more than a thousand miles. Sometimes they stopped at diners or cafés, but mostly they bought food at grocery stores or gas stations and ate from their laps in the car. They talked and talked and sang every song they could think of, went number by number through the musicals they knew by heart from the records Diane used to bring home from London— *My Fair Lady* and *Gigi*, *South Pacific* and *Oklahoma!* And when they grew hoarse, they would switch on the radio and listen to stations so strange they might have been beamed from outer space.

In the afternoons Tommy would start scouring the map and pick a likely town to spend the night and they would check in to some ramshackle inn or motel and huddle together in bed, eating crackers and cheese and apples in front of the TV.

Several times they drove past movie theaters that were playing *The Forsaken* and Tommy pleaded to go see it again but Diane said she simply couldn't bear to. In a restaurant one night in Ely, Nevada, a shy young woman hovered around their table then begged their pardon and asked if she was Diane Reed, the movie star. Diane laughed and said, golly, how she wished she were. Folks often told her there was a likeness, she said.

And all the while the weather grew steadily

351

colder. As they crossed the state line into Utah, it began to snow and just north of Salt Lake City they were caught in a blizzard and would surely have frozen to death had an old and toothless rancher out with his snowplow not rescued them and given them shelter for the night.

It was the most exciting journey of Tommy's life. Looking out with wonder at the vast unpeopled landscape that unfolded before them, the mountains and rivers, the forests of frosted pine, he felt like an intrepid pioneer or wagon train scout from a century before. Flint McCullough in a Galaxie convertible.

With snow swirling around her legs, Diane called Cal from a phone booth in Idaho and she came back to the car beaming and saying it was as if he'd been expecting them. They were to call again when they reached Choteau.

Choteau was a pretty little town on the railroad, with a broad main street lined with trees. Men in pickups touched the brims of their cowboy hats as they drove by. That morning there was a foot of fresh snow and it sparkled in the sun and the sky was a deep, clear blue and seemed somehow to have been stretched wider than a sky should be. They called from the post office and waited there in the warmth for fifteen minutes until Cal arrived in an old pea green pickup. When they stepped out to meet him none of them said a word. Cal just opened his arms and held them both for a long time and Diane started to cry and laugh at the same time then got all embarrassed about it.

John and Rose Matthieson turned out to be every bit as sweet and gentle as Cal was. They welcomed them into their home like family. John was tall and bony and walked with a stick. He wore heavy tweed vests and shirts with no collars and reminded Tommy a lot of his grandfather. Rose, whose Blackfeet name was Little Calf, was a good six inches smaller than Tommy. She had kind, coal black eyes and long black hair that she wore in a braid that reached to her waist. She didn't speak a lot but smiled all the time.

The land around the ranch was flat and scrubby but the view of the Rocky Mountain Front, some twenty miles farther west, took your breath away. It was a giant wall of rock that blazed pink when the sun rose and purple when it set and Tommy came to think of it as having been placed there to keep all that was bad in the world at bay.

The ranch house itself was small and modest. But half a mile along the gravel road that led to the mountains there was a cozy log cabin that Cal had recently done up for himself and this was where he insisted the two of them should stay. He said he still had his old room in the ranch house and was more than happy to be there.

'Just watch out for the grizzlies,' he said, as he showed them around.

'You're kidding,' Diane said.

'You're right. They're all asleep right now. But come April they'll be waking up and rolling on down here. It's no big deal. You just have to keep your eyes open.'

'Oh, we won't be staying that long.'

'I sure hope you will. There's a lot of work to be done around here and I was counting on Tom giving me a hand.'

That first afternoon Tommy helped him load some hay onto the pickup and they drove out to

353

the pasture to see the horses who came loping through the snow to meet them. Chester's coat had grown all shaggy and he kept whinnying and snorting and nuzzling Tommy's shoulder and Cal said that meant he surely recognized him.

Diane made Tommy promise not to breathe a word about what had happened with Ray. She said she would tell him when the time was right and until then they should just pretend they had come on the spur of the moment, that it was a kind of surprise vacation.

The snow melted and the world transformed. The meadows filled with wildflowers and the horses lost their winter coats and shone like satin in the spring sunshine. Tommy went to school in Choteau and made new friends. One day they were shown a film about what to do in the event of a nuclear attack. It was apparently very important not to panic. And just to get everybody used to the idea, the whole school had to do *drop drill*. There was an intercom in every classroom and as soon as the principal hit the button in his office and sounded the alarm you had to dive under your desk, shut your eyes and cover your head with your arms. Nobody took it too seriously.

In the afternoons and on weekends Tommy and Diane helped around the ranch and went riding. The Matthiesons had about a hundred head of cattle, Herefords, and Cal taught Tommy how to rope and ride among them, separating the ones he wanted from the herd. At the end of April the neighbors came around and everybody helped brand the new calves then sat down at a long trestle table outside the barn and ate a wonderful meal that Rose and Diane had prepared.

354

Rose thought it was funny that Tommy knew a few words of the Blackfeet language. She had a high-pitched squeal of a laugh, the kind that always got everybody else laughing too. They all ate together every evening down at the ranch house and Tommy would help (or mostly hinder) her with the cooking and get her talking about her parents and what life had been like growing up on the reservation.

'Oh, you don't want to know about that,' she would always say. And Tommy would say he did, he really did, and pester her until she told him another story. One weekend in July they all drove up to the reservation in Browning for some special ceremony where everybody wore feathered bonnets and danced and sang. They met Rose's brother and his children and everybody made a big fuss of Tommy and wanted to hear him speak their language.

Quite when or how it happened, Tommy would never know. Either he was too young at the time to pick up the signs or else, more likely, Diane and Cal had taken care to disguise it. But at some point during the summer it became clear that they were more than just friends. When the evenings grew warm, after Tommy had gone to bed, they took to sitting out on the little porch behind the cabin and would watch the sun slide down into the mountains. Tommy couldn't hear what they were saying but there was an unmistakable tone to their voices and once he sneaked a look and saw Cal had his arm around Diane, her head resting against him. She seemed happier than Tommy had ever known her.

Maybe it was just the actress in her, but it still sometimes surprised Diane how effortlessly she could slip into a new world and make it her own. On their journey north she had been so full of doubt that she had almost turned the car around. She'd been worried about whether Cal had really meant it when he asked them to come visit, whether it was wrong and presumptuous. But from the moment he showed up to meet them at the post office that first crystalline morning, it had felt like coming home.

This didn't stop her worrying about what people would make of her sudden disappearance. She had called Herb Kanter and told him, in confidence, what had happened and where they were. He was kind and understanding and made her promise to keep in touch. And as the weeks went by, he kept her up to date with what was being churned out of the Hollywood rumor mill.

Herb had put out a press release saying that Diane was *convalescing after a sudden illness*. Despite his efforts, it didn't fool anyone. The word was that she had suffered some kind of nervous breakdown. According to Herb, Ray was the main source of this. Several newspapers quoted him as saying he had become *concerned* about his wife's behavior, that in the weeks prior to her disappearance, she had become *increasingly unstable*. Louella Parsons kept the story going for the best part of a month, with headlines urging readers to *CATCH A FALLING STAR*. She called Diane the *star who never was, a one-pic wonder*, even drew comparisons with the *demented* Frances

Farmer and poor Peg Entwistle (*that other tragic British failure*) who'd leaped to her death from the Hollywood sign.

Diane found that she didn't care. She was only happy to be free of the place, free of all the phonies and the fakery and the trashy venality that was Hollywood. When Herb warned her that her career *could be jeopardized*, she actually laughed. All that mattered was here and now, watching Tommy grow and thrive and turn golden under the wide-angled blue of the Montana sky. And finding a man, at last, with whom she felt safe.

For two weeks, every evening after supper, Tommy and Cal had been breaking in a young horse, though Cal didn't like the word *breaking*. He said the last thing you wanted to do with a horse was break its spirit. He preferred to call it starting. You had to build a partnership, he said, help the animal find the confidence to team up. The horse was a fine cream-colored mare with a proud strut and an almost regal tilt to her head. Though still a hand too big for Tommy, she was to be his. Tommy named her Cloud.

Diane was helping Rose clear up after supper, while John sat watching the news on their ancient black-and-white TV. The picture was like driving in the rain without wipers. The signal had to fly fifty-five miles from Great Falls and by the time it reached the antenna on the ranch house roof it was too tired to deliver any more than Channel Five with no sound and Channel Three with no picture. It was enough however to give an idea of the rampant paranoia that had seized the world beyond the mountains. It sounded as if the Russians were due to invade any moment.

Diane said goodnight and stepped out through the screen door. She stood for a moment on the baked dirt of the yard, staring west toward the mountains. The sun still had some way to travel before it vanished behind them but already the sky was getting ready for its routine show of pink and red and orange swirls. High in the jet stream two intersecting vapor trails drifted west in a vast and crumbling letter X. It had been another clear, hot day without a stir of wind. The air had that smell Diane had come to love, the smoky whiff of dust and sage.

She walked up along the dirt road toward the corrals. She could hear their voices, Tommy calling the mare's name and Cal laughing. They were too busy to notice her arrival and she leaned with her arms folded on the bleached wood rail of the arena to watch. A cloud of sunlit dust glowed like amber around them. They had the horse saddled and Cal was holding her bridle and stroking her neck while Tommy got ready to climb aboard. The little mare scuffed the ground with her front foot and took a few small steps sideways.

'It's all right, sweetheart,' Cal said. 'That's my good girl, that's my beauty. Okay, Tom, slowly now.'

He guided Tommy's boot into the stirrup and hoisted him gently into the saddle, talking quietly all the while to the horse. She tossed her head and took a few quick steps back and to the side. But then she settled and stood and Cal kept stroking her and telling her it was okay, everything was okay.

'Hey, Tom,' Cal said. 'You did that like you'd done it a hundred times before. Congratulations.

358

How does she feel?'

'She feels great.'

'You look like you were made for each other. How about taking her for a little walk?'

'Sure. Hi, Diane!'

'Look at you,' Diane said.

'He did all the hard stuff,' Cal said. 'The guy's going to put me out of work if I don't watch out.'

He led Tommy around the arena a couple of times and then asked him how he felt about going on his own. Tommy nodded gravely and said he felt fine about it and he pushed his hat down firmly onto his head and gathered the reins and when they came near to where Diane was, Cal let go of the bridle and stood back. And they watched him ride slowly around the arena three more times with the little mare blowing and snuffling as if she'd done it a hundred times before.

The sun was slipping behind the mountains now and in the purple twilight they led the horse to the pasture in front of the cabin and took off her saddle and bridle and turned her loose. And the three of them stood and watched her run off with the other young horses, nonchalantly tossing her head as if telling them what she'd just done and how it was no big deal.

Back at the cabin, Tommy had a glass of milk and a cookie then got ready for bed and Cal sat on the boy's bunk and read him a story from an old book he'd had as a child, called *Tales of the Blackfeet Nation*. Diane settled on the old couch that they'd hauled out on to the porch. She couldn't hear every word but the story was about a clever hunter called Little Teeth and his thwarted attempts to catch a wise old bull elk.

When the story was finished, Cal came to find her and she went inside to Tommy's room to say goodnight.

'Boy, did you look good on that horse.'

'Did I?'

'Know who you looked like?'

'Who?'

'Flint McCullough.'

'Oh, yeah.'

'You did, I promise. Spitting image.'

She stroked his forehead. There was a pale band an inch above his eyebrows from the shade of his hat. He frowned.

'Diane?'

'What, sweetheart?'

'How long are we going to stay here?'

'Oh, I don't know.'

'Can we stay forever?'

'We'll see.'

'That's what you always say when you mean no.'

'I don't mean no. I just mean, let's talk about it some other time.'

She kissed him goodnight and went outside to join Cal on the couch. He put his arm around her and kissed her on the cheek and she rested her head on his shoulder and for a while neither of them spoke. The mountains were silhouetted against a sky that would soon be milky with stars. An owl was calling somewhere down by the creek. Diane shivered.

'Are you cold?'

'No. A little.'

She snuggled in closer.

'Did you hear what he asked me?'

'About staying here forever?'

'Yes.'

'I was kind of interested to hear the answer too.'

'You know the answer.'

She kissed him. But later, when they had moved inside and made love and Cal was asleep beside her, she lay listening to the yip of the coyotes prowling the willow scrub beyond the pasture and she thought about what she'd heard on the news.

Old John Matthieson had become so worried about the imminence of World War Three that he was making his own nuclear bunker. He'd dug a big hole out beyond the corrals, twelve feet square and lined with cement. The roof wasn't yet finished, but the provisions stood ready and waiting in the barn: twenty galvanized garbage bins that Rose had packed with hundreds of cans of tuna fish, corned beef and peaches. Another ten stood ready to be filled with water. Cal had helped but made no secret of his belief that the whole enterprise was a comical waste of time. If the bomb ever did go off, he said, they'd all be dead before they knew it.

One of their favorite rides was out to what Cal called the dinosaur graveyard. It was beyond the big pasture on the other side of the creek, a kind of mudstone badlands where there were so many fossils and bones and beautiful pieces of agate, you didn't even have to look for them. You could get off your horse almost anywhere and just pluck them from the ground. Cal said some sudden and great catastrophe must have happened for there to be so many dead creatures in one place.

One afternoon, at the beginning of September when the weather was starting to cool and the leaves on the cottonwoods along the river were turning yellow, the three of them rode there again. Diane found what they later identified in one of John's reference books as the whole toe of a velociraptor. Diane gave it to Tommy. On the way home, while Tommy rode ahead, Diane and Cal got talking about Cuba and the war of words going on between what John called the two K's, Presidents Kennedy and Khrushchev.

'Anyway,' Diane said. 'We'll be safe here. Nobody's going to drop a bomb on Montana.'

'Come with me,' Cal said. 'I want to show you something.'

He called to Tommy and they veered south and urged the horses into a lope, riding up and over the brow of a hill then down into some rolling grassland Diane hadn't seen before. A watery sun was going down and the light was eerie and metallic, the horses' shadows stretching like phantoms across the bleached grass. Diane was beginning to wonder where they were going when, in the middle of nowhere, they came to a chain-link fence topped with barbed wire. There were *Keep Out* signs and through the wire they could see cement lids set into the ground with tracks along which they could be slid aside. In each corner of the fenced area was what looked like a camera. Diane asked Cal what on earth the place was.

'It's a missile silo. There are a whole lot of them, all along the Front. Just been built.'

He said that these silos housed giant rockets called Minutemen that could travel five thousand miles and that each one of them was fitted with a one-megaton nuclear warhead capable of destroying an entire city. One night the previous year, he'd noticed floodlights here and he'd ridden

362

out and seen a long truck with a crane, lowering the missiles into the ground.

'Are there people down there to fire them?' Tommy said.

'No, they say the red button's in Great Falls, at Malmstrom.'

'Will Mr Kennedy come and press it himself?' Tommy asked.

'I guess he'd call on some kind of special phone and tell somebody else to.'

There was a gust of cold wind.

'Maybe that's what happened to the dinosaurs.'

Cal laughed and said maybe he was right. But there was no need to worry. It wasn't going to happen. Having these silos here was supposed to make them all safer. The idea was called Mutually Assured Destruction, MAD for short. And you'd have to be pretty mad, Cal said, to start a war when you knew it would obliterate you and every other living creature on the planet.

A week later came the first fall of snow. It came overnight, just a few inches, and at dawn the sky cleared to show the world remade. After Tommy had gone to school Cal and Diane rode up into the foothills. They stood the horses at the top of the bluff and heard elk bugling. High in the crystalline sky, great flocks of geese were heading south in their V formations.

'I could get used to a place like this,' Diane said.

'So, why don't you?'

'Oh, Cal.'

'Seriously. Hell, Tom's already settled. You'd have a job getting him to leave.'

'I know.'

They were silent a moment, the horses' breath

curling and wreathing in the chill air.

'Cal, there's something I've been wanting to ask you.'

'The answer's yes.'

'I'm serious.'

'So am I.'

'It's just that...if anything were to happen to me. Say, if I had an accident or something, I wouldn't want Ray to have any kind of hold or influence over Tommy. Would you look after him?'

'Of course I would.'

She leaned across and kissed him.

One afternoon the following week, while Tommy was still in school, they drove through the snow into town to the office of the Matthiesons' attorney. Alfred Cobb, a bright-eyed but slightly decrepit veteran of the First World War, had all the papers ready. And in front of a log fire, Diane and Cal sat at his wide oak desk and signed them. In the event of Diane's death, Cal thereby agreed that he would adopt and care for Tommy.

At the very end of October, just two days after the two Presidents K went eyeball to eyeball over Cuba and the world pulled back from the brink of war, a young man drove up to the ranch with a telegram for Diane. It was from her London agent, Julian Baverstock. YOUR FATHER GRAVELY ILL, IT SAID. PLEASE RTN UK SOONEST.

TWENTY-EIGHT

They were having a final dinner—or, as Dutch less than tactfully called it, the last supper—at Marco's. They had their usual corner booth with a red-and-white-check tablecloth and old-fashioned oil lamps. Everyone was trying not to let things get too gloomy. The hearing was due to finish the following day and any hope that it would go Danny's way had faded. That afternoon Brian McKnight had warned Tom, Dutch and Gina to expect the worst. He said that, on the balance of the evidence, Colonel Scrase would have little choice but to recommend a court-martial.

McKnight had promised he would meet them at the restaurant but his place remained empty. Then, just as they were asking for the check, he showed up. He was a little breathless and they could tell at once that something important had happened. Dutch poured him a glass of Chianti and they all leaned in to listen.

McKnight said his office had received a phone call from a young Marine called Travis Wilson, a private first class in Danny's company who had left the corps six months ago. Danny nodded and said he knew the guy but not well. McKnight went on to say that Wilson had seen the TV news the previous night and heard Harker's claim that he and Delgado hadn't conferred.

'He says it's not true. He saw them together in a bar in Coronado. After everyone got flown home.'

'Did he hear what they were saying?' Dutch said.

'Enough. I hope. He's flying in tonight from

Omaha. Kevin's picking him up at the airport at ten o'clock. If it all stacks up, we'll put him on the stand tomorrow.'

Colonel Scrase had barely settled in his plush red throne the following morning when McKnight sprang up to ask permission to call a final witness. Wendell Richards, all set to deliver the government's closing argument, looked both irritated and wary. PFC Travis Wilson wasn't anyone's idea of perfect casting. He was short and had a rodentlike face that was covered in acne. As he took the oath, he looked about as nervous as a man could get without actually wetting himself. What he had to deliver however was the verbal version of a roadside bomb.

McKnight coaxed him through the openers: his rank and experience and what his knowledge was of the incident and of the accused.

'Travis, on the evening of July twenty-third last year, could you tell us please, where were you?'

'In a bar called Dee's Place in Coronado.'

'What were you doing there?'

'Meeting Cindy—that's my girlfriend. Well, she was my girlfriend at the time. We've split up now. Anyhow, we'd arranged to meet at seven thirty, but I got there about twenty minutes early—I'm like that, always early—and I was sitting there, in one of the booths, you know, waiting for Cindy and—'

'Was there anyone else there that you knew?'

'Yes, sir. Sergeant Delgado and Eldon Harker. I realized they were sitting in the next booth.'

'You recognized them?'

'Yes, sir.'

'They were friends of yours?'

366

'No, sir. I just knew them both. In Iraq.'

'And did you say hello?'

'No, sir. Well, I was just about to, but then I, kind of, heard what they were talking about and decided not to.'

'And they didn't notice you?'

'I don't believe so, sir, no. Dee's is a kind of dark place.'

'How clearly could you hear what they were saying?'

'Pretty clearly, I'd say.'

'And what did you hear?'

'I heard Sergeant Delgado telling Harker what he'd have to say if he wanted to get the murder charge dropped.'

Wendell Richards was on his feet immediately to object. And for most of the next half hour he was bobbing up and down like a gopher in a box doing the same. Little by little, however, McKnight patiently extracted from Travis Wilson all he wanted. Wilson said he had heard Delgado, effectively, rehearsing Harker in what he would have to say in order to get off the murder charge and shift all the blame onto Danny. He had even heard the magic words *use your goddamn weapon*.

By the time McKnight was done, he looked a good foot taller than when he'd begun.

Richards had his chance to cross-examine. He tried to cast doubt on what the young soldier had heard, suggesting that he might have some grudge against one or both of the men on whom he'd eavesdropped. But Tom could sense from Richards's demeanor that the poor guy knew the killer punch had been landed. When he was through, McKnight rose portentously to his feet

367

and asked that Sergeant Delgado and Eldon Harker be recalled to the stand and be read their rights under Article 31.

*   *   *

They had to wait almost a month for the investigating officer's findings to come through. Meanwhile, in the first week of June, Kelly went into labor and gave birth to a healthy eight-pound boy. He was to be baptized Thomas David, for his two grandfathers.

On a warm and cloudless morning Tom drove across the divide to the hospital in Great Falls and held his first grandchild in his arms. From the window of Kelly's room you could see the Front Range still dusted with snow and Tom snuggled the baby to his shoulder and pointed to the various peaks and passes and told him their names: Sawtooth, Ear Mountain, Steamboat. Gina and Dutch and Danny were there too and the sun streamed in on them all and there wasn't a dry eye in the room. Gina asked Tom if he'd come back to their place for something to eat but he made an excuse that he had to be back in Missoula and drove all the way home again. Perhaps one day he might be ready for that kind of integration, but not yet.

Brian McKnight called that same evening to say the report had arrived. In two hundred intricate pages Colonel Robert Scrase sifted through the evidence and concluded that Danny had acted in self-defense. He recommended that all charges be dropped. Phone calls were made and everybody exhaled, though nobody seemed inclined to celebrate. Seven innocent lives had still been lost for the one that had been saved. Danny was going to leave the corps and find something else to do.

He called Tom at the end of June and asked if they could get together and talk over his plans. He was thinking of going to college, he said, and wanted his father's advice. On a whim, Tom suggested they go fishing, something they hadn't done together since Danny was a child. Tom hauled the camping gear from the attic and it all seemed in good enough order. But it was years since he'd fished even on his own and when he checked his lines and casts they'd gone brittle and his supply of flies was pitiful, so he went into town and spent a small fortune at the Grizzly Hackle on Front Street.

Danny arrived in Missoula in the afternoon two days later and they drove for an hour to one of Tom's favorite stretches of the Blackfoot. They left the car at the trailhead and hiked with all their gear through the forest until they could hear the rush of the river below. They found a good place at the edge of the trees to pitch the tent and gathered some wood for the fire they'd make later and by the time they'd done this the light was fading and they could see the clouds of flies swirling above the water so they rigged up the rods and put on their waders and fished for their supper.

Danny caught the first, a fine brown trout, some fifteen inches long, and the boy's smile was almost as big. Tom hooked a bigger one but lost it and then lost two more before landing another, two inches smaller than Danny's. It must have taken pity on him.

They lit the fire and panfried the trout and ate them with some tomatoes and the potato-and-chive salad Tom remembered Danny being so crazy about when he was little. The flesh of the trout was pink and sweet and the two of them kept moaning in ecstasy until they were giggling too much to swallow. Tom brewed some coffee and they sat cradling their tin mugs in their hands and watching the light on the river's bend change from silver to bronze to black while an owl kept calling and calling in the pines across the river.

Danny told him his plans. He wanted to go for a bachelor of science degree in agribusiness at Montana State in Bozeman. But he was late in applying for the coming fall and, in any case, liked the idea of getting some practical experience first. Dutch had a friend who ran an agricultural supply outfit and was prepared to take Danny on to show him the business. Tom said he thought that all sounded great, just great.

They fell silent for a while. Just the hushed roar of the water below and the owl still hooting across the river. Tom put some more wood on the fire and the sparks spiraled upward between them. Danny stared at the fire for a long time. In the flicker and glow his face looked suddenly a lot older. When at last he spoke he didn't look at Tom, just kept his eyes on the fire.

'Dad, there's something I need to tell you.'

'I'm listening.'

There was a long pause. The boy took a deep breath.

'I was guilty.'

'What do you mean?'

'You know all that stuff at the hearing, what they

said about me yelling at the women, how I called them *hajji bitches* and ...'

Danny put his head back and stared at the stars for a while, breathing heavily, as if summoning the strength to go on.

'It's okay, son. You can tell me.'

'It's not true I thought the guy had a weapon.'

He stopped again and swallowed. Tom waited.

'The truth is, I didn't care. I just ... hated them. Hated them so much, for what had happened. For what had happened to Ricky and all of us. It was like, when the guy reached down, it was like ... a good enough reason. Maybe it was a weapon, I didn't know. I was, like, totally out of my head. I didn't know. I didn't care. All I knew was ... I wanted to kill the bastards, mow the whole fucking lot of them down ...'

There were tears streaming down his face now.

'And then it was over and I saw them lying there, saw what I'd done. And it was like seeing them for the first time. Women and kids. Babies, for christsake ... And it was me who'd done it.'

Tom shifted around the fire and put his arm around the boy's shoulders.

'It was me.'

'Danny, listen—'

'It was *me*, Dad. I *meant* to do it.'

There was probably something to be said, but Tom couldn't think what it might be. He pulled him close and Danny hung his head and sobbed and Tom just sat there, stroking the boy's hair and holding him. How long they sat like that, he couldn't tell. A half-moon the color of bone hoisted itself above a shoulder of the mountains beyond the bend of the river and the fire crumpled to an ashen glow.

'I want to tell you something now,' Tom said quietly.

'What?'

'I want to tell you about your grandmother and what really happened to her.'

TWENTY-NINE

As soon as the telegram arrived, Diane placed a long-distance call to London. Julian Baverstock told her that her father was in the Queen Elizabeth Hospital in Birmingham. He had cancer of the throat and lungs and it was too advanced for any kind of treatment. The doctors had given him two weeks at most.

Cal made some calls and found that the quickest way was to take the train to San Francisco and, from there, a BOAC flight to London. It was only while they were packing their bags in the cabin that Diane remembered the passports. They were locked in Ray's safe in LA. She cursed herself for a fool but didn't panic. They would simply have to travel by train to LA, she announced, go to the house to collect them, then fly to England as planned.

Cal said, years later, that he had tried to persuade Diane to let him accompany them and that he would never forgive himself for failing to insist on it. But Diane had been calm and clear and adamant about it, he said. She didn't want to call Ray in case he started playing games. No, it was better just to show up. If Ray was there, she could handle it. If he was out (and she would try to time it so that he would be), she had a key to the house and knew the combination of the safe. She would simply let herself in, get the passports and leave.

Saying goodbye to Cal when he put them on the train in Choteau was hard. He made them promise to hurry back and stood there on the platform waving his hat as the train pulled away. And they leaned out the window waving until all they could see of him was a black speck against the snow.

The journey by rail was shorter than it had been by road but it still seemed epic to Tommy. They ate and slept and read their books and stared out in silence at the ever-shifting landscape that grew harsher and more barren by the hour. There was none of the game playing or singing of their trip northward eight months before and it wasn't simply because they were both thinking about Arthur. Another kind of sadness seemed to have fallen upon them and it was all to do with leaving Cal.

'Are you and Cal going to get married?'

'Oh, Tommy, I don't know. He hasn't asked me. Anyhow, I'm still married to Ray.'

'But you're gonna get a divorce, right?'

She smiled at him and stroked his hair.

'You're sounding more like an American boy every day. Yes, I'm gonna get a divorce. Would you like it if Cal and I got married?'

'Are you kidding? Of course I would.'

'Then maybe, one day, we will.'

'Would that mean we could always live in Montana?'

'I don't see why not.'

Tommy was asleep when the train at last pulled into Union Station. When Diane woke him he thought for a moment that she was a stranger. She was wearing a headscarf and sunglasses so that nobody would recognize her. A porter loaded their bags onto his cart and they followed him through the station and found a cab. It was late in the afternoon. His eyes still blurred with sleep, Tommy stared out at the manicured streets, the avenues of palms, the elegant houses with their weedless lawns, the sprinklers making rainbows in the last of the sunshine. And he wondered how he could ever have been excited or impressed by the place for there was nothing here, not a single thing, that was real. It was all for show, entirely contrived and alien.

The gates to Ray's driveway were open and when they came in sight of the house and the rearing bronze horse there were no cars nor any sign of life to be seen. Diane asked the cabdriver to wait and told Tommy to stay there with him. She took her keys from her purse and said she wouldn't be long. Tommy watched her run up the steps to the front door. She stood there a moment listening, then put the key in the lock and stealthily let herself in.

She had been gone no more than a couple of minutes when Tommy heard a car coming up the driveway. When he looked around, his heart missed a beat. It was Ray in the Cadillac. He was peering at the cab, clearly wondering what it was doing there. He pulled up behind it. Tommy quickly turned around, lowered himself in his seat and watched the cabdriver staring in his mirror as Ray got out of the car and slowly walked up to the rear door of the cab and squinted in through the window. He was all in black and wearing sunglasses, even in the fading light. He had to take them off before he could make out who it was. Then he beamed and opened the door.

'Well, for heavensake, look who's here!'

'Hi, Ray.'

'Tommy, old son, how the heck are you?'

'I'm okay.'

'What's going on? Where's your mom?'

Tommy hesitated.

'She's gone inside? Well, what are you doing out here? Come on, ol' pal, let's go find her. Gee, how great to see ya!'

'She said to wait here.'

'Don't be like that, come on.'

He reached in and Tommy realized there was no choice. When he climbed out of the cab Ray gave him a big hug.

'Heck, Tommy, it's so good to see you. I missed you, real bad.'

Tommy swallowed and forced a smile. Ray pulled his wallet from the back pocket of his jeans and paid the driver and told him to go.

'But, Diane said—'

'It's okay, son. Don't worry. Come on, now.'

He put an arm around Tommy's shoulders and they walked toward the house.

'Hey, Tommy, have you grown! Man, just look at the size of you!'

As they reached the front door, Dolores came running out.

'She's back! She let herself in.'

'I know, I know, it's okay. It's great. Look, Tommy's here too. They've come home.'

She glanced at Tommy and switched on a cold-eyed smile.

'Hi, Tommy.'

'Hi.'

'Where is she?' Ray asked quietly.

'Upstairs. She's trying to get into the safe. I told her not to—'

'It's okay, Dolores. Everything's under control, ain't that right, Tommy?'

He slapped Tommy on the back.

'I tell you what, son. Why don't you go with Dolores and she'll make you one of those chocolate shakes you like? How about that?'

'I'll wait here.'

'No, you go with Dolores. Do as you're told.'

Tommy would always blame himself for being so weak at that moment. If he'd stood his ground, stayed in the hallway or followed Ray up the stairs instead of allowing himself to be steered off to the kitchen by Dolores, maybe what happened next might somehow have been avoided. One of the things he would later learn was that in life timing was all. A moment either way could make the difference between happiness and misery, between life and death or eternal damnation.

They went through to the kitchen and Dolores got the ice cream and milk from the refrigerator and asked him questions about where they had been while she made the shake. Tommy wasn't paying attention and didn't volunteer much by way of reply except to say they'd been to Montana. He was trying to listen, trying to imagine what was happening upstairs. He was standing by the table and Dolores told him to sit down and then again more firmly, so he did.

How long it was before Diane started shouting, he couldn't tell. Maybe five minutes, maybe less. But as soon as he heard her, he was on his feet and the chair tipped over behind him and clattered to the floor and he was off and running. Dolores called after him but by now he was in the hallway and heading for the stairs and he could hear Diane shouting upstairs in Ray's bedroom.

'Just open the safe, will you!'

'Diane, for godsake, calm down. Let's just talk for a moment.'

'All I want is our passports!'

'I know, but I told you, they're not in there anymore.'

'I don't believe you.'

'Well, that's up to you, sweetheart.'

'Let me see for myself.'

'No, Diane. I'm not going to do that.'

'Open the goddamn safe, Ray!'

Tommy stopped just outside the bedroom doorway and stood there a moment, listening and trying to peep in without being seen. He could see them at the far end of the room, facing each other in front of the open closet where the safe was. He took a cautious step forward. Ray had his back to him but must have noticed Diane's eyes flicker toward the door because he turned to look over his shoulder and saw Tommy and smiled.

'You go downstairs now, son. Everything's okay. Your mom and I just need to talk a few things over. Go downstairs. Good boy. Do as you're told now.'

Tommy hesitated. He wasn't going to take orders from anyone but Diane. But she nodded her agreement.

377

'Go on, Tommy. Just wait in the hallway. I'll be down in a minute.'

Tommy turned reluctantly and headed back across the landing. They were talking again, but in lowered voices now. He couldn't make out what they were saying but the tone was urgent and venomous. Dolores was at the foot of the stairs and she told him to come down and then headed off again across the hallway toward the kitchen.

He was only halfway down the stairs when Diane screamed. He turned around and ran as fast as he could back up and across the landing and into the bedroom again. And as he came in he saw Ray shove Diane back against the far wall and then step toward her and hit her twice in the face, one-two, backhand and forehand, in quick succession. Tommy yelled for him to stop but Ray ignored him and Diane screamed and leaped at him and tried to hit him back but he was too quick. She clawed at his face then grabbed a handful of his hair and wrenched it and he yelled and grasped her by the wrist and swung her around and slammed her hard against the wall. Tommy heard the breath leave her lungs in a sudden, shocking groan. She saw him at the door and tried to say something but couldn't find her voice and then Ray punched her in the stomach and she doubled up and sank to her knees.

'I said go downstairs, kid, didn't you hear?' Ray yelled, without looking at him. 'Get out of here!'

The command was so fierce that Tommy almost obeyed. He actually turned and began to head out onto the landing. But then he stopped and, in a moment of perfect clarity, knew what to do. He turned one last time and headed across the room

378

to Ray's nightstand.

Ray must have thought he'd gone. He'd taken hold of the lapels of Diane's jacket and was hauling her to her feet. As quietly as he could, Tommy slid open the drawer. Damn it, it wasn't there anymore. Ray must be keeping it in some other place. Diane was crying and pleading now, but Tommy couldn't make out what she was saying because his head was filled with the rush and pump of his own blood. Then he pulled the drawer out a little more and there it was, the dull glint of the barrel, right at the back.

The steel felt cold in his hand as he pulled the gun out. He was trying to be quick and quiet at the same time which wasn't easy because his hands were shaking so badly. But he managed to slip the safety without making a click and then, with both hands, gripped hold of the handle and raised it to eye level and lined it up on Ray's back.

It was Diane who caught sight of him first. Ray had his hand around her throat and was pinning her to the wall. Her eyes were wide and terrified. She stopped struggling and went very still and without letting go of her Ray slowly turned and saw him too.

'Let go of her,' Tommy said.

'Jesus, kid. What the hell do you think you're doing? Put that thing down.'

'I said let go of her.'

Ray shook his head and smiled as if this were the most ridiculous and tiresome thing he'd ever seen. But he did release his hand and Diane slumped and turned to the wall and staggered sideways a little, gasping and coughing and clutching her throat.

379

'Tommy,' she at last managed to say. 'Don't be silly now, put it down.'

But he didn't. He told Diane to move farther away but she still didn't seem strong enough.

'You heard what your mom said, son. Put the gun down. There's a good boy.'

'Get away from her.'

'That's enough, son. Come on, now. Someone's going to get hurt. Give me the gun.'

He took a step toward him and Tommy shouted at him not to move. It was only the bed that separated them now.

'Open the safe,' Tommy said.

Ray laughed.

'You've seen too many westerns, kid. Who the hell are we today? Billy the Kid?'

'Tommy, please, put that thing down.'

'No, he's going to open the safe. Open it!'

He clicked back the hammer. From his westerns, he knew this generally helped to focus attention and it did. Ray held up his palms.

'Okay, okay.'

He turned around and it looked for a moment as if he really intended to go and open the safe. But as he stepped toward the closet he suddenly lurched to one side and grabbed hold of Diane. Tommy knew what was coming. He'd seen it a hundred times on TV and in the movies. The guy was going to use her as a shield. Or maybe he was going to start hurting her again or worse. Either way, in that sliver of a second Tommy knew there was no other choice. He squeezed the trigger and fired.

Watching someone die was nothing like they showed it on TV. The bullet entered Ray's head just below his right eye and he fell back against the wall and slid slowly down until he was sitting on the floor. The look on his face wasn't of agony or even of pain, just a kind of amused surprise that this had actually happened, that this was real life and not some episode of *Sliprock* and that nobody was going to be calling *Cut!*

Time seemed suddenly suspended. There was no blood at first, just a charred black hole. The room smelled of smoke and Tommy's ears rang from the explosion. But he could still hear the rasp and gurgle coming from Ray's mouth. Diane stood there stunned and staring down at him as the life trickled out of him.

'Tommy,' she whispered. 'What have you done?'

'He was going to—'

Dolores was calling from down in the hallway now, shouting Ray's name, asking what had happened. She sounded terrified. Then they heard her outside, calling for Miguel.

Tommy still had the gun in his hand. He couldn't take his eyes off Ray. There was blood now. A lot of it. Rivering down his face and neck, glistening on his shirt. Then his hands twitched and his fingers did a spidery little dance on the floor and he groaned one last time and went still.

'Tommy, quick, give me the gun. Give it to me!'

She snatched it from his hand and he warned her sharply to be careful because the safety was still off. He showed her how to click it on. She grabbed a corner of the counterpane and began wiping the gun down.

'What are you doing?'

'Tommy, listen to me now. Listen very carefully.'

Then there was a scream and they turned and

saw Dolores and Miguel standing in the doorway. Dolores was clutching her face in her hands, her eyes darting from the gun in Diane's hand to Ray's body slumped and bloody on the other side of the room. She murmured something then turned and fled and Miguel backed slowly away across the landing.

THIRTY

The fire had burned low by now and Tom gazed into the embers. He knew Danny was staring at him, waiting for him to go on, but these truths and the pictures they conjured had lain buried for almost half a century and digging them up had taken its toll.

'Dad? Are you okay?'

Tom nodded and glanced at his son but quickly turned away and looked up at the sky. The moon had passed in an arc over their heads and now hung reflected upstream between the steep pinnacled banks where the water ran unruffled.

'I'm getting cold. Are you cold?'

Danny shook his head.

Tom stood up. His knees had stiffened and he limped a little as he walked to the tent. He pulled a sweater from his pack and put it on while Danny fed the fire with the last few limbs of the wood they had gathered. They settled again and both took a drink from Tom's water bottle.

'Dad, you don't have to go on. I can see how hard—'

'I want to.' He laughed. 'Hell, don't stop me

382

now. This is where it gets interesting.'

*   *   *

It had taken Tom many years and thousands of dollars in therapy bills to stop viewing his life as a sequence of *If Onlies*. If only he'd done this instead of that or kept his temper and his mouth shut at certain crucial moments; if only he'd been able to see some important event from someone else's point of view instead of being so damned sure he was right; if only he'd been kinder and more considerate with Gina; if only he hadn't allowed himself to be overwhelmed with anger and self—loathing when she and Danny left. He'd discovered at last that this wasn't a useful way of looking at things—unless, of course, it helped you avoid making the same mistakes over and over again (which, in his case, it hadn't). All it ultimately did was fill your head and your heart with maudlin regrets that sprouted roots and tendrils and clung there like some noxious creeper until there was no room for anything else to grow.

Even so, it was difficult to retrace what had happened to Diane without finding an *If Only* at almost every juncture.

In the late 1990s, just before he died, Herb Kanter had given a long interview to a movie magazine about his life and career. The interviewer had clearly done her research because she'd asked about Diane Reed, a name which by then meant little even to those who considered themselves movie buffs. Herb didn't have a lot to say on the subject except that Diane had been very talented and that what happened was tragic. He

383

reflected that if only Jerry Giesler had still been around, the case wouldn't even have gotten to court.

Giesler was the legendary attorney who was summoned when Hollywood's greatest found themselves up to their hips in trouble. He'd successfully defended a small galaxy of stars, including Errol Flynn, Robert Mitchum and Charlie Chaplin. One of his last triumphs was in 1958, when Lana Turner's daughter plunged a kitchen knife into her mother's mobster boyfriend, Johnny Stompanato. Giesler got to the scene of the killing even before the police and made sure that mother and daughter had their stories in order. The case never got beyond an inquest where Lana gave the performance of her career, clinching a verdict of justifiable homicide. Herb Kanter apparently believed that Giesler could and would have done the same for Diane. Sadly for all concerned, by the time she needed him he was but a plaque on the wall at Forest Lawn Memorial-Park.

The biggest *If Only* by far, however, was the one that Tom alone knew about. If only he had disobeyed his mother and told the truth. But Diane had been so clear and forceful about what was best. In those fifteen minutes before the police arrived, she told him again and again what he should say and made him promise—cross his heart and hope to die—to stick to it. Without yet knowing what she intended, he had watched her clean the gun then grip it firmly in her right hand, even gently press her finger against the trigger, then lay it on the bed. Then she went to the nightstand and wiped the handle of the drawer

384

then pressed her fingers on it.

'Diane, what are you doing?'

'You heard me shouting when you were down in the kitchen with Dolores, right? And you came upstairs and heard us fighting. You stood in the doorway, just the way you did, and you saw him hitting me. Okay? Tommy, look at me. This is very important.'

His eyes kept wandering off to Ray's body, so she grabbed him by the shoulders and made him look her in the eyes.

'I managed to get away from him and run over here, to the other side of the bed, okay? And I got the gun from the drawer—*I* got it, okay? Not you. And I pointed it at him and told him to keep away, just like you did, only remember: it was me who said it, not you. You were just watching from the doorway, do you understand? Tommy, listen to me!'

'I am.'

'Then I asked him to open the safe and get the passports but he came running at me and that was when I fired.'

'But, Diane, that's not—'

'I don't care! That's the story. I did it, not you. If we both say that's what happened everything will be all right. Now go and wash your hands.'

And that was the story they both told the police officers who interviewed them and the one they stuck to long after Tom realized she was wrong and everything wasn't going to be all right.

He knew from the start that Diane was only lying to protect him and he wondered later if there was any connection between this and the other great lie of their lives, the one about who his

385

parents were, the one that was supposed to protect them all from shame. Perhaps she believed it had worked well for all concerned. At least, until it had served its purpose and the truth could safely be revealed. Perhaps she had convinced herself that this new lie would work in their best interests too.

After Danny was born (and long before the question ceased to be altogether hypothetical), Tom had often wondered if he would do the same, wipe his child's fingerprints from the gun and lie under oath to shoulder the blame. He didn't know. How could you ever know until it happened?

Given his fine propensity for guilt, he'd also wondered if he had in some way let Diane down. He knew he should have paid more attention to what she'd instructed him to tell the police, for there were, as it turned out, discrepancies between the statements they had separately made. In particular these concerned what exactly Ray had said and done before Diane fired the shot that killed him.

The officers who interviewed him were friendly and sympathetic but that didn't stop them asking sneaky questions. They got him talking about where he and Diane had been living lately and he probably told them a lot more than he should have. He said how kind Cal had been to them both and even mentioned what Diane had said on the train about how she and Cal might marry once she could divorce Ray. He didn't notice at the time but their ears must have pricked up.

They kept coming back to whether Diane had in any way sought to suggest what Tom should tell them. And it took him a while to realize that this wasn't because they suspected that it was he and not Diane who had killed Ray, but rather that she was trying to make the killing look more like self-defense than it truly had been. And the more he tried to help her, the more tangled his lying became. Finally, he tried telling them the truth. But by now they didn't want to believe him.

'It's her fingerprints on the weapon, Tommy, not yours.'

'I know, because she wanted to take the blame. She wiped mine off—and off the drawer handle. It was me. You've got to believe me.'

'You're a brave boy, son. Trying to protect your mom like that. But it just doesn't figure.'

'But it's the truth!'

Diane was kept in custody. And, until Cal arrived, this meant that Tom had to be kept in custody too. He was declared a material witness and dispatched to the county juvenile hall, about which he could now remember very little except that it wasn't nearly as bad as his boarding school in England. There were some pretty tough kids there and one or two seriously mean ones but at least no psychopaths like Whippet Brent on the staff.

Cal rented an apartment in West Hollywood. Tom remembered them peeping through the shades at the little crowd of reporters and photographers who, for the first few weeks, waited under the trees in the street outside, smoking and laughing then erupting into action the moment they caught sight of anyone coming out of the apartment block. Then they seemed to lose interest. Tommy went back to Carl Curtis and then, in the fall, to the local junior high school.

Diane was duly charged with murder. At a bail

hearing, according to the press clippings Tom later dug up, the prosecution did all it could to paint her as a cold-blooded killer, even darkly hinting that Ray's death might not have been a one-off domestic issue but instead merely the start of some wider purge of Hollywood's thespian cowboys. The judge wasn't convinced. John Wayne and friends, he said, could sleep soundly in their beds. But the bail application was denied. Arthur died a week later, unaware of the crisis engulfing his daughter and grandson.

It was a little over twelve months before the case came to trial.

Reading the clippings many years later, Tom was intrigued by how the plot and the leading characters had been manipulated to fit the Hollywood template. Despite the fact that Ray's seamier side had been an open secret, his demise required that he be remembered only as the valiant cowboy hero, one of the nation's most treasured TV darlings, Red McGraw, righter of wrongs, who *stood alone against injustice*—only now with wings and a halo around his hat.

Diane, by contrast, had to be the wicked temptress. Ambitious beyond all scruple, she was portrayed as the shameless English harlot who'd broken up a happy marriage and lied about her sordid and immoral past, whose illegitimate son dear, sweet Ray had so generously taken in, only to find himself cuckolded by his own stunt double and wrangler, a *half-breed Indian* to boot. Nameless sources spoke of how the *torrid* affair— there could be, of course, no other kind—had started in Arizona, on the set of *The Forsaken*, and (most heinous of all, for everything in Hollywood,

388

in the end, boiled down to money) how the scandal had blighted the movie's performance at the box office.

Cal rented a blue Buick sedan which they kept in the basement garage and every Wednesday afternoon, after school, they drove over into the valley to visit Diane in prison. They were allowed forty minutes with her and had to talk through a glass screen. The only time they were allowed to touch each other during those first few months was when, by special dispensation of a sympathetic judge, Diane and Cal were married in the little prison chapel. Herb Kanter came to give Diane away. The only other people there were the chaplain, who looked about sixteen years old, and a shriveled old man with thick glasses who played the organ. Diane wore a pale blue dress and held a bouquet of cream-colored lilies. She smiled bravely while everyone else tried not to cry.

The trial began in the third week of November in front of a jury of nine men and three women. Tom was not allowed to attend, not even to testify. Both sides agreed that this would be too traumatic and that the sworn statements of his police interviews would suffice. He never found out if there was some other reason. Diane's attorney probably thought there were enough inconsistencies already and that his appearance on the stand might make matters worse.

Not that they could have gotten much worse. The deadliest prosecution witness was, of course, Dolores. On the second day of the trial, according to the press reports, she told the court in *a brave and tremulous voice* that Diane had always treated her badly and been rude and cruel to her; that she had many times seen and heard Diane yelling and swearing at Ray and even throwing things at him; that in a fit of rage she had once broken the living room mirror; how Ray had always tried to calm her and how kind and loving he had been both to Diane and, especially, to young Tommy. On the day of the murder, she said, the accused had barged into the house, shouted at her and threatened her; when Ray arrived she had heard Diane screaming foul-mouthed abuse at him. She said that she'd heard a shot and run upstairs and seen Diane with the gun in her hand, calmly looking at Ray's body; and that when Diane caught sight of her and Miguel in the doorway, she turned toward them, still holding the gun; and that, fearing for their lives, they had fled downstairs and called the police.

From that day on, newspaper and TV coverage of the trial virtually ceased, eclipsed by a murder story far greater, the assassination in Dallas, Texas, of the thirty-fifth president of the United States. And from that day forth, the fate of a young British actress on trial for her life in a California courtroom seemed to hold little interest for anyone except those who knew her. For some years, later in his life, Tom had often thought of doing some research into the conviction rates in murder trials that took place at that time. He'd had this theory that a nation so devastated might well have felt more inclined to seek revenge on all possible assassins.

But there was probably a much less exotic reason for what happened. Many years later, after John and Rose had died and Cal had moved down to Nevada, he told Tom that when she took the stand Diane had seemed vague and distracted. The prosecuting attorney kept tripping her up with the inconsistencies between her statements and Tom's. He said you could almost hear the self-defense theory shattering on the polished courtroom floor and that, the following week, when the jury came back with their verdict, they looked almost bored. It took them just four hours to come up with the unanimous verdict that the rest of the world (or that small part of it that was still interested) had already reached. The defendant was guilty as charged of murder in the first degree. Diane was handcuffed and led away to the cells.

The appeal took the best part of a year to come to court. And during that time there was barely a night that Tom didn't have some terrible dream about what was going to happen. Strangely, it was he who was usually the victim. He was in the gas chamber himself, strapped into a chair while curls of smoke swirled around his ankles and then his knees and hips and then his chest and then he would wake up screaming and Cal would be there and hold him and lie with him until he slept again.

And every Wednesday afternoon, they would drive out together to the prison. Tommy dreaded every visit. Diane was always so brave and funny and full of hope, as if the whole thing were some great misunderstanding that would soon be cleared up. One day, while he sat with Cal in the waiting room, a brown-colored bird flew in through one of the high barred windows. There were four big fans suspended from the ceiling and everyone in the room watched as it fluttered perilously around them. Then one of the guards

391

found a net on a long pole and tried to catch it but all he eventually managed to do was drive the poor creature into one of the fans and it fell dead in a flurry of feathers to the floor.

The appeal was turned down and the date set for Diane's execution. Tom could remember every moment of that last visit. The clanking and the voices echoing along the corridors; how he had followed the fat guard through all those doors and gates; the sight of Diane standing smiling at him in the sunlit cell when the other guard opened the door. And all he had felt was a seething anger that life should be so.

After their time was up, he had to sit in the waiting room again while Cal went to say goodbye to her. When he came back, Tom stood up and Cal put his arm around his shoulders and they walked out of the cell block and out into the warm evening air toward the parking lot. There was a huge Stars and Stripes above the prison, undulating in the last of the sunlight. Tom stared at it all the way to the car and even as they drove away he couldn't take his eyes off it, as if it somehow had the power to stop what was happening.

Two days later, Diane went to the gas chamber.

THIRTY-ONE

Danny didn't ask him anything that night. They sat in silence for a long time until a riffle of wind stirred and sparked the embers of the fire. Tom could see in the boy's eyes that he was shocked and moved by the story of what had happened to his grandmother. Whether it would help lighten the burden of his own guilt about the lives he had taken, Tom couldn't tell. Probably not. Only the passing of the years could do that.

The following day as they drove back to Missoula, Danny asked if Gina knew about what had happened to Diane, and Tom said that all he'd ever disclosed was that his 'sister' had been killed in a car crash when he was thirteen. He said he would tell her, if Danny thought it was a good idea. Danny said he thought it was. He went on to ask a lot of questions about Cal who had died of a sudden heart attack in the same year Danny was born. Gina and Cal had never met. Danny got Tom talking about his teenage years in Choteau, how happy they were and how they probably saved him from being sent off to some reform school or funny farm. He said it as a joke, but it was true.

'What about Cal's parents?'

'John died in the early seventies, two years after I went to UM. Rose lived another five. She wasn't too good after he'd gone. She had what I guess you'd nowadays call Alzheimer's. In the end Cal had to put her in a home.'

'You must have missed him a lot. Cal, I mean.'

'Yeah. He was a great guy. Closest thing to a father that I ever had. I still miss him.'

Whatever else, if anything, Tom's campfire confession might have done for Danny, it seemed to kindle an interest in his family's history. He went in search of the movies Diane had been in. The two she had made in Britain had never made it to video. But about a year later, on some obscure website, Danny managed to find *The Forsaken*. He phoned Tom to tell him and, a little nervously, asked if he wanted to watch it. Tom hesitated for a long time and finally said that if Danny mailed it to him, maybe he'd take a look.

'The movie's not great,' Danny said. 'But, wow, she's sensational. She is so beautiful. And he's such a dork! I dug up some old episodes of *Sliprock* too and... Sorry, Dad. I probably shouldn't have said that.'

The DVD sat on Tom's desk for most of a month before he found the courage to watch it. It was a lousy copy. The picture was all fuzzy and streaked. Someone had no doubt sneaked a dusty old print one night from the vaults. But Danny was right. Diane was stunning. And after he was over the shock of seeing her and hearing her voice, he was captivated. He had imagined that watching the man he had killed would reactivate all sorts of dark emotions, but it didn't. Perhaps that was because he had lifted the lid on the past and told Danny. Or perhaps it was simply because the movie was so bad. More than bad. It was truly, magnificently, dreadful. Ray's performance was hilarious, almost as hilarious as poor old Terry Redfield's attempts to edit him out of the picture.

When he told Gina about Diane, she was devastated. Not so much by the story itself, but by the fact that Tom had never felt able to tell her. She cried and hugged him and kept saying if only she'd known. If only. Tom didn't ask her to follow through with the thought. Would it really have changed things between them, had she known the truth? He doubted it. Unless, of course, its very disclosure had helped him change too. He now realized how corrosive it had been for him to keep the secret for all those years. More than corrosive.

Secrets such as his were like some sort of malign living organism. They thrived on shame and guilt, spawning a fear that gnawed away at your insides. Now, by contrast, for the first time in his life, Tom felt a kind of peace descend upon him.

It seemed to be the same for Danny. Tom couldn't be sure because for many months after their joint confessional, they didn't talk about it. Danny moved with Kelly and young Thomas to Bozeman to begin his studies at Montana State. A few months later, Kelly gave birth to identical twin girls, Rebecca and Diane. Once a month Tom would drive down to see them or they would all come up to Missoula for the weekend.

He bought Danny a new fly rod and reel and one sultry June evening they headed over to fish the Yellowstone. They watched the sky turn pink and orange and the flies dance in smoky clusters over the water. There were trout rising everywhere but neither one of them got lucky. In the end they stowed their rods and sat on the bank staring at the sky's reflection in the water.

'Do you remember that canoe trip when we turned over?' Danny said.

'How could I ever forget?'

'You know, for years I felt bad about it, like it was my fault.'

'*Your* fault?'

'Yeah, that if I'd been better with the paddle or more alert or something, we wouldn't have gone over.'

'You weren't even five years old, for heaven's sake.'

'I know, but I just sat there like an idiot and watched it happen.'

'Man, I can still see every moment of it.'

'Me too.'

'The thing that knocked me out, still knocks me out, is when you bobbed up to the surface, the first thing you said was "Daddy, are you all right?"'

'You just looked so worried.'

'I thought you were gone.'

Neither of them spoke for a while. The light was purple and thickening, the mountaintops to the east aglow with the last of the sun.

'That was pretty much the end of things between you and Mom, wasn't it?'

'Yep. She put up with it for a few more years. Stayed a lot longer than I deserved. She's a great woman, your mom. I count myself lucky to have had those years with her.'

'She said the other day how good it was to see you happy at last.'

'Did she? Well, it's true. I am.'

He smiled and put an arm around his son.

'I'd be a whole lot happier, mind you, if we'd caught one of those damned fish.'

The subject embarrassed him a little. He wore his happiness like new shoes that were still a little stiff but would be fine when they were broken in. He didn't even really want to think about it. In case it took fright and flew off.

For almost a year now he had been spending a lot of time with Karen O'Keefe's mother, Lois. It was she who'd made the first move, rightly guessing that if she left it up to him nothing would ever happen. There was a film festival on in town and one of the organizers, a friend of hers, had given her a free pass to everything. They went to see *Pierrot le Fou*, a movie they had both loved

396

when they were in college. It was so terrible they left after the first hour and laughed about it all the way through dinner.

'How on earth could we *ever* have liked that?' Tom said. 'I mean, is it that we've changed or the world has changed?'

'I guess we like all kinds of things when we're young. I mean, look at old photographs, look at what we *wore* back then, things we wouldn't be seen dead in today. I remember I had this black-and-white op art dress. It was backless with a halter neck and a zipper all the way up the front.'

'I could live with that.'

She laughed.

'Know what I had?' Tom said.

'Go on, shock me.'

'A psychedelic, flare-bottomed catsuit.'

'You did not!'

'And an Afro.'

'You're kidding.'

'I am. But I was pretty cutting-edge, as a matter of fact.'

'I bet you were.'

One Saturday afternoon in Missoula, shortly after the twins were born, Tom bumped into Karen. He knew from her mother that she had been traveling a lot, promoting her movie *Walking Wounded*. It had been winning awards at film festivals all over Europe. American audiences didn't seem to like it so much. She and Tom had never gotten any further with their film about the Holy Family Mission. Nor, come to that, with their relationship.

She was waiting outside Fact & Fiction licking an ice cream cone and when she saw Tom she flung her arms around him and made a big fuss. They stood chatting for a while, then who should come out of the store but Troop. He put a possessive arm around her and kissed her and it was all Tom could do not to fall over in shock.

'I hear you and Mom have been seeing a lot of each other,' she said.

'Yes, that's right. We have.'

'Don't be so coy. She says she may even be moving in.'

'Well, you know, we thought we might give it a go.' Tom could feel himself blushing. 'But *you* two! I had no idea.'

'Oh.' Troop grinned. 'We're just good friends.'

'Strictly business,' Karen said, cuddling into him.

'Don't tell me. You're making a movie together.'

'How did you know?'

'Just guessing. I can't believe Lois never told me about this.'

Karen put her finger to her lips.

'She doesn't know.'

'Your secret's safe with me.' He looked at his watch. 'For about twenty minutes, anyhow.'

By the end of the following month Lois had more or less moved in. There wasn't a moment when it was decided or even a discussion, just a gradual realization that living together worked and was what they both wanted. They made each other laugh and once he'd grown used to having someone else around all the time, everything, in every department, felt right and good. It seemed like the first adult relationship he'd ever had.

On July Fourth of that same year, just after Danny's graduation from Montana State, they held a lunch party for their new extended family. Dutch and Gina came over from Great Falls, Karen and Troop flew up from LA and Danny and Kelly drove up with the three grandchildren from Bozeman. Tom and Danny manned the barbecue and Lois and Gina bonded big-time over the salads.

The weather was clear and hot and Tom had mowed the grass so the air smelled sweetly of summer. After the meal everyone sat around chatting in the shade of the cottonwoods. Dutch was playing with young Thomas and the twins down by the creek and Tom stood watching them from the deck while he waited for the coffee to brew. Thomas was wearing a plaid shirt and a cowboy hat. He had a little stick in his hand that was supposed to be a gun and he kept making shooting sounds, *pish, pish, pish.*

'He's cowboy crazy,' Danny said. Tom hadn't noticed that he'd come to stand beside him. 'Was I like that?'

'No. With you at that age it was all *Star Wars.* I guess he got the cowboy genes from me.'

'It's ever since I showed him those episodes of *Sliprock.*'

'*Lawless heart of the Old West, where the many live in fear of the few ...*'

'*One man stands alone against injustice....*'

They finished it together:

'*His name is Red McGraw.*'

'Lord help us,' Tom said. 'I haven't heard that for about fifty years. Hey, that reminds me. I want to show you something.'

Danny followed him into the house and through to his study where he'd stacked the dusty old boxes that Lois had made him clear from the attic. She wanted to convert the space into an extra bedroom for the twins.

'I was going through this junk the other day. And since you're so into our family history, I didn't dare throw anything out without telling you. I wondered if Thomas might like some of this old stuff. Look...'

He opened one of the boxes and pulled out a big brown paper bag and emptied it onto his desk.

'It's my old cowboy gear.'

Danny picked up the buckskin jacket and unfolded it.

'Wow, that's beautiful.'

'It's an exact copy of Red McGraw's. Ray had it specially made for me. Too big for Thomas just yet.'

'Yeah, but...Boy, he'd love it. And look at the hat! It's fantastic. What else is there?'

'There's this.'

It was in a cloth bag of its own. Tom could still remember the smell of oiled leather. The gun belt was rolled up and he took it out of the bag and opened it up. The fake bullets were all in place, the leg-tie too. The gun in its holster. He handed the whole thing to his son.

'It looks so real.'

'Yep.'

They both stared at it for a long time.

'What do you think?' Danny said at last.

'About giving it to Thomas? I don't know.'

'Me neither. He'd love it.'

'He would.'

'Kelly probably wouldn't like him to have it.'

'Probably not.'

'Let's think about it.'

They put it away without another word and went to the kitchen and got the coffee ready. When they carried it out and down onto the lawn, everyone was fussing around Thomas. He'd fallen and cut his hand and Kelly was on her knees in front of him, dabbing the blood with a handkerchief and trying to soothe him. The boy was trying hard not to cry.

'What happened?' Danny asked.

'He just fell over,' Kelly said. 'It's not too bad.'

Danny put his hand on Thomas's shoulder.

'Okay, son. There's a brave boy.'

Tom was standing to one side, looking on.

'*Semper Fortis*,' he said quietly.

He didn't think anybody had heard but Lois turned and asked him what he'd said. He smiled and shook his head.

'Nothing.'

'Where have you gone?'

'Nowhere. I'm right here.'

She looked at him for a long moment and then reached up and kissed him tenderly on the cheek. And Tom put his arm around her and they turned and walked in the sunlight across the grass and back toward the house.

ACKNOWLEDGMENTS

Many thanks to the following for their kindness, support and help with my research for this book: Bob and Kelly Peebles, Jo Swerling Jr., Stephen Cannell, Clyde Ware, Brett Halsey, Judy Hilsinger, Andy Miller, David Williams, Fred Davis, Noreen Bolam, Sara Walsh, Chris Cobb, Paul Welsh, Bryan Ritz, Geoffrey Sanford, Sylvie Rabineau, Nathan Rostron, Betsy Uhrig, Linda Shaughnessy, Caradoc King, Judy Clain and Ursula Mackenzie.

For their insight and wealth of information about the war in Iraq, I'm indebted to three fine books: *My War: Killing Time in Iraq* by Colby Buzzell, *Just Another Soldier: A Year on the Ground in Iraq* by Jason Christopher Hartley and *Warlord: No Better Friend, No Worse Enemy* by Ilario Pantano. Finally, my thanks to Adolf Hungry Wolf for his brilliantly researched series of books on the culture and history of the Blackfeet.